ONCE BITTEN

TOOTH & CLAW BOOK 3

HEATHER GUERRE

AUTHOR'S NOTE

Once Bitten touches on topics that may be difficult for some readers, including: a heroine who is recovering from an emotionally abusive relationship (includes references to manipulation tactics and grooming), threats of violence between main characters (based on misunderstanding—eventually resolved), violence/gore (multiple acts against main character, perpetrated by side character), and on-page violent death. It also includes mild violence in the form of vampire bites/blood drinking. Sexual content includes both primal play and consensual pain (biting) in addition to explicit depictions of sexual intimacy.

PART ONE

CHAPTER 1

Jules was on her knees in the back corner of the store, restocking cans of baked beans when the bell over the door jingled. Stifling a sigh, she got up, wiped her dusty hands on her jeans, and made her way to the front counter. Over the rows of metal shelving, she spied a familiar shade of vividly red hair, and her stomach sank.

Fixing her expression into calm neutrality, she slid behind the counter. "Hi, what can I—"

"Oh. My. God. *Juliana Wolfe?*" The red-headed woman who'd entered was a gorgeous, heart-faced, petite woman, with a toddler on her hip and another bun in the oven. Her hair was the perfect shade of deepest ruby red. Her skin was smooth as cream, with gentle golden freckles dappled sweetly across the bridge of her nose. Her crystalline blue eyes glowed like sapphires held up against sunlight. Those eyes widened as they took Jules in—rumpled hair, dusty apron, deep under-eye circles, and all.

"Oh, wow," Jules infused her voice was false cheer. "Alicia Fischer? It's been so long!"

Alicia Fischer had been Jules's nemesis in high school. Nothing extreme, nothing traumatic. Just run-of-the-mill mean girl shit. But seeing Alicia like this, in the face of all Jules's recent failures, was a gut punch she really didn't need.

"Well, it's Alicia Schuh now, actually." She gave a twinkling smile as she held her left hand out for Jules to see the glittering diamond on her finger. "Going on three years now."

Jules glanced at the toddler on Alicia's hip, mentally calculating the kid's age. The gingery-blonde child stared back with Alicia's same blue eyes.

"Oh. That's—uh. Congratulations!" she fumbled awkwardly for words. She wasn't good at small talk at the best of times, and these were far from the best. Jake Schuh had been Jules's all-consuming, and *very* unrequited, teenage crush. She'd honestly forgotten he even existed until just now, but hearing that Alicia had been the one to lock him down was just another shovelful on top of a heap of shit.

"So..." Alicia leaned on the counter, giving Jules a *we're-all-friends-here* smile. "What have you been up to? You left Saint Roch, what—ten years ago? And now, all of a sudden, you're back?"

Jules fixed her expression into one of unbothered serenity. She reached for the mental script she'd spent the last week perfecting. "Oh, yeah, you know. Went to college. Did the big city thing for a while. Got married." She held up her bare left hand. "Got divorced."

Alicia's eyes glittered with prurient interest even as she forced her expression into one of sympathy. "Oh *no*, I'm so sorry to hear that! I can't imagine! Jake's just so important to me, and our children are just... *everything*." She laid a protective hand over her pregnant belly, shaking her head sadly. "I could never do it. It must've been terrible."

It was. "Oh. No. Just one of those things. We got married pretty young, and then time passed and we realized we'd grown into different people." She shrugged as if she weren't being crushed by the suffocating darkness that accompanied thoughts of her failed marriage and her ex-husband. "It was for the best."

Alicia nodded as if she were taking that all in, but Jules could see a thousand more questions racing behind those pale, glittering eyes. "And now you're... working at your grandma's store?" she asked, wincing sympathetically, her tone cautious as if they were handling a delicate subject.

Apparently once a mean girl, always a mean girl. Jules didn't miss the implied insult. She was a thirty-year-old divorcee working as a cashier at a backwoods mini-mart. It *was* a delicate subject, though Alicia had no idea how delicate, or why.

Jules had dropped out of college to get married and follow her then-husband to the west coast, where she'd spent the ensuing decade trying to be the perfect housewife. So, she had no degree and no work experience, which had made finding work post-divorce impossible. When she was being honest with herself, she knew, despite her discontent, that she was incredibly lucky that she had a family member who owned a business and needed help. When she had been trying to find work in Seattle right after the divorce, there wasn't a single hiring manager out there who wanted her unemployed ass—at least, not for the cost of a living wage.

So here she was, back in rural northern Wisconsin, her tiny hometown of Saint Roch, living with her grandmother, working the same job she'd had in high school, with nothing to show for the last twelve years of her life except for her age.

"I'm just taking a breather while I figure things out," Jules said, putting the most positive possible spin on *I have no fucking clue what to do with myself and had nowhere else to go.* "And my grandma's getting older, so I've been helping her manage things here."

"Aw, that's so sweet," Alicia cooed brightly. "How long are you staying?"

Jules shrugged. It was hard to see past the dark cloud of her marriage, but even aside from that, she hadn't really liked living in a big city like Seattle. And while she wasn't thrilled to be in her current situation, a part of her had desperately missed the quiet beauty of the forests and lakes where she'd grown up.

"Not sure," she answered, as if unbothered by the uncertainty of her future. "I'm just playing it by ear."

Alicia gave her another sympathetic look.

"Mama," the toddler said, wriggling impatiently. "I want juice!"

Alicia smiled indulgently. "Hold your horses, Miss Rudie-Pants. How do you ask?"

"*Pleeeeeease.*"

"Alright." She set the girl down on the floor. "Go get *one* juice. And get Mama's iced coffee, okay?"

"Okay, Mama."

Jules frowned as she watched the little girl amble off—a kid that young was a walking hazard. To have her pulling bottled drinks out of the cases, possibly from above her head, was asking for an accident. She glanced at Alicia, uncertain if she should say something, but Alicia's interrogation was not about to be derailed.

"So, you were married. Any kids?"

Jules's heart clenched. "Ah, no. No. That didn't happen for us."

In hindsight, she was wildly relieved. If she'd had kids with Eric, she might never have gotten away. But during her marriage, it had felt like a moral failing on her part, even though fertility doctors had determined that the problem was on Eric's end. It wasn't like he'd had *no* viable sperm. So the fact that Jules's apparently fully-functional set-up couldn't make it work with his few useful swimmers had seemed like *her* problem. Eric had certainly seen it that way. He'd constantly questioned her about whether she was secretly using birth control, if she was eating the fertility-boosting foods she was supposed to, if she was drinking the fertility tea, if she was tracking her period correctly...

It wasn't until after the marriage ended, and Jules realized how utterly miserable she'd been, that she wondered if maybe her body had somehow been protecting her—refusing to carry the child of a man who would only make them all miserable. It didn't work that way, obviously, but it was a thought that gave her small comfort. Even during the worst of it, when she blamed herself the most, when she'd twisted herself into knots trying and failing to be who he wanted, when she'd become a shadow of herself in service to her husband's happiness—at least a small part of her had known it was wrong.

"Oh, I'm sorry," Alicia said with too much sympathy. "That's too bad. I can't imagine life without my kids." Her hand went to her stomach again.

Before Jules could think of a response to that, the door jangled and in stepped another unwelcome blast from the past. Jake Schuh. In high school, he'd been a tall, blond, muscular Adonis. He was still tall and blond, but he wasn't a high school athlete anymore, and it showed. Even so, he was still ridiculously handsome, with a square jaw and broad shoulders and a thick head of wheat-blond hair. Jules felt her cheeks heating purely from the memory of the intensity of her old crush.

"Oh, hey! Jules, uh... Wolfe, right?"

"Well, *is* it still Wolfe?" Alicia cut in quickly. In a low voice, she told Jake, "She just got divorced."

"No, it's still Wolfe. I never took my ex-husband's name." Before getting married, she'd told Eric that she didn't see why she had to change her entire identity, just because she'd fallen in love. The irony of that nineteen-year-old girl's naive proclamation still made her cringe. Eric had indulgently agreed with her keeping her last name, as long as their kids had *his* last name. In the end, Jules was still a Wolfe, but she *had* changed her entire identity for love. Or what she'd thought was love.

"Really?" Alicia was appalled. "You didn't want to have the same name as your husband and kids?"

"Well I don't have a husband or kids, so it's kind of a moot point," Jules said, an edge of frazzled anger sneaking into her tone.

"Babe," Jake chided his wife gently.

Alicia huffed, but pressed her lips together, saying no more.

Jules's former crush was defending her from his wife, who'd been a bitch to her in high school, and was apparently still at least a little bit of a bitch. And Jules just had to stand there, waiting to ring them up, in her dirty apron and dusty hands and her exhausted, unloved body.

"Anyway, looks like you've got gas at pump two?" she

said briskly, bringing it up on the cash register. "Anything else?"

"Daddy!" their daughter's voice crowed through the store. She came running over, a bottle of grape juice clutched in her arms. "I got juice!"

"I see that, pumpkin." He scooped his daughter up, making her giggle and squeal, and helped her put the juice on the counter in front of Jules.

"You didn't get Mama's coffee?" Alicia asked, feigning affront.

"Tell Mama she drinks too much caffeine," Jake stage-whispered to his daughter.

"Tell Daddy he doesn't want to see what Mama's like without her caffeine," Alicia shot back playfully, turning on her heel to get her drink.

Jules watched the whole exchange, feeling like a weird voyeur. While they waited for Alicia to get her drink, Jake smiled awkwardly at her and she smiled just as awkwardly back.

"So, Jules, how's life been?" he asked politely.

Not this again. "It's had its ups and downs," she said vaguely, swiping the juice beneath the scanner.

Mercifully, Alicia returned quickly, setting a bottle of iced coffee on the counter. Jules scanned it.

"Well," Alicia said with heavy feeling as Jake put his card in the reader. "I'm *so* sorry about everything you're going through."

That faux sympathy had been the same in high school—except her digs had been a little more artless back then. *It must be so weird to be that tall. Like, you're taller than a lot of guys are. Doesn't that feel weird?* And, *You're so confident, getting a haircut like that. I'd be too embarrassed.* And, *Whoa, you don't shave your legs every day? Good for you, girl!*

"I'm really fine," Jules said as breezily as she could.

"You say that, but it's got to be so tough—"

The door jingled again as somebody new stepped in. Jules wanted to fall to her knees and thank the heavens for this divine intervention, but as soon as she caught sight of the newcomer, her whole body went on red alert.

He was definitely not from around here. She'd have remembered somebody like him. He was tall and broad, with warm, tan skin and short, raven-black hair. A thick scruff covered his strong jaw—too dense to be stubble, not quite long enough to be a beard. Straight black eyebrows glowered over hazel-gold eyes that gleamed like a falcon's. His features were boldly rendered, and alarmingly beautiful in a rough-hewn, rugged kind of way. Like lightning and thunder —awe-inspiring, but dangerous.

As he caught sight of Jules, he went as still as a hunting cat, his whole body tensing, his gaze locked on her. His golden eyes widened, thick brows drawing together.

"*You*," he said hoarsely, staring at her as if she were a ghost.

CHAPTER 2

I t was *her*. The woman whose scent had been driving Max crazy for weeks. The day after he'd arrived in the Cry Lake packlands, he'd gone on a run with the pack and caught the faintest trace of her on one of the walking trails in the national forest. He hadn't been able to track it far —rain had fallen in the time since she'd been on the trail, washing away most of her scent.

But now, completely by accident, he'd found her. She was tall. His wolf liked that. Strong and healthy. A good runner. Her dark hair—almost too dark to qualify as brown, not quite dark enough to be called black—was pulled back from her face in a tidy braid that lay over one shoulder like a mermaid's tail. Halfway down the braid, her hair shifted from dark sable to a deep, emerald green. She was so pale, he could easily see blue-green veins beneath the skin along her throat, her wrists. She had large dark eyes and a high-bridged, aquiline nose. She looked like an empress from the ancient Mediterranean—Greek, or Roman, or Byzantine, maybe.

Well, she would have looked like an empress if she didn't currently seem like she wanted to shrink beneath the counter. She stared back at Max, radiating fear. She'd frozen, as rabbits do, trying to be invisible, too scared to fight, too scared to run. But what was she scared of? *Him?*

A family stood between him and the woman—parents and their pup. The red-headed mother looked between Max and the would-be Empress behind the counter, wide-eyed.

"Oh my god," she breathed, clutching her coffee. "Is this your ex-husband?"

The nosy, delighted question shook the other woman out of her freeze response. "What? No. We've never met." She glanced back at him, but didn't make direct eye contact. "Have we?"

"No," he answered. His voice came out too deep, too gruff. He cleared his throat. "No, sorry. You're—" he cut himself off, scrubbing a hand over his jaw, unable to tear his gaze away from her. He couldn't tell a skinlocked stranger that he recognized her *scent*. "You looked familiar," he finally said.

"Oh." The red-haired woman was obviously disappointed by the mundane turn, lips pursed as she glanced between Max and the woman he'd been trying to find. "Well, it was nice talking to you, Jules. See you around."

Jules. Max tucked her name away like a valuable secret.

"Yep, take care," Jules said faintly. She was looking at the family, but every fiber of her being was attuned to Max. He could feel it. Trying to put her at ease, he turned away from her and headed towards the drink coolers—the whole reason he'd stopped at this little gas station in the first place. He was thirsty and the name had caught his attention.

Wolfe's. It had seemed too auspicious to pass up. And fuck him if fate hadn't delivered in spades.

He had his back turned to Jules, with several rows of metal shelving between them, but he knew she was focused on him in the same way he was focused on her. He was only aware that the other people had left because he heard the bell jingle over the door and their scents faded.

When he returned to the counter with a bottle of water, she had schooled her expression into something more neutral, but stress and anxiety still radiated off of her. Her discomfort was upsetting his wolf, upsetting him. The urge to comfort her had to be suppressed. The wolf only understood physical contact, and the man was terrible at putting nice words together. Growing up in a tight-knit, isolated community, he had no practice at it with strangers.

"Hi," he said gently.

There was just the faintest hesitation before she replied, "Hi. How are you?" Her voice was soft, faded almost. Like she didn't want to be heard.

"Good," he replied, keeping his hands in his pockets and his body language subdued. "And you?"

"Not bad." That sounded like a lie. "Anything else for you?"

"Just this."

She nodded and scanned the water. He paid with cash from his pocket. When he handed it to her their fingers brushed and she flinched away, dropping the money.

"Sorry," she said, not meeting his gaze as she hurriedly plucked up the dropped coins.

His wolf wanted to crawl on his belly and whine, to prove he wasn't a threat. But how could the man prove it? "It's alright. My fault."

"No, it was mine." She put the money into the till and slid the drawer shut. "Alright. Well, you're all set. Have a nice day."

He grabbed the water bottle, then hesitated at the counter, searching for the right words to say.

I've been tracking your scent for weeks.

Absolutely not, you fucking psychopath.

You smell like hope.

Somehow worse.

My wolf likes you.

Nope.

"Uh..." He glanced back at her and found her watching him warily. "Thanks," he said, and pushed out the door. On the way to the truck the Cry Lake pack had loaned him, he resisted the impulse to turn around just to look at her again. He drove back to Cry Lake, ignoring the longing pull of his wolf back towards the woman he'd just terrified.

The Cry Lake pack's territory encompassed a huge swath of northern Wisconsin, northeastern Minnesota, all of Michigan's upper peninsula, and a bit of the lower peninsula. But most of the pack lived in Wisconsin in the town of Cry Lake—hundreds of acres owned in trust by the pack, abutted by thousands and thousands of acres of national forest. Max was living there, temporarily, while he fostered with the Cry Lake pack. He pulled up to the small cabin he'd been given as a pack guest, killed the engine, and sat in the truck for a few minutes, staring into the wooded surroundings.

His connection to his home pack, the Teekkonlit, was still strong in his mind—a pull that made his wolf antsy and restless. But for the first time in a long time, his wolf was no longer whining to return home. He wanted to go back into the small tourist town he'd just left, back to the little gas station, and stare hopefully at a woman who'd stared back at him like he was a known murderer.

With a sigh, he fished his phone out of his chest pocket and called up Caleb. Caleb Kinoyit was part of the reason Max was out Roaming. After his old friend had matebonded, the weight of Max's loneliness had started to get a little heavier. Finally, he hadn't been able to fight it any longer—he'd left the packlands in search of his own mate.

Roaming was an old custom among the wolf kin, with centuries of tradition behind it. Mateless wolves left their home pack, fostering temporarily with other packs in search of a mate. It was how his father had met his mother—though his mother was skinlocked, and not a member of the pack his father had been fostering with. Apparently the apple didn't fall too far from the tree.

"Max," Caleb greeted him in his typical to-the-point way. "What's up?"

"How did you know you wanted to matebond Grace?" Max asked, ignoring the pleasantries.

There was a pause. "You met someone?" Caleb asked.

"I don't know."

Caleb accepted that. He was quiet for a moment, considering his words. "Grace..." He sighed, a sound both rueful and loving. "We got off to a bad start. I smelled strigoi on her when I met her in Anchorage and nobody believed me. I was a dick because I didn't trust her, but..."

"But what?"

"My wolf did. Instantly. Wanted to lick her chin and roll over like a pup."

"So you should have listened to your wolf."

"Maybe. But my sister's wolf loved Nick," Caleb said,

referring to his ex-brother-in-law who'd abandoned his wife and son without a word, and had never looked back.

That very thought made Max's jaw clench, molars grinding together. For wolf kin, losing a mate was damn near a death sentence. There was no coming back from that loss. Matebonds were forever. Abandoning your mate *and* your pup? Unthinkable.

"My mom's wolf trusted my dad, and look how that turned out. And my wolf didn't see a thing wrong with Brenna until... until that all went to shit."

"So, don't trust the wolf." Max sighed.

"I don't know," Caleb admitted. "The wolf wanted Grace in a different way. She felt... important. Not just interesting and new, the way some people were. She was... fascinating. My wolf was obsessed. It was driving me crazy." Another contemplative pause. "Your dad says he knew right away that your mom was the one because of his wolf. And Wade always said the same thing about Dorothy. And... I mean, most the mated pairs will tell you their wolf *knew*."

Max was silent, dwelling on that.

"Who is it?" Caleb asked. "Maybe Joanne knows them." Joanne Lance was a Teekkonlit pack member, married to Harry Lance, but she was originally from the Yellowstone pack.

"I'm not in Wyoming anymore," Max said. "I'm in Wisconsin with the Cry Lake pack. And she's not wolf kin. She doesn't know about us." But then he remembered the way she'd stared at him as if he were a monster, her fear and her wariness. "I don't *think* she knows about us..." he amended uncertainly.

"You left the Yellowstone pack pretty fast," Caleb observed.

He was right. Max had stayed there for barely more than a week. It was borderline offensive how quickly he'd moved on, but the restlessness that had dogged him since leaving Longtooth had urged him beyond Yellowstone. He wasn't exactly right at home in Cry Lake, but the restlessness had become directionless here—neither urging him on, nor allowing him a moment of peace.

Until he'd come across *her* scent, lingering along a deer path. The odds that he would have stumbled across that one little patch of land in the entirety of the Cry Lake pack's territory were nearly impossible.

And yet, here he was. Talking to his friend about a woman he knew only by scent and by name. Nothing else about her.

"I had to," Max sighed. "I knew I was in the wrong place. I just... I had to keep moving."

"You know..." Caleb mused. A faint rasping sounded over the line, and Max could easily picture him scrubbing his hand over his beard. "Grace was originally going to be flown in by a charter out of Fairbanks. For some reason, I decided to change my flight plan and pick her up myself. No reason for it. Just an impulse."

"Was that before or after you decided she was a secret strigoi?"

Caleb made a sound that was half-huff, half-growl, a wolfish noise of exasperation. "Fuck off, I still got her, didn't I?"

"*Maybe* I *got you*," Grace's voice came distantly in the background, mildly affronted.

Caleb chuckled appreciatively. "Got me like a wolf gets a fawn."

Grace murmured something in reply that Max couldn't quite make out, though her tone was clearly suggestive.

"Alright, little fawn," Max said drily. "I'll leave you and your she-wolf to it."

"Hey," Caleb said, suddenly serious again. "I hope you find what you're looking for."

Max did too. "We'll see."

CHAPTER 3

Ten years of marriage to Eric had conditioned Jules to be afraid of anything she wanted. *Everything.* Rich desserts. Pretty clothes. Fun books. Sex. Even simple things like emotional comfort. Hugs. Smiles.

Eric had been big on self-control as a virtue. To him, food was fuel, not an indulgence. So they ate healthy meals of lean proteins and complex carbs and lots of veggies. Eric thought only shallow people cared about fashion, but he also wanted his wife to present a certain image to the world, so Jules had dressed like a minimalist Stepford Wife. According to Eric, reading anything other than educational books was a waste of time, so Jules had had a hidden collection of paperbacks she'd secretly bought from thrift stores and rummage sales. When it came to sex, Eric wanted it only a few certain ways, and that was all he wanted. If Jules suggested anything even slightly out of the norm, he accused her of being brainwashed by porn. If she was having a bad day and needed a hug, Eric called her clingy and emotionally immature. If she tried to make him smile, he got frustrated with her for being ridiculous. If she tried to start a conversation, he got annoyed that she was pestering him.

A year after the divorce had been finalized, Jules had started to dismantle the ways she'd built herself around him. Sometimes she ate ice cream for lunch if she wanted to, instead of a nutritionally balanced, calorically efficient "power bowl." She went for long walks in the woods instead of doing high-intensity interval training and pilates at an expensive gym. She openly read Nora Roberts and Anne McCaffrey and Janet Evanovich novels when the store was slow and there was no other work to be done. She bleached the bottom six inches of her hair and dyed it green. She donated all her old, boring clothes and raided thrift stores for the sorts of eclectic things she'd always wanted to wear, but felt too silly around Eric.

And even though she knew those things were perfectly within her rights to do, she still lived in constant anxiety of being questioned, mocked, criticized. When old men raised their eyebrows at her hair, she had to fight not to cringe in embarrassment, to resist the urge to try to explain herself to them. When strangers cast judgmental glances at her red corduroy bell bottoms, or her denim jumpsuit, or her forest green dirndl bodice worn over a poet-sleeve blouse, or her crocheted sweater made out of multi-colored granny squares, or any of the clothes that made her feel like herself, she had to force herself not to laugh nervously and apologize. Even resisting the minor urge to hide the covers of her books when customers came in sometimes made her hands shake.

And as difficult as it was to embrace those parts of herself, to shrug off the judgment of other people, they were just surface-level changes. The real work was still a snarled knot inside her brain and her heart. She had barely even begun to unravel the emotional fuckery that came with sex and affection and her own sense of self-worth.

So, when the intimidating stranger returned to the store the next afternoon, Jules finally recognized her fear for what it was—*want*. Something about him called to her, and the desire to answer that call was making her sick with anxiety. The fear that he might *know* that she wanted him was the worst of all. Because, while the wanting was scary in itself, it was the rejection that hurt the most. Being shot down, ridiculed, scolded for wanting. Being made to feel stupid and revolting for the things she wanted. Being told she wasn't good enough or smart enough or pretty enough or just plain *enough* to deserve the things she wanted. *That* was what she was afraid of.

It was irrational to think that the stranger could know that she was attracted to him. It was probably even irrational to feel that he'd be angry and disgusted if he found out. But her ex-husband had managed to program rationality right out of her when it came to her own wants and needs.

"Hi again," he greeted her when he stepped inside the store. His voice was a pleasant rumble, almost a growl. The sight of him was just as frighteningly compelling today as it had been yesterday. His eyes gleamed like old gold as he met her gaze. His broad features pulled into an easy smile. He was big, so much bigger than her ex-husband had been. For a split second, the image of herself pinned under the stranger's body flashed into her mind. Mortified, she immediately rejected it. Her cheeks burned. She knew a blush on her pale skin was always ridiculously obvious, which only made her cheeks burn hotter.

"Um, hi," she answered, sounding embarrassingly shy even to her own ears. She was a grown woman. She shouldn't be this unraveled by mere eye contact with an attractive man.

Mercifully, he turned away from her and headed back to the drink coolers. He returned a few seconds later with a bottle of water, same as yesterday.

"Nice weather today," he said as Jules scanned the water.

She glanced out the big window next to the counter. It had been drizzling rain all day, and while it had let up a little, it was still windy, gray, and wet outside. She glanced back at the man, uncertain as to whether he was being sarcastic. He hadn't said it in a sarcastic tone.

When she met his gaze again, his face seemed slightly flushed compared to before. He grimaced faintly. "Actually, it's not very nice," he amended. "Is it? I mean... it's alright?"

"Are you asking me?" Jules was confused. Why did he seem so flustered? Had she done something wrong?

"No. I mean, yes. You can say what you think. About the weather. And then I can reply." He winced again, the flush deepening. "Because that's how conversations go," he muttered, sounding agonized.

Very, very slowly, it dawned on Jules that he was *nervous*. Nervous to talk to her? But why?

"Um, it's alright," she finally answered, still uncertain as to what was going on. But that was okay, because her anxiety had mostly been replaced by confusion. "I like the rain, actually. It's kind of cozy."

The stranger nodded earnestly. "It's fresh. Washes the world."

That was unexpectedly poetic. "I never thought of it that way," she admitted. She liked the darkness. How the cloudy sky made the world feel smaller. Like she was a rabbit snugged up in a burrow.

"It doesn't rain much where I'm from," the stranger said, gazing past Jules to look out the window. "We get a lot of snow. But the warmer months are pretty dry."

"Where are you from?" Jules asked reflexively, surprising herself by maintaining a conversation.

"Alaska. The northern interior."

"Oh, wow. You're far from home. What brought you to Wisconsin?"

"Visiting friends," he said. "What about you?"

Jules blinked. "Me? I live here."

"Right. Of course." He flushed again, and now Jules was certain—he was nervous with her. But *why?*

An awkward silence lapsed until Jules realized she was still holding his water and hadn't told him the total. "Oh! Um, is there anything else you need?"

He hesitated. "No," he finally said, seeming frustrated.

He paid with cash again, and this time when his fingers brushed Jules's hand, she didn't flinch. She felt the rough pads of his fingers against her palm as his golden gaze held hers. It took the space of a second, but it felt prolonged and intimate. She nearly dropped the money again. Overheated, anxiety rising, she tore her gaze away from him and focused on putting the money in the till. She counted out his change and dropped it into his open palm without touching him.

"Thanks for stopping. Have a nice day," she told him with practiced politeness.

He stood at the counter, holding his change and his water bottle, looking oddly reluctant. He didn't speak, simply gazed at her, brows drawn together. The silence turned uncomfortable, and Jules felt the panic rising again.

She tried to batten it down, to let logic overrule emotion, but it wasn't working.

The man stepped back suddenly, casting his gaze downward. "Sorry. Didn't mean to—" He swallowed whatever he'd been about to say. "Never mind. I, uh... thanks. Bye."

And then he was gone.

Much later that night, as she lay in her bed in the silent darkness in her grandma's house, she thought of the stranger and the way he'd gotten flustered trying to make small talk with her. Years ago, when she was younger and not quite so worn-down, Jules might have assumed he... *liked* her. But the Jules of the present day wasn't so optimistic. She wanted to believe it, though. And that made it worse.

CHAPTER 4

The next day, the stranger showed up again, the same time as the last two days—five-fifteen in the afternoon. Jules wondered if he worked somewhere nearby before she remembered he'd said he was only here visiting. But why would he be driving by every day at the same time?

"Hello," he greeted her as he stepped inside, those hazel-gold eyes as arrestingly bright as always.

"Hi." Jules blushed reflexively.

He went to the drink coolers and got a bottle of water, as usual.

"You know, you'd probably save yourself some money if you got a refillable bottle," Jules said as she scanned it. She wasn't sure why she'd said it. She cringed inwardly, waiting for him to tell her to mind her own business.

"You're probably right," the stranger agreed.

Even though he wasn't angry, the urge to placate was second nature at this point, and Jules quickly tried to backpedal. "Well, maybe not. What do I know? After all, you said you're only visiting. You probably don't want to, like, pack a water bottle. It'd take up space in your bag, and if you're flying that's a pain, and it's probably just easier to—"

Jules broke off abruptly as the stranger's big hand descended on hers, warm, gentle, strong. His gaze held hers, painfully acute. "Hey, it's alright," he said. "It's a good idea. I should get one."

Jules knew she should pull away, but the gentleness of his touch felt so good, she could only stand there, speechless, staring back at him. When was the last time a man had touched her to offer simple comfort? To be kind?

She couldn't remember.

"Your name is Jules?" the stranger asked.

Instead of worrying that he knew her name when she'd never told it to him, the vast majority of her brain cells were focused on the feel of his warm, rough hand over hers. She nodded mutely.

"I'm Max. Maxim Freeman."

She swallowed. "Jules—uh, Juliana. But usually just Jules. Jules Wolfe."

His brows rose. "Wolfe?" he repeated.

"Yeah. Do you know my family?"

"No. I don't think so. Do you own this gas station, then?"

She felt her face heat at the unwelcome turn in conversation. "My grandma does."

"Well, Jules Wolfe," he squeezed her hand and released it, "you've motivated me to go get a reusable water bottle. Where's a good place to get one around here?"

Grateful for the change of topic, she gave herself a few seconds to really overthink it. "Don't go to any of the chain stores. None of that money stays in town, you know?"

He nodded, watching her with total absorption. It was intimidating, but the panicky feeling didn't rise anymore.

"The sporting goods store on Main Street is locally owned, and they have a ton of that kind of stuff, but everything there is really, uh… high end," she said diplomatically, instead of *overpriced*. Beauchamp's Sporting Goods did a lot of business with tourists—rich tourists from Chicago and Milwaukee who threw money around like it grew on trees—and their prices reflected that. "But if you take Main Street over the bridge, then turn left at the second stoplight, you'll be on Dawson Street. At the end of Dawson, towards the water tower, there's a grocery store and a hardware store and a bunch of stuff like that."

He nodded, still following intently.

"The hardware store is locally-owned. They'd probably have a decent selection of water bottles in the housewares section."

"The hardware store on Dawson," he repeated in that velvety, rumbling voice. "Got it. Thank you, Jules."

She flushed again at hearing her name in his deep voice. "You're welcome."

He stood for a moment, just looking at her, like he'd done the last two days. He seemed on the edge of saying something more, but never did. Instead, he ducked his head almost ruefully, flashed Jules a smile, and headed for the door.

"See you around," he said.

"Goodbye, Max." His name slipped out unexpectedly. At the sound of it, he brightened, his smile widening.

And then he was gone.

Long minutes after he left, Jules could still feel the imprint of his hand gripping hers. She stared at the door, stricken by a sudden realization—once he got a reusable water bottle, he wouldn't be coming back anymore to buy water. If it had all happened before he'd held her hand, she'd probably be feeling relieved right now. But instead, his warmth had soaked into her skin, and she wanted him back.

THE NEXT DAY, A LITTLE PAST FIVE, THE STORE WAS QUIET. JULES stared out the window at the empty street, expecting nothing, and disappointed by it for the first time in a long time. It was silly—the delusional hopes of a drab, unwanted nobody—but she wanted to see him again. Max. She wanted to hear his voice and maybe pluck up the courage to ask him more about himself. It wouldn't go anywhere. She knew that. He was only here temporarily, and she wasn't the sort of person who made anybody want to stick around. But it would be nice to talk, anyway.

At five, she glanced out the window again. A few cars went by on the street, but none pulled into the parking lot. At ten-past, the bell over the door jangled, and Jules looked up excitedly—only to see two teenage girls.

"Hi," Jules said to them, pretending not to be disappointed.

The girls bought sodas and went on their way, leaving the store in silence again.

The usual post-work rush followed, until around seven when the store quieted down again. Max never showed. Of course he didn't. He had a stupid reusable water bottle now.

At nine, Jules was in the back, restocking the soda cases when the bell jingled over the door. She set down the case she was flattening and stepped out of the cooler to make her way to the counter. Halfway there, she froze.

Max was standing in the middle of the rows of shelves, looking at bags of beef jerky.

Why don't you tell him to go buy his own cow? her inner voice demanded snidely.

His attention lifted, catching sight of her, and a sweet, warm smile stretched his mouth. "Jules," he said happily, as if they were the oldest of friends.

It should have been weird, this instantaneous familiarity between them. She didn't care. She was too starved for any kind of affection to let it go.

"Hi, Max. How are you?"

"Alright. I took your advice." He held up a big water bottle. It had the sort of design that could be found on everything in the Northwoods—a loon sitting on peaceful water, silhouetted against pine trees. It was printed on shirts, mugs, bumper stickers, magnets, shot glasses, key chains, dish towels, hats, and anything else tourists might buy. She knew he'd gone where she'd recommended, though, because the backside of the water bottle had the hardware store's logo on it.

"Oh," she breathed. The fact that he'd taken her advice, down to the letter, filled her with a disproportionate level of joy. She wanted to throw her arms around him and thank him for treating her like someone worth listening to. Which would be a bit much, so she quickly scuttled behind the counter, where a physical barrier would prevent her from giving in to that impulse.

A second later, Max sidled up with a bag of beef jerky, sliding it across the counter towards her. "Can I ask you a personal question?"

Jules hesitated. Her stomach fluttered nervously. "Um..."

"Never mind," Max said quickly, casting his gaze down. "It's none of my business."

"No, go ahead," Jules found herself saying. "Ask me."

"Have you lived here your whole life?"

"Oh. No." She sighed, wistfulness, shame, nostalgia, and grief all contained in that single exhalation. "I grew up here, but I lived in Seattle for the last ten years, and before that, I lived in Milwaukee. I only moved back here a few weeks ago."

"I thought so." Max nodded.

"You thought that I lived in Seattle?"

"No, just that you're a wanderer."

She was struck by the romanticism of the word he'd chosen. She sometimes felt like she didn't belong anywhere, like she just went wherever the wind blew her. And not in a fun, free-spirited kind of way—more of a spineless, directionless kind of way. But "wanderer" made her sound like somebody who did it on purpose, who *had* purpose.

"What makes you say that?" she asked.

"Just something about you. You're always looking far away. You smell like running water."

"I... what?"

"Figuratively speaking," Max said, straightening abruptly. "It's an expression. Is it not an expression here? It is in Alaska."

Something about that was ringing false, but Jules couldn't imagine why he'd lie about it. "No, it's not an expression here. It sounds nice, though."

Max relaxed slightly, but he reached into his pocket for his cash, looking suddenly restless to get out. "It is nice," he assured her. "What do I owe you?"

He paid for the jerky, and then with a nod and a slightly

nervous-looking smile, he was out the door. Jules watched through the window as he got into his truck and drove away. There was a lightness in her chest that she hadn't felt in such a long time, that she hadn't been sure she'd ever feel again. A crush. She had a crush on a boy.

But with that lightness, came the edge of fear. Because the last time she'd had a crush, she'd ended up married at twenty, to a man fourteen years older than her. In hindsight, all the red flags had been there from the beginning. And even so, she'd felt just as light and giddy about Eric as she did now about Max. And that was dangerous.

CHAPTER 5

"**B**ut she's skinlocked!" Andrew Kirsch, a Cry Lake pack member, said incredulously.

Max gave him a low warning growl. "My mother's skinlocked."

Another growl sounded a few feet away. "So's my mate," a woman's voice cut in.

Andrew shook his head in disbelief. He was a sturdy, freckled, barrel-chested man, near Max's age, and also unmated. "Why would anyone *want* a mate who's skinlocked? They'll never be able to run with you. Never hunt with you. You'll never see their wolf."

To be fair, Max had wondered what Jules's wolf might've looked like if she'd had one—and been momentarily disappointed that she didn't. But then he'd seen her again today, inhaled her compelling scent, and he forgot all about that. His wolf didn't care if she couldn't do those things. He just wanted to nuzzle her, lick her chin, show her his belly.

Max didn't care to explain all that to Andrew, who was, as far as Max could tell, one of the thicker-skulled members of the Cry Lake pack. He regretted even mentioning Jules to the others at all. Wolves were insatiably curious, and now he was going to be hounded about her. He'd at least had the sense not to reveal her name or where he met her. All the pack knew was that he'd met a skinlocked woman who'd caught his wolf's attention.

"Don't listen to Andy," Lara Delacroix told him with a roll of her eyes. "He's inbred."

"I am not!" Andrew said hotly.

"Your grandparents are cousins."

"*Second* cousins!"

Laughter from everyone else broke the tension, and Max slipped out of the conversation. A good portion of the pack was gathered at what they called the Lodge—a big community building that sat on the shore of Cry Lake. It was Friday night, and while the pack was self-sustaining in a lot of ways, and didn't generally observe the seven-day work week, plenty of pack members still had nine-to-fives in the outside world. They tended to congregate on Fridays, just like outsiders, to unwind.

The Lodge was a big open building, with a low stage in one corner, a counter that served as a bar in another, a central fireplace hearth with a huge stone chimney, and a long bank of windows overlooking the lake. Max drifted towards those windows, stopping to stare at the water. It was so smooth. Like glass. The water back home was a wide, rushing river, and thousands of fast-running streams of snow-melt in the spring. Only puddles were this still. But Cry Lake had over a thousand acres of surface area, and it was as smooth as glass. It was a mirror in the night, reflecting the dispersing clouds, the glittering stars, and the sliver of the waxing moon.

"Andy's as dense as they come, but he has a point," Luke Mercier said, coming to stand beside Max at the windows. Luke was quiet and steady, and mated to the most hectic hurricane of a human being Max had ever met—Iris Eriksen. The two of them together were like night and day, but somehow they made it work. Iris was well-meaning, even if she was sometimes overwhelming. Luke was not a man of many words, but when he spoke, people listened.

"What point is that?" Max asked, feeling his hackles lift.

"Skinlocked humans aren't like us."

"And?"

"I'm not saying that's a bad thing, or that you shouldn't see what your wolf likes so much about this woman." Luke paused, and Max didn't rush to fill the silence. Finally, Luke continued his thought. "They court differently than we do."

Max's hackles smoothed. "I know."

"They don't like being followed. It's not 'chase' for them. It's stalking."

Max pressed his mouth into a thin line. His wolf rejected that outright. Logically, Max, the man, understood the distinction. And as a man, he did nothing more than stop in the gas station where she worked. But when he was in his wolfskin and the wolf was in control? He couldn't stop himself from trying to track her. So far, she'd proved elusive.

"And they're not as quick with physical touch as we are."

He knew that in a logical sense, but he wasn't sure where the line was drawn. While he understood what was okay among wolf kin, the rules for skinlocked humans were vague and uncertain. His mother had talked about it somewhat, but knowing what had been proper and respectful in rural Poland in the nineteen-eighties wasn't terribly helpful in the present-day U.S.

"How do you know so much about it?" Max asked, fixing Luke with a questioning gaze. As far as he knew, Luke and Iris, also wolf kin, had mated young. There wouldn't have been much time for Luke to figure out all the courting customs of skinlocked humans.

"Your pack is pretty isolated up there in Alaska," Luke said. "You don't deal with outsiders unless you intentionally bring them into your community. Our packlands aren't so remote. We have neighbors and friends and even kin among the outsiders. We have to teach our young ones how to court skinlocked kids respectfully."

"Hm." He didn't object to any of Luke's advice, necessarily, but hearing it right now was almost pointless when his wolf was sitting so far forward in his mind.

"Don't frighten her, is all I'm saying. Wolf kin like eagerness, straight-forwardness. Humans find it aggressive."

"I hear you," Max said.

Luke clasped his shoulder, a friendly gesture, and left him to his brooding.

With the rumble of too many conversations at his back, Max felt himself getting overly warm, cagey, restless. He slipped quietly out of the Lodge and walked in the dark down to the edge of the lake. Grass gave way to a thin slice of sandy beach. The faintest little waves lapped against it.

It was early spring, too cold in this climate to not have a jacket. Max peeled his clothes off and tossed them onto a nearby picnic table. He took a deep breath and shifted into his wolfskin. On four paws, covered in thick warm fur, he gave into the restlessness and ran.

He circled the shore of the lake, where the forest on the other side turned into public land. He passed other wolves running, and they called for him to join with howls and yips, but he chose not to. Running alone, he went deeper into the national forest, following deer trails and streams and occasionally human-cut trails.

He ran so long and so far, that he eventually found himself approaching the scents of human habitation. And then the faintest thread of familiarity tickled his nose—*her*. Jules's scent. Warm and earthy, the usual human muskiness cut with something crisp and bright that made him think of spring snowmelt and autumn winds.

He chuffed happily. Max knew he ought to pull back, but his wolf had the reins now, and the wolf wanted to find the woman who'd fascinated him, who smelled like the warm earth and running water, who smelled like constancy and change in the same breath.

Her scent was thicker upon a maintained walking trail. Max followed it until he emerged at the dead-end of a single-lane road. A few houses lined each side, small, still, and dark in the night. The silence was all-encompassing. There were no humans awake in this little corner of the world. Moving cautiously, keeping to the shadows, Max went on, following Jules's scent to one of the houses. He circled the small yard, learning everything his nose could tell him. Jules lived here with another female—a family member. An elder. They had no pets, though they liked to put suet and seeds out for the birds. Deer, raccoons, possums, coyotes, and squirrels all came frequently into their yard, as well as an occasional black bear. There were no men living with them, though a neighboring male—another elder—and his mate had recently been on the back patio.

The distant sound of an engine interrupted the stillness of the night, growing gradually louder as it drew nearer. The vehicle slowed and bright lights stretched down the length of the one-lane road. Max retreated to the edge of the yard, sinking into the bracken and brush, and waited for the vehicle to pass.

Jules was stuck working late that night. Grandma always opened the store at five a.m., and Jules came around two in the afternoon to relieve her, manning things until the store closed at ten. It usually took her another hour after closing to empty the trash, clean all the coffee carafes, balance the till, and all the other end-of-day clean-up. Usually she could get the big stuff—mopping the floors, cleaning the bathrooms, restocking—done during the slow parts of the afternoon.

Tonight had been an especially long night. Fridays always were. After five, she had a steady stream of customers picking up cases of beer, soda, and bottles of liquor. It meant she was constantly behind the counter, ringing up sales, unable to do the regular clean-up throughout the night. To add to it all, somebody had puked in the men's bathroom right before closing, and had missed the toilet bowl with most of it. When she'd finally gotten the store cleaned, her back and her feet ached from standing all day and her shoulders ached from scrubbing vomit off the baseboard heater in the bathroom. She had worn gloves and a disposable apron, but she felt absolutely filthy. She wanted nothing more than a shower.

Her grandma's house was a small, post-war ranch, a little ways off of a county highway, settled on a one-lane road in a mostly-undeveloped stretch of woods near the national forest. There were only four other houses on the lane, all inhabited by elderly people around her grandma's age. As Jules pulled onto the road, a little past midnight, all the houses were dark. The only lights to see by were her headlights, and the small one grandma left on for her above the side door.

She pulled into the driveway and parked beside grandma's old Buick. Killing the headlights, Jules clambered out of the truck with a weary sigh, tilting her head back to watch her breath steam in the cold air. Overhead, the sky was cloudless and bright with stars. Tall pines surrounded her, needled boughs rustling in a mild wind, trunks creaking softly as they swayed. Even for early spring, it was cold. Somehow, the colder air always made the stars seem brighter.

She'd missed this. The quiet. The beauty. The lack of people. She hadn't seen the stars this brightly since leaving Seattle. Theoretically, she'd been living in a nature lover's wonderland. Puget Sound, Olympic National Park, Mount Rainier, the Cascades, the ocean, had all been only a brief drive away from the city. But Eric had wrinkled his nose every time Jules suggested it, telling her she didn't need to become some "crunchy, granola type" just because of where they lived. In the whole ten years she'd lived there, Jules had only ever seen Mount Rainier from a distance, on days when the sky was clear enough to see it from the city.

There were no mountains in her hometown, or anywhere near it. But the air was clean, scented of pine and freshwater, the night sky was jewel-bright, and the world felt *quiet*. Peaceful.

Unfortunately for Jules, that peaceful quiet also felt incredibly lonely. Or... it had.

She was leaning against the truck door, thinking of Max,

when a subtle twitch of motion at the edge of the yard, just behind the garage, caught her attention. She looked towards it, letting her eyes adjust to the dark. An indistinct shadow slowly took shape. At first, she thought she was seeing a much smaller animal—a coyote, maybe—surrounded by dark undergrowth. Slowly, the realization dawned that this was no coyote. It was a wolf. The most *massive* wolf she'd ever seen in her life. As tall at the shoulders as a pony, and as broad in the chest as a brown bear.

Jules stiffened, afraid to move, afraid to even breathe. The tawny brown wolf stared back at her with eyes of striated gold.

The giant wolves were a local legend—had been for eons. Everyone knew someone who claimed to have seen one. Every old man had a story about spotting a pack of them during deer hunting season. Every other teenager had a story about seeing one while they were off in the woods drinking. Jules wasn't a hunter, and she hadn't been the sneak-off-to-go-drinking kind of kid, so she'd never seen one. And she hadn't really believed in them either. She'd put about as much stock in the giant wolves as she did in the Hodag.

But now, here one was, staring her in the eye with an unnerving degree of acuity. There was something more than animal in that golden gaze. Jules couldn't do anything but stare back.

Slowly, with obvious caution, the wolf took a step toward her. Jules was too scared to run, to scream, to do anything. She just stood frozen in place, watching as the most massive predator she'd ever seen inched closer and closer to her.

The wolf approached like a hopeful, but shy, lapdog.

Head low, tail low but wagging gently, gaze cast down. It let out a soft whine as it approached, sounding for all the world like a lost puppy.

Jules's heart hammered in her chest. This was how she was going to die. She wasn't going to go down swinging, or anything brave. She was going to lay there and take it. Because on the day they handed out everyone's fight or flight responses, Jules had apparently been absent. Instead, when she was scared, her whole body just went into lockdown and she turned into a sweaty, trembling mannequin.

The massive wolf went still, lowering itself further to the ground, whining placatingly. If this were just a strange dog, she'd be perfectly at ease. But this wasn't a dog, it was a pony-sized wolf. Her primordial monkey brain was screaming *GET INTO THE TREES!* But her useless sense of self-preservation operated along the logic of, *if I don't move, it can't see me.*

The wolf whined again, sinking all the way onto its belly and crawling forward in hopeful wiggles, tail sweeping the ground. It reached Jules's ankles, big nose snuffling happily along her boots while she stood there like the world's best impersonation of Lot's wife. The wolf raised its head and nosed her limp hand. A big wet tongue lapped at her palm.

That feeling triggered an instinct that overrode her paralyzing fear.

"Ick!" she scolded, pulling her hand away. She wasn't averse to puppy kisses, but she didn't like her hands being licked.

The wolf cringed down, nudging its nose against her ankle, looking up at her with hopeful golden eyes.

"Oh my god," Jules breathed, as the ridiculousness of what she'd just done hit her. She'd just yelled at a wolf.

The creature whined again, tilting its head up, licking at its muzzle in a playful, beseeching way, holding eye contact with her in a distinctly non-wolfish fashion. Maybe it wasn't a wolf? Maybe somebody's monstrously terrifying dog had gotten loose?

Without thinking, Jules lowered her hand to the massive, furry head. The wolf-dog groaned, eyes closing, tongue lolling. Jules scritched behind its ears, her heart rate slowly falling. This couldn't be a wolf. It was too tame, too friendly. Whatever it was, it panted happily as Jules petted it.

"Where are your people, buddy?" Jules asked, working her fingers down into its ruff, seeking a collar. There was none. "What are we going to do with you?" She didn't want to leave him out in the cold, but Grandma would have an absolute fit if Jules brought a giant, strange dog into the house.

What if she closed him off in the laundry room, where the floor was all linoleum? It would keep him warm until Jules could bring him to the animal shelter when it opened in the morning. Grandma still wouldn't be happy, but at least there was nothing the dog could really damage in there.

She gently gripped his ruff, testing his reaction. When he only leaned against her, she gripped him tighter and tried to guide him forward.

"Come on, buddy. I've got a warm laundry room for you. And maybe a can of tuna if that's okay for dogs to eat. I have to look it up. Come on, this way—"

In the distance, the long, ululating howl of a wolf sounded. Several others joined, forming an eerie chorus. Jules wasn't alarmed—they sounded far away. But the wolf-dog leapt to his feet, suddenly alert. Standing, Jules was struck by the size of him all over again. His shoulder was nearly as high as hers. His head was as big around as her truck's hubcaps. She wasn't sure he'd actually fit in the laundry room.

He stared towards the source of the howls, nose working, ears pinned forward.

"Hey, come on," Jules asked, tugging gently on his ruff. He'd fit in the garage, and while it wasn't as warm as the house, it was still warmer than outside.

But shelter wasn't in the cards for him. The wolves' howls sounded again, and even to Jules's human ears, they sounded noticeably closer. With a low growl, the wolf-dog butted his head gently against her stomach before springing away. He ran with great loping strides and disappeared into the trees, leaving Jules with nothing but a fistful of his fur.

"Bye," she said softly, looking into the darkness where he'd disappeared.

The wolves' cries sounded again. Jules finally stirred into motion, hurrying into the house.

CHAPTER 6

Wolfe's was always busy on Saturdays. The little mini-mart was the closest place to get gas, food, or bait, for anybody between Lac Bonne Vue and the Aster Flowage. Summers were the worst, when the Northwoods was flooded with tourists. But in early spring, the lakes were still covered in ice, so the Saturday traffic was limited to locals and weekend ice fishermen.

By seven, things had slowed somewhat. In between customers, Jules couldn't help wondering when Max would show up. *If* he would show up. By eight, the sun was down, the store was mostly quiet except for the occasional drop-in looking for beer, and Jules had to admit to herself that Max wasn't going to show today.

At nine-thirty, Jules was in the back, breaking down boxes to go in the recycling when the door jingled. She knew it was going to be just another random customer, but she couldn't help hoping. She wiped the cardboard dust from her hands and made her way back to the front. Immediately, she knew it wasn't Max. The man waiting at the counter was too stocky, with a short blond buzz cut, dressed in the heavy insulated coveralls that ice fishers favored. It was too late in the season to be safely ice fishing, but as long as there was ice on the water, there were plenty of idiots who thought they were too special to fall through.

He looked Jules up and down as she approached, a mean gleam in his lazy perusal. She instinctively stiffened, shoulders rising defensively. His gaze roved over her black overalls and dark red boots, drifting up to the white crop top that revealed a bit of skin on her sides where the overalls didn't cover. She'd left her heavy cardigan in the back, and the urge to turn around and go get it almost stopped her in her tracks. Repressing that defensive instinct, she slid behind the counter.

"Hi," she said to the guy, pretending nonchalance as she woke up the register. "Gas on pump two?"

He didn't say anything, an amused smile tugging at his mouth as he continued to look her over. His posture was loose, his eyes a bit bloodshot. He was either a little drunk or a little high, but Jules would've put her money on drunk. There was a belligerence in the way he looked at her that seemed more in line with booze than with weed. His attention settled on her hair, wrapped around her head in milkmaid braids, and the vivid green ends.

"Did you get gas?" Jules repeated, feeling her face heat.

"Yeah," he finally answered, laughter in his voice as he met her gaze. "Yeah, pump two."

"Anything else for you?"

"Nah, that's it."

"Okay, that's fifty—"

"Hey, I got a question." The amused drawl in his tone

told Jules everything she needed to know about this question.

"What's that?" She pretended to be focused on the register.

"Did you know your hair's green?" He grinned at her, real proud of his wit.

"Nope," she said flatly. "Had no idea. Your total's fifty dollars even."

His eyes crinkled as his smile grew. Patting at his jacket, he fished around unhurriedly for his wallet. "You know what they say about girls with unnatural hair colors, right?"

"'Watch out, they're usually armed'?"

The guy blinked. "What?"

"Hm?"

He shrugged off the momentary confusion, smile returning with its predatory slant. That look reminded Jules of the boys she'd known who liked pulling the wings off flies, and the sort of men who went hunting just to shoot anything that moved. Not terribly bright, but totally unaware of it. Casual cruelty was their favorite form of humor. They likely never developed the part of the brain that recognizes that other people have different thoughts and experiences from theirs.

"They say they're real good at... you know."

Jules felt herself flushing hotter. It was a mixture of discomfort and anger. But she was alone in the store, and he was bigger than her, so she couldn't tell him to go fuck himself, because he seemed like a good candidate for the sort of guy who liked to punish women who dented his ego.

"*You know*," he prompted. He raised his eyebrows, surveying her flushed face with satisfaction.

"No, I don't. Your total is fifty dollars."

"Hmmm." He finally pulled his wallet out of his inside pocket, flipping it open and pulling out a few twenties. He handed them over to Jules, but as she reached for them, he pulled them back. "You single?"

Jules stared at him.

"Come on, mermaid hair. What time do you get done here? I'll take you to the Carriage House." The Carriage House was a supper club on the shore of Lac Bonne Vue, popular with tourists and the old folks who'd retired up here. The food was good, but the prices were steep.

Regardless, Jules had no intention of taking him up on it. It didn't even matter. This late at night, it'd be closed soon, anyway. "It's nine-thirty."

"Aw, shit." He grinned. "Guess we'll have to skip dinner. Come on, what time do you get off?"

Jules had no idea how to shut this down. She'd spent all of her early adulthood married. Something about the person she'd become with Eric had radiated a kind of forcefield that kept creeps from propositioning her. She'd never learned how to deal with them the way so many other women had.

"I'm sorry, I'm not looking to date," she said uncomfortably.

He laughed. "Who said anything about dating? I'll show you a good time."

"No, I'm sorry." She pinned her gaze on the cash register's screen. "Fifty dollars—how do you want to pay?"

The door jingled, and Jules nearly sagged in relief. When there was someone else in the store to witness their behavior, the pricks usually mellowed out.

"Hey man, what's taking so long?" the newcomer demanded, immediately crushing Jules's hopes. He sounded drunker than the first guy.

"Just talking to my new friend here. Right, honey?"

"Sir, I need you to pay for your—"

"*Ooohoohoo!* You hear that, Danny? She called me *sir.*"

"She can call me anything she likes," the other guy said, sidling up with a grin. "What's your name, gorgeous?"

"None of your business." She was sweating now, hands shaking. She curled her fingers over the edge of the counter to hide it. "You need to pay for your gas and get out of here."

"Oh no, don't be like that," the first guy said with false dismay. "Come on, what's your name, honey? We got a nice room at the Timberline. You can come party with us."

"Two double beds," the other guy said, waggling his eyebrows suggestively.

"I'm going to call the cops if you don't pay." An embarrassing tremor made her voice fragile.

Like sharks scenting blood, both men laughed.

"Aw, you don't want to do that. We're just trying to make friends. Don't you want to—"

The door smashed open suddenly, hitting the bell so hard it nearly flew off the hook. A sound like a revving engine cut through the men's laughter. It took Jules a second to realize she was hearing a deep, vicious, animalistic growl.

Max.

He stormed into the store like an avenging angel, golden eyes gleaming like bright hellfire. "She said *no*," he snarled at the men, his voice distorted with anger—deeper, hoarser.

They stared at Max in stunned silence. The tallest of the two men was as tall as Max—and it'd be two-on-one in a fight. But something about the look on Max's face, or the fury in his stance, cowed them.

"Ah, sorry, man," the first guy said. "Didn't know she was taken."

"Why are you apologizing to *me*?" Max growled, looking ready to tear them limb from limb.

The first guy turned, not quite looking Jules in the eye as he slid three twenties towards her. "Sorry about that, honey. Just playing around."

She made his change without responding, slapping a ten on the counter in front of him. He took it, and both guys left immediately. She watched through the window as they got into their truck and pulled out. When they were gone, she breathed out a sigh of relief.

Max approached the counter, still tense, eyes still bright with anger. "You okay?"

She nodded. "Fine now. Thank you."

"You know those guys?"

She shook her head. "They're out-of-towners. Just here for ice fishing."

He leaned against the counter, and unlike the other two men, his closeness, his size, was comforting. His strength was a shield and shelter, not a weapon. As his gaze tracked over her, Jules got the distinct sense that she was being examined for injury. She was so used to hiding imperfections—and her ex-husband had definitely taught her to see her own pain as an imperfection—that she turned away, pretending to orga-nize a stack of mail. It was all just junk that needed to be recycled, but it gave her something to do with her hands, and somewhere to look other than Max's penetrating gaze.

"Jules."

"Hm?"

"Does this sort of thing happen a lot?"

"No. Not really. I mean, there's always a few creeps to deal with, but they're not usually quite *that* persistent."

Max made a grumbling sound deep in his throat. "And you're here by yourself?"

"It's not usually that bad." None of it was her fault, but her broken brain couldn't help reacting like it was. She needed to defuse the situation, convince Max she wasn't incompetent, change the topic. The therapist she'd seen for a little while had called it complex PTSD—this constant vigilance, feeling obligated to manage everyone else's emotional reactions, the instinctive self-blame, the insecurity, the intense fear of criticism.

But then Eric had cut her off from therapy—saying it was a selfish indulgence for bored housewives—and Jules had never learned what she was supposed to do with all those feelings. She couldn't give them up. She'd needed them to survive her marriage. But now the marriage was over, and she was still stuck with these defective coping mechanisms.

"Hey," Max said gently.

Something in his voice called her attention, and she looked up, meeting his gaze. The intense gold had receded to a darker hazel-brown. How was that possible?

"It's not your fault," he told her. "Don't feel bad, okay? Those guys were assholes, and they deserved a lot more than the easy scolding they got. Where I'm from—" He cut himself off, seeming to consider his words. Finally, he said, "My mother and my aunties and all the rest of my community would've come down on them like a fucking hammer for treating you that way. You shouldn't have to put up with that shit."

Something brittle and sharp that Jules had been carrying in her chest for a long time suddenly cracked a little—just enough that pieces of it could fall away, lessening the burden.

"I—" She didn't know what to say to him. "Um."

The intensity of his expression softened. "How was your day otherwise?"

"Um... it was alright." *Spent most of it wondering when you were going to show up.* "How was yours?"

"Not bad. I spent the day in the woods."

"Yeah? What for?"

"Just roaming. Went from Cry Lake to Lac Bonne Vue, then over to Arrow Lake."

Jules blinked. "In one day? Were you on the ATV trails?"

"No, just on foot." He went preternaturally still for a second, his face turning into a blank mask. "Uh, I was running. I do a lot of running."

"I guess so. That's, like, two marathons in one day."

He shrugged, looking cagey. "It's beautiful here. I could run all day long just to see all the lakes and the trees."

Jules puffed out a wistful sigh. "Me too. Well, maybe not *run* all day. But I could easily spend the whole day just rambling around."

"Yeah?" Max's eyes brightened as he leaned closer. "Where's the best place to ramble, then?"

Jules thought for a second. "My favorite is the trail that runs from Possum Lake to Hemlock Lake. They're both smaller lakes and motorized boats aren't allowed on them, so they're really quiet. The trail follows an old, disused railway for a while, and there's this huge train bridge you take across the outflow below the narrow part of the Aster Flowage, just below the Falls..." She trailed off, suddenly self-conscious as she heard the enthusiasm in her own voice.

This was the point where Eric usually told her she talked too loud.

But Max didn't look annoyed. "I'll have to check that one out," he said, sounding sincerely interested.

Every broken instinct in Jules was screaming at her to shut up, stop being annoying, stop being attention-seeking. But she didn't want to be that person anymore—the quiet shadow who existed in the background of other people's lives, never taking up anybody's space or energy or effort. She was allowed to have a voice, and interests, and passions. That didn't make her bad, or silly, or "too much."

Ignoring the pounding of her heart and the slight tremor in her hands, she went on, "Yeah, after the Falls, it goes upland, and there are all these gorgeous granite formations surrounded by huge pines. It's really peaceful. There's a little creek, too, with lots of pretty rocks."

"Pretty rocks, huh?" Max smiled, such open fondness in his expression that Jules's heart started hammering for a totally different reason.

She flushed. "Yeah. I like... nature things."

Max's smile grew. "I like nature things too."

They kept talking, and it might have been the easiest, most natural conversation Jules had ever had in her life. Before she realized it, too much time had passed. It was ten-thirty—half an hour past closing time. She'd just stood there and chattered at Max for nearly an hour. He was probably desperate to get away but too polite to end the conversation.

"Oh my god," she interrupted herself, embarrassed and apologetic. "It's so late! I'm so sorry, I've been talking your ear off. You probably—"

"It's okay, Jules." Max's hand closed over hers. Again, his comforting warmth, his solid strength, seemed to imbue itself through her skin, calming her, reassuring her. "I'm the one who should apologize. I've been holding you up while you probably have work to do."

"I was supposed to close the store already," she admitted, instantly regretting it.

"Do you need help?" Max offered, surprising her. "It's the least I can do, to make up for keeping you late."

And like that, the last of her anxiety melted away. "It's sweet of you to offer, but I couldn't accept your help. Way too much liability for the store."

"I understand." He squeezed her hand and released it, stepping back from the counter and shoving his hands in his pockets. "Have a good night, Jules."

"You too, Max."

There was a weighted moment where it felt like either one of them might say more. But the moment stretched out, and neither of them spoke. Max broke it, stepping back to the door. With one last glance, he left.

Jules sighed and went to lock the door behind him, turning the "open" sign off. She was halfway through taking down the coffee carafes when it dawned on her—he hadn't bought anything. She paused, a dirty carafe in each hand, and for a moment, she wondered. Had he come by just to see her? Or, more likely, had he just gotten distracted after chasing those creeps off? *Yes*, her pragmatic, dour side insisted. *You're not that interesting.*

MAX DROVE DOWN A QUIET SIDE ROAD AND PARKED THE TRUCK before running back to Wolfe's Quick Mart, where he could keep watch while Jules closed up. He knew this was borderline unacceptable behavior, but he didn't care. His wolf especially didn't. After chasing off those two assholes, he couldn't leave knowing she was alone and unprotected. This was what he did, who he was. Back home, that was his whole purpose—he was a protector of the pack and a guardian of the borders.

He'd felt a bit adrift since leaving home, with no pack of his own to protect. But now there was Jules, and all that directionless protective instinct had a point of focus. As he kept watch over her, his mind went back to the leering drunks. He'd heard a fair amount of the conversation before he'd made it through the door—he knew the name of the motel they were staying at. He also knew their scent. After Jules was safely home, he could go find them and lay down the law.

Except this wasn't his pack territory and those men weren't wolf kin, so it wasn't his law to lay down or his place to do so. Frustrated at his uselessness, he was only marginally comforted by the fear he'd instilled in them. In his fury, his wolf had started to emerge. Just a little. He hadn't quite begun to shift, but he'd let his wolf dangerously close to the surface. It had been enough to make the two men reek of fear. The skinlocked strangers wouldn't have consciously noted the change, but deep in their primordial monkey brains, they recognized the threat of a *much* stronger predator.

He stifled a satisfied growl as he stood in the shadow of the trees across the street from Wolfe's. He could see Jules moving around inside the store, cleaning and shutting things down. He wasn't really watching her, though. His attention was mostly focused on the immediate surroundings of the gas station, eyes attuned for any motion near the building, ears pricked for the sound of approaching threats.

When she was finally done, he watched intently as she emerged from a side door, turning her back to the rest of the world while she locked it. He was poised to race over at the slightest provocation, but the world remained quiet and peaceful. Jules got into her old rusting truck and drove away.

Max sprinted back to his truck, where he ripped his clothes off and threw them onto the driver's seat. He swung the door shut and threw his body forward—landing on four paws. In his wolfskin, with his wolf in control, he sprinted towards the end of the street, where the woods waited. Jules had to follow the county highway back to her house, but Max could run a straight line through the forest. If he ran at his top speed, he could beat her there.

And he did. Panting raggedly, he watched from the tree line as her headlights swung into the driveway. When she stepped out of her vehicle, he whined, letting her know he was there before he trotted out to greet her. She stiffened at first, but when she recognized him, a wide smile crossed her face.

"Hey, buddy," she greeted him in a cooing voice. "I was worried about you."

Max chuffed, amused by the irony. He leaned against her as she scratched his ears, content with her touch and her nearness. He couldn't stay too long. He didn't want any of the Cry Lake wolf kin to track him here—he wanted to keep her to himself for now, and nosy wolf kin would ruin that with glee. If he was gone for too long, others would notice, they'd go looking for him, and his scent trail would lead them straight to Jules. If he hadn't needed to take the straightest course to beat her here, he'd have led a more discreet trail. When he didn't want to be tracked, he could make himself a ghost.

But for now, he had to content himself with the fact that Jules was safely home, and depart. He drew back from her touch—though it took some effort from the man before the wolf conceded.

"Hey, where're you going, honey?" Jules asked, frowning. "Don't you want to come into the garage? It's nice and warm. We can find your people in the morning. Come on, you fluffy giant. Come with me," she coaxed.

He whined, hating that he had to leave, but wanting her safe inside, and needing to leave before he was tracked. He pulled away from her, loping back into the woods. From the tree line, he watched as she sighed, straightened, and went to the house. When she was safely inside, he turned and ran. This time, he retraced his own trail, laying false leads, back-tracking, doubling over, and circling until he was sure that anyone trying to follow him would end up with their legs tied in knots.

When he made it back to where he'd parked the truck, he was panting hard. He shifted back into his human form and quickly dressed, forced to pull his clothes on over sweaty, hot skin. He didn't mind. It was worth it to make sure Jules was safe.

CHAPTER 7

Sunday evenings were the only nights that Jules and her grandma were at home together and both awake, since the store closed at five on Sundays. So Grandma always fixed a big dinner, and they usually played a few rounds of rummy or cribbage after. After more than ten years of living off of tasteless, "healthy" meals (and secretly sneaking junk when Eric wasn't around), Grandma's home-cooked meals were the height of luxury. While she savored scratch-made Salisbury steak and mashed potatoes with gravy and roasted green beans, Jules tried telling her grandma that she'd seen one of the giant wolves—twice—and petted it both times. But before she could even get to her theory that the "giant wolves" were actually just one large, but tame, dog roaming around, Grandma had cocked her head, fixing Jules with a worried look.

"Maybe I should take the evening shift for a while," Grandma said gently. "A little more daylight might do you good, Jujube."

"No, really, I—" Jules cut off her objections. Grandma

had seen how defeated and hollowed out Jules was when she'd first moved back from Seattle, and she had fretted ever since. Jules didn't need to add more worry to the heap. "I'm fine, Grandma. I like the evenings—you know I'm not a morning person."

Grandma considered her for another moment, openly skeptical. "If you say so…"

"I'm fine," Jules insisted.

Her grandma was in her late seventies now, but could easily pass for being more than a decade younger. Her face was expressive, her eyes bright. Her silvery gray hair was cut in a short pixie style that emphasized her strong cheekbones and large eyes. In her younger days, she'd looked much like Jules did now—except happier. She and Jules were temperamental opposites. Grandma was outgoing and chatty and loved visiting with friends, while Jules was a quiet introvert who lived mostly inside her own head.

"How's Mike and Tammy's house coming along?" Jules asked, diverting Grandma's attention to something else. A windstorm had knocked a big pine right onto one of the neighbor's houses, smashing in the roof. Grandma knew every detail and didn't spare a single one in the telling.

"Well, you know that contractor they were having trouble with?"

Jules nodded. "The one who tracked dirt all through the house?"

"That's the one. You'll never guess what they found two days ago in one of their window wells."

"What?"

"Garbage! All the workers' garbage! Fast food wrappers, cigarette butts, empty soda bottles—you name it! And you know what Tammy saw on the dashboard of their truck?"

"What?"

"A marijuana pipe!"

Jules bit her lip, trying not to grin. "Oh no."

She listened in contented quiet, eating her dinner while Grandma went through a laundry list of unprofessional behavior and minor crimes. After dinner was over, they played a few rounds of cribbage before Grandma went to sleep. Jules normally watched TV or read a book to fill the lonely quiet, but she was too restless tonight. The TV was on, but she wasn't paying attention. She paced around the house, straightening and tidying things that didn't need to be straightened or tidied.

She had just tossed the damp kitchen towel in the laundry room hamper when something outside the narrow little window caught her eye. She froze. In the dark of the backyard, along the tree line, a hulking shadow paced. It was the time of year when bears were starting to come out of their dens, and they were happy to raid backyard bird feeders to fill their hollow bellies. Jules went to the window, eyes narrowed as she peered into the darkness.

After a moment, her eyes adjusted to the dark, and unexpected happiness flooded her. It was the dog—the giant dog that her Grandma thought she was hallucinating. Jules hurried to the living room and slipped out the patio door.

"Hey, buddy," she called softly.

The massive dog perked at the sight of her, loping over happily. He whined as he butted his big head against her belly.

"Hey, you." Jules smiled as she scratched behind his ears. "How are you *always* here at midnight? Do you have a watch or something? Hm? You got an important doggy appointment?" She scruffed her hands through his fur, fluffing up his face as she continued to gibber at him in a ridiculously sweet voice. "I hope I'm not keeping you from your business. I wouldn't want to interfere with important canine matters. Or are you here because you're eating the peanuts Grandma puts out for the cardinals? She's not going to like that, you know."

The dog looked up, licking her chin. His tongue was huge, and his breath steamed her whole face.

"Ack!" She wiped his spit off with the backs of her hands. "Ugh, no dog kisses, *thank you*," she said archly, pulling her sleeve over her hand and using it to wipe away the last of his saliva. "Only *I* give kisses, okay?" She bent and smooched the top of his furry head.

He lolled back happily, tongue hanging out, eyes bright. He seemed to accept her terms. In fact, there was something in his gaze that was almost *too* astute. It gave Jules a moment of pause. She was just about to shrug it off and keep petting her giant new friend, when a single wavering howl cut through the night, coming from the not-too-distant south.

The dog jumped up to all four feet with a quickness, all playfulness gone. He nudged his head affectionately against Jules's hip before he disappeared back into the woods.

Suddenly alone, with the wolf's howl echoing in her mind, Jules shivered and hurried back into the house. She locked all the doors and windows, and went to the bathroom to brush her teeth and do her nighttime skincare routine.

As she lay in bed, waiting to drift off to sleep, it suddenly struck her that she hadn't gotten to see Max today. She wondered if he'd gone to the store without realizing they closed early on Sundays. Would he have been disappointed?

Don't be so self-obsessed, a voice that was a little bit her own and a little bit someone else's sneered in her mind. *He doesn't care where he buys beef jerky.*

But a different voice—a quieter voice that sounded a lot more like Jules, whispered, *I think he does.*

MONDAY NIGHT, JULES WAS ALL NERVOUS ANTICIPATION AS NINE o'clock drew nearer. That was around the time Max usually showed up—or at least it had been for the last few days. But she hadn't seen him yesterday, and for some reason, that struck her as important. Had the disruption ruined everything? Maybe he was never going to show up again. Maybe it was over.

Nine o'clock came and went with no sign of Max. The store was quiet, leaving Jules free to stare out the window at the parking lot. At nine-thirty, he still hadn't shown up. At nine forty-five, she had to accept reality and admit to herself that he wasn't coming. With a sigh, she left the window and went to start emptying coffee carafes.

She had just dumped out the decaf when the bell above the door jangled. She turned, looking past rows of shelves to catch sight of familiar golden eyes.

"You're late!" she blurted. Mortified heat immediately suffused her cheeks. Good god. At what age could a grown woman expect to stop blushing like a neon sign every time she felt even the slightest hint of embarrassment?

But Max grinned, looking nothing less than pleased by her indignation. "Sorry," he said with false chagrin. "There was a party today that I had to be at."

"Oh. Well. That's... you're obviously not late," Jules said awkwardly.

He made his way back to the coffee station, still smiling. Without the counter between them, Jules was even more conscious of his presence. He was big and broad, and he radiated warmth like a space heater.

"I'm a little late," Max conceded. He tilted his head, watching Jules while she pretended to be engrossed in wiping down the coffee carafes. "You're closing up in a few minutes, aren't you?"

"Um, yeah. But, I mean, it's not a problem. No rush," she said hurriedly.

Max was quiet for a second, considering her with a thoughtful, assessing gaze that made her want to fidget. At long last, he finally looked away. "I ran the trail you told me about."

Jules immediately forgot her nerves, turning to him eagerly. "Yeah? What'd you think?"

"Beautiful. I can see why you love it."

"I walk on it pretty much every day. My grandma's house is close to Hemlock Lake, so it's an easy walk."

"Every day?" he asked, a thread of something stronger than mere curiosity in his voice.

"Pretty much. Right after I eat breakfast." She hesitated, torn between knowing she was reading too much into his interest, and wanting to believe in it anyway. "Um... around ten o'clock in the morning most days."

"Ten a.m.?" Max repeated casually, but there was a glimmer of something *more* there. Jules's heart sped up.

"Yeah," she said faintly, nerves returning in full force.

"What if you happened to run into someone you knew while you were on your ten a.m. walk?" he asked in a tone of idle curiosity, though a playful smile lit his eyes.

"I, um... I would be... happy?" Her face flushed hotter than the sun.

"You don't sound very sure."

"No, I am." Her heart was going to pound right through her sternum. "I would be happy to see... um, someone."

Max smiled. "Well then, I hope you see someone."

"Me too," Jules replied without thinking.

Max's smile turned into a broad grin. "Alright, well, I'll get out of your hair so you can close up. See you, Jules."

"Bye," she said, slightly dazed by everything that had just occurred.

She watched him leave, staring out the windows until his truck pulled out of the parking lot and disappeared down the road. When the road was dark and empty, and the silence of the store pressed in on her ears like cotton, Jules suddenly became aware that she was staring vacantly. She lurched back into motion, going to the front of the store to turn off the OPEN light and lock the doors.

When she was finally done and ready to leave, it suddenly occurred to her that Max hadn't bought anything. Again.

Had he... had he come just to see her? Her stomach did a nervous flip, but the rest of her was filled with a warm, contented glow.

CHAPTER 8

Guard Jules while she closed the store.

Race to beat her home in his wolfskin.

Give in to the wolf's urge to play for a bit.

Then race back to Cry Lake before any of the pack noticed he'd been off on his own for too long.

It was fast becoming a routine. And looking after Jules for an hour or so every night gave his restlessness an outlet. He missed home. He missed his family and his pack. He missed his role as a protector and guardian. But for the short time that he spent with Jules or watching over her, the homesick, cagey feeling vanished. And now he'd gotten her permission to see more of her. Tomorrow. Ten a.m. It played on repeat in his brain, as if he might otherwise forget.

When he made it back to Cry Lake, he was reluctant to go into the small cabin where he slept. It was unnatural for wolf kin to live alone. Technically, he had neighbors to his immediate left and right, but the idea of being the only occupant in an entire dwelling, no matter how small, was uncomfortable. He was used to the Spruce—the boarding house and hotel that his parents ran—where he lived and ate and spent his downtime in the company of his packmates.

The Cry Lake pack was hardly any different—most of them lived in large, multi-generational family households. But they didn't have a central communal dwelling like the Spruce, so fosters and visitors ended up sleeping alone in the little bachelor cabins behind the Lodge. The sense of remove, the isolation, made it hard to sleep. He spent every waking minute outside of the lonely little cabin.

He occasionally ran patrols with the Cry Lake guardians, though he was little more than an observer since he had no authority in the pack. More often, he offered his help wherever it might be needed. He'd spent several days felling dead standing trees in the pack's managed forestlands, dug a new culvert to divert flooding, hauled old appliances out of the Lodge and hauled new ones in, changed the oil in multiple pack-owned vehicles, drove in new fence posts around an apple orchard the pack was expanding, and a million other little odd jobs meant to keep his mind off the fact that he missed his pack like a phantom limb.

Although, lately, what he needed to be distracted from was Jules.

He'd spent yesterday afternoon replacing shingles on the roof of the Lodge with a handful of Cry Lake wolves—including Iris Eriksen, who was incredibly persistent about learning more about Max's "new skinlocked friend." He'd managed to evade any real answers, but he knew it was only a matter of time before the pack figured out who she was and started following the courtship like fans at a sporting event.

So the next morning, when he was due to meet Jules on her favorite walking trail, he left well ahead of time. He shifted into his wolfskin and carried a bag of clothes in his mouth. It was uncomfortable, but he felt pretty certain that showing up totally nude would scare Jules off for good. But the wolfskin was necessary—he needed to lay a track that couldn't be followed, and the truck was too easy to follow.

As soon as he set out, he knew he had followers. No doubt Iris was among them. Partially annoyed, and partially amused by the challenge, Max set to losing them. Among the Teekkonlit, he was the best tracker—and that meant he was the best at keeping others off his trail, as well. Even as a kid, when the wolf kin version of hide-and-seek involved a heightened sense of smell, Max had been the best—the best at finding others, and the best at hiding from them.

Huffing around the bundle clutched in his jaws, he ran a circuitous, labyrinthine trail that used every trick in the book —backtracking through bodies of water, soaring leaps across ravine gaps, crossing over his own trail in cloverleaf formations, creating dead-ends by doubling back.

When he was sure he'd lost his extra tails, he continued to be cautious as he made his way to Hemlock Lake, pausing now and then to disrupt the trail. At the lake, he spat the clothing bundle out and sat at the water's edge, sides heaving as he panted. Judging by the sun, Jules wasn't due for another hour. But Max shifted into his human skin— sweaty and flushed—and jumped into the lake. This early in spring, the water was brutally cold—there was still snow on the ground in the shadier parts of the woods, and ice on the bigger lakes. But it doused the furnace inside of him, turning panting breaths into chattering teeth.

He got out, shivering in the open air while he waited for his skin to dry. Despite the chill, he was content, enjoying the quiet. The little lake was surrounded on all sides by steeply sloping land covered in thick forest. The world smelled of fresh water and pine sap and clean air. The sky above was rich, bright blue, studded with puffy white clouds. Squirrels and birds chattered from the forest. The water lapped ever so faintly against the shoreline, driven by the gentlest of westward breezes. A single red-tailed hawk circled overhead, riding thermal updrafts in lazy swoops.

His shivering eased as he dried. Steam rose faintly from his skin. Wolf kin ran hot, and the nearly-freezing air temperature only felt bracingly cool, rather than the stark discomfort a skinlocked human would feel. He dressed anyway, not keen on being found naked by passing strangers. He hadn't been able to fit a winter coat into the bag of clothing he'd brought, but hopefully Jules wouldn't be too suspicious of the fact that all he had for outerwear was a lined flannel.

He was just lacing his boots when the wind carried the first hint of Jules to him. Her scent was faint, almost a ghost. But then he heard the sound of footsteps—almost inaudible against the soft, needle-padded bedding of the forest floor. He hastily finished his laces and got to his feet, hiking up the slope to where the walking trail circled the lake.

He saw Jules through the trees before she saw him, her attention turned to the opposite side of the trail. When she looked forward again, he was there, and she nearly jumped out of her skin at the sight of him.

"Sorry!" he said quickly, stooping his shoulders, shoving his hands in his pockets, doing everything he could to not seem big or looming. "Didn't mean to startle you."

She smiled, but it was obviously a nervous smile. "Oh, hey, it's somebody I know," she said with badly-acted surprise. "How unexpected!"

Playing along, Max nodded earnestly. "Yes. What a shocking coincidence that we are both here at ten a.m. on this particular trail."

As she drew up beside him, her scent more concentrated, Max inhaled discreetly. Beneath the usual fresh, homey scent of her, there was the astringent sourness of anxiety. But coupled with it was something else—not quite arousal, but... attraction. Interest. His wolf was thrilled. But Max knew he had to tread carefully. She might be interested in him, but she was also wary. Her heart was racing, her pupils dilated. He wanted her at ease, comfortable, smiling with genuine laughter instead of nervous politeness. He had to prove she could trust him.

Jules was so excited and so freaked out, she was astounded that she was managing to string coherent sentences together, let alone *joke* with Max. Eric had once pulled her aside at a big faculty event and gently but firmly told her that her sense of humor was missing the mark—that her lack of education was showing, and that she was embarrassing him in front of his colleagues. Jules had been mortified, but it had seemed obvious to her at the time that Eric had just been trying to help her out. Though, in the years that followed, the gentle reproaches eventually turned into stern scoldings, into outright hostility, until Jules gave up on trying to goof around at all.

The fact that she'd tried it with Max had her whole body prickling with nervous sweat, and she couldn't help searching his face for some sign that his smile was forced—an attempt at politeness in the face of her awkward unfunniness.

But, unless he was an *amazing* actor, it seemed like he actually found her at least marginally amusing. His golden-brown eyes were bright with laughter, and he'd added on to her joke, instead of giving it a weak smile.

Relaxing a little, Jules started walking again. Max fell into step beside her. As the familiarity of her routine resumed—a peaceful walk on her favorite trail in the quiet of the forest—some more of the anxiety fell away.

"So, how long are you staying in Cry Lake?" Jules asked, immediately wincing because it sounded like she was angling for something more than just polite conversation.

"I don't know," Max said, casting her a thoughtful look. "Until it's time to move on, I guess."

Jules tilted her head. "Don't you have a job you have to get back to?" Immediately, the rudeness of that question hit her, and she flushed. "I'm sorry, I mean—"

Max smiled, waving his hand in a wordless gesture of no-harm-done. "I'm on a leave of absence, I guess you could say. My life will still be waiting for me when I decide to go back."

"What do you do, then?"

"Mostly community safety. But I do other work where it's needed. We all do."

"So you're like... a cop?"

Max frowned. "No. We don't have cops."

"Oh." Jules flushed again, cowed by the firmness of his tone. "Sorry, I didn't mean to offend you."

He shook his head, expression softening. "I'm not offended. It's just, our community doesn't have that. And what I do is different from what cops do. But, we do have to deal with the state troopers sometimes, and I'm the liaison for that, so I guess I'm 'law enforcement' in a sense."

"Wow. You sound important." Jules knew she was fawning—it was a habit she'd picked up with Eric that she hadn't yet managed to break. Whenever she'd offended someone or disturbed the peace somehow, the compulsion to smooth it over with flattery and ego-stroking was impossible to resist. It was how she got back into Eric's good graces. It was how she made a miserable, cold, oppressive home environment turn back into a light, peaceful, affectionate one.

Max shrugged. "We're all important."

Without meaning to, Jules puffed out a derisive huff.

Max's brows rose. "You don't think so?"

"I'm not important." She was speaking truthfully, but she also knew that kind of self-deprecation made people uncomfortable, so she generally didn't give voice to it.

Max staggered to a halt, turning to face Jules full-on. "You don't think you're important?" he echoed, incredulous.

"I know I'm not," she said plainly. "If I vanished off the face of the earth today, a few people would be sad about it, but it wouldn't change anyone's life in any meaningful way."

"Jules," Max breathed her name, face stark with disbelief, clearly at a loss for what to say to her.

Her well-honed people-pleasing skills kicked in. "I'm just being dramatic," she said with a laugh, trying to wave away the heaviness of the conversation. "Anyways, how does somebody from the interior of Alaska have friends in Cry Lake, Wisconsin?"

Max considered her for a moment. He looked like he was going to keep arguing about her importance (or lack thereof), but instead, he faced forward and resumed walking. Jules kept pace with him, wishing he would break the silence. Her anxiety was vibrating like a piano wire about to snap, and if he didn't say something, she was going to have a panic attack. She couldn't cry in front of him. Eric hated when she cried, and Jules had learned to hate it just as much, if not more.

"I have, er... extended family in Cry Lake."

Jules hadn't realized how high her shoulders had risen until he spoke, finally breaking the taut silence. Muscles all down her back relaxed. "Oh. Interesting."

"Is it?"

Her tone had accidentally betrayed some of her feelings about Cry Lake. Not that she disliked the people there. Truthfully, she didn't know any of them. But, like most other locals, she found them a bit odd. A bit mysterious. Everybody knew somebody who knew somebody who knew a Cry Lake resident, and they generally had only good things to say about individual Cry Lakers, but as a whole, the community kept to themselves and it made everybody else... wonder.

"Um, well, they really keep to themselves," she said as diplomatically as she could. "I guess I don't know a lot about them. There are rumors, but who knows what you can really believe."

"What kind of rumors?" Max asked, suddenly intent.

Jules paused, trying to explain without offending him. "Some people think Cry Lake is... um, an 'alternative' religious community." It was about as delicately as she could reframe the word *cult*. "And some people think they might be, like, end-of-days preppers? Or sovereign citizen, off-grid types?"

Max laughed, genuinely amused, and it put Jules at ease.

"No. They're none of those things. It's hard to explain, but I'd say they're more like a cultural community. They live a little differently than outsiders, but they're not crazy. And preserving their culture means living a bit removed from the rest of the world."

"Like the Amish?"

Max shook his head. "It's not religious. And we have electricity and all of that."

"'We?' So your home is like Cry Lake?"

"We're even more isolated, to be honest. But we have more outsiders living *in* our community than Cry Lake seems to."

Jules digested that, and they walked for a while in comfortable silence. The trail wended its way along the top of a basaltic ridge that ran from Hemlock lake all the way to the Aster Flowage, rising and falling in height. At its base, a creek ran, flowing fast and high with the snowmelt. Jules paused when the trail dipped down to the creek's banks, crouching at a slow-moving bend to examine the soil.

"What's wrong?" Max asked.

"Nothing. These spots, where the water pools, are good places to find arrowheads." She dragged her fingers through the shallow water. It was ice cold, and the sandy creek bottom rasped against her fingertips. She turned up small pebbles and stones, but no arrowheads. She wasn't completely disappointed, though. She found a chunk of bright white quartz the size of a plum and plucked it up happily.

"What's that?" Max asked.

Jules startled. She had almost forgotten about him. Feeling a bit foolish, she held the quartz out in her palm for him to look.

"A... rock?" He glanced at her uncertainly.

"A pretty rock," she said defensively, pocketing it.

"Hey, wait, I wasn't done looking."

Still mildly embarrassed, but playing like she wasn't, she huffed and pulled it back out. "Here." She handed it to him.

He took it, looking closely, then holding it up to the light to turn it slowly. "It is pretty," he agreed before handing it back to her. "Like ice."

"There's lots of granite around here," Jules said, mollified, crouching back down to comb through the creek bottom a little more. "So, you can find a lot of quartz."

"You told me before about the pretty rocks. I didn't expect to get a payout so soon."

Jules was stunned that he remembered. Why would he remember something so insignificant? "Do you want this one? I've got a ton of quartz."

His smile grew. "Really?"

"Yeah. Here." Still crouched, she pulled it out of her pocket and handed it up to him.

"Thank you," he said earnestly, as if she'd just given him a diamond.

"You're welcome," she said bashfully.

She resumed combing through the creek bed and the edges of the bank. She turned up a small, jagged orangey-red stone with a glassy, translucent quality, about the size of a kidney bean. She examined it for a second, uncertain. Max crouched down next to her, peering at it.

"It might be garnet," Jules said. "You can sometimes find it around here." She handed it to him. "There you go."

"For me?" he asked.

"Yeah." Her cheeks burned and she stared back down at the water.

"To keep?"

"Yeah. Of course."

"But aren't garnets... expensive?"

Jules shrugged. "I don't think this one is jewel-quality. Sorry. You can just toss it back."

"No, I like it." Max pocketed it. "What other kinds of rocks can you find?"

"Um..." Jules thought for a moment, working her fingers around a big, submerged rock. "Supposedly there's opal at the bottom of a bunch of the deeper lakes around here. I've never found any, though. There's mica. It's mostly just a brownish color, but it's still shiny and pretty. There're lots of fossils. I mostly find corals and bivalves, but this is a good area to look for trilobites."

"You collect all of that?"

"Sort of. I've never found a whole, intact trilobite fossil. I'd like to find that one of these days. I've got a couple broken arrowheads, but I'd like to find a whole one, too." She finally pulled the big rock free, disappointed to find it was just a plain chunk of basalt. She tossed it back in. Drying her hand on her pants leg, she stood up. Max stood with her.

"Ready?" he asked.

She nodded, and they resumed their walk. It wasn't long until they reached the railroad bridge that spanned across the narrow connection between the upper and lower parts of the Aster Flowage. Pickerel Falls loomed over them—not the largest of waterfalls at only twelve feet, but impressive enough in the spring when melting snow put water levels at their highest. In the summer, it was more like two or three smaller waterfalls that streamed over a well-worn granite formation. Just now, it was a thick curtain of rushing water that pounded into the pool below. The water boiled and churned as it passed beneath the railroad bridge, and Jules and Max stood at the rail, watching it for a moment.

"I want to jump in," Max said suddenly.

"Oh my god, don't you dare!" Jules gasped. She realized very suddenly that she'd just given him a command as if she had any right to, and instinctively prepared herself to be verbally swatted back into her place.

But instead of taking offense, Max grinned. "Come on," he teased. "Jump in with me."

Jules coughed out a skeptical sound that was half laugh, half cat-with-a-hairball. "Absolutely not. You'll crack your head open!"

Max waved her objection away. "What's a little brain damage for the sake of a good time?"

This time, Jules laughed for real. "I'll pass."

"Suit yourself." He grabbed the rail and made to hoist himself over.

"Max!" Jules grabbed his arm automatically, a split-second before her brain processed that he was just joking.

Laughing, he let her pull him away from the rail. "Alright. No jumping. Maybe tomorrow?"

"Maybe never," Jules grumbled, releasing his arm.

"You grew up here and you *never* jumped off this bridge?"

"Not in April!" There was still ice on most of the lakes. The only reason there was none here was because of the fast-moving water.

"When? May?"

"*No*. The water's still freezing in May."

"June?"

"Kids are usually brave enough in June, but I'm not."

"July?"

"July's a possibility," she conceded.

"So if I wait until July, you'll jump in with me?"

She started to answer, then paused. "Are you going to be here that long?"

The playful expression faded as he held her gaze. "I could."

"Oh." Jules was suddenly overwhelmed. She couldn't look straight at him. She stared at the falls, clinging to the rail like she might fall overboard otherwise. "Um. Maybe. If you're still here in July, then... maybe."

Max's smile returned. "I can live with maybe."

The rest of the walk passed too quickly. All too soon, Jules and Max found themselves back at Hemlock Lake, standing at the fork in the trail that would take Jules back to her grandma's house.

"I like this trail," Max said. "I think I might walk on it again tomorrow. Around ten a.m."

Jules smiled, and she knew it was too bright, too wide, eating up her whole face with both happiness and nervous anxiety. "Yeah?"

"It would be a real shock if I ran into someone I knew. Again."

"Yes," Jules agreed with over-acted sincerity. "That would be completely unexpected."

Max grinned. "Bye, Jules."

Jules tried to get her own manic smile under control. "Bye, Max."

CHAPTER 9

Back at the house, Jules had to jump in the shower because of all the nervous sweating she'd done. Then it was straight to work. The day passed slowly. She wasn't expecting Max to come by, since they'd spent nearly two hours together that morning, so she had nothing to look forward to except closing up at the end of the night.

Or so she thought. Ten minutes to closing, Jules was mopping when the bell over the door jangled. She looked up to see Max's honey-brown eyes gleaming as he made his way back to her.

"Oh hey," she said, feeling like a giddy teenager with her first crush. "It's somebody I know."

Max squinted at her. "You *do* look familiar. Have we met?"

"You might recognize me from earlier today when I stopped you from concussing yourself on the rocks beneath Aster Falls and drowning."

He clasped a hand over his heart as if fatally wounded. "You wouldn't have jumped in to save me?"

"So we could both drown?"

Max laughed. "I appreciate a pragmatic woman." He leaned against the coffee station, smiling down at Jules the way she had always wished Eric would look at her.

The thought triggered alarm bells in her head. Hadn't she felt this way at one time about Eric? Special. Admired. Excited by the attention.

Look how that had turned out.

She turned away from Max abruptly, pretending she needed total mental absorption to ring out the mop.

You're not a naive eighteen-year-old girl anymore, she reminded herself. And Max wasn't Eric. And most importantly, she wasn't going to let the scars of her past mar any hope of a better future. She looked back up at Max.

"So, how was your day?" she asked.

"Well, I had a nice morning. But the rest of the day was boring." He shifted to keep facing her as she rolled the mop bucket to the other side of the coffee station. "How was yours?"

Max ended up staying long past close, watching as she finished all the closing tasks. He offered to help multiple times, but Jules waved him off each time. She should've been booting him out of the store entirely, but she liked talking with him while she finished shutting everything down.

When she was done, Max followed her out the rear door and waited while she locked it up. He was in the middle of describing his family's hotel and boarding house back in his hometown, Longtooth, and she didn't want him to stop talking. She didn't want him to leave. She stood under the eaves, in the cold and the dark, imagining a place that was cozy and warm and welcoming in a world that was dangerous and beautiful and so far away from her small little life in Wisconsin.

"You're shivering," Max said suddenly, cutting himself off. "Jules, you should've told me to shut up and leave."

She smiled. "Shut up and leave."

"Wow. Rude."

She laughed, punching him on the arm the way she used to horse around with her brothers before they'd all grown up and gone their separate ways. She'd never felt this easy and light around Eric. She'd always felt like there was some important, but unknowable standard that she was constantly failing to live up to. Talking to Max, laughing with him, it was just... easy.

"I should go anyway," Jules said, fishing in her pocket for her truck keys. "I've got to make sure I get up on time for my morning walk."

"Right. Me too. Wouldn't it be weird if we took our walk at the same time?"

"It'd be even weirder if we walked in the same place."

"Absolute madness," Max agreed. A big, wolfish smile lit up his face. "See you tomorrow."

Jules flushed, happy and nervous and excited and a little bit incredulous. "Bye."

The next morning, Max appeared on the trail in the same place as he had the day before. This time, Jules was ready for him. She smiled, still nervous around him, but not so overwhelmed by it anymore.

"Oh, hey," Max said brightly, as if astonished to see her. "What a coincidence."

"Truly unprecedented," Jules agreed.

They fell into step together, walking the same trail as yesterday. The conversation flowed easily, and Jules couldn't stop marveling over how simple and pleasant and safe Max's company felt. She wanted him to like her, but she never felt like she had to *prove* her worth to him. She wanted to make him laugh, but she never felt like she had to rehearse witty lines in her head ahead of time—she could just be herself, silly and spontaneous, and Max met her with the same energy. It didn't feel like a performance with him. It felt like collaboration. Reciprocation. It felt like friendship.

When she'd been married to Eric, she'd always thought people who said they'd "married their best friend" were just reciting a meaningless platitude. But with Max, she could see how that could be real. It was way, *way* too soon to be imagining marriage with him. And the still-wounded parts of her psyche couldn't quite comprehend the idea that the person she wanted might want her just as much. But whoever Max ended up with, they'd definitely tell people they'd married their best friend, and they'd mean it.

When the trail dipped down to the creek, Max crouched with Jules and fished for arrowheads. They found empty snail shells, which Jules kept, some boring rocks, which Jules did not keep, and no arrowheads.

"Oh well," she said, flicking water off her hands and wiping them dry on her jeans. "Someday."

Max stayed for a few seconds longer, combing through the creek bed with a furrowed brow. Eventually, he relented as well, following Jules as they continued on their walk.

"How are you not cold?" Jules asked, plucking at the quilted flannel Max was wearing for a coat. "It's thirty-six degrees out."

His expression went stiff for a second, and Jules worried

that she'd somehow inadvertently insulted him, but then he shrugged and with a smug look, said, "I'm from Alaska. This is tropical to me."

"Right. That must be why you wanted to go swimming when there's still ice on the water."

"Other people here do it. One of the Cry Lake wol —*people*—" He cleared his throat abruptly. "Someone from Cry Lake was telling me about 'polar plunges.'"

"Those are for charity. Nobody does them for fun."

"People surf on Lake Michigan in the winter."

"Those people are crazy."

Max was quiet for a moment, seeming thoughtful. "Do you dislike the cold?"

"Just because I don't want to go swimming in freezing water doesn't mean I can't handle the cold."

"So you like it? You like the long winters? And the ice and snow? All of that?"

Jules grew warm as the significance behind those questions occurred to her. "Yeah, actually. That was one thing I didn't like about Seattle. It never got cold enough to accumulate much snow. The winter was so *wet* and it didn't feel like actual winter."

"There's plenty of snow where I'm from."

"Oh." Jules didn't know what to say to that, but her stomach flipped nervously.

"What brought you to Seattle?" Max asked, changing the topic before nerves consumed her entirely.

"Uh, my ex-husband. He got a job out there."

Max tore his gaze from their surroundings, looking so intently at her that she stopped walking. "You're not married anymore?"

"No."

"You're... single?"

Her stomach flipped again. "Yes."

He nodded as if she'd only confirmed what he already knew and resumed walking, the intensity of his gaze fading as he returned his focus to the surrounding forest. "How long were you married?"

"Ten years."

He looked back at her, brow furrowed. "Ten years? How old are you?"

"Thirty. I got married at nineteen."

"That's young. High school sweetheart?"

"No, um..." Mortified shame burned her cheeks and crushed her lungs. "I met him when I was eighteen, when I started college. He, uh... he was my professor."

"Your *professor?*" Max repeated, unable to hide his shock.

"I know, I know." She cringed, mortified, as always. She knew what he was thinking—what kind of gullible idiot married the man who'd obviously been preying upon her?

In hindsight, how could she not have realized how fucked up it was that this thirty-three-year-old man was pursuing her? A man who was in a position of power over her? She had been too naive, too optimistic, too trusting. She wasn't any of those things anymore, but the silly girl she used to be still haunted her like a recurring nightmare.

"He was— I mean, I didn't—" She didn't have the words to explain it in a way that didn't make her sound like a fool.

"Jules," Max said, suddenly gentle. "I'm not judging you. I'm definitely judging *him*." He paused. "Maybe that's not fair of me. You said you were married for ten years?"

"It wasn't a good ten years," Jules said quietly. It was the first time she'd said it so plainly to anyone other than the therapist Eric had stopped her from seeing.

"I'm sorry," Max said gently, though his voice was rough.

"I made the choices that got me there." She shrugged. "Can't really blame anyone but myself."

Max stopped walking, pivoting sharply to face her. He caught Jules by the shoulders, gripping her tightly as his gaze bored into hers. "You were *eighteen*, Jules. Fresh out of childhood. He was a grown-ass man. And he was your professor—he had power over you in more ways than one. The blame is *all* on him. Okay?"

She knew that. Logically she knew that. Emotionally, she still hadn't quite internalized that idea. Because all the while it was happening, she'd known it looked bad from the outside. She'd been well aware that other people wouldn't understand. But instead of tallying all the red flags and wising up, she'd rushed headlong into the relationship. Instead of seeing Eric as a predator, grooming one of his students, she'd seen herself as so irresistibly desirable that she'd made a good man throw away his morals. Instead of recognizing that all the secrecy and lies were signs of a bad person, she'd reveled in the thrill of being a part of something so deliciously forbidden. She'd known it was wrong, she'd done it anyway. She'd made her bed, and then she'd had to lie in it.

But Max's intensity was contagious, and she found herself nodding in agreement. "Yeah. You're right. He... he wasn't a good person."

Max suddenly pulled her against him, wrapping her tightly in a vise-like hug. She could barely breathe, but it felt like some of the poisonous feelings that thoughts of Eric always brought up were being crushed out of her along with the last of her air supply. She held onto him for a few seconds, savoring the feel of his arms around her before she started to feel light-headed.

"Max," she wheezed.

He released her, stepping back to give her space. "Sorry," he said gruffly, his voice oddly distorted—deep and growling. His eyes were brighter than she'd ever seen them, gleaming like molten gold. "That was out of line. Sorry, Jules."

"You're fine," she said, still a little breathless. "Don't apologize."

Max looked so guilty, she went to him, looping her arm through his, and tugging to keep him walking. He came along, a quiet, hulking presence at her side. As the silence stretched on, Jules's anxiety started to rise. She'd ruined things by telling Max about Eric. Now he wasn't going to want—

"What'd you go to college for?" Max asked, voice subdued, but not angry.

"Biology. I never finished my degree though. I dropped out when we moved to Seattle. I was going to enroll at a university there once we were settled, but it just never happened."

"What do you mean?"

"There was always some reason why it wasn't the right time for me to re-enroll. First, Eric didn't want me taking out more student loans when we'd just taken on a really expensive mortgage. When I offered to get a part-time job so I could pay a big chunk of tuition out-of-pocket, he said it would be embarrassing for him if his wife was doing menial labor when all his colleagues' spouses had advanced degrees. Then I suggested a two-year degree or an apprenticeship program in something, and he hated that idea even more."

Max made a sound that was eerily similar to a growl. He stifled it with a cough.

"Anyways, every solution I came up with just didn't work for Eric. After a while, he just told me flat out he wanted me to be a stay-at-home wife who took care of the house and the children."

"You don't have children," Max said, with surprising certainty. Jules glanced at him, wondering how he could tell. He looked away sharply.

"Um, no. No kids."

"Do you want them?"

Jules hesitated, anxious dread twisting her stomach.

"Sorry," Max said quickly. "That was too personal."

Not any more personal than talking about her miserable marriage or the other disappointments of her life thus far. "No, I... I'm not really sure I want kids." She still hadn't figured out if that aversion was because of the trauma of her marriage and the endless stress that trying to conceive had been, or if she truly just wasn't meant to be a parent.

Max shrugged. "I have lots of nieces and nephews. I love them, but they're a *lot* of responsibility."

"You don't want that responsibility?" Jules asked, faintly hopeful.

He shrugged again. "If I had to rise to the occasion, I would. I think I'd even be good at it. But I like being an uncle."

Relief flooded her. Not that Max was anywhere close to

asking her to bear his children, but the knowledge that he wouldn't insist upon it was such a relief.

"I have a nephew and two nieces," she said, "but I don't see them very often. One of my brothers lives in Minneapolis and my other brother lives in Chicago." Both of which were more than four hour drives from their tiny northern hometown.

"It's a good time. You get to do all the fun stuff, the cool-uncle stuff, and then send 'em back to their parents when they start getting out of hand." He grinned unrepentantly.

They reached the railroad bridge and they paused on it again, watching the falls. Max turned to look out over the lower portion of the flowage. Suddenly, he did a mild double-take.

"That island wasn't there yesterday."

Jules followed his line of vision. "Oh, yeah, it probably wasn't. That's a floating bog."

"A *what?*"

Jules grinned. Explaining the floating bogs to out-of-towners was one of the best things about living up here. "Floating peat accumulates into these huge mats that plants can grow out of."

"A *tree* is growing out of that one," Max said skeptically, pointing.

"Yeah. The big ones can support multiple trees."

Max turned to look at her, a disbelieving half-smile on his face. "Is this a joke that locals pull on outsiders?"

Jules laughed. "No! Floating bogs are *real*. Look it up on your phone."

He patted at the pockets of his flannel, then his jeans. "Left it behind. I'll have to take your word for it." He gave her a dubious look.

"Alright, you know what? Meet me early tomorrow. We'll paddle out to one of them and you can see it's real." The boldness of what she'd just done—openly demanded more time with him—hit her like a slap.

Before she could backpedal on her own impulsiveness, Max said, "Alright. Deal. Where am I meeting you?"

She needed a second to gather her nerve before she said, "Meet me at my grandma's? I'll need help loading the truck."

Max nodded, cool as you please, as if Jules hadn't just rocked her own world by being daring and confident with a man she liked—a man she *wanted*.

"What time?"

"Is eight too early?"

"I'll be there."

"What's your number?" Jules asked, pulling her phone out with another little flash of panic at her own bravado. "I'll send you directions."

Max blinked. "Right. Directions."

He recited his number and Jules saved it to her contacts. When she pocketed the phone again, it somehow felt heavier.

THAT NIGHT, MAX SHOWED UP AT THE STORE AT TEN MINUTES before closing, as had become his habit. Jules had gotten comfortable enough to expect him.

"Hey," she said happily, pausing from wiping down the glass on the drink coolers.

"I have something for you," he said, boyish delight shining in his eyes.

"What?"

"Close your eyes and hold out your hand."

Surprising herself, Jules did so without questioning him. Her trust in him was weird, considering she'd known him for, like, two weeks. She didn't feel like examining it too closely right now. She stretched her hand out, palm up, no idea what to expect.

Something cool and light landed against her skin, along with the faintest brush of Max's fingertips. Goosebumps raced up her arm, making her shiver.

"Open your eyes."

She blinked them open, taking a second to recognize what was in her palm.

An arrowhead. A whole, intact arrowhead.

Her gaze flashed up to his, lips parted, eyes wide.

"Do you like it?" he asked.

"Oh my god," she breathed, pulling it close to examine it. Silly, overwhelmed tears pricked her eyes. She blinked hard, ignoring them, turning the arrowhead this way and that as she examined the notches and the fluting. One fat tear spilled over her cheek, and she swiped it away, still engrossed by the gift.

"Jules," Max said urgently, "I'm sorry! Please don't cry. I'll take it back. Here—"

She snatched it out of his reach. "These are happy tears."

"They smell like distressed tears," he said worriedly.

She finally looked up from the arrowhead. "They... what?"

Max went rigid. "They seem like distressed tears," he said, his expression shuttered.

"Oh." She gave a watery little laugh. "I thought you said 'smelled like.'"

Max laughed weakly in return.

Swiping hastily at her wet cheeks, Jules got a hold of herself. "Sorry, I just... this might be the sweetest gift anyone's ever given me." She looked up at Max. "Thank you."

The worried creases smoothed from his forehead. "You're welcome."

"It's definitely going to be front and center in my collection when I get home."

"What do you collect?" Max asked, visibly relaxing now that she was no longer weeping over his gift.

"Just... things. Like pretty rocks and feathers and other found things."

"Big snail shells?"

She nodded, remembering the ones they'd found that morning. "Yeah."

"So, nature things?"

She tilted her head. "Well, mostly. But other found things, too. I have an old skeleton key—I have absolutely no idea what it opens—but I found it in the field behind my school when I was in fifth grade. And I have a nickel with Jefferson's face carved to look like a skull. I found it on the floor of my dentist's waiting room when I was a little kid. I also have just the innermost doll from a set of gold-leafed Russian nesting dolls. I found it in a box of free things at a flea market."

Max smiled. "A flea market sounds like cheating."

"It is a little," Jules admitted, not at all offended. It was uncanny that Max had picked up on it—she saw it that way herself. "Anyways, *now* I also have an arrowhead."

He regarded her warmly, obviously pleased by her pleasure. It was a foreign feeling, but she wanted to wrap it around herself and drown in it.

Just like the night before, Max kept her company while she closed—offering to help and being denied—and then walked her out to her truck when she was ready to go.

"Remember, you promised to show me a floating swamp up close and personal," Max reminded her as he held her truck door open for her.

Jules laughed. "Floating *bog*."

"Yeah, that. Eight tomorrow morning?"

Jules nodded. "See you then."

"See you then," he promised softly. He closed the truck door for her and then stepped back, keeping watch until her ignition started and she pulled away.

MAX WATCHED JULES DRIVE AWAY, A FEELING OF GLOWING contentment that was at complete odds with the desperate need for *more*. Every time he was with her, he wanted so badly to touch her. He wanted to take her into his arms and put his scent all over her. He'd succumbed to the urge briefly this morning when he'd heard the brokenness in her voice as she talked about her ex-husband. His protective instincts had overwhelmed him. But it had only been a few seconds, and his wolf was still deeply unsatisfied. This courtship was ridiculously slow by wolf kin standards.

All the same, he was coming to live for the moments he spent with her in easy conversation, seeing her world through her eyes, sharing some of his and watching the fascinated way she listened. As her wariness around him lessened, her personality emerged more and more, revealing complexities and nuances that Max could spend eons trying to unravel. She was both somber and playful, a quiet observer of the world who wasn't afraid to laugh at what she saw, but who also found significance in the smallest pieces of it. She seemed so fragile, wounded, with her pensive silences and her big, dark eyes, but then she would surprise him with sarcastic wit and a beautiful laugh. She was a rabbit—fleet and darting, hard to catch, but soft to hold.

If only he could hold her.

CHAPTER 10

Half an hour before Max was due to show up, Jules was staring out the window like a golden retriever with separation anxiety, watching the road for his truck. When he finally pulled up she had to make herself count to ten before she burst out the side door so she didn't look like an over-eager, clingy loon.

Even so, his feet had only just hit the ground when Jules reached his truck, unable to hold back her excited smile. Normally she *hated* waking up early. But this time, she'd hardly been able to fall asleep in anticipation of the morning.

"Hello," she said cheerfully when she reached his truck. Nervousness still crackled through her like electricity, but she'd decided to channel it into enthusiasm. "Fancy meeting you here."

"A real mystery how this keeps happening," he said with an answering smile.

She rocked on her heels, restless, antsy. The impulse to give him a hug battled with the still-potent fear of *wanting*. Fear won, and she shoved her hands into her jacket pockets.

"Well, let's get the truck loaded up and then we can get going." She turned away from him, leading him around to the back of the garage.

"Kayaks?" Max asked, following her.

Jules almost laughed. "Even better. We've got—" she rounded the corner, and held out her hands with a flourish "—a fifty-year-old aluminum canoe!"

Max played along gamely, making an impressed face. "*Oooh*. Vintage."

Turned upside down, mounted on cinderblocks, the old canoe looked every bit its age. The weathered, dull silver body was covered in large, irregular dents. Powdery white corrosion bloomed around all the rivets. Near the bow, a softball-sized hole had been roughly patched with a piece of scrap metal that was entirely covered in a fine coat of rust, joined to the rest of the canoe by the world's ugliest weld.

"This is the Good Ship Beulah. She isn't pretty, but she gets the job done." Jules patted the canoe's hull fondly. She had memories all the way back to earliest childhood of sitting in the middle of the canoe while her parents or her grandparents sat at either end, paddling along lakes and rivers and flowages.

With Max's help, they got it flipped off the cinder blocks and carried it to her truck, the tailgate already down and waiting. When the canoe was loaded and tied down, Jules hopped into the driver's seat, and Max slid in on her other side. She was struck, once again, by the differences between Max and her ex-husband. If Jules and Eric were in the same vehicle, Jules was never the driver. Once upon a time, she had thought it was chivalric. Now she knew better. It was about control. It had always been about control.

"How'd you sleep?" Max asked as she backed out of the driveway.

Like some sort of repressed Victorian nun, the idea of Max thinking about her in bed made her blush. "Good," she said, staring at the road with fixed determination. "How about you?"

"Honestly, I haven't slept very well since I left home. I'm used to sleeping at the Spruce, surrounded by other people. Here, I'm in a cabin all by myself."

Don't like sleeping alone? I can help with that. Jules bit her lip, amused, but not brave enough to say the words out loud, even if the reawakening of her libido was cause for celebration. Sex had become a tedious, high-pressure obligation during her marriage. After the divorce, she hadn't wanted her own touch, let alone anybody else's. But, Max? Oh, yes, she wanted his touch.

He looked at her suddenly, alert, as if she'd called his name. For a split second, she was terrified she *had* said the words out loud, but then just as quickly, Max looked away.

"You should try a weighted blanket," Jules said, managing to sound like she hadn't just been picturing herself in bed with him.

He glanced at her again, a thoughtful, lingering look that Jules felt over her entire body, like a bucket of warm syrup had been turned over her head.

"Maybe I will," he said.

Discreetly, Jules squeezed her thighs together.

They reached the boat launch and put in alongside the L-shaped dock. Max got in first since he was heavier. The canoe rocked as he stepped into it. Gripping the edge of the dock for balance, he sank gingerly onto the hard metal seat. Jules took the stern, getting in with a little more grace than

Max—but not much, considering it'd been at least a decade since she'd last clambered into this old thing.

"This is a lot more wobbly than I expected," Max said, swaying his weight so that the canoe rocked back and forth.

"Stop!" Jules squealed, gripping the gunwales. She'd always hated when her brothers did that.

Max stopped, but he flashed her a smile that was anything but apologetic. "Is this what they meant by 'don't rock the boat'?"

"What they meant," Jules said sourly as she steadied herself, "was 'don't rock the boat because I might smack you with my paddle if you do'."

"Ah, yes, I remember that old proverb."

Jules's heart swelled in her chest. She wanted to launch herself at Max, wobbly canoe be damned. She was so used to being put in her place any time she dared to tell her ex-husband to do or not do something, so used to frosty silences and cold shoulders whenever she got the slightest bit sarcastic with him. Max's sanguine good humor was a shock. The idea that she didn't have to constantly guard her thoughts around him, massage his ego, reinforce his masculinity through her own performance of fragility, was a lot to process. She wasn't really sure she knew how to "be herself" anymore. But whoever she really was, being with Max was freeing.

"Well, keep it in mind," Jules said primly, then ruined the effect with a smile. "We're headed that way." She pointed northwest.

Together, they paddled. It was a gorgeous day, unseasonably warm and sunny, with only a mild breeze rippling the top of the water. At not-even-nine in the morning on a Wednesday, the lake was quiet, with only a few fisherman anchored here and there. The sun glittered over the water, spangling and bright, while the pine trees surrounding the lake *shush*ed gently in the wind. Jules closed her eyes and lifted her face, letting the sun's warmth sink into her skin, feeling the breeze as it ruffled her hair. The whole world was quiet, holding its breath with her.

When she opened her eyes, she found Max turned toward her, watching her, something intense and heated in his eyes. That warm syrup feeling came over her again. A delicious shiver ran down her spine as she held his gaze. The urge to go to him made her hands tighten on her paddle until the skin stretched thin over her knuckles.

"If I tell you you're beautiful, will it make you uncomfortable?" Max asked, his voice low and gentle.

Yes, but in a good way. Instead, she said, nervously, "Um…"

"Never mind then." He turned away with a sly smile.

"Wait—"

"Too late, you're hideous to me now."

With an offended scoff, Jules skipped the tip of her paddle forward over the surface of the water, sending a small spray of water towards him. It mostly splattered against the side of the canoe, but a few sprinkles landed on his sleeve. He swiveled around, open-mouthed with incredulity and wicked amusement.

"Juliana Wolfe!" he gasped as if appalled, but the way he drew out the syllables of her whole name set a horde of butterflies fluttering in her stomach.

"Oh look, we're getting close to one of the bogs!" Jules said quickly, paddling hurriedly in an effort to distract him from retaliating.

Max gave her a look that promised later retribution

before he turned around and resumed paddling. The floating bog they were nearing was smaller in surface area than her grandma's two-car garage, but it had three small trees growing on it, and an abundance of grasses and wildflowers. They glided up to the edge of it, the canoe rocking gently as they nudged against it.

"This has *got* to be an island," Max said, poking the edge with his paddle. "It's firm."

"Well, yeah, there's a whole root system in there and everything. But I promise, it's a floating bog. There are no fixed islands in the Aster Flowage."

Max stared at it, continuing to push and prod with his paddle. After a moment, he leaned over to press his hand on the edge. The whole canoe leaned with him, and Jules shrieked again, clutching the gunwales.

"Max!" she objected in an embarrassingly high-pitched voice.

He grinned back at her. "You can splash me, but I can't rock the canoe?"

"Yes. I'm glad you understand. Now *stop!*" The last bit came out in a childish whine, but she didn't care. A rocking canoe made her stomach flip the same way leaning too far back in a rocking chair or missing a step when going down the stairs did.

"Hang on, I just want to—" He shifted his weight, making the canoe sway wildly again. He was trying to swing his leg out so that he could step onto the bog.

"*No!*" Jules said urgently, forgetting her fear of capsizing for a moment.

Max froze.

"Don't ever walk on them. They look like they can hold your weight—and probably they can in most places. But all they're made of is peat. If you hit a weak spot, you'll sink through and get tangled in the roots where you'll die a horrible death, suffocating on mud."

"Well." Max drew his foot back, eagerness gone. "Thank you for the warning."

"Sorry," Jules said, anxiety rising in the face of his diminished enthusiasm. Was he angry that she'd yelled at him? She did that nebbishy thing she always did when she'd annoyed her ex-husband, trying to apologetically explain why she'd dared to tell him what to do. "Our parents really drill it into us when we're kids that we don't play on the floating bogs. It's super dangerous. I didn't want—"

"Jules," Max said earnestly, holding her gaze. "It's okay. I meant it—thank you. I wasn't planning on dying today." He smiled wryly, and her nerves settled.

A small part of her was ashamed that she needed such constant reassurance. Eventually, he was going to get annoyed by her, tired of tip-toeing around her anxieties and continually insisting that he wasn't angry.

"Oh, good," she said, aiming for unbothered and slightly missing the mark. "I had the same plans."

"Great minds think alike." Max picked his paddle back up. "Do you want to head toward the falls? I want to see it up close."

The last of Jules's anxiety faded. He had seen a floating bog up close, so calling it quits would've been perfectly reasonable. But he still wanted to spend time with her— even after she'd told him to stop doing what he wanted to do. It suddenly occurred to her that Max was the kind of guy who'd never get irritated at her for being better than him at assembling IKEA bookcases, or telling him he was driving in the wrong direction, or being able to fix the leaky kitchen sink after he'd failed to.

"Um..." She tore her mind away from thoughts of her ex. She didn't want him in her head anymore. She didn't want him poisoning every interaction she had with Max, even if Max came out better in the comparison every time. She wanted to let go of the ugly, unhappy past and live in the contentment of the present and the hope of the future. "Yeah," she finally said. "Let's go."

They couldn't paddle directly up to the falls—the current was too strong. But they had fun struggling against it, paddling as hard as they could, only able to make it to just under the railroad bridge. Jules's coat was splattered and her thighs were soaked with water from the spray of the rushing current, but also from the splash-back of Max's ferocious paddling.

"Hey!" she cried, every time he got her.

"Sorry!" he called back, singularly focused on battling the current. He was unbelievably strong, and at a certain point, Jules gave up on paddling and just watched the impressive movement of his powerful body. He was deeply invested in his fight, completely oblivious to the fact that Jules was lounging with her paddle across her lap.

Somehow, despite Jules's lack of participation, he managed to gain another few feet. But the current grew wilder the further upstream they went, the jutting peaks of a large granite formation punctuating the flow of the water with bubbling rapids. Max pushed against one of them with his paddle, trying to use it for leverage, but he ended up anchoring his end of the canoe, while the stern, with Jules, swung wildly out.

"Hey!" she cried again, stomach flipping as the canoe dipped steeply to one side.

"Sorry!" Max called back again, still entirely focused on paddling. He shoved against another jutting rock, trying to straighten out. He lost control, and the bow got caught in the swiftest part of the current, spinning the canoe like a top.

"*Max!*" Jules gripped the canoe, heart pounding.

"I've got it!" He paddled wildly, trying to straighten them out, but all he was doing was fighting against the current in an erratic fishtail that made the canoe rock like a metronome.

Even though Jules was terrified, she was laughing, caught in hysterics at the sight of Max struggling this way and that while the canoe careened from rapid to rapid. She clung to the gunwales and shrieked each time the edge dipped too close to the water, but then she was straight back to gasping for breath and laughing at Max.

"You could help paddle!" he called over his shoulder.

"But you're doing so well!" she shouted back.

The canoe dipped as they went over a small rapid, taking on water. Jules didn't have time to scream before they went over another, steeper rapid—the canoe pitched over sideways, dumping them both into the lake.

Ice cold water closed over her head, silencing the world. The life jacket that she'd had casually draped around her neck popped over her head as she sank, gone in an instant. *Probably why you're supposed to buckle those things,* she thought wryly as she oriented herself underwater. The current pushed her away from the falls, thankfully, and she fought against the counterweight of her clothes to get to the surface. When she broke through, she hauled in a gasping breath. The water was so cold it was hard to make her lungs work.

"Jules!" Max was there immediately, strong arms pulling her body against his. He held her tight, swimming for both of them. "I'm so sorry!" he said, over and over again. "God, I'm so sorry. Are you alright? Hang on, we're almost to the canoe. Just hang on. I'm so sor—"

"Max." Jules pushed out of his arms, fighting a smile despite the painfully frigid water. His frantic concern was sweet, actually, but it was unnecessary. "I'm fine. I'm not injured. I know how to swim."

"Right. Sorry." He let her go. His brows were drawn together, his normally full lips compressed into a thin line. He looked so miserable, Jules just wanted to hug him.

"Max," she said his name beseechingly, treading the frozen water while the foreign feeling of heavy wet clothing bloomed around her body. "Honestly, it's alright. It's funny!"

"It's funny that I nearly drowned you in a freezing cold lake?"

She laughed. "Yes! I mean, no offense, but I am going to tell everyone I know about this."

Finally, a glimmer of humor returned to his expression. "I deserve that."

She started swimming towards the canoe, which was drifting rapidly away from them. Max followed. When they reached it, retrieving the drifting paddles along the way, Jules was shivering. She clenched her jaw so that Max wouldn't hear her teeth chatter. She didn't want him to go into another self-recriminating spiral.

They had to tip the canoe several times to get as much of the water out as possible. Max did what he could to hold it steady while Jules clambered back in. Then she had to try to counter his weight by leaning on the opposite side while he tried to haul himself up.

It didn't work. Jules was flung into the lake for a second time. She didn't get a chance to swim to the surface—one of Max's big hands caught her by the arm and he hauled her up like a minnow trap.

As soon as she broke the surface, she was laughing.

"Jules," Max said, aghast.

"I'm fine," she assured him, shivering as she treaded water.

"You're freezing!"

"Well, y-yeah," she stuttered through chattering teeth. "Aren't you?"

His face went blank for a second. He shook it away, brow furrowing with consternation. "You're going to get hypothermia. We'll get you back in the canoe and you'll paddle for shore, okay? I'll swim back. No, I'll push the canoe while you paddle, that way—"

Jules would never know where she found the nerve to do it—she slung one arm around Max's broad shoulders and pressed her lips to his. He froze, speechless. Just as Jules was beginning to regret giving in to the impulse, Max growled deep in his throat and pulled her body roughly against his, kissing her back with desperate hunger.

The kiss went on, breathless and urgent and more intense than Jules had expected or intended. She was clinging to him with both arms now, climbing his body with her thighs, spurred by a fire that chased the cold out of her skin and turned her blood to steam. Max gripped the edge of the canoe with one hand, keeping them afloat, while his other arm was wrapped around her back, keeping her pinned tightly against him.

But no matter how hot the kiss, eventually, the reality of their circumstances had to intrude. They both realized at the same time that Jules was shaking from the cold, her teeth chattering even while her lips were pressed to Max's. He broke the kiss with a soft curse.

"In the canoe with you," he said, breathing raggedly as he hoisted her towards it.

Jules didn't have the breath to speak. She scrambled gracelessly back into the canoe, shivering like a chihuahua. With shaking hands, she took the paddle Max handed up to her.

"Sh-shouldn't you g-get in?" she asked, becoming increasingly aware of the painful cold in her extremities despite the lingering warmth simmering in her blood.

"I'll just tip you out again if I try."

"Max—"

"I've got more mass than you. I'll be fine. Start paddling." He gave the stern a shove, sending her gliding toward shore.

CHAPTER 11

The Aster Flowage was huge, but fortunately, they were only about a quarter mile from the launch. Jules paddled with shaky, weak arms. Out of the water, the cold wasn't so bad. Her body heat warmed her drenched clothing, gradually creating what was, more or less, a wetsuit. Max swam alongside the canoe with powerful strokes of his flannel-covered arms. Occasionally, he paused to give the canoe another shove, but within seconds he caught up to her feeble paddling again.

When they reached shore, Max was already on his feet, grabbing the bow and dragging the canoe out of the water. He hurried back to Jules, helping her out of the canoe. "Go get the truck started," he told her. "Blast the heat. I'll load the canoe up."

"By yourself?"

In answer, he bent over, grabbing the gunwales on each side of the centerline, and hefted the entire thing into the air, settling the left gunwale on his shoulder for balance, basically wearing the canoe like a giant hat. Jules knew lots of people carried canoes like that when they were portaging from one lake to another, but those people usually had lightweight, modern canoes. This old beast weighed more than most people could carry on their own.

But, apparently, Max wasn't most people. "Go on," he prompted. "Get the heater going."

She hurried over to the truck, glancing back at him periodically. He picked his steps carefully across the launch and parking lot, but seemed otherwise unburdened by the heavy canoe.

By the time Jules got the truck started and the heat turned up all the way, Max was already sliding the canoe into the truck bed. He secured the ratchet straps Jules had initially tied it down with, and then he joined her in the cab. The heater wasn't terribly warm yet, but Max laid his hands over the vents and sighed.

"Jules, I'm so sorry," he started again. "I'm an idiot."

The fact that he was back on the apology wagon after she'd kissed him so desperately was a bit of a blow to the ego. But instead of letting it drag her into insecurity, Jules decided to embrace the rash, impulsive side of herself that had prompted her to kiss him in the first place. She pulled her knees up and crawled across the bench seat until she was nearly on top of Max while he continued to ramble on.

"—shouldn't have done something so reckless and stupid. I'm not—"

She grabbed his soaking wet flannel by its sodden collar and pulled him in for another soul-searing, mind-melting, breath-stealing kiss. Max groaned deep in his throat, a sound that was more growl than anything, as his arms wrapped around her, hauling her onto his lap.

Jules forgot about the cold and her wet, heavy clothes

and the fact that it was broad daylight and they were parked at a public boat launch. There was only Max. His feverish heat and woodsy, musky scent and big body enveloped her in a haze of just... *goodness*. She wanted to melt into him. She *was* melting into him. The taste of his mouth and the feel of his beard rasping against her cheeks and throat, the crushing strength of his arms holding her close and the gentle ferocity with which he kissed her—it all overwhelmed her to a state of pure impulse and sensation. There was no anxiety over how she *should* be, there was only the languorous pleasure of the moment.

A sudden tap at the window jarred them both apart. Breathing heavily, arms still looped around Max's neck, Jules turned to see an older man peering through the window at them. With an amused expression, he made the *roll down your window* gesture.

Face burning, Jules scrambled off of Max and lurched back into the driver's seat. Grandpa's old truck was from the early nineties, and she had to literally roll the window down.

"Er, hello," she said awkwardly.

"Everyone alright here?" His bright blue gaze flickered between the two of them, lingering momentarily on Max.

"We're fine," she said quickly.

"Saw your canoe flip, but we were above the falls. We docked and drove over here quick as we could."

"*Oh.*" Grateful she wasn't about to be lectured for public indecency, Jules sighed in relief. "Yeah. That was us. We're good."

A smile twinkled in his eyes. "I see that." He stepped back from the truck. "Well, just wanted to make sure. You two take care."

"You too," Jules said, trying not to succumb to death by mortification.

She cranked the window back up, and Max let out a derisive snort. "Probably for the best," he grumbled.

"What was?" she asked, faintly uneasy with the cynical note in his voice.

His eyes were fire and gold as he met her gaze. "That we were interrupted before I lost my mind and begged you to fuck me in a public parking lot."

"Oh." Her face burned again, but that burn simmered through the rest of her as well, a pulsing heat deep in her core that made her clench her thighs together. "That *is* for the best, because I probably would've said yes."

"*Jules*," her name came out as a rasping growl. He took a deep breath, clutching the door handle. With visible effort, he looked away from her. "We should get back to your house. You need dry clothes."

She bit her lip, grinning as she clicked her seatbelt on and shifted the truck into reverse.

THE WOLF WAS SMUG AND MOSTLY CONTENT. MAX'S SCENT WAS ALL over Jules, her taste was in his mouth, and she'd more or less confirmed that sex was in the future. While the primal side of his nature was anxious to move forward, to have all of her, to claim her, the fact that he'd finally gotten to touch and taste and hold her had taken the edge off of the turbulent need.

He watched Jules as she drove, struck by the change in just the short time he'd known her. When he'd first seen her she'd seemed so shy, terrified of her own shadow. He would never have guessed at the fire contained within her—fiery joy, fiery passion, and a nearly-fiery temper. His wolf approved. Clear terms and well-defined boundaries suited wolf kin nature. Guessing games and subtle implications and unspoken wishes were confusing and discouraging. Even as a bystander, witnessing Caleb's resistant, convoluted courtship of Grace had been torturous.

Even if Max had to handle the complication of courting a skinlocked woman, at least he could anticipate a fairly straightforward courtship. Jules knew he wanted her, knew he liked being with her. All that was left was time—time for her to grow comfortable with him, time for her to feel secure with him. When they got there, he'd call his mom, tell her he wanted to break Silence so he could claim his mate. He had no doubt the aunties would approve it. Max was known for being level-headed and reliable. Well, except when he was trying to impress a woman with his ability to row upstream against the force of a waterfall, apparently.

He suppressed a wince at that, casting another discreet glance at Jules. Her attention was on the road, but the sweet scent of her arousal was perfuming the air in the truck. He'd been hard basically since she'd pounced on him, and the lingering evidence of her need was keeping him hard. His wolf bristled at the knowledge that he'd left her wanting and unsatisfied. The urge to finish what they'd started simmered beneath his skin, thrummed like a drumbeat in his veins.

They reached Jules's place and as she put the truck into park, Max prepared himself to make a polite goodbye.

But Jules turned to him and said, "Come in, I'll throw your clothes in the dryer. I've got some of my grandpa's old stuff you can wear until yours are dry."

"Alright," Max agreed, working to keep his voice steady as his wolf surged in his awareness. Being invited into her home, her den, was a significant thing for wolf kin. The scent of her arousal strengthened, heady and rich, and Max nearly choked suppressing the hungry growl that rose in his throat.

The house was small and cozy, decorated with decades of accumulated art and knick-knacks and mementos. There was a series of photographs of Jules on the hallway wall, school portraits starting with kindergarten and going all the way to her final year of high school. Above and below her row of portraits were two other rows, each belonging to two boys who were obviously family to her—probably the brothers she'd mentioned.

Max paused to examine Jules's row, finding youth-softened versions of her current features in the happy, bright-eyed child in the pictures. This was who she'd been before she'd become the shy, defeated woman Max had first met—sunny and hopeful and unencumbered. Whatever had happened to her in the time since the last photograph was taken and the woman he first met only a couple of weeks ago, it had robbed her of that brightness.

It wasn't a good ten years... He wasn't a good person. Her voice echoed in his mind, filling him with a sudden and uncharacteristic flash of murderous rage. He clenched his jaw, grappling with it, controlling it. He calmed himself with the knowledge that she was slowly regaining that brightness —that he was lucky enough to witness it as it happened.

"*Ugh,*" Jules groaned when she noticed what he was looking at. "Don't look at grades six through ten. Puberty was not kind to me."

Max's gaze went there immediately. The age range she'd forbidden was filled with photos of an adorably gawky girl with too-long limbs and colorful braces and heavy eyeliner and increasingly experimental hairstyles. Max grinned.

Jules shouldered in front of him to splay her hands over the photos. "Don't! I looked like an emo giraffe."

He laughed, but took mercy, and turned away from the pictures. "You were adorable." Prompted by her embarrassment, he added, "When I was a teenager, I had a wispy mustache and patchy little chin-beard that I could *not* accept was anything less than magnificent. My mom has all the pictures."

She lowered her hands, moving further down the hall. "I find it hard to believe you were ever anything other than gorgeous."

Max raised his eyebrows suggestively. "You think I'm gorgeous?"

She snorted a derisive laugh. "Of course I do. You think I just throw myself at any man who dumps me in a frozen lake?"

Max winced and started to apologize, but Jules cut him off.

"Do I have to kiss you to shut you up again?"

He closed his mouth, opened it, then closed it again. A wolfish smile took over his face. "Well, now you're just incentivizing me."

She laughed. The sound was like a salve over his entire nervous system, calming everything about him. Even his wolf, hungry for her, desperate for more, settled at the sound.

She opened a small closet in the hallway and rummaged among the shelves until she pulled out a pair of navy blue sweatpants and a green sweater.

"Hm." She examined them. "These still have the sticker on them—looks like you get *brand new* borrowed sweatpants."

Max accepted the clothes from her. "I've only ever dreamed of such luxuries."

"Play your cards right and I'll find you an unopened bag of the finest Dollar Store tube socks." She gestured to a door just past the closet. "You can change in there."

It was a small bathroom. Max stripped off his wet, cold, heavy clothes and pulled on the loaned sweats. Jules's grandfather had apparently been relatively tall for a skin-locked man because the sweatpants were only slightly short on Max, and the sweatshirt was only a little tight on his chest and shoulders. The Mardi Gras-themed design on the sweatshirt said SUPER BOWL XXXI CHAMPIONS with the Packers logo underneath. He stepped back into the hall, wet clothes bundled in his hands.

"All set?" Jules peered out from yet another doorway further down the hall. "Bring them here."

He did as she said, but froze in the doorway, arrested by the sight of her. She'd stripped out of her wet clothes—because of course she had—and was wearing only an over-sized gray t-shirt, the hem high on her thighs, the sleeves hanging down to her elbows. Obviously a man's shirt—probably an old hand-me-down from her grandfather, like she'd loaned to him. But even so, Max couldn't help imagining her in one of *his* shirts, with his scent surrounding her, marking her.

"This everything?" she asked, taking his wet clothes.

He nodded, betraying none of the rising hunger simmering through his veins. She was already turning away from him, oblivious to his struggle. He watched as she threw his clothes into the dryer and started the machine.

When Jules straightened, he stepped into her space without thinking, pulled her into his arms, and kissed her.

His mouth was on hers, tasting, devouring. She kissed him back without hesitation, holding onto him with a need that felt as fierce as his own. He pressed her back against the dryer, feeling every inch of her body flush against his. She groaned, arching against him, nails curling into his skin, then suddenly broke away.

"Upstairs," she said breathlessly, pushing against his chest.

He nodded, incapable of speech. He followed her out of the small laundry room, down the hall to a set of narrow stairs that led to an attic room with low, sloping ceilings. There was an old wooden dresser, a narrow bed made up with a colorful block quilt, a nightstand covered with a crocheted lace doily, and a turnkey lamp with a floral-painted glass shade. It reminded him a great deal of the homey furnishings at the Spruce, and for a moment, he was overwhelmed by something that should have been home-sickness—but instead of sadness, he felt contentment. This room reminded him of the Spruce, his home and his pack, but now Jules was with him and her scent filled the space, and the two together was the perfect combination.

Jules had his hand in hers, and she pulled him over to the little twin bed. He had to duck as he sat down on it, coming close to cracking his head on the low ceiling. Then Jules was there, sliding astride his lap like she had in the truck, except now she was warm and dry and wearing next to nothing. Max could feel the heat of her skin through the thin cotton t-shirt, seeping through the borrowed sweatshirt and sweat-pants to warm his own skin, fire his blood.

Her mouth met his again, and she clung to him as she kissed him, hungry little noises rising in the back of her throat, close enough to growls that Max kept breaking away to bare his throat to her—confusing his wolf when he didn't feel the sting of her teeth. Instead, her lips traced over the thunderous beat of his pulse, the touch of her tongue teasing his feverish skin.

Max held her tightly, rolling them both until she was on her back and he was poised above her. The kiss deepened as their bodies rocked together. Jules locked her thighs around Max's hips, arching up against him with each panting breath. Max was hard and aching, grinding himself against her sweet, hot core, hindered by the layers of fabric between them.

Freeing one hand, he stroked down her body, tracing her curves, feeling the soft skin of her inner thigh and following it up to the damp heat of her pussy. She had a pair of thin cotton panties on, and they were soaked through with her arousal. Max cupped that hot flesh through her panties, feeling as if he might explode when she moaned and arched up against the heel of his hand.

"Oh, god," she breathed, clinging to him.

Her intoxicating scent was filling his head, stealing his sense. But threaded through the delicious perfume of her arousal was a tinge of something less appealing—fear. At first, it was too faint to identify, but it slowly intensified, until arousal and fear battled in equal measure. Without the accuracy of his nose, Max would never have guessed. She clung to him no less eagerly than before, rolling her hips to grind on him, kissing him like she needed his taste to survive.

He wanted her, desperately, but not like this. Gently, he broke the kiss, pulling back. Jules still held onto him, flushed and panting, looking for all the world like a woman who wanted to fuck. Was she even aware of the anxiety radiating off of her right now, or had she spent years training herself to ignore it?

It wasn't a good ten years... He wasn't a good person.

"Max?"

He shook his head, centering himself, bringing himself back to the present—to the scent and feel of Jules.

"Are you alright?" he asked.

"I'm fine," she said quickly—too quickly. A flash of fear entered her eyes, there and gone in a second.

"Are you sure?" He spoke gently, softly.

"I..." Her gaze darted away from his. "Did I do something wrong?"

"No! No, of course not. You just—" He couldn't tell her he could smell her fear. "You tensed up on me. If this is too much for you, then we'll stop, okay? I don't want anything you don't want."

"I..." She bit her bottom lip, lush and red from kissing him. "I'm not sure I'm ready for, um, you know... full-on sex." Her gaze met his again, hesitant and uncertain. "I'm not saying no forever. But a little more time..."

He leaned down, nuzzling her cheek, unable to resist leaving one last scent mark on her. "I'm in no hurry. I'm here *at least* until you jump off the train bridge with me, remember?"

A soft smile broke through the worried mask. She leaned up, pressing a soft, sweet kiss to his lips. "Thank you."

"Don't thank me, sweetheart. I'm over the moon to be here."

He nuzzled her other cheek before pushing up to sit, freeing Jules to sit up next to him.

"I also didn't really want our first time to be a rushed

quickie before I have to go to work," she said, adjusting her t-shirt to cover her thighs.

Max suppressed the pleased rumble in his chest. The fact that she referred to "their first time" implied that she wanted more than just a little fun, that she was thinking about a future with him, and that she wanted sex between them to be special. It was enough to make him want to push her down to the bed again—not to fuck, just to hold her and bask in her warmth and scent.

"In case it matters," Jules went on, fidgeting with a crocheted pillowcase, "I've only ever been with my ex so I'm not, like... super skilled."

"Skilled?" Max repeated, baffled.

"At sex."

"It's a skill?"

"I mean, yeah. People have *moves*. Everyone talks about 'being good' in bed. But I don't have any moves and I don't think I'm that good."

Max turned to face her. "Just kissing you has gotten me hotter than I've ever been in my life. I think we'll be fine."

She finally looked up from the pillowcase, meeting his gaze uncertainly. "Really?"

"I'm not expecting a Cirque de Soleil performance—I hope you're not either. I'm from a small town in a remote part of Alaska where I'm related to most of the other residents. I'm not exactly running out of room for notches on my headboard."

Jules bit her lip.

"I just want to be with you," Max said, cupping her cheek, stroking his thumb along the crest of her cheekbone.

She smiled, a faint blush turning her face pink. "Okay."

Max gave into the need and pulled her into his arms, resting his chin atop her head. "Okay."

CHAPTER 12

"So, are you ever going to tell me about the man you've been sneaking into the house for the last couple weeks?"

Jules froze, a forkful of potato salad halfway to her open mouth. She blinked. "Um. What?"

"Don't play dumb with me, Jujube," Grandma said impatiently. "It never worked when your mother tried it, and it's not going to work for you, either."

Jules was still frozen. "But, how...?" Had one of the neighbors ratted her out?

"I've got one of those camera doorbells," Grandma explained impatiently. "You never noticed?"

She had, actually, in a sort of vague way—not distinctly enough to plan around it, though. "Um..."

Grandma cackled. "Well, at least tell me his name."

"Um." It was the only sound she seemed capable of producing. Getting a hold of herself, Jules set her fork down, took a drink of water. "Max," she finally said. "His name is Max."

"*Well.*" Grandma raised her eyebrows, an impish smile plumping her cheeks. "He's a looker, in'so? Can't blame you for sneaking a little afternoon delight."

"Grandma!" Jules's face went hot, and she buried it in her hand.

"What? Am I supposed to pretend you bring him here to play Parcheesi?"

Jules laughed, scrubbing at her still-warm face. "Maybe we're discussing international politics."

Grandma snorted and rolled her eyes. "Don't tell me you found yourself another *intellectual.*" She'd hated Eric from Day One, and aside from the fact that she knew damn well he was preying on a girl too young to know better, the thing she'd hated most about him was the "fake, phony way he goes on and on about shit without ever actually saying a single goddamn thing."

"No," Jules said, then quickly corrected herself. "Max is smart. But he's not in academia. He's..." He'd told her about what he did back in Alaska, and the closest way she could think to describe that Grandma would understand was "police." But Max was insistent that he wasn't police, and Jules didn't want to call him that if he didn't like it. "He works in public safety," Jules said vaguely.

"What, like a cop?"

"No... more of like a first responder kind of deal."

"A paramedic?"

"Um... sort of?" What he did sometimes involved providing emergency care "in the field." But he also patrolled the boundaries of the community. And investigated crimes. And helped clear roads after accidents. And ran search and rescue missions. And just about anything else that meant somebody was in danger and needed help.

"Well, I tell you what, he's a cut above that prick you were married to."

Jules's brows drew together. She shot her grandma a skeptical look. "How would you know? Maybe Max is terrible."

"He's not," she answered confidently, sawing away at her pork chop. "He always holds the door for you."

"Lots of men do that."

"He makes you smile like I haven't seen since you were a girl."

Jules had no answer for that one.

"And he looks at you like you make the sun rise and fall. Here." Grandma pulled her phone out and pulled up a photo. She handed it over to Jules. "Scroll through 'em. I saved a few."

They were screenshots from the doorbell camera. The first image was of Jules laughing while Max grinned, obviously pleased that he'd made her laugh. The second was from a different day, Jules smiling up at Max with happy abandon. The third was mostly just Max—Jules's shoulder blocked the left third of the picture while she unlocked the door, with Max standing just behind her holding the screen door open, gazing at her with such soft, sweet tenderness that it took her breath away.

"Oh." She managed to breathe again. She handed Grandma's phone back. "Um. He's... yeah. He's a good guy."

Grandma smiled fondly. "You deserve a good one, Jujube. Bring him over next Sunday for dinner."

"I'll have to see if he's free."

Grandma gave her a knowing look. "That man'll make himself free for you."

. . .

Contrary to Grandma's suspicions, Jules hadn't had sex with Max yet. To be fair, they weren't playing Parcheesi or discussing global politics, either. Every morning after their walk—which they'd started taking a little earlier, to leave more time for them at the house—she and Max went up to her bedroom and just... kissed. Sure, they talked some. But they did plenty of that on the walk. Once they were in her bed, they just cuddled and made out like teenagers. Every time it started to escalate into something more, Max would eventually break it off, pulling back and just holding her until it was time for her to leave for work.

She stood by what she'd originally said—she didn't want their first time to be a sloppy quickie ten minutes before she had to go to work. She also didn't want it to be in the rattling little twin bed that had been her mother's childhood bed. But with each passing day, the kissing got a little closer to turning into something more, and every time Max put a stop to it, she was just a little less relieved and a little more frustrated.

As they lay in her narrow bed, Max inhaling deeply with his face pressed against her neck, Jules's whole body throbbing with unrelieved arousal, she came to the conclusion that she was going to have to move things along or Max would let them both wither and die before he'd risk pushing her too far.

"Max."

"Hm?"

"When are you going to let me get in your pants?"

His surprised inhalation turned immediately into a hacking cough as he choked on her hair. It took him a few seconds to get himself under control, and when he did, his voice was a husky rasp. "I've been waiting until you're ready. I want you to be—"

"I am going to be nervous no matter what," she said firmly, twisting in his arms to face him. "Not only are you the first person I've been with since the divorce, you're the only other person besides my ex-husband that I'll ever have been with. Unless you're willing to wait, like, a couple *years*, there's no way I'm going to be a hundred percent casual and cool about this. So, either, you put up with the fact that I'm a little nervous and let me get past it in my own way, or you get real comfortable with a *long* stretch of celibacy."

Not even a month ago, Jules wouldn't have had the guts to be so forthright. She was proud of herself, but she also knew it had more than a little to do with the patience of the man holding her in his arms—patience she was currently ready to strangle and dump in a lake.

Max was quiet, his gaze traveling over her face as he considered her words, the beginnings of a mild smile curling one corner of his mouth. "When's your next day off?" he asked finally.

Excitement filled her stomach with butterflies. "Thursday." Two weeks ago, her grandma had hired Jules's younger cousin, Levi, on a part-time basis, allowing both Grandma and Jules to have a couple days off during the week.

Max's eyes lit with excitement. "Want to go camping?"

Jules kept her expression as neutral as possible. It was early May, so the weather was erratic, and the nights were still frigid. "Isn't it kind of cold?" she asked uncertainly.

His smile grew. "I'll keep you warm."

As if confirming his promise, her whole body flushed with languid heat. "Oh. Well, alright." She curled into him, pressing a kiss to the part of his neck that always made him arch and groan. He liked when she nipped him a little, so she did it now, trying to entice him into another round of making out and dry-humping before she had to go to work.

"Easy," Max panted, gripping her tightly. "Thought you didn't want to do it in this rickety bed."

She chuckled against his thumping pulse, licking a long stripe up the side of his throat. "You're right." She rolled away from him. "Time to get ready for work."

Max growled, catching her around the waist and hauling her back against him. "You've got ten more minutes."

"Hmm, do I?"

"Do I have to convince you?"

It turned out, he was very convincing.

Max was in heaven, and he was in hell. Jules was perfect. She was everything. He wanted to claim her so badly, his teeth ached with it. Every time she kissed and nipped his neck, he had to clench his jaw shut to keep himself from begging for her claim mark. He hadn't known her very long, but he knew enough. He loved every little quirk and nuance he discovered about her. The more he discovered, the more he loved. His wolf was desperate to claim her, riding too close to his skin whenever he was with her. But he hadn't gotten the pack's agreement to break Silence, and that needed to be rectified before Thursday.

After Jules went to work, leaving Max hard and wanting, but deliriously happy, he drove to the public parking lot at a quiet lake where he could have a conversation that wouldn't be overheard by sensitive Cry Lake wolf kin ears.

He waited while the simmer in his blood subsided somewhat, gazing out at the rippling surface of the lake, watching a loon as it dove beneath the surface and resurfaced several yards away. When his pulse had settled and he could think more clearly, he rang his mom on a video call. It was mid-morning in Longtooth, so she'd be done with the breakfast rush, free to talk for a little while.

She answered his call quickly, her smiling face filling his screen. His mom was a petite, auburn-haired, blue-eyed, Polish woman. Max took after his dad in appearance, tan-skinned and dark-haired, his features a distinctive creole blend of several different ethnic forebearers, but his mother's influence had come through in the lightness of his eyes and the scattering of freckles that came out in the summer sun.

"Kochanie!" his mother greeted him happily. "You look well. Where are you now?"

"Still in Wisconsin."

"The Cry Lake pack is treating you well, then? Are you eating enough?"

"I'm good." He was a little surprised that his mom wasn't showing the slightest inkling of knowing what he'd called for. It'd been a few weeks since he'd spoken to Caleb about Jules, and while he knew Caleb would never rat him out, he wouldn't have blamed Caleb's mate, Grace, for accidentally letting something slip to his mother. Grace had become the daughter his mother never had, and the two were thick as thieves.

"I'm happy to hear from you. It's been weeks! I know you're out Roaming, but is a weekly phone call too much to ask for?"

Max winced. "Sorry, Mom. I'll try to call more often." He paused, striving for casual. "So, ah, where's Dad?"

"Fixing the radiator in one of the short-stay rooms."

"Can you get him? I want to tell you something."

His mother went totally still for a moment. Her eyes went wide. An eager smile took over her face. "Oh! Yes! Just—hold on. Just wait. One second."

The screen blurred as his mother raced through the Spruce to find her husband.

"Arthur? Arthur!"

In the distance, his dad's voice rumbled back, "*What's wrong?*"

"Nothing! Nothing. It's Max." The camera suddenly found his mother's face again, held at a distance so that he could see his father standing next to her. "He wants to tell us something!"

His dad's brow furrowed in a moment of confusion before sudden comprehension lit his eyes. "Oh, does he now?"

Max smiled at his parents' eagerness. "Do I really have to say it? You seem like you've figured it out."

"Tell us!" his mother ordered impatiently.

He bit back a laugh. "I've met someone."

"Maxim!" His mom clutched happily at his dad. "What's her name? Tell me about her. Who are her parents? I want to talk to them."

"Her name is Juliana. Jules. And I need you to tell the aunties I want to break Silence for her."

His mom drew in a surprised breath. "Oh! She's skinlocked?"

Max nodded. "Yeah."

His dad's brow furrowed. "How long have you known her?" he asked gently.

"A little over a month. I know it's short..."

"If she was wolf kin, I'd ask you what was taking so long," his dad said. "But if she's not kin... if she doesn't even know about us? That's a big risk to take, son."

"I'm not going to claim her right away. But I need to give her time to know about us if she's ever going to accept a claim. She's been hurt in the past, and I don't want to spring anything on her."

His dad's expression softened. "That's fair."

"You have permission!" his mom blurted eagerly, eyes shining.

His dad grinned, shaking his head. "Tasha, you can't speak for the whole pack."

His mom shot his dad a mutinous look, but she relented. "I'll handle it. You know the answer will be yes, though."

She was right. The next day, shortly after leaving Jules's house, his mom called again to let him know the aunties were in unanimous agreement. Max wasn't surprised—partly because he knew how persistent his mother could be, but also because he knew the pack was still dealing with the guilt of keeping Grace in the dark for too long.

"Margaret will call to give you the 'official' approval later today. Probably once school gets out. Now tell me more about this Juliana."

With a warm fire stoked in his chest, Max described Jules to his mom—including the shy, wounded shell he'd first met, and the wonderful woman he'd discovered beneath all the armor. He explained, in broad strokes, that she'd been married to a man who had mistreated her, and even through the phone line, he could feel his mother's righteous outrage. She was a protector and caretaker to her core—Max was fairly certain he'd gotten those qualities from her, though his more easy-going nature was definitely courtesy of his dad. Just like Max, she couldn't abide the unhappiness of her loved ones, and she especially couldn't stand for abuse.

"What's his name?" his mom asked tightly.

"I don't know his full name," Max said, grateful that it was the truth. "There's nothing to be done about him, Mom. As far as I know, he lives in Washington and Jules hasn't even spoken to him in over a year."

"Hmm."

Max moved the conversation onto happier topics— speaking fondly of Jules' collection of "found things" and how often on their daily walks she picked up some new little treasure to add to the collection.

"She gave me a garnet."

"She bought you jewelry?" his mom asked, both puzzled and excited. Gifting was an instinctive part of wolf kin courtship, an almost irresistible impulse. It was a good sign when a skinlocked human started acting on the impulse.

"No, she found a piece of raw garnet in a creek bed and gave it to me."

"And have you given her anything?"

"I found an arrowhead for her. I'm keeping my eyes peeled for an intact trilobite, too."

"A... what?"

"A fossil."

"You're giving her rocks?" his mother asked flatly.

"Caleb got Grace with *yarn*," he objected.

"Gracie loved the yarn."

"Well, Jules really likes rocks."

"Hmm." After a moment, she sighed. "Well, who am I to argue? Your father gave me a hammer."

Max knew the story, but he pretended to be appalled anyway. "A *hammer?*"

His mom laughed. "It was a very nice hammer!"

CHAPTER 13

Jules was waiting at the kitchen window, staring at the road, when Max's truck pulled into view a little after noon. With a happy squeal, she grabbed her backpack and hurried to the door. Per Max's instructions, she'd packed light—mostly just several layers of clothing and a few toiletries. He'd assured her he'd take care of everything else.

Before he even had the truck in park, Jules was at the passenger door, pulling it open and hopping in.

"Well, hello," he said warmly.

Jules surged across the center console, grabbing his face and kissing him deeply.

"Happy to see you too," he said, voice husky, when she pulled away.

"Let's go!" She sank back into the passenger seat, buckling her seatbelt and settling her backpack at her feet.

Max reached over to brace himself against Jules's seatback as he looked over his shoulder to back out of the driveway. She couldn't explain why she liked it so much, but seeing him do that made her want to throw herself at him again. Max seemed to know it, too. He glanced briefly at her, a knowing grin teasing the corner of his mouth, before returning his attention to the road.

They drove north, to Lac Bonne Vue, and parked at a public lot on the eastern shore. Max had planned a hike along the trail that ran through the national forest from Lac Bonne Vue to Cardinal Lake. Cardinal Lake was deep in the woods, accessible only by the trail, so visitors were few and primitive camping was permitted. Jules had only ever camped at actual campgrounds, so she didn't really know what to expect, but she was thrilled nonetheless.

They were halfway between Lac Bonne Vue and Cardinal Lake when Max stopped and turned to face her. Tall pines grew close on either side of the trail. The air was bright with golden sunshine, and filled with the chatter of songbirds and insects. There was nobody around but the two of them, and Max's face was so serious, so intent, that Jules thought for a brief moment that he might throw her down on the trail and fuck her right there.

Her breath hitched at the thought. She wasn't exactly opposed to the idea.

But then Max said, "I have to tell you something about myself," in a tone of such gravity that all thoughts of sex left her mind.

"Okay…" she said nervously, wondering if she was about to find out she'd skipped merrily into the deep woods with a prolific serial killer. "What is it?"

"I don't even know where to start." He raked his fingers through his hair, looking agitated. Suddenly, his eyes grew wide. "It's not bad," he said urgently. "Don't be scared. It's really not bad. It's just… different."

Serial killers are different, Jules thought faintly.

"I told you that my family, my community, we have a unique culture."

A culture of murder?

"We're, uh... we're not like most humans."

The murder train in her mind suddenly derailed. "Most... *humans?*" Jules asked uncertainly.

"We're human!" he said quickly, defensively. "But also... ah, shit. I should probably just show you."

"Show me what?"

Max slipped his arms out of the heavy hiking pack and set it on the ground. Jules stared in baffled alarm as he began stripping out of his clothes.

"What are you doing?" she asked, the words coming out strangled.

"Just a second," he said as he shoved his pants down his legs. "You'll see."

And then he was stark naked. It wasn't exactly how Jules had anticipated first witnessing his nude body, and her gaze shot to the sky, mortified.

But then, Max wasn't there anymore. From the edge of her vision, it seemed like he'd crouched down, but then the shape blurred, condensed, and when she looked at him again, there was a massive ruddy-brown wolf staring back at her.

The massive brown wolf. The one who'd been visiting her after work every night.

"Oh my god." She stared at him. One part of her brain immediately understood. The other part was adamant that she was actually having a psychotic break. After ten years with her ex, she was probably overdue.

The wolf approached her, as bright-eyed and friendly as

always, and nosed her limp hand. Instinctively, she began to pet him. He let out a happy chuff, rubbing his cheek against her hip. After a moment, he stepped back. In a blur of motion that Jules couldn't quite fathom, the wolf shifted back into Max—naked and crouching on the ground.

"Do you see?" he asked, gazing up at her with a fraught mix of anxiety and hope.

"You're a werewolf." She heard her voice as if it belonged to someone else, speaking with inexplicable calm.

Max stood slowly. "We call ourselves wolf kin. The myths about werewolves are... not totally accurate."

"But you can *turn into a wolf.*"

"Yes."

Jules stared at him, at a loss for words.

"I promise you have nothing to be afraid of. I'm still *me*, in either form." He paused. "But if this is too much for you, I understand. I won't pressure you or bother you if you don't want to see me again. But I wanted you to know about me before we... before... I wanted you to have full knowledge of who I am before you made a choice you might regret." There was a quiet resignation in his voice as he spelled it out for her.

Jules was quiet for a long moment. The hope in Max's expression began to fade into defeat.

"Can you..." Jules had to swallow, willing her throat to work. "Can you turn into a wolf again?"

"Sure," he said cautiously.

Jules's brain once again failed to comprehend the shift happening in front of her, and then there was a giant russet wolf sitting politely in front of her like a well-trained collie.

"Give me your right paw," she said.

The wolf raised a paw to her.

"That's your left."

He set the paw down hastily and gave her the other.

Okay. So he definitely understood her.

"Can you speak?"

He answered her with a low whine, which she assumed meant "No."

"But you understand everything I say?"

He chuffed at her, tail wagging, sweeping brown pine needles across the trail.

"I need to sit." She sank to the ground unsteadily.

The wolf—Max—rushed to her, circling behind her and bracing his weight against her back, supporting her. He rested his head on her shoulder and licked at her cheek.

"Ick! What did I tell you about that?" She wiped wolf slobber off of her cheek as Max whined apologetically, tail swishing anxiously.

The comfort of having her big wolf-dog at her back was at complete odds with the bizarreness of knowing that it was Max.

But why should it be? She let herself lean against him. She'd known from the start that there was something different about Max. Something wild and even slightly dangerous. She'd been afraid of him at first. But time had proven him neither wild nor dangerous. At least, not in the ways that mattered. He was steady and patient and funny and sweet. He never made her feel small or annoying or stupid. She was nobody, but Max made her feel special. She couldn't give that feeling up. She couldn't give *him* up.

Steadier now, she turned to look at him. "I'm done freaking out. If you want to, um... change back? So we can talk?"

He drew away gently and shifted back into his human

form. Jules averted her eyes from his nakedness. Never mind that the whole reason for this camping trip was to finally have sex with him. Ogling him just felt rude in this context.

"I'll just get dressed first," Max suggested gently.

"Yep. Okay."

He walked past her. In her peripheral vision, she watched as he pulled his clothes back on. When he had his pants buttoned, Jules turned to him.

"So... you're a wolf man."

"Wolf kin."

"Wolf kin. And that means... you turn into a wolf sometimes?"

He dusted pine needles from his bare feet so that he could pull his socks back on. "Whenever I want, really."

"How did you become a were—I mean, wolf kin?"

"I was born this way. All of us are. It's inherited."

"Were you born in human form or wolf?"

"Definitely human. We're not able to shift until we're older. Plus, my mom's skinlocked."

"Skinlocked?"

Max stood up, fully dressed again, and went to grab the heavy backpack loaded down with camping supplies. He slung it easily onto his back and then held a hand out to Jules. She accepted it, letting him pull her to her feet.

"Can't change skins. Locked into one. Like you."

"Oh."

They were standing dangerously close—close enough to kiss. Jules could see the same thought in Max's eyes, but he didn't move to initiate. That same uncertainty that had been in his expression after he first showed her his secret was still there.

She couldn't have that. She rose up onto her tiptoes and

pressed a soft kiss to his lips. "So, are we going camping, or what?" she asked, a faint, silly blush heating her cheeks. "Camping" meant more than just sleeping in a tent. They both knew it.

"I..." It took Max a second to process what she was saying. "Oh. *Yes*. Absolutely," he said earnestly. "We're going to camp all night long. And then maybe camp some more in the morning."

Jules suppressed a slightly hysterical giggle. "Are you sure your... *tent* can handle it?"

"Sweetheart, after experiencing my tent, you'll never want to sleep in a house again."

Jules couldn't contain the giggle this time. The metaphor was getting away from them.

As they continued down the trail, Jules peppered Max with questions about wolf kin, and he answered them all, some with total seriousness, others with a laugh.

When they finally reached Cardinal Lake, she had more or less come to terms with the fact that Max was... wolf kin.

I'm about to fuck a werewolf, she thought, watching as he set the backpack down and unfastened the tent from it. The thought did little more than make her grin.

"What's so funny?"

"My entire life, to be honest," Jules answered, crouching beside him to help pull the tent out of its case.

They worked together, setting it up in less than ten minutes. Innuendo aside, it was a nice tent. It was sturdy and spacious enough to be comfortable, but snug enough to be cozy. Max took other rolls off his backpack—spreading a foam mat across the bottom of the tent, then two large sleeping bags, unzipped, one on top of the other. He topped their simple bed off with two foam pillows that he took out of unbelievably tiny bags. Unconfined, they expanded to normal pillow size.

When the bed was done, he set the backpack in the corner of the tent and stood back to admire his handiwork. Jules's stomach dipped as she took it in, eager anticipation mixed with nerves. Max glanced at her, his expression gentle.

"We won't do anything you don't want," he said. "We can just hang out, stargaze, whatever. Or we can go back."

Jules shook her head, forcing herself to meet his gaze. "I don't want to go back."

"So you're saying you just want to stargaze," he concluded, a teasing note in his voice.

"*You* can stargaze when I have you on your back," Jules said sweetly, turning away to trot down to the water's edge. "But I'll be a little too busy to—*oof!*"

Max's arms locked around her, pulling her tight to his chest and lifting her briefly off her feet. "Busy doing what, sweetheart?" he growled against the curve of her ear.

A hot shiver ran down her neck. "Oh, you know... exploring your *tent*."

Max growled again, a distinctly canine sound coming from his seemingly human throat. He bent his head to nip lightly at the tender skin on the side of her neck. "Not yet," he said roughly. "I have plans for today. I'm going to seduce you so subtly and so artfully, you won't even know what happened. By the end of the night, you'll be begging to explore my tent."

She didn't bother telling him she was already seduced. She just laughed and turned in his embrace so that she could wrap her arms around his neck and kiss him. "How are you going to seduce me, exactly?"

"Well, first, we're going to have dinner, so I'm going to impress you with my manly vigor while I set up the camp stove."

Jules bit the inside of her cheek as another manic grin threatened to take over her entire face. He was too good to be true. So what if he turned into a wolf sometimes? At least he didn't turn into a condescending, gaslighting, soul-destroying narcissist like her ex had. Max could turn into a slug and still be an improvement over Eric.

CHAPTER 14

After a simple dinner of chicken dumpling soup heated up over a small propane camp stove, Max and Jules sat on the grassy bank along the edge of Cardinal Lake, and watched the sunset over the tree tops. The sky turned a brilliant mix of pink and orange, making the clouds look as if they were on fire. As the sky darkened and the stars appeared, Max turned to Jules. He cupped her cheek, leaned in, and kissed her.

It was soft, tender, undemanding. But it was also slow and deep and drugging. When he leaned back, Jules went with him, clutching the front of his flannel. His arms circled her waist, hauling her against him as he sprawled back on the grass. She could feel him getting hard, a thick ridge pressing against her hip. It was just like their daily make-out sessions in her bedroom, except there were no time constraints today, and they both knew it wasn't going to stop at kissing.

Suddenly, a thought occurred to her, and she pulled

back, breaking the kiss. "You're not going to turn into a wolf in the middle of this, are you?"

Max laughed, a slightly strained sound. "Trust me, my wolf doesn't want to do anything that would interrupt this."

"Is he separate from you, then?"

"No." Max paused, choosing his words, his hands coasting slowly up and down her back. "I'm the same mind, the same soul, in both forms. When I talk about 'my wolf,' I'm talking about the side of myself that is primal, instinctive, intuitive, and... less civilized. I feel those traits more intensely in my wolfskin, but it's still me."

Jules often thought of her own mind as having multiple "sides." It wasn't a psychiatric disorder, just a compartmentalized way of viewing her own self. Max's explanation of his wolf made perfect sense to her.

"If you bite me, will *I* turn into a wolf?"

He laughed at her again. "No. If I bite you hard enough to draw blood, it means I'm marking you as my mate. You'll still be skinlocked, but you'll be mine. Forever."

"Oh." She felt her eyes getting wide. Her heart thumped strangely.

"Don't be scared. I'd never do it unless you wanted it."

Was it crazy that she *did* want it? Yes. "And what if I bite you?"

"Same thing," he said, sounding slightly strained. His cock was an iron brand, hot and hard, pressing against her. "Skinlocked humans can claim wolf kin mates. You do it with a bite, just like me."

What a strange power to be bestowed with. "What if you don't want to be claimed?"

"Then you'd just be gnawing on me like a cannibal, I guess."

Jules laughed a little at the image.

"But, sweetheart, be careful—if you tried to claim me, it would take."

Her smile faded. The weight of what he was telling her seemed to settle on her chest.

"And it's not something you can back out of," he went on, expression grave. "It's an irreversible lifetime bond."

"You would want that with me?" she asked softly, incredulous.

"Of course I would. I know this is a little fast for you, but I'm ready whenever you want to take the leap. If you ever do."

Jules's heart squeezed. "How can you be sure? What if I'm a psycho?"

Max smiled fondly at her. "You're not."

"What if I've been putting on a really good act?"

"Nobody's that good an actress." He lifted his head, kissing her briefly. "My wolf knows. *I* know. You're amazing, Jules, and I would be lucky to be your mate."

Jules stared at him, stunned. It took her brain several long seconds to put together anything in coherent language. "I... Max— I really need to see your tent now."

He grinned. "My tent, or *my tent?*"

"Both."

Max somehow managed to sit bolt upright and toss Jules over his shoulder in one fluid motion. She shrieked as he got to his feet and carried her to the tent. A second later, he was crouching through the tent flap, sinking to his knees and spilling Jules gently onto the waiting bedding. She stared up at him, flushed and laughing and so desperate to have the feel of his body against hers again. He clicked on a dim light hanging from the peak of the tent, then turned to zip up the flap.

As soon as he turned back, Jules grabbed his shirt and pulled him down on top of her. His mouth met hers, hot and hungry, while his hands roved over her body, slipping beneath the hem of her shirt to trace up her sides. His thumbs coasted over her ribs to the underside of her breasts, teasing those curves in soft strokes. Jules arched up against him, all but thrusting her breasts into his hands.

"Can I take your shirt off?" Max asked. "I want to see you."

"If you take yours off."

"Deal."

Jules grabbed the hem of her shirt and tugged it over her head. Max hurriedly unfastened buttons down the front of his flannel while Jules reached behind herself to open the fastening on her bra. She flung her clothes off into the corner while Max continued unbuttoning his shirt with suddenly clumsy fingers. His gaze lit on her bare skin, his eyes so hot, she should have been scorched.

"*Juliana*," he growled, abandoning his shirt buttons to descend on her.

His big hands gripped her waist and slid roughly upward to cup her breasts. He bent so that he could nibble at the side of her neck, then trailed lower, leaving hot, wet kisses on her collarbone, the upper slope of one breast, teasing closer and closer to her nipple. She arched her back, instinctively pushing into his touch. The soft abrasion of his beard teased her peaked nipple, but instead of taking the sensitive point into his mouth, he moved his attention to the other side of her body, beginning at her collar bone, and blazing a new trail with his lips and tongue along the slope of her other breast before finally dragging his tongue across one peaked nipple, and then the other. Jules moaned, arching up, hands gripping the back of his head as she clutched him to her.

"*Max,*" she sobbed his name, a gasping plea.

"We'll get there," he promised, lips brushing against her breast as he spoke, breath fanning across her skin.

His hands roved further down her body, grasping her hips, one hand sliding between her thighs to cup her roughly, working the heel of his hand against her clit. Jules gasped as brilliant sensation lit her up from head to toe.

"You don't need these jeans," Max decided, hand slipping up to unsnap the button. "It's way too hot."

It was fifty degrees outside, but Jules wouldn't have noticed if they were in the middle of a blizzard. Max's heat was burning her up from the inside. She fumbled to help him get her jeans off, kicking them down her legs.

"What about these?" His index finger hooked inside her underwear, tracing the low waistband from hipbone to hipbone. "They look way too warm."

"You're still totally dressed," Jules complained, spreading her hands inside his half-unbuttoned flannel. He was thick and muscular, with coarse black hair covering his chest and arrowing down his abdomen. She followed the trail to the edge of his pants.

"I got distracted," Max said with a saturnine smile. He sat back on his knees, his weight on Jules's thighs, pinning her in place. His gaze raked over her mostly naked body with feral desire as he ripped his flannel open, sending the last three buttons pinging against the sides of the tent. He shrugged out of the shirt and tossed it aside. Still eyeing Jules with a hunger that made her shiver, he opened his belt.

Watching him do it, naked and pinned beneath him, felt lewder than actual nudity.

When the belt was open, he unzipped his jeans. He eased forward, his weight lifting from her legs as he braced himself on one arm above her. The other arm worked his pants down his legs as his mouth found hers again. Slowly, he lowered himself over her. His bare skin felt feverishly hot against hers, his chest hair a delicious abrasion against her nipples, his cock a heavy, burning weight against her hip.

The hand that had pulled his jeans off was back at her underwear, easing them down. Jules lifted her hips to let him slide them over her ass and down her thighs. He swept them the rest of the way off her legs, and instead of throwing them aside with the rest of their scattered clothes, he pulled back from her and brought her panties to his face.

Jules nearly choked on her own tongue as he inhaled, burning gaze meeting hers over a fistful of pale blue cotton.

"I've been smelling this sweet scent from a respectful distance for weeks," he growled, flinging her panties aside. "And I can't wait for the real thing."

He came back down on top of her, both of them fully bare now, hot skin against hot skin. He took her mouth in a rough, needy kiss, then trailed hot, open-mouthed kisses down her throat, her collar bones, the valley between her breasts.

With his hands braced on either side of her body, he closed his mouth around her nipple. He stroked his tongue over the stiff, sensitive peak in rough passes that made her gasp and arch with each one. He sucked gently, and when she whimpered, he sucked harder. He kissed his way across her chest until he found her other nipple, and lavished it with the same attention. When she was gasping and arching, and nearly certain she was going to come just from having her nipples played with, he kissed his way back to the delicate skin above her sternum. He dragged his lips lower, then lower still, following the centerline of her body down, and down, and down.

As he kissed her belly, drifting lower and lower and lower, Jules suddenly realized where he was going and what he intended. With instinctive shame, she snapped her legs together, but it was too late—his head was already there, and she ended up clapping her thighs over his ears like cymbals. The hot, sweaty, desire fled and suddenly she was cold, clammy, and exposed.

"I'll take that as a 'no'," Max said, voice muffled, head still trapped.

"Oh my god." She released him and scrambled backwards until she was pressed against the tent wall. "I'm so sorry. That was— I mean, I don't—" Mortified she buried her face in her hands. "I'm sorry."

"It's okay." Max kept his voice gentle as he moved back, giving her space. "If you don't like that, I won't—"

"No, it's not that. I mean, I don't know if I like it. I've never—it hasn't really—um..." She couldn't look him in the eye, her face burning hot. "Nobody's ever done that to me before."

"Your ex *never* went down on you?" Max asked, incredulous.

"No," Jules said in a tiny, shamed voice. Strong women didn't put up with men who didn't want to please them in bed. Strong women definitely didn't spend *ten years* married to men who didn't want to please them in bed. Jules wanted to be strong, she wanted to be the sort of person who demanded respect, but she kept being reminded that she was not.

Max crept closer to her. He came slowly, giving her every chance to tell him to stop or ward him off. Slowly, gently, he pulled her into his arms, turning her so that her back rested against his chest. He sank down to sit, Jules cradled between his thighs, his strong arms wrapped around her. He rested his chin on her shoulder and simply held her. Slowly, she felt the tension leech from her body as she relaxed against him.

"Can I?" he asked after a quiet moment.

"Hm?"

"Can I taste you? You smell amazing, Jules. I want you on my tongue."

A jagged shiver ran down her spine. Lust tightened deliciously in her core, making her breath stutter and her pussy throb. Max inhaled deeply, which was both unbearably arousing and mortifyingly direct. Jules shivered again, even as her face burned. He nuzzled against the side of her neck, teasing sensitive skin with the tip of his nose and the scruff of his beard.

"*Please,*" he whispered directly against the shell of her ear. His breath tickled her skin, sending goosebumps down her neck and back.

"Alright," she said faintly, still nervous, but too turned on to let it hold her back. "Yes. Just... if you don't like it, don't pretend for my sake, okay?" The end of her sentence was lost in a startled shriek as the world spun around her. In a split second, she found herself laying on her back. Max braced himself over her on hands and knees, grinning.

"Juliana," he chided her, shaking his head in pretend disappointment. "I don't think I've ever heard something so ludicrous."

"I just—"

"There is no question of whether I'm going to like eating your pussy—"

"*Oh my god.*"

"—the question is, how will I ever get enough? Because I have been starving for a taste for weeks, sweetheart. *Starving.*" His golden eyes burned into hers, intently focused.

"Max," she breathed his name, staring up at him, helplessly aroused. She didn't know what to say, because her brain had stopped thinking in words.

Luckily, Max didn't seem to need coherent language. The corner of his mouth curled up, apparently in satisfaction at whatever he read in Jules's expression, and he leaned down, taking her mouth in a deep, slow, all-consuming kiss. When he broke away, she was clinging to his shoulders and panting for breath. He dipped back down, his lips tracing a new trail down her body.

He made his way lower and lower, big hands cupping behind Jules's knees and spreading them wide so that he could sink his broad shoulders between them. He pressed a kiss to each hip bone, making Jules's skin shiver, her legs tremble. With his arms hooked beneath her thighs, hands gripping her hips, Max cast her a roguish smile before bringing his lips back to her overheated skin.

He kissed the inside of one thigh, working his way higher and higher until his mouth was nearly on her pussy. But he didn't touch her there. Breath ghosting over slick, sensitive flesh, he turned his head to the other thigh, and began kissing his way up.

When he reached the top, he paused again, breath fanning against her, his lips just shy of touching her.

"Max!" Her fingers slid into his hair, tugging on what she could grasp of the closely-cut strands.

He made a rumbling sound deep in his throat as he rubbed his beard against the delicate skin of her inner thigh. "Pull harder."

She couldn't help but do as he asked, her whole body clenching on the hot spear of arousal that his words sent through her. Max growled his approval, and brought his mouth to her pussy, his lips sealing over her skin as his tongue swept from her entrance to her clit, slicking through flesh so tender that even his soft touch made her cry out. Her back arched up from the bed, but Max's hold was strong on her hips, keeping her positioned for him to feast.

He licked her again and again, moaning against her skin as he did. The vibrations of his voice nearly set her off right there. Her hands clenched again, inadvertently tugging harder on his hair, but that only seemed to motivate him.

He lifted his head for a second, lips glistening, eyes burning. "Knew you'd taste good," he told her gruffly.

"What, like strawberries and champagne?" Jules joked breathlessly, distantly amazed that she'd managed to put a coherent sentence together.

"Like hot, raw pussy," Max growled before filling his mouth with her again.

His tongue found her clit and circled it, working her higher and higher into a state of wordless, overwhelmed need. She gasped and moaned, all shame forgotten, hips rolling to grind herself against his tongue. She was *so* close to the peak. *So* close—

Max tightened his lips around her clit, sucking hard, and she was gone. A blinding, body-shaking, sobbing orgasm took hold of her, working through her in powerful waves, one after another after another, each one peaking higher than the last, until she felt like she might die from the pleasure of it.

When she came back to her senses, Max was crawling up her body to lower himself beside her, pulling her into his arms. His erection was pressed between them, hard and throbbing.

"Give me a second," she panted, "When I catch my breath, I'll return the favor."

"There are no favors between us," Max said, kissing the top of her head. "There's no tally, okay?"

She sagged against him, unable to believe a man like him truly existed. Was this all some delirious fever dream? That would explain the wolf thing.

A sudden spark of fear ignited within her.

"Jules?" Max lifted his head. "What's wrong?"

"I'm afraid this is a dream. I'm afraid *you're* a dream."

A sharp pinch on her ass made her startle.

"Hey!"

"See, not a dream."

"People in comas can feel and hear things from their surroundings without being fully—"

Max shifted hips behind her and lifted her knee so that his cock slipped between her thighs. "Can coma patients feel the dick they're keeping warm?"

She was still hot and slick and sensitive, and his shaft slid easily through the soft pressure of her thighs.

Jules swallowed a whimper. "Maybe it would feel like that when they're being...you know, cleaned by the nurse, or—"

Max bent his head to press a hot, open-mouthed kiss to

the side of her neck. "Don't mind me, just the nurse, checking your vitals."

Jules let out a breathy laugh that hitched when he rocked his hips, gently thrusting between her thighs. One hand came up to cup her breast, his thumb stroking over her nipple until it was peaked and hard again.

"Gotta replace your IV," he said, lightly pinching her nipple.

She gasped. "Nobody puts IVs there."

"You were in a terrible accident, it was the only usable part."

"How am I even alive, then?"

He slid his hand from her breast down to her pussy, gently circling his fingers on her mons—not directly on her clit, thankfully, but providing enough stimulation to make her arch against him.

"Because I am a very talented doctor," Max whispered against her ear.

"I thought you were a nurse."

"I'm both. I have multiple degrees."

Jules laughed. "I see."

He slid his cock from between her thighs and urged her onto her back. "Time for your exam." He slid on top of her, bracing his weight on one arm so that he didn't crush her. With his other hand, he reached for his cock.

"What kind of hospital is this?" Jules demanded, trying to hide the fear and nerves that apparently Max's stupid wolf kin nose could easily detect.

Max smiled at her, the look both fierce and fond. He dipped his head to kiss her. "Ready for me?"

She nodded, circling her arms around his neck.

"Are you sure?" he asked gently. "I can wait. I want you to want it as bad as I do."

"I want you so much, Max. Just let me be nervous, okay?"

He nodded, some of the heat banking in his gaze, but he kept going. As the blunt head of him nudged against her entrance, Jules steeled herself for the unavoidable discomfort. But Max sank into her with an intensely slow, gentle pressure. He didn't have to force himself in and even though he was intimidatingly big, she stretched without feeling like she was being split apart.

"Oh my god," Jules gripped his shoulders, wide-eyed.

"Are you alright?" Max asked, going totally still.

"Yes—*oh*, wow. Yes. I just... I didn't know it could be like this."

"Like what?" he asked, smiling, though there was a strained edge to his voice.

"Painless. Easy."

For a moment, something between grief and rage flickered in his eyes. He shook it off, leaning down to kiss her again. "I will *never* hurt you," he whispered against her lips. "I promise you that."

Jules's heart turned a somersault, and she had to swallow a sudden knot in her throat. "I know."

Max kissed her again, holding her in his arms as his hips began a subtle rocking motion that put rhythmic pressure on her clit while his cock nudged gently inside her. She couldn't get over how good he felt. Sex with Eric had often felt like she was having a pelvic exam done by a broomstick. But with Max she felt filled up in the best way, like a missing piece of her had been fitted into place.

Every time he retreated, she wanted him back. And every time he slid in deep again, her toes curled and her breath sighed out and everything felt right. The motion of his body worked with hers to stretch and massage and stimulate, not just where he was inside her, but everywhere they touched. Hot skin against hot skin, strong arms holding her tight, her own hands roving over the contours of his body, thighs wrapped round his hips, lips and tongues and teeth tasting and delving and nipping and sucking.

Max was a full-body, whole-mind experience. There was nothing but the taste of him, the scent of him, the feel of him. In this moment, he was the whole world, and Jules never wanted it to end. But he felt too good, and soon, Jules fell over the edge into another explosive orgasm. As her inner muscles clenched down on him, Max groaned and shuddered, thrusting with short, urgent strokes until he slid in deep and stayed there, his cock pulsing inside of her as he gasped his way through his own climax.

When he slumped over her, Jules wrapped her arms and legs around him, holding him tight, feeling their pounding heartbeats thump against each other as they gasped for breath. Max's lips were on her shoulder, and very, *very* briefly, she felt the lightest pressure of his teeth. A wild part of her almost told him to do it—bite down, claim her. But she kept the words inside, saving them for later... some day.

Max kissed the skin he'd just had his teeth pressed against, and rolled to the side, taking his weight off Jules, sprawling on his back. He pulled Jules in tight against him and kissed her deeply.

"Good?" he asked when he finally broke the kiss.

"Better than good," Jules told him. She was glowing with an impossible feeling of mellow contentment mixed with ecstatic joy. She'd never felt like this before in her life. Satisfied, treasured, safe, but also electric with hot, heady desire.

They lay in each others' arms, dozing in that blissful contentment, murmuring to each other now and then as they listened to the forest sounds around them—wind through branches, the gentle lap of water, the hum of insects, and the steady, mellow call of a great horned owl.

With a little time, the contented tangle of their bodies turned heated again, and Jules found herself sitting astride Max's hips, sliding her needy core along his erection—a lot sooner than she would've expected.

"Already?" she asked, impressed.

He grinned at her. "Wolf kin have more stamina than skinlocked humans—in a lot of ways."

They came together again and again that night, proving Max's words true. Jules couldn't seem to get enough of him, and as much as she needed, he was able to give. By the early hours of the morning, they were both sweaty and spent, their skin coated with too many layers of sweat, and more come than Jules wanted to think about.

"Let's go clean up," Max urged her, voice hoarse with exhaustion.

Jules sprawled bonelessly across the bed, eyes closed. "Did you bring wet wipes?"

"No, in the lake."

She slotted one eye open. "It's, like, fifty degrees outside."

"Yeah. Refreshing."

Jules laughed weakly. "Absolutely not."

"You just want to sleep covered in... *us?*"

She groaned. "No."

"Then the lake's the only option. I brought towels, and I promise I'll warm you up afterward."

She sighed and reluctantly pushed herself up. "I think

you fried my brain with too many orgasms." That was the only explanation for why she was letting Max take her hand and tug her out into the bracingly cold night air, naked as the day she was born.

"A dip in the lake will help," Max said.

The moon and the stars were bright overhead. Faint gray light on the eastern horizon hinted at the approach of dawn. They walked down to the water. Max strode into it unflinchingly, all but dragging Jules with him. She shrieked as the cold water rose higher and higher on her body. It was warmer than the night air, but that was hardly an improvement. With a sudden flourish, Max swung her into his arms bridal-style—

"Max, don't you—"

—and then plunged them both beneath the surface of the water. The cold was so sudden and so all-encompassing, that the unpleasantness was almost imperceptible beneath the shock. A second later, Max surged back up, holding Jules in his arms as water poured off of them both. Jules hauled in a ragged, gasping breath, clinging to Max.

"You son of a—"

He dropped them both into the water again. The clarifying cold was less brutal the second time. In fact, the warmer water temperature was almost preferable to the air on her wet skin. But when Max hauled her back up out of the water, she squirmed out of his arms and dove for his leg. Grabbing his calf with both hands, she lifted it fast and hard, throwing him off balance, and sending him splashing back into the water.

As soon as he rose up, laughing, she tackled him again, sending them both careening into the cold wet. Max caught hold of her and hauled her up against the furnace-like warmth of his big body, laughing as he spun her around. A moment later, he stopped and frowned down at her.

"You're shivering," he said, striding out of the water with her in his arms.

"Yeah, because it's cold. I believe I raised some objections along those lines. But *no*, you wanted—"

Max silenced her with a hard kiss. "I thought you were so meek when I first met you," he said, an incredulous laugh in his voice.

She *was*. But Max made her feel safe enough to be honest and playful and opinionated in ways that she hadn't for *years*. She arched up, kissing him again—a wordless expression of gratitude and happiness and... love. She couldn't quite bring herself to say that one out loud just yet, but it was there, and she couldn't lie to herself.

Too fast, the pragmatic side of her warned.

She ignored it.

Max fished towels out of the backpack and helped Jules dry off. Cleaning her feet carefully first, Jules dove back into the warmth of the tent and immediately slipped beneath the top sleeping bag. Max joined her a second later, zipping the tent flap closed before slipping beneath the sleeping bag and pulling Jules into his arms.

They fell asleep, wrapped in each other's warmth.

WHEN JULES WOKE, THE SUN WAS HIGH IN THE SKY, AND MAX WAS still wrapped around her. She shifted in his arms, looking for her phone. She knew she'd left it in her jacket pocket, but she wasn't sure where she'd discarded her jacket last night. Her stirring woke Max.

"Good morning," he said muzzily, rubbing at his eyes as he sat up.

"I think it might be afternoon," Jules said.

She finally found her coat beneath Max's flannel and fished her phone out of the interior pocket to check the time. It was just past noon. She felt Max's warmth at her back as he looked over her shoulder.

"Afternoon?" he said, incredulous. "I *never* sleep that late."

"Guess I wore you out," Jules said smugly.

He kissed the top of her head. "And here I was bragging about my stamina."

"Trust me, your stamina is brag-worthy." Jules stretched. "I'm not going to forget it anytime soon."

"Good." Max nipped her shoulder before pulling away from her to hunt for his clothes. "Hungry?"

"Famished."

"How do pancakes sound?"

Jules stared at him. "I'm back to thinking I'm in a coma dream."

"Would it help if I dumped you in the lake again?"

She glared at him, but ruined it by breaking into a giddy smile. "Don't you dare," she said, less severely than she meant to.

Max scrubbed at his face ruefully. "Even if I wanted to, I think my legs would give out. It's not healthy to come that many times in one night. I think I need electrolytes. And a multivitamin."

"I bet pancakes have electrolytes."

"You're probably right."

Max mixed up a just-add-water pancake mix and cooked them over the little propane cookstove in the same collapsible pot he'd heated up last night's dinner in. They were the best pancakes Jules had ever had in her life, even though Max realized he'd forgotten to pack syrup and they had to eat them dry.

After breakfast, they broke camp together—quick and easy considering how few things they had—and set out on the hike back to Lac Bonne Vue, where Max's truck was parked.

"We should've thought this through better," Jules complained, not even twenty minutes in.

"I hadn't planned on having my muscles fucked to jelly," Max said, looking just as unenthusiastic as Jules was. "Otherwise I would've picked a shorter hike."

"So if I asked you to carry me...?"

Max groaned and Jules laughed.

They walked on in exhausted silence. Several minutes later, Max abruptly broke it.

"I want you to meet my parents."

Jules blinked. "Your parents?"

"I want you to meet my whole pack," he went on. "Could you get some time off from the store? A couple weeks?"

"You want me to go to Alaska with you?"

"Yeah. I mean, not tomorrow. But, eventually?"

Jules thought on it. "Alright," she said, a spark of warmth kindling in her chest. "I'll meet your family. But you have to meet mine."

"Sure. When?"

"Sunday dinner with me and my grandma?"

Max smiled. "I'll be there."

CHAPTER 15

The following weeks were some of the happiest of Jules's life. Max came to Sunday dinner, and Grandma had immediately adored him—and essentially ordered him to be present at every subsequent Sunday dinner.

"He's a good one, Jujube," Grandma told her after Max had gone home the first Sunday.

"I know," she said softly.

"You deserve a good one." Grandma hugged her and returned her attention to clearing the table. Jules stood at the sink with half-washed dishes, watching out the window as Max got into his truck and drove away. She'd see him again tomorrow, but her heart already ached at the separation.

Her body ached, too—in a sensual, constantly aroused kind of way. Since their camping excursion, they'd been taking advantage of every possible stolen moment, and it still wasn't enough. Their after-walk make-outs had turned into after-walk sex. Every night after work, when Jules finished closing down the store, Max drove her to an over-grown fire lane in the state forest near Cry Lake, where they steamed up his truck windows.

With Max, sex wasn't a performance she put on in order to earn affection and approval. It wasn't something that was done *to* her. It was something they did together, because making each other feel good was all that mattered. She'd stopped caring about the faces and noises she made, or if her breasts looked weird in certain positions, or if she was doing the "right" thing, because there were no right or wrong things. There was just Max—his warmth, his strength, his comfort, and his passion. Everything they did together felt good and right, even when they didn't go exactly according to plan. They just laughed at the missteps and even that felt good.

She'd lost all sense of inhibition when it came to things like letting him go down on her. In fact, she was almost starting to think she was doing him a favor. To be fair, she felt pretty lucky herself when their positions were reversed. She'd always hated giving blow jobs before—it made her choke, made her jaw ache, and it tasted awful. But with Max, it was different. He didn't direct her like she was a voice-controlled fleshlight. She was free to taste and play at her leisure, eliciting pleasured groans and growls from him with everything she did. And while he didn't exactly taste like candy, he *did* taste like Max, which was hotly intoxicating in its own pheromonal way.

It was more than physical, though. Sex with Max felt damn near spiritual. And the afterglow was almost as good as the main act. As they lay in her narrow bed in the after-noons, or sprawled across the bench seat of his truck at night, they talked. Max told her about his home, his family, and she didn't miss the pride and the longing in his voice. They swapped stories about their childhoods. Max held her when she shared some of the harder details of her terrible marriage. He listened when she spoke—anything she spoke about—with rapt attention. He was as fascinated with her as she was with him, and that kind of mutual regard was so alien to her, but she couldn't get enough of it.

"You must've seen some interesting things, though," Max mused one night after she'd told him about moving cross-country after her quickie marriage. "Traveling across the country."

Jules shook her head. "We flew. Eric had his furniture and things shipped to Seattle by a moving company."

"Seattle is in a beautiful part of the country. The ocean, the sound, the rain forests, the Cascades..."

Max trailed off as Jules shook her head.

"No. Eric never wanted to do anything like that. Whenever I brought up going to see Mt. Rainier or anything, he'd act like I only wanted to go because it was 'trendy'."

"Mountains are trendy?" Max asked, nonplussed.

"Anything I wanted to do was somehow frivolous or vain or shallow or juvenile, no matter what it was. I could've walked on water and healed lepers, and Eric would've said I was doing it for attention." She sighed. "And I would've believed him. He made me think so many bad things about myself."

A vicious growl rose in Max's throat, but he quickly stifled it. He squeezed Jules a little tighter against him. "My mom wants to know his full name and address. I'm starting to think I should get it for her."

"Your mom knows about me?" Jules asked, surprised.

"Of course. Do you think I've been going to Sunday

dinners with your grandma, but keeping you a secret from my family?"

"No." Actually, yes. She hadn't consciously thought it. But she'd subconsciously expected it. "I don't know."

"They know about you, Jules. They want to meet you."

He'd asked her to meet them on the hike back from their camping trip. Jules had been flattered, thrilled even, but she'd assumed he was speaking from a post-sex endorphin haze.

"Really?"

"Yes. You said you'd go to Alaska with me, to meet them. Did you change your mind?"

"No," she said quickly. "I guess I just didn't think you were serious."

"I'm very serious where you're concerned."

Happy warmth flooded her from the inside. She felt like she should be glowing like a nightlight. "I could probably take some time off in June. My cousin Levi will be out of school for the summer, so he could take my shifts at the store for a bit."

"Perfect. Take as much time as you can get. We'll drive there and we'll take the scenic route."

"What's the scenic route?"

"We'll loop through a few National Parks. I'll make damn sure you get to see Mount Rainier."

Jules buried her face against the crook of his shoulder. "Man, I'm going to be so unhappy when I wake up from this coma."

Max rumbled with amusement, a deep chest sound that was more canine than human. "Hey, it's me, your doctor. I need to do another examination."

Jules giggled as he flipped her onto her back, thighs

spreading around the welcome weight of his hips. As he sank into her, their bodies joining, she was certain the world couldn't get more perfect.

"WOULD YOU LIKE TO MEET SOME OF THE CRY LAKE PACK?" Max asked, sweeping the floor while Jules refilled the coffee creamers. It'd been a couple of weeks since he'd finally bullied his way into helping with the closing tasks.

Jules's eyebrows shot up. "Wait, *they're* all wolf kin too?"

"Shit." Max looked cornered, furious at himself. "I just assumed you knew, since you know what I am. I shouldn't have said anything."

"I won't say a word," Jules said. "I promise."

"I know you wouldn't." He sighed.

"Don't feel bad." Jules went to hug him. "I probably would've figured it out if I ever spent a minute thinking about anything besides you."

Max's grim expression dissolved into a smile. "I probably wouldn't have run my stupid mouth too much if I ever thought about anything besides you." He bent to kiss her. "But, yeah, some of them would like to meet you. On Friday, after work, if you want to come to the Lodge, there'll be a bunch of them there."

"Okay," Jules agreed.

WHEN FRIDAY NIGHT ARRIVED AND THE STORE WAS CLOSED UP, Jules somewhat nervously got into Max's truck for the drive over to Cry Lake.

"Don't worry, they'll love you," Max assured her.

When they reached the Lodge—a large, timber-sided building with big windows that looked out over the lake—Max held Jules's hand as they walked inside. Heads swiveled at their arrival, dozens of pairs of eyes lighting on Jules with acute interest. Jules, used to being the tallest woman in the room, suddenly felt average height. Everyone here was tall and sturdy-looking.

A tall, lean, blonde woman pushed her way through the small crowd, pale blue eyes bright with excitement. Without so much as a hello, she grabbed Jules by the shoulders and pressed her face against Jules's hair, inhaling deeply.

Max's hand tightened on Jules's, a soft growl rumbling in his throat. "*Iris*," he said warningly.

The woman stepped back, still holding Jules by the shoulders. "Yep," she declared cheerfully, ignoring Max's growl. "You're the one I've been smelling on him. I've been trying to find you for *weeks*."

Jules glanced uncertainly at Max, who looked flatly back at Iris.

"Iris," another man said impatiently. He was big and broad, slightly shorter than Max, but wider, with dark hair and muddy green eyes. "She's going to think you're insane." He looped his arm around Iris's waist, pulling her back from Jules.

"She *is* insane," Max said.

"I prefer the term 'spirited.' 'Unconventional.' 'Lively' is also acceptable," Iris said, affecting a prim demeanor.

"You're all of those things," the other man told her, "*And* mentally unhinged."

Iris grinned at him.

The man smiled fondly at her before he turned his attention to Jules. "I'm Luke Mercier," he said, extending his hand.

Jules shook it. "Jules Wolfe."

"*Wolf?*" Iris echoed incredulously.

"It's just a surname," Max put in.

"It's fate," Iris decided, looking at the two of them with a satisfied smile.

"Anyway," Luke cut in. "This is my m— my wife. Iris Eriksen"

Jules was certain that he'd been about to say "mate." But she wasn't supposed to know the Cry Lake residents were wolf kin—never mind Iris's completely unsubtle introduction—so she didn't react to the slip. She couldn't help but notice, though, that both Luke and Iris had silvery-white scars on their necks, in the telltale shape of a bite mark.

She shook hands with Iris, who returned the gesture enthusiastically with a very firm grip and intent eye contact.

"Nice to meet you," Jules said, both charmed and overwhelmed by the intensely friendly woman.

"Wonderful to finally meet you!" Iris replied. She threw an arm around Jules's shoulders, pulling her away from Max and steering her towards the bar. "Forget Max, he sees you all the time. It's my turn to get to know you."

"Uh..."

Max gave her a helpless shrug. "Blink twice if you need help."

Jules laughed. "I'm fine."

"Yeah," Iris said, offended. "She's fine. Come on, Jules."

She spent the night being cheerfully interrogated by Iris, being introduced to other people when they managed to get a word in edgewise, and just generally enjoying herself. Time passed quickly and before Jules knew it, it was nearly three in the morning and she was more than ready for bed.

"Hey, I'm no good to drive," Max said, his gaze a little

blurry, his smile a little loose. "Do you mind spending the night in my cabin? I can drive you back home in the morning."

"Sure," Jules agreed. It'd be nice to spend the night with him. They hadn't slept together—literally slept together—since the camping trip. She shot her grandma a text telling her not to worry, and then she followed Max out into the cool night air.

The walk to his cabin was quick. They stumbled inside, struggling to get their shoes off without tipping over. When Max had finally succeeded, he pressed Jules against the door, nearly tripping over the rug as he did so. He laughed as he kissed her, clumsy and playful.

"Max," Jules said gently. "How much have you had to drink?"

"Four beers."

"You're *this* drunk off of four beers?" He was a big guy. Jules had also had four beers, and she wasn't nearly as tipsy as him.

"Wolf kin— we— our metabolisms." He grunted, losing focus as he tried scooping her into his arms.

Jules laughed and evaded his grasp. There was no way she was letting him carry her right now. She darted through the small, studio-style cabin to the big bed on the back wall. Max followed her with a lascivious grin.

"What about your metabolism?" Jules prompted.

"Oh. Right. Fast metabolism. We get drunk super fast. Super easy." He clambered onto the bed, eyeing her like she was the last slice of cake. "We sober up fast, too."

If he was implying that he was not still terribly drunk, that illusion was quickly shattered when he lost his balance trying to crawl across the bed and face-planted into the coverlet. Jules fell back against the pillows, helpless with laughter. Max growled as he righted himself, clambering up the length of her body and draping his weight carelessly over her. Jules clung to him, laughter subsiding, and buried her face in the crook of his neck.

They fell asleep like that, fully dressed, holding each other close.

In the morning, Max woke her with slow, lazy morning sex and then took her to the Lodge for breakfast where she met more of the Cry Lake pack—friendly faces who welcomed her heartily and smiled knowingly at Max. After breakfast, they took their usual walk, but around Cry Lake instead of their usual trail. Halfway through their walk, Iris came bursting out of the underbrush, a leaf in her hair and a wide smile on her face.

"Well, lookee here," she said with an indulgent smile. "My new friend Jules, out for a stroll with our grumpy foster."

"Iris," Max said tiredly, "You can't talk about that stuff. Your elders are going to skin you."

Iris scoffed. "What, fostering? Like you haven't spilled the beans already, loverboy."

Max flushed slightly, red flagging his cheekbones above the dark line of his beard. "I got the okay from my people. Did you?"

Jules couldn't quite follow the conversation, but she knew it was about wolf kin stuff. She pasted a blank look on her face, trying to pretend she had no clue what they were talking about.

Iris shrugged off Max's question, unconcerned. "Where are you guys going?"

"Just for a walk," Jules said.

Iris brightened. "I'll come with."

SOMEWHAT TO MAX'S CONSTERNATION, JULES QUICKLY FORMED A friendship with Iris Eriksen. Iris stopped by most days to chat at the store for a bit, and on Friday nights at the Lodge, she usually stole Jules away from Max for at least half the night. As much as Jules looked forward to every minute she got with Max, it was nice having a friend. She hadn't had any close friends since college—Eric had made it impossible—and Iris's all-out, open-hearted friendliness soothed a raw part of Jules's soul.

Max didn't begrudge the friendship in any way, though she could see that more than a few minutes of Iris's company started to irritate him. When he'd reached his limit, he'd find someone else to talk to, leaving Jules to soak up Iris's company alone. Iris was talkative and energetic and kind of a lot to take in sometimes, but for Jules, that was a good thing. She was getting ten years of missed friendship condensed into a one-woman tornado of camaraderie. And with Iris's friendship came tentative friendships with others in Cry Lake. Jules's heart was nearly full to bursting with all the happiness that knowing Max had brought her.

So, when he asked her to meet his parents on a video call, she did so with nervous joy. Within minutes, her nerves receded. His mother was a warm, sweet woman with a slight Polish accent that made everything she said seem more charming. His father was quieter, but no less warm.

"It's so nice to meet you, Mr. and Mrs. Freeman. Max has told me a lot about you."

"No, no, you call me Natasha," his mother chided.

"Arthur's fine," his dad added.

"It's so wonderful to finally meet you, Juliana," Natasha said happily, clutching Arthur's arm. "Max had told us some things, but I want to hear it from you. Tell me about you."

The conversation flowed easily, buoyed by Natasha's excitement, and the easy rapport Max had with his parents. Jules didn't have nearly that kind of relationship with her parents. She loved them, and they'd been good to her, but she didn't miss them in the way that she could tell Max missed his family.

"You'll get to meet her in person pretty soon," Max said at the end of the call.

"Oh!" Natasha straightened. "When?"

"Jules got a few weeks off in June."

"Ah! So soon!" Natasha said happily. Arthur smiled indulgently at her. "Wonderful! We'll have a party! We—"

"Easy, mom," Max said lightly. "We don't want to over-whelm her."

Natasha gave him a slightly sullen look, but it didn't last long. "I can't wait to meet you in person, Juliana! You're coming at a good time of year."

Eventually, Max managed to bring the call to a close, bidding both his parents goodbye.

"Sorry," he said to Jules when he'd ended the call. "She gets excited about this kind of thing."

"Your mom? Don't apologize. She's lovely."

"I'm glad you think so." A thoughtful look crossed his face. After a moment, he asked, "Would you ever consider moving to Alaska?"

Jules didn't know how to respond at first.

Before she found words, Max rushed to say, "Not right away. Obviously, you want to see it first. But, maybe someday? If you don't want to, I'd be willing to join the Cry Lake pack and we could stay here..."

Jules should have been alarmed that Max was already planning their long-term future together. But she wasn't. She was pleased.

"I love it here, but I'm not as close to my family as you obviously are to yours. I mean, there's my grandma, but she has my Uncle Paul and Aunt Jeannie and all the grandkids and great-grandkids to love on, so it's not like I'd be leaving her by herself."

Max listened raptly, gaze intent on hers.

"Moving to Alaska would be an exciting adventure, I think. Some day, I might be up for it."

Relief and joy seemed to crash over him, and he pulled her into his arms, hugging her fiercely. "You'll love it, Jules. The pack's going to love you, too. Wait until you see it. It's so beautiful."

CHAPTER 16

For the first time in a long time, Jules had to close the store by herself. Max was at a celebration of some sort at Cry Lake—one he couldn't politely get out of, and one which Jules, as a skinlocked person who wasn't supposed to know about wolf kin, wasn't invited to. Since the celebration was for a Cry Lake wolf, whose pack Max didn't belong to, he wouldn't tell her what the celebration was about. But in an oblique way, he later mentioned that wolf kin have a celebration called a "First Moon" that celebrates a young wolf kin's first shift.

So, Jules did all the closing tasks alone. It took her longer without Max. It also felt creepy without Max. She'd forgotten how quiet the store was after closing. And how dark the windows seemed at night. And how empty the streets were.

After she bagged the garbage and carried it to the door—her last task for the night—she paused to send Max a text.

All done at work. Have a good time at the party.

He responded immediately, *Text me when you get home so I know you got there safe.*

With a pleased smile, she slipped her phone back into her pocket and fished out her keys. She dragged the garbage bags out with her, and turned to lock the door. All she had to do was toss the bags in the dumpsters, and then she was good to go.

But when she reached the dumpsters, something shifted in the shadows between them. Jules jumped back, expecting a raccoon to come barreling out at her. They were exceptionally bold when they could smell good garbage and Jules had a bunch of expired deli sandwiches in one of the bags. But after a second, her vision adjusted to the low light, and she realized there was a *person* huddled back there. A girl—shivering and pale.

"Oh my god," Jules gasped. "Are you okay?"

The girl's gaze jerked up to hers. She got up unsteadily. She was short, with a young, round face, straight black hair, and southeast Asian features.

"Do you need help?" Jules asked, reaching for her phone. "Let me call—"

The girl moved so fast that Jules couldn't even track it. One second she was crouched between the dumpsters, the next she had her hands fisted in Jules's shirt, shoving her back against the hard metal side.

"I'm so sorry," the girl whispered hoarsely. And then she attacked.

THE FIRST MOON PARTY WAS IN FULL SWING WHEN HOWLS FROM the sentries on watch rotation cut through the music. Iris

Eriksen and a few others came barreling into the Lodge in their wolfskins. Iris shifted to her human form.

Gasping for breath, she managed to raise her voice enough to hoarsely shout, "Strigoi!"

A ripple of sudden alertness went through the entire party. The music died.

"We found a strigoi trail at the eastern boundary," Iris explained roughly. "Headed towards Saint Roch. Five sentries are tracking it right now."

Saint Roch was the tiny town where Jules and her grandmother lived. Where their store was. Max shifted instantly. His drink hit the floor, glass shattering. His clothing shredded, torn apart by his much larger form. He bolted through the open door and raced towards Saint Roch.

He found the strigoi's scent trail on the edge of the county highway that ran from Cry Lake to Saint Roch—the highway that ran past Wolfe's Quick Mart. Dread turned his blood to ice. He dug into the ground harder, running as fast as he possibly could.

When he reached Wolfe's, all the lights were out, the store appearing to be locked up. He told himself that Jules was peacefully driving home, far from the strigoi's path of travel. But when he rounded the corner of the building, her truck was still parked there. The breeze coasted softly along the side of the building, bringing with it the scent of blood—Jules's blood.

Frantic, he raced towards it. As he rounded the back of her truck, he scrabbled to an abrupt halt.

No.

No.

Please, no.

Jules was laying on the concrete, perfectly still. Her eyes

were open, staring up at the sky as if she were simply stargazing. But her throat was a terrible mess of red pulp.

Max stared. He heard the cries of the Cry Lake wolves drawing closer. He finally managed to make himself move—surprised to find it was on two feet. When had he shifted? It didn't matter.

He dropped to his knees beside Jules, hands outstretched helplessly. A wide pool of dark, gleaming blood spread around her head, forming a gruesome halo.

"*Jules,*" he whispered brokenly, voice cracking into a sob. "Sweetheart. Please." He pressed a shaking hand to the mess of her throat, but there was nowhere to search for a pulse. Everything was shredded. She was gone. His Jules was dead.

A savage, shattering howl tore from his throat. One after another—brokenhearted cries that sounded neither human nor animal.

When the others finally reached him, they found him cradling her body, face pressed to hers, tears tracking from his eyes onto her bloodless cheeks. They stood back for a moment, shocked. And then for another moment, giving Max time.

But after a while, one of the wolves shifted into human form and approached him, slowly, gently.

"Max," a woman's aged, rasping voice called his name gently. It was Dina, one of Cry Lake's elders. "You have to let her go, honey."

He didn't respond to her, didn't react to her presence. In the distance, a siren sounded. The other wolves looked towards it, shifting restlessly.

"Max," Dina tried again. "The police are going to come, and you can't be here when they find the body."

He ignored her.

With a sigh, she glanced back at the small crowd of wolves. She made a subtle gesture, and a second later, three young sentinels were in their human form, wrestling Max to the ground and pulling Jules from his arms. He fought to keep hold of her, shouting incoherently, but three-on-one was insurmountable odds, and they managed to drag him away.

"No! Jules! Please! No!"

"Iris, figure out if there are surveillance cameras here and deal with them," Dina said, leading the way back towards the woods.

"Yes, ma'am," Iris said quietly, her voice a hollow whisper.

The three sentries dragged Max with them. He had one last glimpse of Jules's sprawled body before the forest closed around him.

THE DISCOVERY OF JULES'S DEATH WAS A STRANGE AND STAGGERED thing. Evelyn Wolfe, Jules's grandmother, called him at one in the morning, frantic and sobbing. He had to pretend to be shocked by the news, which wasn't difficult given that he still hadn't processed it.

"Jules?" he asked faintly, voice breaking on her name. "Dead?" Saying the word out loud was like a gunshot. He flinched.

"I have to identify the body," Evelyn sobbed. "Tomorrow morning after... after the coroner..." She broke down into tears.

Max cried silently with her.

"Will you come with me?" Evelyn asked tearfully.

"What?"

"You don't have to. It's a horrible thing." She let out a gasping little sob.

"I'll come with. What time?"

THE COUNTY MORGUE WAS HOUSED IN THE BASEMENT OF THE RURAL county's only hospital. Max and Evelyn drove there in silence, punctuated by Evelyn's occasional, quiet sobs. Max was numb. He parked the car and walked inside with Evelyn. They met the coroner at a small reception area outside of the actual morgue, along with a deputy from the Sherriff's department.

The coroner and the cop were both talking, explaining something, but Max couldn't hear a word of it. He stared at the wall just behind them, feeling cold and empty.

After the talking finally ended, the coroner led them down a short hall and through the steel doors of the morgue. As soon as he stepped inside, he froze.

"What the—"

Max walked into him, not aware enough to realize the man had stopped. He looked up, wondering what the hold-up was.

The back wall was lined with multiple large, square, steel doors. One of them hung open. A long metal tray extended from the empty interior.

"What's going on?" Evelyn asked, confusion and fear overriding her grief for a second.

"The— It's got to be the wrong one," the coroner said to himself. He moved past a steel table with a drain in it to go examine the open door. He glanced at whatever the label said. He shook his head and read it again. After a moment, he began opening all the neighboring doors. They were all empty.

"This is— this is impossible," the coroner sputtered, turning to face them.

"What are you talking about?" the cop asked.

The coroner stared at him, wide-eyed and frantic. "She's gone!"

Max stiffened. In his world, there was only one reason a dead body went missing. If he thought he'd been cold before, it was nothing compared to the razor-sharp chill that ran through him now. He felt his canine teeth elongating. He felt his claws lengthening.

Strigoi.

CHAPTER 17

J ules was lost. She knew she was somewhere in the Chequamegon, but beyond that, she had no idea. As soon as she'd fought her way out of the cold, dark box she'd woken in, an insatiable hunger had overwhelmed her. It was so all-consuming, she hadn't even been confused by her surroundings or concerned as to how she'd ended up there. A hospital of some sort? A *morgue?* Who cared when she could *smell* the most deliciously appealing aroma that promised to take away all her pain. Just around a corner, down a hallway, and the hunger could be assuaged. An awful, gut-clenching, painful hunger that dried her mouth and made her hands shake and left her dizzy and unbalanced.

It wasn't until she'd followed the trail of that scent through blinding white hallways reeking of astringent disinfectants and found herself staring at an unsuspecting stranger, his back turned to her, with visions of ripping open his throat and gorging on the spurting fountain of his blood, that she'd realized what the scent was.

Him. A man. A person, but also an easily opened vessel, filled to the brim with the most appealing flavor her mind could conjure.

Blood.

She'd wanted it so badly. So badly it frightened her, the things she imagined doing to him. The hunger made her want to forget any semblance of morality. So she'd run.

And now she was huddled somewhere in the forest, no idea how far she'd run or in which direction, naked and dirty and aching with an unappeasable hunger. Her whole body was wracked with violent tremors, like she was going through the worst withdrawal. All of her senses were in overdrive, drowning her in a chaos of sensory input. She could smell pine and earth and wood and a dozen different kinds of animal urine and musk. She could hear the buzz and chirp and chatter of insects and tree frogs and bats and other night creatures. There was the wind whispering through the trees, making leaves and pine needles rustle and shush, making branches clatter together. The moon was only a slim crescent overhead, but its silvery brightness was like a needle in her eye. She curled into a shivering ball, eyes squeezed shut, hands clutched over her ears, breath held.

She wanted desperately to go to Max—she knew Max would help her. But the hunger for blood was so strong, she was afraid she'd attack him and do to him what had been done to her. She couldn't bear the agony of even thinking about it.

In the distance, a wolf howled. She wondered if it was Max and immediately pictured herself running into the safe warmth of his arms. But then the picture transformed, and instead of curling into his embrace, she was attacking him, tearing out his throat, drinking every last drop of his sweet, hot, rich blood. Horrified revulsion had her scrambling to her feet, fleeing the sound of those howls. She couldn't go near him. She couldn't hurt him.

As she ran further into the forest, further from the possibility of harming Max, a small part of her mind was stunned by the speed at which she was running. It was dizzying and unnatural, and multiple times, she nearly ran into trees as she zig-zagged rapidly between them. She couldn't stop though. She couldn't let herself give in to the urge to find Max. The image of his loving smile turning to shocked betrayal as she drained the life from him wouldn't leave her mind's eye. She ran faster and farther.

Sometime later, the sky began to lighten on the eastern horizon, and with it, Jules felt a leaden weight come over her body, dragging her down like an anchor. The compulsion was even stronger than the bloodlust, and she couldn't fight it—instinct drove her to dig into the earth itself, burrowing deep and pulling the soil back over herself. When the weight of the earth was heavy over her and not a speck of light could reach her, she gave into the dragging pull of sleep.

QUITE SUDDENLY, JULES AWOKE. SHE JERKED IN THE CONFINED space, crushed beneath the weight of the earth, choking on dirt. She clawed her way out of the shallow grave she'd buried herself in, coughing and gasping for air as she broke free. A foreign hand closed around one of her wrists, and she instinctively flinched away, but the stranger's grip was strong, hauling Jules upward from the earth.

Doubled over and kneeling, she wiped dirt from her face. When her eyes were clear, she opened them to find the same young girl who'd attacked her last night. Jules instinctively recoiled, scrambling backward.

"Oh, whoa, you're naked." The girl snatched her hands back, as if embarrassed. "What happened to your clothes?"

Jules stopped scrambling. "Good question." They'd been taken from her at the... *morgue?*

"Oh, god, this is so crazy," the girl said, Jules's nudity already forgotten as she cringed apologetically, obviously flustered. "I'm so, so sorry about last night. I don't know what the fuck is going on. I don't even know where I am. How far away is Oshkosh?"

Jules blinked. "What?"

"I'm just trying to get back home. I live in Oshkosh, but I was at a concert with my friends in Chicago, and then some asshole jumped me when I went for a smoke, and then I woke up in somebody's fucking shed! Covered in blood! And I think I have rabies! I just... I can't stop thinking about biting people. And, like, I finally gave in when you surprised me at that gas station. I'm so fucking sorry about that, by the way. You should probably go get a rabies shot—"

"Honey," Jules interrupted her, more resigned than scared at this point. "It's not rabies. I think you're a vampire."

The girl blinked. She'd been crouched with her weight on her heels, and she suddenly slumped back, landing on her ass. "Oh, fuck."

Jules trembled. "I think I'm one, too."

"Oh, shit."

They stared at each other, both at a loss. The girl looked no more than twenty at the oldest. Her face was stark with fear. Jules wasn't feeling particularly capable herself, but one of them had to do something.

"What's your name?" Jules asked gently.

"Bee Moua."

"I'm Jules Wolfe. How old are you, Bee?"

"Eighteen."

"Do you have family?"

Bee nodded vaguely, clutching her knees to her chest and staring through Jules like she wasn't even there. "Yeah." Her gaze suddenly sharpened, brows flying up in alarm. "I can't go back to them! I'll hurt them. I'll do...*this* to them. I can't! I've got baby nieces and nephews and—"

"Shh..." Jules moved closer to Bee, reaching over to give her arm a comforting squeeze. "It's alright. I know someone who can maybe help." She was still scared to go to Max, scared of what she might do when this desperate hunger had her in its painful grip. But Max was the only supernatural being she knew. He was the only person she could ask about other supernatural creatures—about herself.

Bee looked up, hope shining in her eyes. "Can they fix us? I don't want to be like this."

Jules swallowed hard. "I don't know." She doubted it, but she didn't have the will to crush Bee's hopes. "We'll find my friend. He's not a vampire, but he probably knows about them. Okay?"

Bee nodded, choking back a snuffling sob as Jules pulled them both up to stand.

"We just have to find a road so I can figure out where we are, okay?"

Bee nodded. "There's a road that way," she pointed past Jules's shoulder. "Not far."

"Alright. Let's go."

Jules only managed a few strides before a snarl sounded

behind her and a massive body crashed into hers, bringing her to the ground. She rolled, and her attacker rolled with her, pinning her on her back. It had all happened so fast, Jules didn't even have time to scream before she realized she was staring up into the familiar golden eyes of a massive, russet-brown wolf.

They stared at each other, both stunned.

The sight of him, the familiar warmth of him, was such a welcome sight. She nearly burst into tears. She moved to throw her arms around him, desperate to bury her face in the soft warmth of his ruff, but he jerked back with a hair-raising snarl.

"Max?" she said uncertainly.

He answered her with another snarl, his golden eyes gleaming with unmistakable fury.

"Max, it's me," she said, pleading with him to recognize her. "It's Jules."

MAX COULDN'T MOVE. HE COULDN'T THINK. HE WAS STARING INTO the face of the woman he'd loved, and instead of a lifeless corpse, she'd become something much, much worse. She looked just as she had in life, but her sweet scent—summer rain and earthy musk—was tainted by something foreign and monstrous. It didn't smell like anything else in the world. It was the scent of cold, eternal death. The smell of pain, suffering, and cruelty.

He knew he needed to dispatch the monster occupying her body and put Jules to rest once and for all, but he couldn't do it. He kept her pinned, trying to work up the nerve. He knew it was a mercy, it was what Jules would have wanted—she wouldn't have wanted a cold, merciless killer using her body to visit endless cruelty upon the world. But he just couldn't.

She wasn't even fighting him. The monster with her face was staring at him with those same soft, sweet eyes and he just... he *couldn't*. But he couldn't let her go either.

An unexpected snarl rent the air as a small body crashed into his, throwing him off of Jules as dangerously strong arms wrapped around his neck. It was the other strigoi. He'd completely forgotten about her, so stunned by seeing Jules. With instinctive self-preservation fueled by unbearable grief and rage, he twisted back, closing his jaws over the strigoi's shoulder, ripping her off of his back and flinging her away with all of his strength.

She slammed against a wide tree trunk with a heavy crunch and fell to the ground, motionless.

Jules moved so quickly, it was a dizzying blur. She rushed to the other strigoi, crouched beside the lifeless body. She turned her horrified gaze on Max.

"What did you do?" she asked, appalled.

For a moment, he felt ashamed and guilty. Then he remembered that these were strigoi and he was being manipulated. He snarled, advancing on them.

"Max?" Jules looked at him, shaking her head, tears filling her eyes. He froze.

No, *not* Jules, he had to remind himself again. This was only the monster inhabiting her body. That was who was looking at him. A creature. A thing.

"What are you doing? Why..." her voice cracked into a tear-strained rasp. "Why won't you help me?"

The monster had Jules's face and Jules's voice and even Jules's mannerisms. It was tearing his heart apart. He knew that *his* Jules was dead and gone, that this was just a demon wearing her face. But the raw pain in her voice was killing him. He shifted into his human form.

"Get out of here," he ordered, his voice a jagged, broken growl.

Her eyes widened. "What?"

"I said *leave*. Leave this territory. If you come back, I'll kill you."

"Max, please, I need your help. I—"

He surged forward, tackling her to the ground as he shifted into his wolf form. He pinned her, snarling in her shocked face. He shifted back to human, one hand around her neck, the other fisted in her hair so she couldn't go for his throat.

"I said *leave*," he gritted out in an inhuman voice, twisted with hate and grief and fury and shame. "Don't make me kill you, strigoi."

MAX SHIFTED BACK TO WOLF FORM AND BACKED OFF OF HER. JULES had heard that tone of voice from a man before, and she knew exactly what it meant. She'd never expected to hear it from Max, but her old instincts from Eric hadn't completely vanished, and she automatically moved to obey him.

She got up, silently crying, willing the pain away. Max's scent called to her like it never had before—there was his familiar warm scent, now underlaid by the allure of his blood. He smelled even better than the stranger in the hospital had. In his wolf form, there was another dimension of scent that reminded her a bit of wet dog, but it wasn't off-putting—if anything, it added another layer of comfort and familiarity.

But the crushing pain around her heart and lungs, the

choking pressure that threatened to close her throat entirely, allowed her to resist the desperate hope and hunger for the man she'd thought she loved.

She'd been through this before. She should have seen it coming. Max's words echoed her ex-husband's when she'd finally decided to stand her ground with him—*Leave, then, you ungrateful bitch. I don't want to see you again.*

Jules gathered Bee's limp body and gently hoisted her over her shoulder. It was shockingly easy to do—not because Bee was unbelievably light, but because Jules had become unbelievably strong.

The wind shifted, bathing her in the maddeningly delicious lure of Max's scent. She turned towards him one last time. She wanted to say something, but she didn't know what. In the distance, a chorus of wolves' howls filled the air. Max snarled again, hackles rising, fangs bared.

Letting herself go numb, just like she had in past to survive, she turned and ran. She ran and ran and ran and ran. She passed forests and small towns, then farm fields and cities. She carried Bee over her shoulder the whole time, and even though she was stronger and faster than she'd been before, eventually, her strength began to fail her. By the wee hours of the morning, she was only trudging along, clinging shakily to Bee. She was following the edge of some farm fields with a thin, scrappy forest on her other side, when the eastern sky began to lighten. As the pull to darkness overwhelmed her, she trudged into the cover of the spindly trees and laid Bee down so she could dig.

When she had a suitable burrow, she dragged Bee's body in with her. She knew it was crazy, but she didn't know what else to do with the girl. Carrying her had been a strange impulse that Jules hadn't thought through at the time. But now, at the very least, the body needed to be found so that her family could have closure. Jules just didn't know where to leave it to be found without bringing more trouble down on herself. She was too exhausted and too numb to think it through. She'd deal with it when she woke the next night. She pulled the earth over them both and slipped into the empty oblivion of deathly sleep.

CHAPTER 18

She awoke with a jolt again, cold panic slicing through her as she clawed her way free of the shallow grave she'd dug herself. To her surprise, Bee crawled out beside her, coughing up dirt. For a few seconds, sheer relief overwhelmed the crushing weight of grief and fear.

"Bee! Oh my god!"

Bee grimaced, rubbing at her neck. "My neck broke when I hit that tree. I felt it snap like a glow stick." She turned her head from side to side. "It's better now."

"Apparently so," Jules said faintly.

"So," Bee brightened, "are we going to find your friend?"

Instantly grief, rage, fear, shame, and sorrow all came crashing down on her so hard it drove the breath from her lungs in a single harsh breath. "No," Jules said, her voice a barely audible rasp. "He can't help us."

"Then what do we—"

"Well, well. What do we have here?"

Jules and Bee both whirled around to see a tall, thin, pale man standing behind them. His eyes were a shocking shade of bright red, seeming to glow in the silvery moonlight and somehow managing to clash with the bright red of his shoulder-length hair. He was dressed like a Yacht Club member, in a striped white and blue polo shirt and neatly pressed chinos. Despite his benevolent smile, there was something incredibly sinister about him. Maybe it was the eyes, maybe it was the fact that he was alone in a random strip of forest in the middle of nowhere, or maybe it was the intensity with which his focus flickered between Jules and Bee.

"Who are you?" Jules asked, grabbing Bee's arm instinctively.

"You're the fucking weirdo who jumped me at the concert!" Bee gasped. She turned to Jules. "It's him! The one I told you about! He—"

"Quiet," the man said impatiently, and Bee fell immediately silent. He tilted his head as he regarded her. "It seems I have accidentally sired progeny." His gaze flicked to Jules. "And my progeny has begotten her own progeny. A double blessing." His dry, flat tone suggested otherwise.

"You're a vampire?" Jules asked, her voice shaky with fear.

"Yes, my dear. As are you."

It was on the tip of her tongue to ask him if he could help them, but there was something cold and snake-like in the way he looked at them, and a cruel amusement hidden in the dryness of his speech.

"Okay. Well. Nice meeting you. We're going to head out —" Jules pulled on Bee's arm, trying to lead them in a safe berth around the stranger.

He moved so quickly that Jules, even with her supernaturally enhanced speed, couldn't follow. He was in front of her so suddenly, she ended up walking into him. She staggered backwards, still holding onto Bee, who was holding tightly to her in return.

"I'm afraid that won't be possible." His accent was crisp, precise, and unrecognizable. It sounded Germanic, maybe Dutch, but also… not. Something about it felt out of place, uncanny, like it didn't belong in this world or time. "You, my darlings, are loose ends. And you know what loose ends do."

Bee's brows drew together and she shot a look at Jules that clearly said, *What the fuck is he going on about?*

Jules slanted an equally confused look back at her.

The stranger sighed in a much-beleaguered way. "They unravel the entire tapestry," he explained, as if the two of them were unspeakably dense for not having completed his archaic little proverb.

God, that feeling was familiar. Jules almost instinctively apologized, but caught herself before the words slipped out. She didn't do that anymore—not since Max.

Visceral pain cut through her at the very thought of him. Her last memory of Max would be his beautiful face cast into a mask of hate and revulsion, snarling at her to leave and never return, warning that he'd kill her if he ever saw her again.

Beside her, Bee whimpered. Her hand flew to her chest, and she looked up at Jules with a tortured expression on her face. "Is that *you?* Why am I feeling your—"

"You have much to learn," the stranger declared imperiously. "And unfortunately, I will have to be the one to teach you both."

He stepped towards them, but Bee recoiled, knocking Jules back a step with her.

"We're not going anywhere with you," Bee said sharply, her voice thin with fear.

"Child." He gave Bee a fond, doting smile that sent a cold, slithering feeling over Jules's skin. "You will do exactly as I wish, because you are too weak to do otherwise."

"Please, just let us—" Jules never got to finish what she was saying.

He moved so quickly, she didn't even realize he'd done so until she felt his hand grip her neck. He twisted hard, and she felt the vertebrae separate with a sudden, wet pop that echoed in her skull before everything went dark.

JULES REGAINED CONSCIOUSNESS WITH A SCREAM. SHE JERKED upright, fighting to get away from—

Nobody. She was in a dark, windowless room. Despite the darkness, she could make out the details of the room without difficulty. The floor and walls were plain cement, with a solid metal door with no handle embedded in the far wall. The small space was sparsely furnished with only four narrow cots. Two of them were empty. Directly across from Jules, Bee sat on the fourth, her face tear-stained as she regarded Jules with bleak hopelessness.

"Oh, good, you're awake," she said flatly.

"Where are we?" Jules asked. Her voice came out as a hoarse rasp. Her mouth was so dry, her tongue felt like sand and the roof of her mouth like tissue paper. Hunger was a constant, desperate, debilitating ache that she felt not only in her stomach, but through her whole body. It coursed through her veins like slow poison, making her feel weak and shaky and dizzy and fragile. Her mind instantly conjured the memory of Max and his delicious, comforting, inviting scent. Her mouth prickled as if saliva wanted to pool, but she was too parched to produce any. Instead, she swallowed, embracing the raw pain of her desiccated throat as a distraction from the pain in her heart.

Across from her, Bee rubbed anxiously at her chest. "Stop doing that," she whimpered. "It hurts."

"Sorry." Jules swallowed again, trying to force Max out of her thoughts. "Do you know where we are?" she asked again.

Bee shook her head. "I don't—"

Suddenly, the door slammed open and bright light filled the room, momentarily blinding Jules. She hissed, blinking against it. When her eyes had adjusted, she saw the stranger who'd attacked them in the woods now filling the doorway. She hissed again, an animal sound of pure rage that she'd never made before in her life. It came so naturally and unexpectedly that she surprised herself into silence.

"Oh, stop," their captor said with benign indulgence as if she were a grumpy kitten. He tossed something at them both. A bag of some kind landed in Jules's lap. She picked it up, confused for a moment until it registered—a bag of blood. Exactly like the kind she'd seen at blood drives when she'd donated blood in the past.

Without thinking, she brought it to her mouth and bit in. The lukewarm blood spilled across her parched tongue and it was the greatest thing she'd ever tasted. Every ache and pain in her body, every discomfort, every bit of exhaustion and weakness, faded away as she drank. She sucked on the bag until it was completely empty, and then she ripped it open to lick the last few droplets from the plastic.

"Thirsty, aren't we?" The stranger chuckled.

She couldn't answer him or look at him. Now that the worst of her hunger had been abated, she stared at the torn open bag in horror. Her lips and chin were sticky with blood. It was all over her fingers. There was no denying it—she wasn't human anymore.

"Where are we?" Bee demanded, her voice shrill with fear. "What do you want from us?"

"You're in civilization, pet." He paused as if waiting for them to intuit meaning out of that oblique response. He sighed when they didn't. "Chicago," he answered dryly. "My home. And I really don't *want* anything from you. I'd rather you didn't exist. But unfortunately for me, that progeny-bond is hard to overcome. Killing you would've been much easier but, alas, I can't seem to find the will to do it."

Bee and Jules stared at him in horrified silence.

"But," he went on, "I suppose it's past time that I furthered my line. I'm the patriarch now, ever since Markov decided to go commit suicide by wolf." He laughed dryly. "The two of you have been bestowed with an honor you cannot even comprehend. Since I gain no benefit from your existence as I do from my thralls, you will repay me for the gift I have given you."

"That's not how gifts work," Bee said shakily.

A dangerous smile stretched his lips. His eyes remained cold, gleaming as he glanced between them. "It is with me."

PART TWO

CHAPTER 19

Jules's funeral had been closed casket. Max had stood through the entire thing feeling numb and detached, a strange ringing in his ears, his face a blank mask. He finally met Jules's parents—under the worst possible conditions—and it was all he could do to make himself speak, to express his condolences to her sobbing mother and teary-eyed father, before he had to tear himself away. His skin was too tight, his lungs too small, his throat filled with rocks. He tore at the borrowed tie strung round his neck, loosening it as he hauled in desperate breaths, leaving the church on stumbling, heavy feet.

He broke out into the open air and stood in the bright sunshine, breathing raggedly while his blood pounded in his ears and his head spun.

"Max? Honey?"

He turned to see Jules's grandmother, Evelyn, coming down the steps, brows drawn together as she took him in. That she could spare concern for him when she was also grieving the loss of her granddaughter almost crushed him.

Evelyn didn't know how badly he'd failed Jules. He hadn't protected her when she'd needed it. And when he'd encountered the consequences of that failure, he hadn't done what needed to be done.

She was still out there, restless, never to find peace, because he hadn't had the nerve. As far as her family knew, her body had been stolen from the morgue for some unknown reason. There was an active investigation to that end, for which Max had been questioned—but as far as all official channels were concerned, Jules was legally dead.

And she *was* dead. Spiritually, psychically, mentally, emotionally—Jules was gone. Her body was still roving around, possessed by a monster, because Max had been too weak to do the right thing. But the real Jules was dead.

"Sit down," Evelyn urged as she reached him, laying a gentle hand on his back. "Put your head between your knees."

He did as she said, mostly because he had no fucking clue what else to do. Even with Evelyn's gentle soothing, he couldn't catch his breath. How could he let her comfort him when all of this was his fault?

"Here. Drink." She handed him a crinkled water bottle from her purse.

He accepted it unthinkingly and held it, twisting the cap back and forth without actually taking it off, staring at the ground. Slowly, gradually, his breathing evened. Still ragged, but at least he was getting some air in.

"That's better." Evelyn squeezed his shoulder. She gazed down at him, heartbreak and wistfulness shining in her eyes. "I'm so sorry, honey. Jules was..." Her voice failed, and she took a second to gather herself. "These last few months with you... She was so broken after that man. Then she met you, and she healed. And we got to see our happy, wonderful Jules again." She muttered a quiet *shit* and reached into her purse for tissues. Blotting at her leaking eyes, she hauled in a shaky breath. "I'm glad she got that time with you. I know it hurts to lose her, but I'm so happy she got to know you before she left us."

Max's throat tightened on a choked sob that sounded more animal than human. "It's my fault," he said hoarsely, eyes blurring with tears he couldn't seem to shed. They built inside him, a painful tension in his sinuses and skull, but they just wouldn't fall. He didn't deserve to weep over her.

"Oh, baby, no." Evelyn bent to cup his cheek, forcing him to look at her. "Don't you dare fall down that dark hole. I felt that way after my husband died, and for years after he passed, I couldn't think of him with anything but shame and regret. Why hadn't I pushed him harder to go to the doctor? Why hadn't I noticed the symptoms sooner? But it's not fair to me or to Jim to think that way. Jim deserves to be remembered with love and joy, and so does Jules."

"Evelyn—"

"So you're not going to do that bullshit, Maxim Freeman. If you love Jules—and I know you do—you're going to give her what she deserves. After all she's been through, she deserves peace and joy and love. So when you think of her, that's all you hold in your heart, alright?"

She did deserve peace—and he'd robbed her of it by failing to act. But he couldn't explain that to her grandmother.

"Alright," he said hoarsely.

Jules deserved peace, but as long as the monster inhabiting her body still lived, she would not have it. So if Max owed Jules anything, it was to find the strigoi and dispatch it. He might have failed once, but he wouldn't fail her again.

Tracking a strigoi was next to impossible, especially one that had been on the move for days, but Max was the best tracker in the Teekkonlit pack, and the best of any pack he'd fostered with so far. If anyone was going to find her, it was him.

He drew in a slow, steady breath. Finding strength in the core of himself, where his love for Jules resided, he got to his feet.

"That's better." Evelyn patted his arm, leaning against him briefly. "Come over to the house. We're having lunch with just close family. Laura and Kevin and the boys would like to get to know you a little better. They know how happy you made their girl."

A vision of the strigoi flashed into his mind—Jules's face, stark with fear and shock, then dawning realization, then grief, then bitter acceptance. It twisted in his gut like a knife.

Just a performance, he told himself. His heart wouldn't stop pounding, though. *Just a monster trying to survive.*

"Sure," he told Evelyn hoarsely. "I'll be right over."

CHAPTER 20

Jules's new master was named Ragnvaldr. In a lot of ways, being his captive was not terribly unlike being married. She still never did anything right. She was still too stupid to be trusted with any autonomy. She was still shamed and scolded for expressing any of her own wishes or needs. The difference this time, was that Jules at least *knew* he was wrong. Instead of making herself smaller and quieter and weaker to suit Ragnvaldr's wishes, she let herself be as stupid and useless as he said she was.

In fact, living under Ragnvaldr's thumb even had some advantages over her marriage. Instead of a gradual but steady evisceration of her sense of self through years of subtle psychological manipulation and emotional abuse, Ragnvaldr just called her a stupid cunt and broke her bones to punish her. Bones healed more easily than souls did, so who was the real monster?

Max, actually. Max was the monster. Because no matter how awful Eric was, he'd never been anything other than himself. Jules was the one who'd built a delusional fantasy around him. But Max? Max had tricked her into believing that good men existed and that happily ever afters were possible—and then he'd ripped it all away. If being with Eric had been a slow death by a thousand cuts, then Max had been a knife plunged right into her heart.

Her current circumstances were infinitely more painful because she'd fallen from the dizzying high of Max's love. Or what had seemed like love. How many times was she going to hurt herself by loving men who didn't deserve it? Never again. Even if she managed to escape Ragnvaldr, she would spend the rest of eternity trusting no one. She'd find some quiet place in the forest, far away from people or other vampires, and she'd never leave. She'd have to figure out some way to get bagged blood since she'd never be able to feed from humans. She'd seen what Ragnvaldr did to his thralls—the half-turned slaves who had no choice but to obey his every whim. Jules could never do that to someone else.

The thought of the thralls' dead-eyed stares and ice-cold skin and their listless faces when Jules went in to clean their rooms haunted her mind whenever she wasn't dwelling on her past or fantasizing about escape. They were all too young, not one of them over the age of eighteen. They screamed when Ragnvaldr came for them—blood-curdling, tortured begging that bled through the sound-proofed basement walls. It was the sound that Jules heard every night as she lay in her cell, waiting for the oblivion of the daysleep to give her a temporary reprieve from her misery.

She'd tried helping them. Tried escaping. After a week, she gave up on that. She was a coward, but she couldn't bear the punishments anymore. The first time Ragnvaldr had caught her and Bee whispering together in their shared basement cell, he'd separated them after knocking a few of Jules's teeth out with a backhanded slap. She only saw Bee in passing after that, both of them confined to separate parts of the house, slaving over different chores.

The night after that, he'd caught Jules trying to silently ease the locks open on the back door. She'd cringed, expecting another hit to the face and more teeth she'd have to regrow, but instead, he'd torn off her hands and feet as easily as snapping asparagus stalks. Then he'd made her finish her cleaning duties on her elbows and knees, trailing viscous, sluggish pools of blood behind her.

A few days later, when he'd caught her whispering to a few of the thralls, asking them if he left the house routinely, he'd ripped out her tongue and crushed her throat. She couldn't breathe through her wrecked windpipe, but she also couldn't die, so she'd spent hours in suffocating agony until her throat healed enough for her to draw in thready, gasping breaths.

The final time, the time that had cured Jules of her delusions of escape, he'd caught her trying to slip a kitchen knife to the thrall he'd been favoring the most lately. She'd tried to convince the girl to gut him while he was distracted by the sick torments he visited upon her, but Ragnvaldr—too fast and silent for Jules to ever compete with—had crept up on her, listening to every detail of her whispered plan. He'd taken the knife from her and then used it to flay every inch of her skin off of her body. The thrall girl had been forced to watch, and she'd screamed until she fainted. Jules had been left on the floor, writhing in unspeakable agony, wishing she could die, but unable to.

It had all healed. A few pints of blood, a few days of sleep, and she was back in working order. Her extremities showed no sign of having been severed. Her tongue worked as well as it ever had, and her voice emerged from a perfectly functional throat. She had all her skin, with only the scars she'd already had before being turned. But she'd more than learned her lesson. Escape was futile, and this was what the rest of her life was going to be—an eternity of mindless servitude to a sadistic monster.

She had two ways out—either she died, or he did. And while the first one was easier said than done, the other option was *impossible*. Ragnvaldr was just physically superior to Jules in every possible way. His senses were more acute—he heard and scented her long before she even knew he was nearby. He was infinitely faster. Even with her unbelievable speed, Jules could only perceive him as a sudden blur when he chose to move quickly. He was immeasurably stronger. Jules had tried to fight the knife out of his hand as he'd flayed her, and he'd laughingly let her try—it had been like trying to pull a mountain loose from the earth. Now that she was a vampire, Jules could hear a whisper from the opposite end of the house, move faster than any human, and lift things ten times her weight with ease, but she was as helpless as a newborn against Ragnvaldr.

So, like it or not, this was her life now.

CHAPTER 21

Max knew he should go home, but he couldn't leave Cry Lake. Not when he was meant to be returning home with Jules, introducing her to his family and his pack, potentially making the decision that would bind them together forever.

His parents understood, though his mother's hints that he should come home anyway were gradually turning into pleas.

"You need your pack, kochanie."

"I know, Mom," he said quietly, simply. "But not yet. I need... I need to finish some things before I can come home."

His parents knew that Jules had been killed by a strigoi, made one of them. They didn't know that he'd knowingly let her go, and that he had dedicated himself to finding her and putting her to rest. He let his parents think that staying in Cry Lake, in the place where he'd known and loved Jules, was helping him grieve. In reality, he was investigating. Researching. Planning.

And some of the pack were planning with him. He'd

noticed when he first arrived in Cry Lake that there was a bit of friction between the younger pack members and the elders, but he'd shrugged it off as generational differences. Every pack experienced it. But with the strigoi attack and the loss of Jules, that friction had turned into a minor rebellion. The younger pack members had long wanted greater integration into the outside world and a move away from the pack's old isolationist policies, among other things. Jules's death had been the spark that set fire to the simmering powder keg. *If Max had been able to tell her more about their world, she would've had the knowledge to prevent such a tragedy,* they argued. Max didn't necessarily agree, except in the broader sense that he'd failed to protect her.

But the younger pack members were hungry for a fight, and the strigoi who'd killed Jules was a perfect outlet for the discontent they couldn't take out on their elders. Parallel to Max's goals, the Cry Lake rebellion was planning their own course of vengeance. So when Max set out to follow the weak trail left by Jules's strigoi, he'd had several other noses assisting—all watchers and peacekeepers in the Cry Lake pack, which told Max more than a little about the strictness of the elders here. But that wasn't his problem—Jules's strigoi was. And he wasn't interested in company while he tracked her down, but as a guest in their territory, he couldn't rightly tell them all to fuck off, either.

So, with help he didn't want, he went to the clearing where he'd failed to do his duty to Jules. Shame curdled his stomach as he watched the other wolves investigate the scents—they'd detect Jules's fear and his adrenaline, the anxiety and turmoil he'd been drowning in. None of them gave any indication that they judged him for it, but it didn't matter. Max blamed himself entirely, and there wasn't a soul alive who could make him feel worse than he already did. Iris was the only one who reacted at all, and she only cast Max a gently sympathetic look that made him want to rip his own heart out and crush it.

When everyone had Jules's scent, as well as the other strigoi's, they set off to follow the trail. It was faint, and the others lost it at times. But Max was easily able to bridge the gaps where the scent trail faded, keeping them on course.

They'd gotten as far south as Waupun when a third scent joined the first two. Another strigoi—male, and much older. The scent of Jules's fear was still present, acrid and sharp, lingering in the soil she'd been buried in.

Not Jules's fear, he had to remind himself, again and again, fighting the desperate urge to save her, protect her. *The strigoi's fear. A monster's fear for its own survival. And the fear of a stronger, older monster. That's all.*

The male strigoi's scent was tangled with city smells—concrete, car exhaust, and other air pollution—and the strength of those scents told Max he came from a large city, and that he spent the majority of his time there. The nearest two were Milwaukee and Chicago, but the fading trail left by the male strigoi, in which Jules's scent was only the faintest whisper, headed in Chicago's direction before it was lost entirely just outside of Beloit.

But it was enough to go on.

Traveling to a major city in their wolfskins required a circuitous route that took them in a wide berth around Chicago's sprawling suburbs. They journeyed through farm fields and thin stretches of forest and bracken. Due west of Chicago, they reached a forested preserve near a state park, where they could hunker down and rest. In the morning, Max would go in his human form to rent a car that would take them the rest of the way into Chicago. Because they'd long since lost the strigoi's trail, they'd have to canvass the entire city in hopes of picking it back up again.

Before Max had even managed to fall asleep, their night of rest was interrupted by the brutal screams of a terrified woman in the distance. Leaping to their feet, they surged towards the sound. Max's heart thundered as they raced towards the river, then fought against its current as they crossed into the state park where the screams had come from. Too much time had passed—whatever damage was being done was likely complete. But as they clambered onto the opposite river bank and up towards the high ridge, they picked up the scent of another strigoi. A completely different scent from the three they'd been trailing—but the combination of a strigoi and a woman's screams didn't bode well.

Running next to Max, Andrew Kirsch let out an enraged howl that carried across the park like a siren. Max and Iris reacted at the same time, both delivering warning bites to his thick ruff, choking off his howl. If they'd had any chance of finding and dispatching the strigoi, Andrew had just ruined it.

Still, they had to try. In the near distance, Max could see a blur of speed racing down the ridge—the strigoi. The rest of the wolves saw it, too. Ears pinned back, heads low, they moved in unison as they raced to intercept the monster.

The strigoi had a car waiting for him—he threw his human victim into the passenger seat, and then raced around the vehicle to take the driver's seat. The headlights flared to life and the car raced backwards, the strigoi frantically backing himself towards the driveway out of the park.

They couldn't let him get away. Moving in a defensive formation, they surrounded the vehicle. Max caught a flash of the passenger's terrified face, and he wished he could somehow convey to her not to be afraid—they were trying to help her.

But the strigoi outmaneuvered them—Max saw it coming, too. He barked out a sharp warning call to the rest of the pack just as the strigoi slammed on his brakes. The pack tried to regroup, but the vehicle was already gunning forward past their scattered formation. Wolf kin were fast, especially on four legs, but not as fast as a car barreling at its top speed.

Frustrated howls filled the air as several of the wolf kin continued to the chase the quickly disappearing car. For the first time, Max felt an edge of anger building towards his foster pack. If he'd come alone, he could've already been in the city instead of accommodating everyone else's need to rest. He would've never crossed paths with a random strigoi and he wouldn't be trying to recall the hotheaded idiots who thought they could chase down a speeding car.

He shifted into his human form. Luke and Iris were the only two who hadn't run off. Max slanted a furious glare at both of them. "What is this?" he demanded.

Both wolves looked back at him with flattened ears.

"We're supposed to be here for Jules!" he snapped.

Luke and Iris both shifted to their human forms. Luke looked sympathetic, Iris looked annoyed.

"We know, Max," Luke said calmly. "But if we could've saved that woman, we had to try."

He should care. He should care about other innocents being harmed by strigoi. But he only cared about finding Jules and... the image stopped there. He knew what he had to do, and this time he wouldn't fail, but he still couldn't carry the image in his mind. He'd have to carry it for the rest of his life once the deed was done, but until then, he'd let himself live without it.

"I need to find Jules on my own. I need to do this on my own. We should go our separate ways."

"Max," Iris began, clearly ready to argue.

"No. There's no need for any of you to have come this far." There wasn't a single point in tracking Jules that their help had been even remotely necessary. If he stayed with them, they would only continue to slow him down. And if one of them found Jules before he did—if someone else put her to rest... he didn't think his reaction would be rational or defensible.

"Jules was my friend, too," Iris put in. "I have—"

"She was going to be *my mate*," Max snarled the words, feeling his teeth extend into pointed canines. His skin prickled as fur sprouted over his arms and chest. Wicked black claws grew from his fingertips as he took a furious step towards her.

Luke stepped between Max and Iris, his face a stony mask. "You're right, Max. Okay? Jules is yours, and we won't interfere with that. But if you come at my mate half-shifted again, I'll rip your throat out."

Max drew in a ragged breath. He never lost control like this. Never.

"Sorry," he said hoarsely, turning abruptly away from them both, sinking into a crouch and clutching his head. His claws and fangs and fur slowly retracted. "I'm sorry," he said again, his voice heavy with shame, regret, self-loathing. Every darkness he'd ever felt weighed down on him now, an anchor tied around his neck. He needed to find Jules. He needed to—

He couldn't finish the thought.

After a moment, Luke's big hands descended on Max's shoulders.

"Max," Luke said softly. "I understand. If something happened to Iris..." He sighed, lost for words. After a moment of fraught silence, he said, "You find Jules. Do what needs to be done. I'll take care of the others."

Max nodded, not quite able to speak. Luke's hands lifted from his shoulders. He returned to Iris, murmured a quiet explanation.

"What about the woman we just saw?" Iris objected heatedly. "We're just going to leave her to a strigoi's tender care? We have his scent! We can find him—we can save her!"

"Pursue that woman all you want," Max said tiredly, rising to stand. "I'm going my own way from here. You're free to go back to Cry Lake—"

Iris started to object, but Max spoke over her protesting growl.

"—or chase down that strigoi. Do not pursue Jules. If you catch her scent, I'd appreciate a call letting me know the location, but do not track her. She's mine."

"Of course," Luke said calmly.

Iris frowned, but she finally nodded her stubborn acceptance.

"Will we see you again?" Luke asked.

Max shrugged. Just as he couldn't quite bring himself to imagine the actual task he'd come here to complete, he also couldn't really picture a life without Jules. She'd been his mate in all but the final formality of a claiming bite, and wolf kin didn't suffer the loss of a mate well.

"I don't know," he said.

CHAPTER 22

Despite never being allowed to leave Ragnvaldr's house, Jules still managed to get a piecemeal sense of the world outside—the vampire world, that is. Vampire society was deeply entrenched in Chicago, to the extent that they had a Council, with laws and courts and economic policies. She also came to realize that most other major cities had similarly developed vampire networks. And Ragnvaldr was connected to all of those lines of power. He was a member of the ruling Council in Chicago, which Jules figured out when she was made to serve a small gathering of Ragnvaldr's fellow councilors. He'd made her dress in crisp black trousers and a black button-down that allowed her to fade into the background, as all good servants should.

"And who's this one? She's a bit old for your tastes, Ragni."

Jules froze as a slim finger trailed along her throat. The vampire it belonged to was a dark-haired woman with coppery-tan skin and long, elegant limbs. Her raven-black hair was pin straight, and hung down to the small of her back in a perfect, shining curtain. She was dressed in something that looked vaguely like a dark red toga, but she wore modern black stiletto heels with it.

"Take a sniff," Ragnvaldr answered with a smirk. "But trust me—don't bite."

Jules was still frozen in fear as the woman leaned in, pressing her nose against Jules's jugular and inhaling deeply. She breathed out in a surprised snort, finally freeing Jules from her touch as she leaned away.

"A *vampire!*" the woman exclaimed in shock. "And so young! Her eyes haven't even reddened—she can't be more than a few weeks old! Don't tell me you've finally turned some progeny?"

"Indeed I did. And, while *this* one—" he nodded at Jules who had shakily resumed placing blood-filled goblets before all the guests at the table "—is *of* my line, I wasn't the one to turn her. She was turned by *my* progeny. Bee? Bee, come here, darling. Come say hello to my guests."

Bee got up from where she'd been quietly sitting on a chair in the corner. Ragnvaldr had dressed her like one of the elaborate porcelain dolls Jules's Aunt Lisa collected—a frilly white silk blouse with an equally frothy blue skirt that looked fussy and hyper-feminine in a childish, puritanical way.

Bee's face was a dispassionate mask as she approached the table, but her gaze flicked briefly to Jules's, just long enough to convey a message of sympathy. It was the first time they had seen each other in days. Ragnvaldr kept them in separate parts of the house, and any attempts for them to reach each other had been painfully thwarted.

"Here she is, my lovely girl." Ragnvaldr threw an arm

around her shoulders, beaming at the table as he tugged her in close. "Very spirited. It will take time to teach her discipline, but she'll be a fine addition to my legacy. What do you think, my girl?"

Bee stared flatly at him and said nothing.

The rest of the table—five other vampires with the same blood red eyes that Ragnvaldr had—laughed merrily. "Oooh, I don't think she's pleased with that, Ragni!" a tall, thin, raven-haired man crowed. His gaze traced over Bee with prurient interest, the red irises shockingly lurid against the paleness of his skin.

"She'll come around," Ragnvaldr said, shooting the black-haired vampire a distasteful look as he released Bee from his embrace. "You can tell me more about progeny when you've got any of your own."

"Ludolf will never have progeny," an older-looking vampire with silver-white hair declared. "Have you seen him eat? There's never enough body left to resurrect."

Jules tried not to flinch at that visual.

"That's a deliberate choice," the black-haired vampire returned sourly. "If I wanted progeny, I'd have turned one by now."

More laughter followed that.

"Ludolf," the elegant woman who'd sniffed Jules tossed her head as she laughed, "you can't keep a thrall alive for more than a year. How would you manage progeny?"

The rest of the table laughed at the glowering vampire, while Jules stared at him in horror. She thought of Ragnvaldr's thralls, the torture he put them through, and the fact that they were still alive. She hadn't thought it could get worse than his sadistic pleasures. But apparently, it could.

Unable to look away from the monster at the far end of

the table, Jules accidentally knocked Ragnvaldr's goblet of blood over as she withdrew her hand.

"Ah!" he hissed in dismay. "You clumsy idiot!"

Jules cringed, expecting physical punishment—broken fingers at the very least—but apparently, corporal punishment wasn't fit for company, because he only glared at her.

"Well?" he snapped impatiently. "Don't just stare at me. Get a towel and clean it up!"

Jules rushed to obey, hands already shaking with anxiety. He would probably just wait until they all left and then he'd dish out a punishment. That's what Eric had always done—he'd always dressed Jules down in private. Meanwhile, he had the whole rest of the party to stew over it and really build up a head of steam.

When she came back, she rushed to Ragnvaldr's side, hand already outstretched to clean the spilled blood with a kitchen rag. She froze before she reached him though, stricken by another panicked fear—he never let her get this close to him, this quickly. He was going to snap her neck or otherwise incapacitate her.

But he didn't. He was expecting her to clean the mess, and so he simply leaned back, gesturing impatiently for her to get to it.

That was a useful piece of information. He didn't react defensively when he was *expecting* her to get close to him. She could use that.

But later.

She couldn't tip her hand, so she continued to play the meek but bumbling slave as she muttered apologies and cleaned up the spilled blood.

"Now get me a fresh glass," he snapped when the mess was mopped up.

Jules darted off to obey. She could still hear Ragnvaldr speaking, extolling the virtues of the blood as he were a sommelier at a Napa vineyard.

"This was tapped from Eugenia. You've had Eugenia, Pravi."

"Ah, I think I remember. The one who cries so beautifully?"

"Mmmm. Yes. Even after all these years—fifty now? Sixty? Bah, it doesn't matter. I've had her for a while now, and she still hasn't totally broken. Still tries to get away, still begs for mercy."

An appreciative murmur resonated from the other guests as Jules returned with a fresh goblet for Ragnvaldr. The desire to smash it into his smug, grinning face was almost impossible to resist. She knew Eugenia—the doe-eyed, shivering girl who never spoke and stared right through Jules like she wasn't even there.

But she wouldn't help Eugenia and she'd only bring more pain on herself. So she carefully placed the goblet in front of Ragnvaldr on the table, and silently withdrew to the kitchen. She stood in front of the sink, holding the rag that had soaked up Eugenia's blood. Hunger coiled in her gut, sharp and urgent. The scent was delicious and the urge to drink briefly overwhelmed her with dizziness. Before she could give in to it, she turned the sink on and ran the rag beneath the water. Bright, scarlet blood slipped down the drain, out of Jules's hands. Those hands shook as she rinsed it over and over, scrubbing it with harsh soap until no scent of blood remained and her hands were chafed raw.

The conversation from the dining room washed over her distantly. She was aware of it without really hearing it.

"And when will their induction be?"

"Soon. Though I think just Juliana will suffice."

"Growing soft in your old age?"

An indulgent chuckle. "Perhaps."

Then suddenly, the voices jumped into stark clarity as her name rang out. "Juliana!" Ragnvaldr called from the dining room. "Put Bridget on the warmer!"

She moved automatically to obey. She got the glass decanter labeled "Bridget" out of the fridge, stashed amidst a racks of blood bags. The bags, she knew now, were mostly for show. Jules and Bee both relied on them, but Ragnvaldr subsisted off his thralls, and there was enough blood in the fridge for a dozen vampires.

"*Juliana!*" Ragnvald barked impatiently. "Even humans move faster than you!"

"Sorry," she murmured, hurrying to get the decanter in the warmer, but careful not to mishandle it. She didn't want to add to her tally of errors—she knew she was already due some sort of retribution for spilling the goblet earlier. She wished her timid docility were just an act—like she was only lulling him into a false sense of security. Like it was part of some clever master plan. But the reality was that she *was* timid and docile. She was afraid of the pain he dished out and she behaved how he wanted so that she wouldn't be punished. Just like with Eric.

RAGNVALDR—*RAGNI,* AS HIS MONSTROUS FRIENDS CALLED HIM— had another party the following week. All the familiar faces were there, plus a few more. And Jules was the night's enter- tainment. All the thralls were dressed up like frilly little dolls and made to serve the guests as live decanters of blood. Jules had been "inducted" to her new life and her new abilities through a series of torments that made the older vampires laugh and laugh.

She already knew that she healed unnaturally fast, that she could survive injuries that should've been fatal. She knew that she craved blood and that it was the only thing that eased her hunger. But she hadn't known that a vampire could feel their progeny's pain. So Bee was chained to the wall and forced to watch as Jules was tortured.

They'd ripped her fingernails off and then broken her fingers one by one. They cut off an ear, pulled several teeth, and more or less vivisected her abdomen. In between each torment, they chatted casually—gossiping about other vampires, musing on Council politics—and fed on the listless, defeated thralls.

Bee had howled with the same pain Jules was feeling, but it was so overwhelming that, after the hands, Jules couldn't even make noise anymore. She couldn't beg them to stop, couldn't sob at the pain. Bee sobbed for her. Bee cursed and screamed and spat at the other vampires, but no matter how hard she fought, she wasn't strong enough to break free of the heavy iron chains they'd wrapped her in. She'd dislocated both shoulders and broken her wrists trying, but it was useless.

"Oh, come now," Ragnvaldr scolded his progeny—apparently the pain that Bee felt on Jules's behalf didn't continue up the line to her progenitor. "You're only feeling a fraction of what Juliana feels, and she's not making a scene, is she?"

Jules lolled weakly against the chair they'd chained her to, half-dead. Her mouth was full of her own blood, tasteless and thick. Nerve endings all over her body screamed in agony.

"You're sick," Bee hissed venomously. "And you're a coward. You're only doing this to Jules because you can't feel it."

Ragnvaldr's eyes narrowed at the insult. "Introducing a new vampire to their indestructibility is an ages-old tradition. I suppose I was a bit soft in wanting to spare you twice the pain, but we can make the arrangements if you're feeling envious, my dear."

Bee, already vampirically pale, blanched further. "Fuck you," she said unsteadily.

Jules didn't blame her. There was no point for both of them to suffer. Or, no point in making Bee suffer twice.

By the end of the night, Bee's face was swollen with crying, and Jules was a bleeding mess, only able to sit upright because of the chains holding her in that position.

"Oh dear, sunrise approaches," Ragnvaldr observed after pulling a hissing hot poker away from Jules's cheek. The scent of burning flesh was deeply unpleasant, but Jules was past feeling the pain. Her body reacted instinctively, cringing away from it, but her mind was far away.

In her mind, it was still May. In her mind, she'd waited for Max before she took the trash out at the end of the night, so she never met Bee. In her mind, she wasn't a vampire. In her mind, she was still human, and Max still loved her, and she was in his arms, asleep and safe.

"Release her chains," Ragnvaldr declared. "If she makes it to her chamber before the sunlight gets her, then I daresay she'll live on. If she doesn't—"

Bee began to twist violently against her chains, swearing and crying anew.

"—then she wasn't meant to be one of us."

The other vampires cheered and clapped as Ragnvaldr unlocked the chains. Without their support, Jules slipped from the chair and fell to the ground. The others stepped over and around her crumpled body, making their way to the door, bidding Ragnvaldr cheerful goodbyes as they departed to their own homes for their daysleep.

Ragnvaldr bolted the door behind his guests. Just like the others, he stepped over Jules, making his way to Bee.

"Less than a minute to sunrise," he told his progeny. "Better move fast." He released her, and then with a careless laugh, went to the stairs to go to the safety of his locked, light-proofed bedroom.

The windows began to glow with faint, gray light. It was the brightest Jules had seen the sky since she'd been turned. She lay on the floor, watching the glow of the windows, hoping she got to see just a little bit of the sun before it killed her.

She got neither. Instead of fleeing to the safety of her basement cell, Bee raced to Jules and hoisted her from the floor. Jules groaned at the pain, and Bee groaned with her.

"Sorry," Bee panted as she dragged Jules towards the basement steps, leaving a thick streak of dark blood in their wake. "Sorry, Jules. I'm so sorry about all of this. I'll kill him. I'll figure out how. I'll kill him and we'll—"

They both hissed as the first faint rays of the risen sun filtered through the windows. Their skin sizzled and smoked where the light hit them.

"We'll get away," Bee promised, grunting as she made it to the top of the stairs. "I'll kill him and I promise we'll get away."

CHAPTER 23

Several weeks had gone by, and while Max had picked up countless strigoi scents, none of them were the ones he was looking for. He'd followed yet another fresh scent trail, hoping it would lead him to a congregating point with multiple other strigoi scents, but he'd only ended up at the end of a quiet street in an obviously rich neighborhood. Century-old brick mansions lined both sides of the street. The scents were mostly human, but a few houses obviously belonged to strigoi. If the metal exterior shutters on the windows didn't give it away, their scents did.

His phone buzzed in his pocket and he pulled it out, sighing when he saw Luke's name.

"Hello?" he answered impatiently, starting to walk back the way he came.

"We're going back to Cry Lake." Luke's voice was heavy, resigned.

"Good," Max said, meaning it. Cry Lake was their home. It was where they were needed.

"We caught up to the strigoi from the state park."

Max's stride faltered for a moment. "What happened?"

"He still had the woman."

He hesitated to ask. "Was she…"

"Still human. Still alive."

"Did you—"

"No," Luke growled. "No. The strigoi had a… partner? Another strigoi. A female. The male got ahold of Iris."

Max said nothing, chest tightening uncomfortably.

"Iris is fine," Luke answered the unspoken question. "He released her on the condition that we leave."

So they'd left the human woman with the strigoi.

"Andy attacked a human." Luke's voice cracked with barely contained fury. He was probably on the verge of shifting—claws extending from a white-knuckled fist.

Max froze. "*What?*"

"A human. He reeked of strigoi—we all thought he was one. But he bled like a human."

Max let out a long, slow exhale. Harming humans was a taboo on par with assisting a strigoi. Even doing so much as using wolf kin strength and speed to best a human in sports was forbidden.

"Is the human—"

"We don't know." Luke sighed heavily. "We don't know anything for sure. We had to leave to save Iris. But… probably. Andy tore his throat out."

Max didn't know what to say, but his horror must've come through in his prolonged silence.

"We're dealing with it," Luke said darkly. "We're in a tough spot—Cry Lake pack law calls for the execution of anyone who kills a human in anything other than self-defense."

So did Teekkonlit pack law—though the aunties would

confer and decide on the actual course of punishment, as they did with any major violation. The Cry Lake pack was ruled by their elders, and their methods had struck Max as slightly more rigid than his pack's, though not nearly as rigid as the Yellowstone pack. Either way, it wasn't Max's concern. He was sorry for the dead human and the still-captive woman, but his duty was to Jules, and until he fulfilled that, he couldn't focus on anything else.

"This shouldn't have happened," Max said, too distracted and frustrated for diplomacy.

"You're right," Luke answered, his voice heavy with regret. A small eternity passed, grim reality weighing them both down in a deafening silence. Finally, Luke broke it. "That's not the only reason I called. While we were tracking, we came across a building that *reeked* of strigoi. Iris is certain she picked up the scent of the male strigoi we tracked from Waupun to Beloit."

"Nobody else is certain?" Max asked, not daring to get his hopes up.

"Iris has the best nose in the pack. I'll give you the address, you can check it out yourself."

Max stood before a neo-gothic fortress that looked a great deal like a human church, with stained glass windows and elaborate stone masonry and a massive entry with a peaked arch and a bronze door depicting a surprisingly beautiful forest scene. Strigoi were urban dwellers. Why would a building of theirs venerate nature?

And there was no mistaking it—this was most certainly a strigoi building. The air reeked of their scent. If he'd had to describe it to another person, he wouldn't have been able to.

There was some inexplicable quality that distinguished strigoi from human. Perhaps it was the smell of death. Not rot, not decay, but just bleak emptiness. It reminded Max a bit of winter, when the air became so dry and cold that scents were somehow both sharper and more muted. Crisp, but subtle. It wasn't a *bad* scent, necessarily, but it went hand in hand with the presence of cruel, sadistic predators and made his hackles rise instinctively.

Max tilted his head back, pretending to admire the architecture while he inhaled deeply, mentally sorting and cataloguing the scents he picked up. He went preternaturally still when he identified a familiar scent. It was a faint thread, tangled amidst so many other faint threads, but Iris was right. The male strigoi they'd tracked through southern Wisconsin was here. Not particularly recently, but regularly enough that his scent hadn't blended entirely into the general miasma of other strigoi.

He tried to follow the trail, but it died within two blocks, lost in all the other city scents. However, it had been pretty conclusively headed north, which was something, even if it meant very little in a metro of nearly ten million people.

Frustrated, Max walked northward, hoping for another hit of that scent, but mostly just inhaling exhaust fumes. Under normal circumstances, his wolf would've been fascinated by the chaotic new scents. Instead, the wolf was so far forward in Max's consciousness, he was surprised he wasn't fighting off a partial shift. His dual nature must've recognized the urgency of the situation, remaining wholly in the form that best served his current needs. But even in his human shape, he had the acuity of the wolf's ears and nose, and he relied on the wolf's intensity and focus as he stalked his quarry.

Only a few blocks from the massive gothic strigoi build-ing, as he strode past a small stretch of greenspace, his phone buzzed in his pocket. He pulled it out, expecting a call from another Cry Lake wolf. Instead, it was his mother. Heart sinking, he left the sidewalk. Leaning against the trunk of a tree, he answered the call.

"Hi, Mom."

"Maxim," his mother said softly, heavily. No *kochanie* for him this time. That meant she was dreading this conversa-tion as much as he was. "Are you in Chicago?"

"Someone from Cry Lake told you?"

"What are you doing there?"

He swallowed, trying to find the right words. There were none. "I have to find Jules," he said, unable to keep the faint edge of desperation from his voice.

"You're hurting yourself," she said, worried, pained. "Slaying this strigoi will hurt you more. Let her go, kochanie. Come home."

Max let out an unhappy sigh. "I can't."

His mother was quiet for a moment. Finally, she murmured, "Your father wants to speak to you."

A second later, the somber resonance of his dad's deep voice came down the line. "I'm afraid your mother's right," his dad said. "Doing this will hurt you more than losing her already has."

"I have to do it," Max said bleakly.

His dad sighed. "I understand. If you have to, you have to. I wish I could..." His dad broke off with another sigh. "You should talk to Grace. She lived in Chicago while she was under that strigoi's influence. Maybe she'll know something that'll help."

He'd thought of calling Grace, but he hadn't wanted to

tip off the pack that he was searching for Jules. He'd been trying to put off this conversation for as long as possible. His mom's worry weighed on him, but there was nothing he could do about it. He *had* to do this. And she would probably tell him she *had* to worry about it.

"Yeah. I'll give Grace a call."

His dad was quiet for a moment. Max was used to it—Arthur Freeman wasn't a man of many words. He waited in quiet contemplation until his dad figured out what he wanted to say.

"Be safe, son," his dad finally said. "Be safe, and come home to your pack when this is all done."

Max's throat tightened with emotion. He swallowed it away. "I will."

"The details of my time with Alex are... hazy," Grace told him apologetically. "But he brought me a few times to meet friends of his. I don't remember their names or the addresses or anything like that, but they both had big old mansions up in Lake View."

"Thanks, Grace." He'd been hoping for more to go off of, but a specific neighborhood was better than just a vague sense of "north."

"I'm so sorry about everything. I wish you didn't have to... I don't know. I'm just sorry."

"Me too," Max said quietly.

After they'd bid grim goodbyes, Max immediately pulled up the map on his phone, trying to find Lake View. When he had his destination, he pocketed his phone and started walking. It was getting close to sunset. He should be heading back to the cheap room he'd booked in a shabby little motel.

A pack of wolf kin could take on a strigoi or two, but a single wolf in a city filled with strigoi? He was asking for death.

He didn't care. He had to find Jules. He had to end this. As the streetlights blinked on and the sky turned black behind the glow of city lights, Max continued to walk. He reached Lake View a few minutes before the sun officially set, and he could feel that looming deadline like a cold breath against the back of his neck.

He kept walking. A few blocks in, he picked up the scent of strigoi—not the one he was looking for, but it was still something. The sun was down now. He felt the change in the air—a sudden electric tension as all the undead awoke. They would be aware of him. Their senses were keen, though not so keen as wolf kin. They made up for that disadvantage with speed that wolf kin couldn't compare to.

As he went on, he found two homes that undoubtedly housed strigoi. At the second one, he stiffened, freezing in place as soon as the scent hit him. His quarry had been here. Not Jules, but the male strigoi who'd joined her in Waupun. This wasn't his house—a different strigoi scent was stronger, more recent, more frequent—but he had visited not very long ago. A few days, maybe. It hadn't rained in the last week, so the scent trail should be strong.

He followed it at as close to a run as he could without attracting too much attention. The sun was down, the strigoi would be alert and active now. He should return to his rented room, but he couldn't. Not when he was so close.

CHAPTER 24

J ules woke with a jerk, nearly falling off the narrow cot. Frantic, she ran her hands over her body, checking her injuries. But there were none. They'd all healed. Her fingers were unbroken and she had all her finger-nails. She had all her teeth. The skin on her stomach was closed and unmarked, no sign that she'd been eviscerated. Every injury she'd been dealt was gone. She knew enough by now to have expected it, but it still shocked her. She shouldn't have been able to survive what they'd done to her.

A small part of her wished she hadn't.

Her cell door banged open, and Ragnvaldr stood in the doorway, looking cheerful. He was dressed in a bright blue polo shirt and pressed khakis with a braided leather belt. He looked like someone's inoffensive soccer dad.

"Ah, she lives." He tossed a cold bag of blood at her, and she snatched it up like the mindless monster she'd become. "Welcome to your new life, Juliana. You're officially a vampire now. You can thank your dam for dragging your inert carcass into your bedchamber. I doubt you would've survived all day in the sun."

Jules emptied the blood bag, feeling strength and vitality return to her body. She'd exhausted herself by healing from all the damage.

"You made quite a mess last night," Ragnvaldr went on, mildly annoyed. "You're all over the rug. Go clean it. If you leave a single speck of blood behind, you'll enjoy a repeat performance of last night. Understand?"

She got up without speaking and followed him upstairs. The parlor where they'd tortured her was still a mess. Blood stains marked the furniture where the guests had fed on thralls. The wall where Bee had been chained was a mess of gouged-out wall paneling and scratched flooring. The chair where Jules had sat was drenched in blood, and the floor around it—including an antique Turkish rug—was covered in a thick red circle of dried blood and crusted viscera.

Ragnvaldr took the seat next to the bloodied one—a pair of wingback chairs poised before the fireplace—and settled in to stare at his tablet screen. Jules knew he was sitting there just to make her job more difficult. She'd have to work around him without disturbing him, lest she get another punishment.

"Don't forget the fireplace tiles. I don't want the grout stained with blood."

Jules went to the kitchen to get the cleaning supplies from beneath the sink. She had to pull out the big jug of muriatic acid that she used to clean the thrall's cells in order to get at the carpet cleaning solution and grout cleaner at the back of the cabinet. But as her hand closed around the wire brush she'd use to scrub the grout, she froze. Slowly, she turned to look at the jug of acid.

The first time she'd had to mix it up—diluting it in water so it wouldn't eat straight through the concrete—she'd spilled some of the full-strength acid on her hand. It had melted her skin like candle wax and gone through to the fat and muscle below. After that, she'd always been extremely careful not to get it on herself or the thralls.

She stared at the jug of acid, indecision gnawing at her. Last night, she'd thought she was going to die. If she tried this and failed, and he killed her in retribution, she'd be no worse off than she'd expected to be.

Steadying her hands, blanking her face into an emotionless mask, she pulled the mop bucket out and began pouring the acid in. She didn't bother filling the bucket with water first. She didn't want it diluted this time. When the jug was empty, she pulled a backup jug from the broom closet and emptied the entire thing into the big mop bucket. The fumes were powerful enough to burn her eyes and nose. She blinked away the sting, keeping her breathing even, her movements unhurried.

As she made her way back to the parlor, carrying the bucket full of acid, she made sure to move with the same defeated sullenness with which she did all her slaving. As she neared Ragnvaldr, her nerve began to fail her. He would know—he would figure out what she was doing and react too quickly for her to counter. He'd punish her and she didn't think she could bear another—

"After you're done here, you'll need to go down to the thralls' chambers. Our guests were a little too enthusiastic last night and drained Marguerite. The body needs to be disposed of."

Jules threw the contents of the bucket without thinking. Ragnvaldr moved, but not far enough. The wide arc of acid still caught him, splashing across his face and chest with an audible slap.

For a second, Jules didn't think it'd done anything at all. Ragnvaldr came at her, all rage and power, but just as she attempted to dart out of his reach, the acid started doing its work. He roared in pain, dropping to his knees to claw at his face and chest.

"You stupid bitch!" he snarled, the words contorted by rage and agony and the steady deterioration of his face.

Jules stared for a second, horrified and astonished as the acid ate through his flesh with sizzling, bubbling alacrity. But then her sense of self-preservation kicked in, and she remembered that she wasn't done. He was old and powerful, and if she didn't finish the job, he would heal and her living nightmare would become infinitely worse.

With her bare hands, she tore him apart. He was stronger than her, but that didn't mean the tissues of his body were impervious to her supernatural strength. Bit by awful bit, she broke him into a thousand soft, wet pieces. She crushed his skull and dropped his head into the mop bucket, letting it dissolve in the few inches of acid that remained inside. While she worked, a frantic pounding sounded in her ears and a distant screaming filled her mind.

She thought it was herself, until the ceiling overhead began to crack, then bulge, then broke open in a spray of timber and plaster and lathe. Bee dropped through the opening, breathing hard, looking around frantically. She saw Jules —wild-eyed and soaked in blood—and her panicked expression faded into dismay.

"Aw, Jules, I said *I* was going to kill him."

Jules laughed. It was a hysterical, horrified, sharp-edged stream of laughter that she couldn't get under control. But it felt good. She held up her bloody, acid-eaten hands, sat back on her heels, and laughed until it hurt.

Bee crouched beside her, touched her shoulder gently. "Jules? Take a breath."

"He's dead," she said breathlessly. "He's dead. I... I have to go outside. I need to breathe."

Bee nodded. "You do that. Stay close, though, okay? I'm going to let the thralls out and then we'll... I don't know. We'll figure something out."

Jules couldn't answer her. She got to her feet and walked numbly to the front door. She almost hesitated to reach for the locks before she remembered—he was gone. He was gone and she was free. She flipped all the heavy latches and bolts, ripped the door open and stepped out into the night.

It was the first time she'd stood in the open air since Ragnvaldr had snapped her neck over a month ago. She stumbled down the broad front steps to the sidewalk, staring at the city beyond the rooftops. There were so many sounds and lights and scents, and they hit her all at once, completely overwhelming her. They crawled inside her skull and filled her brain until she couldn't think at all.

In the midst of it, she was almost certain she heard Max's voice. She turned—and there he was, standing on the sidewalk, as if he were just out for a stroll. That was impossible. She knew it was. Ignoring the mirage, she sank to the ground, pressing her hands over her ears and squeezing her eyes shut, burying her face in her knees and willing all the chaos away.

She knew she couldn't go back in time. She knew she couldn't fix any of this. But she wished she could erase it all. She wished that Bee had just killed her.

CHAPTER 25

Max followed the strigoi's trail south again, a few blocks east of the route he'd taken northward. The scent grew stronger—strong enough that he knew he was close. He was within a block of the strigoi's home.

Suddenly, four houses down, the front door swung open. The harsh scent of acid overwhelmed his nose to the point that he couldn't scent anything else about the house.

But the scent didn't matter, because the figure emerging from the house was *Jules*. She walked down the steps, looking dead and empty.

"Jules?" he called. He couldn't help himself. He knew what he was here for, but he hadn't let himself focus beyond the immediate moment. And now that he was seeing her again, his mind had gone staticky.

Jules looked at him, her expression gutted and broken. Not an ounce of recognition flickered in her eyes. Turning away from him, she crumpled to the ground, clutching her head and curling in on herself like a wounded animal.

Instinct took over and he ran to her, dropping to his knees beside her. "Jules?"

She wouldn't answer him. Wouldn't look at him. Wouldn't uncurl. She was covered in blood and trembling. Beneath the sharp tang of acid, he smelled the blood of the male strigoi he'd been tracking. And a bit of Jules's own.

Max didn't know what to do. He picked her up—she didn't resist—and started walking. Nobody stopped him. There weren't many people out on the sidewalk at this time of night, and anybody who was out made sure to give him a wide berth. He carried her in his arms like a human groom carried his bride across the threshold of their home, but Jules was curled up like a wounded rabbit, silent and unmoving.

He reached the ratty motel where he was staying and went into the fenced lot where his rented vehicle was parked. Not entirely sure what he was doing, he put Jules in the passenger seat. She remained curled up, but he buckled her in as best he could. In the driver's seat, he pulled out of the lot and drove out of the city. Instinct made him head east, opposite the direction anybody would have expected him to go. He crossed the Indiana border and kept going. Somewhere south of Gary but north of Indianapolis, he pulled off the highway.

In a small factory town, he found a quiet little motel just off of a county highway. He paid cash for the room, heart hammering the whole time. When he got back to the vehicle, Jules hadn't moved from the passenger seat. He opened the door and pulled her out, holding her as if she were an injured dove instead of a blood-crazed killer. He carried her into the room and set her on the bed, then turned to bolt the door and drag the dresser in front of it.

He knew he was an absolute idiot—every second he kept her alive, he put countless people at the risk of a brutal death at her hands.

He turned from the dresser, gazed down at her, feeling as if he were being torn apart from the inside. Even the wolf was conflicted—it was a strigoi. But it was also *Jules*.

But it wasn't Jules. The strigoi stared blankly back at him, no longer curled into a ball, but still totally non-responsive.

God, he'd loved her. It hurt so much to see a monster wearing her face. He stepped closer, risking his life to cup her cheek, stroke his thumb along the crest of her cheekbone. She flinched away from his touch, the first sign of life she'd shown since he'd taken her off the sidewalk. It shouldn't have hurt as much as it did. He wasn't being rejected by Jules —just the creature who'd taken her body.

Aside from the flinch, she didn't seem terribly alert. Her knees were drawn to her chest, her arms looped around them, bloodied hands clenched together. Not sure what to do, he stepped back, blocking the door, and called Luke.

"I found Jules."

Luke let out a heavy breath. "I'm sorry man. I'm sorry you had to do that."

"I didn't," Max said flatly.

"You let her go?"

"No."

A beat of silence. Then, "What are you saying?"

"I've got her with me."

"Why haven't you slain her?" An edge of uneasiness crept into Luke's voice.

Max sighed. "I don't know."

"Max—"

"I shouldn't have called." He hung up. He remained where he was, staring at the strigoi who used to be Jules, while she stared blankly at the wall.

A moment later, a call came in. He didn't recognize the number, but it was from the Cry Lake area code.

"Hello?"

"Maxim," a hoarse, aged voice greeted him, somber and grim. It was one of the Cry Lake elders—Reynold Delacroix.

"Hello, Reynold."

"You know why I'm calling."

"I suppose I do."

"You know what you need to do."

Max didn't answer.

Reynold sighed. "Maxim, I understand this is impossibly difficult for you. Tell me where you are. I'll send a few wolves to meet you. They'll take care of the strigoi so that you don't have to."

"No. Nobody touches her but me."

"Please, be sensible. Imagine if anyone else were doing what you are right now."

He'd assume they'd been compelled by strigoi magic, influenced to act against their own sense. But Jules had done nothing. She hadn't spoken to him. Hadn't even made eye contact with him.

"I will handle this in my own way," Max finally said, gaze still fixed on Jules's blank face.

"Maxim, don't make us track you. Tell me where you are."

Max laughed bitterly. "If I don't want to be found, you'll never pick up my trail."

"Maxim—"

He hung up. As he tucked his phone back into his pocket, Jules's head turned, her eyes tracking the motion. It was the first real sign of awareness she'd shown so far.

"Jules?" She wasn't Jules, but he didn't have anything else to call her by.

She looked up at him. As she searched his face, poring curiously over his features, recognition slowly replaced the vague emptiness in her eyes. Her expression shifted from blank nothing to barely suppressed fear. She tried to scoot backward, away from him, but as soon as she put her hand down on the rough bed cover, she hissed in pain and snatched it back, holding it against her chest.

Max looked at her hand, and for the first time, he realized they weren't just covered in some other strigoi's blood. They were stripped raw, nothing but red open wounds, the fingertips eaten down to bare bone.

"What the *fuck*, Jules!" He went to her on instinct, reaching for her hand. She moved too quickly for him— darting out of his reach in the blink of an eye. As a human, Jules would've never been able to move that fast.

Jules is gone, he reminded himself for the billionth time. *This is a strigoi.*

Max stepped back, resuming his post in front of the door. "What happened to your hands?" he asked, needing to know, wishing he didn't care.

She looked down at them. "Acid. I killed him with acid." She spoke faintly, her voice sounding far away, even though she was right here in the room with him. "Got some on me, I guess." She laughed weakly.

Max's stomach flipped unpleasantly. "Killed who?"

"Hm?" She was still staring at her ruined hands. When she finally looked up at him, it was as if she'd just remembered he was there, and the fear came over her again. She cringed back until she was pressed against the headboard, ruined hands curled protectively against her chest. "Ragnvaldr," she answered faintly.

"*Who?*"

"The vampire," she said, her voice weak with fear. "The one who took me and Bee. I killed him. You said if I stayed away you wouldn't kill me," she blurted suddenly, trembling. "I stayed away. I don't—I'm sorry. I didn't mean to see you. I wasn't looking for you."

But I was looking for you. But he couldn't say that. He also couldn't tell her he wasn't going to kill her. He didn't know what he was going to do. He knew what he *should* do. But even with her in his possession, he couldn't make his mind go to that place. He'd already held her cold, lifeless body once before. He wasn't sure he could do it again.

"I know you weren't," he said, ashamed that he couldn't resist comforting her.

"Then... why?"

He couldn't answer her. He didn't have an answer for himself.

"What are you going to do to me?" she asked quietly, nothing but terror in her voice. It gutted him.

"I don't know," he answered honestly, gruffly.

She paled, making the blood streaking her face look even more vivid in comparison. It was clumped in her hair and soaked the front of her shirt. It should have made her look like the bloodthirsty monster that she was. Instead, she looked lost and hurt and scared, and Max wanted nothing more in the world than to pull her into his arms, pretend she was still his Jules, and comfort her.

"You should wash all that off," he said, gesturing at her. "There's a shower there." He pointed to the back of the room.

"Why?" she asked fearfully. "What does it matter?"

It didn't. It shouldn't. "Just go wash off," he barked.

She flinched and it made his chest want to cave in. But he said nothing, watching silently as she edged off of the bed and back to the bathroom, never turning her back on him.

"I don't have any clean clothes to change into."

"I'll get you something."

She shook her head, not objecting, just at a loss. "*Why?*"

He didn't know. He didn't speak. He just stared at her until she nervously lowered her gaze and darted into the bathroom. When he heard the shower running, and the sound of her body stepping beneath the spray, he went out to the car and pulled the small bag of necessities he'd carried from Cry Lake to Chicago. In it were a few changes of clothing. She'd have to make do with one of his old t-shirts and a pair of athletic shorts.

When he stepped back into the room, the shower was still running. He could hear Jules shifting beneath the spray, and then the faint sound of a pained whimper.

"Jules?" Max called out, going to the bathroom door. "What's going on?"

"Nothing."

"Why are you crying?"

"I'm not crying."

"Yes you are!" he snarled, angry for too many reasons to count. Angry at himself, at the world, at her—but not even really at her, which only made him angrier with himself.

"My hands hurt," she said so faintly he could barely hear her.

Her ruined hands, skin eaten away, bone visible at the

tips. Who'd done that to her? *She did it to herself. Killed another strigoi with acid, remember?* He needed to remember. He couldn't let himself forget what she was.

Still, his heart ached, and he wanted desperately to step into the shower with her, gently clean her so she didn't have to hurt her hands doing it, and then take her to the doctor to get her hands fixed. But he couldn't do that—she'd eat the fucking doctor. She'd eat *him*. For fuck's sake, what the hell was he doing?

The water turned off, and the strigoi emerged from the bathroom, hair wet and pasted to her skull. She had a tatty towel wrapped around her body, held closed by ruined hands that were leaving bloody prints on the bleached white terrycloth. She looked too thin. Deep, bruise-purple shadows ringed eyes that looked too big in her pale, hollowed face. Her lips were colorless and cracked. The bones in her shoulders jutted starkly beneath her skin. It was all probably just the look of a strigoi, but that strigoi had Jules's face, and Jules's freshwater scent, and Max wanted to fix it so badly his hands were shaking with the need to reach for her, comfort her.

Instead, he reached into his bag and pulled out a t-shirt and a pair of athletic shorts. He set them on the foot of the bed.

"You can change into that."

"*Your* clothes?" she asked, surprised.

"It's all I've got. Take them and get dressed."

She obeyed without argument, meek and timid in a way that made his anger rise again. It reminded him too much of the Jules he had first met—a quiet shadow who couldn't make eye contact and was afraid to talk. Strigoi were known for their ability to influence minds—Grace had spent years under the power of one, and even now that she was free, she could hardly remember anything about him. Max had to acknowledge that it was very possible he was being manipulated, influenced.

He should slay her. Now. While he still had any sense left.

But then she stepped out of the bathroom, dressed in his clothes, and he could only stare at her. The last time he'd seen Jules wearing one of his t-shirts, they'd been cuddled together in bed in the bachelor cabin in Cry Lake. Everything had been warm and safe and perfect.

"Jul—" he started to say her name, overcome by desperate longing, but he managed to choke himself off.

"Thank you for the clothes," she said softly, not meeting his gaze. Her ruined hands were clutched together in front of her chest, still looking no better. Weren't strigoi supposed to heal quickly?

"Let me see your hands," he ordered.

She hesitated, eyeing him with obvious fear. But fear of disobeying him must have won out—which sent a cold, unpleasant sharpness through him—and she approached, hands held out.

He handled them gently, turning them to examine the damage. "Why haven't you healed?"

"I need to sleep," she said, staring at the floor. "And..."

"What?"

"Nothing."

"Tell me," he snarled.

She hissed in pain as his grip tightened on her hands. Feeling like an absolute monster, and furious at himself for feeling that way, he dropped her hands and backed away from her, blocking the door again. She stood where he'd left her, looking uncertain and terrified, sick with misery.

"I don't know what you want from me," she said said weakly, hoarsely.

That makes two of us. But he said nothing.

"I... I need to sleep soon. I can feel the sun rising. If you're going to kill me..." she swallowed hard, looking away from him "...will you do it while I'm asleep?"

Max wanted to scream. He wanted to howl. His wolf wanted to burst through his skin and trash the motel room and then tear the entire world apart.

"Just go to sleep," he managed to say thickly, speaking past the choking rage.

She nodded in defeated acceptance. She pulled the rough coverlet from the bed and took it into the bathroom.

"What are you doing?"

"I'm sorry," she said immediately, standing uncertainly in the middle of the bathroom. "I need to get away from the light. It's... it's instinct. The bathroom is the darkest place."

He scrubbed at his face. "Fine. Take the bathroom. I'll be guarding the door, though, so don't try anything."

She didn't respond to that. With wordless acceptance, she gathered up the coverlet and pushed the flimsy bathroom door shut. There was a shuffling sound as she pushed rolled-up towels against the crack at the bottom of the door, then the screech of the shower curtain being pulled back. Was she going to sleep in the tub? After she just showered?

In answer to his question, he heard the sound of her feet stepping into the tub, then the screech of the shower curtain being drawn shut again. He doubted it would offer any meaningful light protection, but instincts were instincts. He and his wolf knew it well.

There was a moment of shuffling, the tub squeaking as she shifted herself within it, then the rustle of the coverlet being adjusted. Finally, there was silence. A long, long stretch of silence. Max went to the window, lifting the shade to peer out. The sky was pink and gold as bright light crested the eastern horizon.

The sun had risen.

He dropped the shades. The room was dark, but was it dark enough? He drew the dusty curtains over the shades. He went to the bathroom door—listened. No noise. Not even the sound of breathing.

He paced the small room. What was he going to do with her? He couldn't keep her indefinitely. He either had to slay her, or he had to let her go. Both were impossible.

He stopped at the bathroom door to listen again. The deathly silence was unnerving. Giving into an overwhelming need, he eased the door open and slipped inside. No movement, no noise. He crept to the tub, gently drew the curtain back. There was nothing to see but the dusty floral bed cover. Cursing himself for an idiot, he took hold of it and gently drew it back.

Jules lay beneath it, as still and pale as death. She looked just as she had when he found her behind the store, except her throat was intact and there was no more blood. But, still, the sight of her like that made his heart pound and his hands sweat. He tucked the coverlet back over her, pulled the shower curtain into place, and slipped out of the bathroom, rearranging towels on the other side of the door to cover the crack.

What was he doing?

What the fuck was he doing?

He sat on the bed. He hadn't slept properly in weeks—

had barely slept at all since arriving in Chicago. Getting some sleep would help him think. Giving in, he set an alarm to wake him well before sunset and laid back on the bed. It was small and lumpy and smelled of mildew, but Jules was in the next room, and even though nothing was right and his world was still in shambles, something about the current circumstances allowed him to finally close his eyes and sleep.

CHAPTER 26

Jules was surprised to wake up. She hadn't expected to do so again. Max had promised to kill her if he ever saw her again, and he hadn't seemed in a wildly different frame of mind about it last night. She was afraid to get up, to face him again. Blood hunger was a fire burning beneath her skin, a painful need leaching through her entire body like poison. She wasn't afraid she would lose control. She knew she could control herself. She was mostly afraid that he would notice her hunger and get angry.

She was so tired of angry men.

"I know you're awake," Max's voice came through the bathroom door, flat and hard. "Might as well get out."

Jules closed her eyes against the tide of pain that accompanied his voice. She was wearing his clothes, surrounded by his scent, and she was trapped in a conflicting storm of nostalgic comfort and crushing dread. With concerted effort, she hoisted herself up out of the bathtub. Her hands had mostly healed—covered over in tight, shiny new skin. The rest of her felt like shit, though. She was weak, slow, and unsteady. All the healing had taken a great deal of energy, and she desperately needed to feed. Until she got blood, her body would cannibalize itself in a contradictory effort to keep her alive.

When she stepped out of the bathroom, Max stood in front of the entry door, his whole body poised as if for a fight. Jules instinctively looked around the room for his opponent, but there was nobody else there. A moment later she realized —he was prepared to fight *her*. Was this it, then? She stood in the bathroom doorway, defeated, resigned to her fate. She hoped he'd make it quick. She wished he'd done it during her daysleep when she would've been oblivious to the pain.

When Max made no move to attack her, she lifted her head, looking at him in confusion. "What are you waiting for?" she asked.

He frowned. "What are *you* waiting for?"

A frustrated growl escaped her throat. Max stiffened, and she choked it off immediately. "I'm waiting for you to decide if you're going to kill me or not," she said plainly.

He flinched, some of the aggression easing from his posture. Straightening, he scrubbed at the back of his neck, an indecisive gesture she recognized immediately. The wistful longing was almost painful. She tamped it down immediately.

"Just... take care of whatever you need to take care of. We've got to get back on the road."

She stared at him. "Why?"

"We're being followed." He didn't meet her gaze, turning his attention to the dresser as he shoved it back to its original position on the wall, freeing the door.

"But... why are you taking me? And where?"

Max was quiet for a second, still gripping the top of the dresser, head down. Finally, he pushed away from the dresser, his face a hard mask. "Just get ready. What do you need to do before we leave?"

Feed. "Nothing."

His brows raised skeptically. "You're ready to go?"

Did he want her to tell him she needed blood? She didn't dare risk asking. "I guess."

Max shepherded her all the way to the truck like a body-guard—though she knew he was protecting the rest of the world from her, not the other way around. When she was settled in the passenger seat, seatbelt buckled, he got into the driver's seat and started the car. She was too exhausted to be scared anymore. She was passive and silent as he pulled out of the motel parking lot, still confused, but aware that he wasn't going to give her any useful answers. He got them onto the highway, headed east. Why? Where were they going? She was starting to think that Max didn't actually know what he was doing.

"Who's following us?" she asked, bracing herself for his withering response.

"Don't worry about it," he said flatly, living up to her expectation.

She couldn't stop worrying about it, though. She was afraid it was Bee following her. She wasn't optimistic about what Max had planned for her, but she was downright terri-fied about what he might do to Bee. She hoped that wher-ever Bee was, she and the thralls were safe, though Jules doubted she'd live long enough to find out.

They rode in silence. The cab was filled with Max's

enticing smell, and her entire body ached with the need to feed. She ignored it, forcing her attention elsewhere. Her gaze drifted around the vehicle's interior. It was a plain, midsized sedan, probably only a year or two old. It was nothing like the eighties-era pickup truck he'd been driving in Cry Lake.

"When did you get this?" Jules asked, skimming her fingers over the armrest.

"It's a rental."

"Oh."

Max glanced at her, his attention landing on her hands. "You healed."

"Yeah."

He nodded once, rigidly. Jules had no idea what it meant. Another tense silence stretched out. She stared at the road. Max would have to stop at some point to either eat or relieve himself. When he did, she'd run. She should've run when they left the motel, but she'd been so confused by his behavior, and too aware of how weakened she was, she hadn't dared. She was still too weak, and growing weaker, but the longer she waited, the less chance she'd have of getting away. She had to take her next opportunity whenever it came.

"Why were you messing with acid?" Max asked suddenly, startling her out of her planning.

"What?"

"You got acid all over your hands when you... when you slew the other strigoi. How? Why?"

She'd never heard the word strigoi until Max had said it, but she could figure out what he meant. A strigoi was what she was. A vampire.

"It was the only way I could kill him. He was faster and

stronger than me. I had to catch him unaware, from a distance."

"*Why,* though? You can't feed on your own kind."

Jules grimaced. She'd never considered it, and something inside her instinctively recoiled from the thought. "It wasn't to feed. It was the only way I could get away from him. He was a monster."

"You're all monsters," Max said. He didn't seem angry. He mostly seemed confused.

"I don't know what to tell you, then. He was bad and he deserved to die."

Max murmured a dark agreement, but it didn't feel good to have him on her side. It felt like an insult, a threat.

Another stretch of silence, in which Jules fell to planning her escape, interrupted by Max again. "Your hands healed— why does the rest of you look like hell? You look even worse than last night."

That statement shouldn't have rocked her as hard as it did. The man had threatened to kill her, and somehow, this hurt worse. Max had *never* criticized her appearance. Ever. She flipped down a visor to look at herself. He wasn't wrong —she was gaunt and pale, her face hollow, her skin stretched too tight over her bones.

"I'm hungry," she said honestly, too hurt by his words to bother censoring herself.

Max stiffened. She shouldn't have said anything.

"You get any ideas about attacking me, I'll show you why strigoi stay out of wolf territory."

"I don't want to attack you," she said.

The blood hunger was making her head spin, her body shake, and Max's delectable scent was filling the car, calling to her. But she hadn't lied—she didn't want to attack him.

She wanted to drink from him, more than she'd ever wanted any taste of blood, but she wanted it in the way she wanted to go back in time and undo everything that had led to this point—not as a violent, rapacious desire, but rather, a sorrowful longing for something that wasn't hers anymore and probably never had been.

The silence lasted much longer this time. They crossed into Ohio and drove straight on towards Pittsburgh, but as they neared the city, Max got off the highway and gave it a noticeable berth. They'd been on the road for over six hours, and he showed no signs of wanting to stop. A bit west of Pittsburgh, he got back on a highway, headed south this time.

"Where are you taking me?" she asked, unable to keep it in anymore. "My family's all in the midwest and yours is all in Alaska. This makes no sense!"

Max glanced at her, brow furrowed, obviously thinking. He didn't answer her right away. After a moment, instead, he asked, "What do you know about Jules?"

She frowned. "What?"

"How much of the person does a strigoi retain? You've got some of her memories at least—you knew my name. You know where I'm from."

Jules shook her head. "I... I don't understand the question."

Max let out a beleaguered sigh. "Of course you don't."

"Where are you taking me?" she demanded again, frustrated, confused, scared, and steadily growing angrier.

"I don't know."

"Are you going to kill me?"

A bleak silence. In a low growl, he answered, "I don't know."

Jules sat back against her seat, seething with the unfairness of it all. She was already in unbearable agony from the blood hunger, tormented with each breath by the allure of Max's scent. She'd already suffered under Ragnvaldr's cruel and capricious rule and finally escaped him only to fall into the hands of another mercurial, threatening captor. She couldn't take anymore.

"This isn't fair!" she cried, balling her hands into white-knuckled fists. "I didn't ask for this! I didn't ask for any of this! You told me to leave, and I left. And now you're going to kill me anyway? Why? *WHY?* I didn't do anything wrong! I get it—you're wolf kin and you hate vampires. Well, guess what, I fucking hate them, too! I hate what I am! But I didn't ask for this! For Christ's sake, just let me go, Max!" She worked herself into a frantic panic, tears streaking down her face. She reached for the door and jerked on the handle, ready to throw herself out of the vehicle and hope for the best, but it wouldn't open.

"Stop," Max snarled. His hand shot out, grabbing her wrists and pinning them to her lap. "*Stop!*"

"Let me go," she begged on a sobbing breath. "*Please.* Just let me go."

A wolfish sound of pain—half whine, half snarl—rose in his throat. "I can't," he said hoarsely.

Max found a hotel in some nowhere town in West Virginia, just before the sun rose. As Jules tried to walk inside the open door, it was like she'd hit a wall.

"Oh. That's right," Max said grimly, expression tightening with revulsion. "You need an invitation. Well. Come in, then."

Jules was out of words and out of fucks to give. She crossed the threshold, snatched the coverlet off the bed, went into the bathroom, blocked the crack under the door with rolled-up towels, and crawled into the bathtub. She pulled the coverlet over herself and surrendered gladly to the oblivion of her daysleep.

CHAPTER 27

An unnerving suspicion was beginning to take hold in Max's mind. He knew it wasn't possible. It was a combination of lack of sleep, grief, wishful thinking, and probably even strigoi manipulation.

He couldn't stop thinking it, though.

The next night, when Jules awoke, looking even worse than the night before, he ushered her into the car and they hit the road again.

He drove them south through the Appalachians, taking a meandering route between a dozen different medium-sized cities that were too big for a wolf kin presence, but too small for strigoi to comfortably settle. The Cry Lake pack would expect him to go back to Alaska, so he'd gone in the opposite direction. He couldn't cross into Canada. Even if Jules had her passport on her, a legally dead woman would probably have a little trouble trying to cross international borders. So he went south.

He glanced periodically at Jules as he drove. She stared steadfastly out the side window, face turned away from him.

Despite the fact that she'd healed from the acid injuries on her hands, she looked even worse than she had yesterday. She looked sick. She looked like she was dying. It made him anxious. Every time he took note of all the fine bones in her hands, standing in stark relief beneath her papery skin, every time he realized how deep the hollows beneath her cheeks had sunk, every time he catalogued the exhausted slump of her posture and the tired dullness in her eyes and the unsteady weakness of her movements, a whine began to rise in his throat that he had to consciously stifle.

He still had no idea what he was doing, what his end-game was. He couldn't take the strigoi back to Longtooth. He was beginning to come to terms with the fact that he couldn't kill her. But he also couldn't let her go. Was he just going to spend eternity driving around with her?

"What do you remember about Jules?" he asked somewhere in the middle of the night, unable to fight the need to hear her voice.

The strigoi turned to look at him, an expression of almost comical confusion on her face. "What the hell are you talking about?"

The suspicion that he couldn't acknowledge grew a little stronger.

"Tell me what you remember from her life."

She stared at him a moment longer, gaze traveling intently over his face before turning away from him again. For a while, he was sure that she wasn't going to answer him. Then, tiredly, her voice a dry rasp, she said, "Juliana Wolfe was a gullible idiot. She probably got what was coming to her."

His heart twisted, but not for the right reason. He should be angry at the monster for disparaging the woman he loved.

Instead, he wanted to reach out, soothe the monster, hold her until that pained edge left her voice.

HE'D HAD THE STRIGOI FOR THREE DAYS NOW. SHE NEVER TRIED attacking, never betrayed an interest in doing so. She ignored him. Spoke in single syllables when he demanded a response from her. Every morning they stopped at a new motel, and after he invited her inside, she grabbed the coverlet off the bed and secured herself in the bathroom where the sun's rays couldn't get her. He checked on her while she was asleep, discomfited by her breathless, deathly stillness— made worse by the increasing gauntness of her features. Her scent—Jules's familiar scent of summer rain and autumn wind, mingled with the cool nighttime scent of strigoi—was tainted with a smell of illness, decay. Something was wrong. He should've been relieved that she was wasting away. It spared him the trouble. Instead, he was growing increasingly frantic.

That's not Jules, he reminded himself on a daily—hourly —basis.

They'd hit Louisiana yesterday, and now he was driving idly northward along the Mississippi's twisting banks.

"Oh!" Jules said suddenly, brightly, leaning forward to peer at the sky.

Max followed her line of sight in time to see intermittent, arcing streaks of light—a meteor shower. He slid his gaze to Jules, discreetly watching her, observing the happy wonder on her face with a sinking feeling in the pit of his stomach.

Would a soulless, bloodthirsty killer care about shooting

stars? Would a monster be able to look up at the night sky with the same breathless wonder as Jules always had?

Jules caught him watching her, and as soon as she realized, the soft, awe-struck smile faded into flat, blank emptiness. She sat back, averting her gaze from the sky to stare out the side window again, giving him her back.

The strigoi was either a masterful manipulator or...

Max turned his attention back to the road. He couldn't finish the thought. His palms turned slick against the steering wheel. His stomach churned. His heart thundered in his ears.

"What's wrong?" Jules asked, suddenly alert.

She could hear his heartbeat. *Strigoi.* The stark reminder of what she was eased some of the panic and he was able to take a steady breath.

"Nothing," he answered roughly.

She didn't try to speak to him again after that. The rest of the night passed in stiff silence.

With little more than an hour before sunrise, Max pulled off the highway in a poky little factory town in Arkansas. He found a motel on the town's quiet main street. Jules went to stand listlessly beside the door, waiting for him to unlock it and invite her in. He took a small risk, letting her out of his sight as he popped the trunk and got his bag out of it.

When he straightened up, about to slam the trunk shut, his attention was caught by Jules. She still stood by the motel room door, but she was digging in the shrubbery that grew along the front of the building. Remaining still, hand poised on the trunk, he watched as she very carefully pulled something out of the branches. At first it looked like a clump of dirt, but as she tilted it gently in her palm, he realized it was a bird's nest. She picked something out of it, something small and even more delicate than the nest. An eggshell.

She stood in the silvery moonlight, examining the empty little eggshell, her expression as soft and wondering as it had been when she'd found rose quartz in the creek bed, and turkey feathers in the woods, and big snail shells on the lake shore. There was something so purely *Jules* about her expression and her absorption and her delicate admiration of such a mundane piece of the world that was impossible to deny.

Max stared, stricken, as it suddenly hit him with total certainty—Jules wasn't gone. She was still here. She'd always been here.

He flushed hot and then cold. His skin felt too tight, his lungs too small. His heart pounded against his sternum like a hammer. Cold sweat broke out across his whole body.

What had he done?

He'd *left* her. Worse—he'd threatened her. He'd chased her straight into the clutches of other strigoi—who'd been so monstrous, she'd had to kill him to get away. Max had failed her as utterly as it was possible to have done. He was supposed to be a protector. That was what he did, it was who he was. But for the woman he'd wanted as *his mate*, he'd denied his protection and forced her into danger and suffering. She wasn't a monster. She never had been. *He* was the monster.

Max didn't know what to do with that. He was frozen in place, paralyzed by the unfathomable magnitude of his failure.

Jules turned, keeping the eggshell carefully in her palm. When she saw Max over the lip of the trunk lid, she startled slightly. Her expression shifted from the calm contemplation with which she'd examined the eggshell to a stony mask.

Fear and unhappiness radiated from her, turning her fresh-water and autumn night scent slightly bitter, sharp.

Once upon a time, her face had lit with a smile when she saw him, and her scent had become warm and enticing. He'd ruined that.

"Jules..." His throat tightened around her name, and he couldn't get anything else out. Which was just as well, because he had no idea what to say.

Her hand dropped to her side, her loosely curled fist keeping the eggshell protected. She didn't show it to him. She would have done that, before. But not anymore. He'd ruined that. He'd ruined everything.

HER MOUTH WAS AS DRY AS DESERT SAND. HER BONES ACHED WHEN she moved. Her thickened blood moved sluggishly through her veins. The hunger was sharper and crueler than it had ever been. Max's scent was the most appealing thing she'd ever smelled in her life, and the desire to taste the sweet, rich, vital flow of him was making her dizzy and shaky with want and fear. Every night she felt more of herself wasting away, her strength failing, her body shutting down. She wouldn't succumb to the hunger. She would never hurt Max —never hurt anybody the way Ragnvaldr and his ilk had hurt people. She'd rather die. But she was also afraid that it was quickly coming down to that.

So many times since Bee had turned her, she'd thought she'd reached the end. And she'd made her peace with it each time. But every time she'd managed to survive, and she'd been grateful for it. She didn't want to die. She didn't want to live like this, but she didn't want to give up, either. She was afraid. She didn't know how much longer she could go on like this. When she caught glimpses of herself in a mirror, she was shocked by the shadowed, hollow face staring back at her. She needed blood so badly, she couldn't think about anything else. The pain was constant. The need was constant. If it didn't kill her soon, it was going to drive her insane.

As she stood at the motel door, waiting for Max to come over with the key, her gaze dropped to the dark green shrubs growing along the front of the building. Nestled in the top branches, just below the cover of the uppermost leaves, was an abandoned robin's nest with one nearly perfect eggshell still resting inside. Forgetting Max and the pain of hunger and the fear of death for one brief moment, she reached for the nest.

The eggshell was a perfect sky blue, limned with silver in the bright moonlight. She turned it carefully in her hand, examining the hairline crack along the equator. She carefully opened it along the crack, hinging like a clamshell, to see the empty inside.

For a moment, instinct overrode common sense, and she looked up at Max, about to show it to him. But then the crushing weight of reality intruded. She remembered that Max hated her, that she was his prisoner until he decided to kill her, or until she succumbed to starvation and spared him the trouble.

He was watching her, she realized, staring with wounded eyes and a stricken expression on his face.

"*Jules...*" he rasped, looking as if he'd been shot.

What had she done now? Some irrational part of her was convinced he'd try to take the eggshell away from her. Or that he'd scorn her for it. *Why are you always picking up trash? Stop it. You're not a toddler.* Those words were Eric's, not

Max's, but the contempt in Max's eyes had been the same ever since she'd become a vampire. She tucked her hand against her side, hiding the eggshell. Max's gaze tracked the movement, and the anguish in his expression only deepened.

"Jules," he said again, coming around the car towards her, his expression bleak. "What have I done?"

Jules retreated from him until her back hit the door, the little blue egg falling from her nerveless hand. This was it—he'd finally made the decision to end her. She was too weak to run, too starved to fight back.

But at her retreat, he froze, raising his hands in a gesture of surrender. "Jules, no, I—don't be afraid, okay? I was wrong. I get that now. I'm not going to hurt you."

She laughed. The sound emerged as a crackling rasp from her parched, desiccated throat before turning into a pained cough.

"Jules?" Max rushed to her. She flinched away from him and he froze again. "I'm so sorry," he said in a low, agonized voice, a hint of growl roughening the words. "I'm so, so sorry."

"Are you serious?" she asked when she could finally stop coughing. Her voice was raw and hoarse. "You're *sorry?* Sorry for what?"

He winced. "Let me get the door open. We can talk inside."

With nothing else to do, Jules stepped aside so that Max could unlock the door.

"Go in," he bade quietly, gesturing for her to enter first, and she did so with a prickle of suspicion. His scent washed over her as she passed him, and blood hunger twisted its hold on her so fiercely and suddenly that she doubled over in pain.

"Jules?" Max's hands were on her—one on her back, the other on her arm, bracing her up.

She stiffened, icy panic and wistful longing at war inside her. "What are you doing?"

He ignored her question, guiding her to sit on the bed. "Are you alright? What do you need?"

Confusion, resentment, exhaustion, and most insidiously of all, *hunger,* forced her to snarl at him. "I need *blood,* Max! Did you forget what I am? I'm fucking starving to death!" The outburst shredded her already aching throat, and the last few words emerged as a nearly silent hiss.

Instead of being angry, or revolted, or frightened, or appalled, Max just nodded calmly. As if he hadn't been threatening to kill her just days ago because of that need. As if she'd told him she wanted pizza.

"You can drink from me," he said.

Jules stared at him, her mind going briefly blank. There was no way he'd just offered—

"Drink from me," he repeated. "I'm strong enough to stop you before you kill me."

"No," she said instantly.

Wanting was terrifying, and she wanted to taste Max so badly it was literally killing her. But she couldn't take his loathing anymore. She couldn't bear it if sating her hunger made him even crueler. Or worse—what if she killed him? Bee had killed Jules, not because she was cruel and violent, but because she was desperately hungry. If Max hated her as a vampire, what would he do if she accidentally turned him into one as well? And what if he didn't turn? What if he was just... gone? She'd have to live with the fact that she'd killed him for the rest of her unnatural, eternal life.

"Jules," he said her name softly, beseechingly, the way he used to say it before her world turned dark and cruel and ugly. "Trust me."

"I can't," she answered bluntly. As much as she longed for the happiness she'd had with him in the last of her mortal days, he'd proven that she didn't know him like she'd thought she did. She would never have guessed at the heart-breaking coldness he was capable of—how he could just shut off the way he'd felt about her as soon as he realized she wasn't human anymore. The way he could refuse her pleas for help. The way he sent her away from everything she'd ever known, upending her world even worse than it already had been.

She hated him for that. If he hadn't run her off, maybe Ragnvaldr never would have found her. Maybe things wouldn't have gotten so bad. Maybe she wouldn't have suffered so cruelly and needlessly.

"You have no choice," Max said gently. "You need blood. I can't let you kill anyone. But I can defend myself, so I'm your only option."

Jules had no response to that. She stared at her hands, at the faint tremor she couldn't suppress even when she clenched them together, at the bones and tendons standing out like cords beneath her too-pale, too-thin skin.

Max's hand slipped into her field of vision, closing gently over her clenched fists. The warmth of his skin was like a furnace against hers.

"Let me help you, Jules."

She couldn't look at him. She continued to stare down at his hand clasped over hers. "Why?" she whispered hoarsely.

"I... I have to. I have to take care of you."

Her gaze flashed up to his. "*Now* you have to take care of me? What happened to killing me?"

He flushed, his expression turning shamed. "I was wrong. I was so wrong, Jules. Let me do this. I won't hurt you. I promise."

He had made that promise before. Months and months ago, when they'd first been intimate together. He'd promised to never hurt her. Wounded resentment bubbled up, sickening and hot, almost strong enough to make her tell him to go fuck himself. She'd rather die than take any help from him. But she didn't want to die. No matter how much she hated Max, she wanted to live more.

"Fine," she said faintly, ashamed of her weakness, her lack of pride.

Max let out a relieved sigh. "Okay, how do we do this?" He rose from his crouch, sitting beside her on the bed.

Jules shook her head, at a loss. "I don't know. I've never fed from anyone before."

He did a nearly comical double-take. "How is that possible?"

"We had blood bags. Like the kind from a hospital. We drank those."

"Are you telling me you never killed anyone?"

"I killed Ragnvaldr."

"A strigoi," he said dismissively.

Yes. Like me. She swallowed the resentful words, saying nothing.

"I think you need to go for the throat," Max said when she had been silent too long.

Jules shook her head, cold and nauseous with anxiety. "I can't."

"I'm not a normal human, Jules. I'm stronger, I heal faster. It's okay. If it's too much, I'll pull you off, okay?"

He tilted his chin up, baring his throat to her. His neck was strong and muscular, corded tendons drawing straight lines down his throat. His pulse ticked beneath his skin, a hypnotically rhythmic beat. His scent was rich and warm and familiar, enveloping her in its intoxicating pull. She couldn't resist any longer. Obeying instinct, she leaned across his body, cupping the back of his neck, and bit.

CHAPTER 28

The first sting of her bite was a sharp pain, but Max remained still, determined not to make a sound of objection. Jules was dying, and if this was the only way to save her, then he'd make the sacrifice. It was the very least that he owed her for how monumentally he'd fucked up. He prepared himself for pain. He prepared himself to resist his own instincts. What he hadn't prepared for was pleasure.

After she broke his skin, her lips sealed over the bite—a touch so familiar, his body couldn't help but react. But it was more than that. A languid warmth was stealing into his veins, spreading from the spot where she bit him. It intensified until his whole body felt light and floating and warm, a heady euphoria scattering his thoughts so that all he could do was *feel*. The feeling of Jules's hand clasping the back of his neck, her lips pressed to his throat in the sharp-edged imitation of a lover's kiss. The feel of her body pressed to the front of his. The feel of his blood, his vitality, slipping from him and into her. It was a shockingly pleasant sensation, an intimacy so deep, he'd never experienced its like.

He was still strong, still fast, still wolf kin—but none of that mattered when he had no desire to resist her. He never wanted to give up the high-flying feeling of Jules feeding from him. He melted back until he was laying on the bed, and Jules followed him down, drinking in slow, steady draughts. Who was moaning so loudly? Was it him? He didn't care. His hands went to Jules's waist, holding her to him, urging her to drink, to keep drinking. Vaguely, he was aware that *this* must be the strigoi magic that wolf kin warned of, but he couldn't find the will to break away.

Too soon, she eased her fangs from his throat, lapping gently at the wounds before she pulled away entirely. Max remained sprawled on the bed, still floating on the high of the feeding.

"Max?" Jules said his name hesitantly.

Even through the euphoric haze, he noticed that Jules's voice was no longer a crackling, fading rasp, but rather, the warm, slightly smoky tenor he remembered from before she was turned. He laughed, exalted. He had his girl back.

"Max?" she sounded worried now, leaning over him to peer into his eyes. She cupped his face, holding him steady. "Max, are you alright? Please answer me."

"Good," he said drunkenly, breathlessly. "I'm good." He should feel drained—he'd been fed from, his blood diminished, his vitality consumed—but instead, his whole body was filled with invigorating strength.

He made a concerted effort to focus his eyes, bringing Jules's beautiful face into sharp relief, hovering just above his. She looked good—she looked like herself. The hollowness was gone, her color was healthy, her eyes no longer dull, no longer ringed by bruise-dark shadows. She looked like *his* Jules, beautiful and cared for and *alive*. Her scent was no longer underlaid by that unsettling thread of sickness, decay. She was clean water and tree bark and forest air. That strigoi edge added an inexplicable darkness to her scent, but he no longer found it appalling. It was mysterious and unknown, but it braided into her natural scent, adding complexity and depth to the familiar comfort.

"Are you sure?" She was so close, examining him fretfully.

He lifted his head, closing the scant distance between them, and kissed her. She made a faint sound of surprise, but she didn't flinch or turn away. Wrapping his arms around her, Max rolled them until Jules was on her back and he was poised above her. He dipped his head, kissing her fiercely, desperately, possessively. He tasted his own blood in her mouth, coppery and bright, and it drove his arousal higher. The place where she'd bit him was still tender, like a claiming mark. The intensely primal part of his mind—his wolf—loved that he had her mark on his throat and his taste in her mouth. They belonged to each other. It was natural and right.

But Jules broke away suddenly, breathing hard, eyes wild. "No," she said shakily, pushing against his chest.

He released her immediately. His head was no longer fuzzy with the high of her feeding, but his blood was racing hot and hectic through his body. Need for Jules had him rock hard. His skin ached to press against hers.

"Are you okay?" he asked, pushing himself up to sit.

"I don't want that from you," she said quietly. "Ever."

The pain that tore through him almost made him howl.

But he had no right to be upset. He'd done this. He'd brought it on himself. Brought it on both of them.

"I'm sorry," he said, words thick in his throat. "I lost my head." He almost laughed. He'd been so worried about Jules losing control, but in the end, he'd been the problem. After a moment of shamed silence, he asked, "Why did you stop drinking? I wasn't stopping you."

"I got what I needed," she answered quietly. "I wasn't hungry anymore."

Max frowned. Strigoi killed their victims—drained them entirely. "That's not how it works," he said, confused.

She shrugged. "I don't know what to tell you."

He stared at her, the crushing weight on his chest growing heavier with each breath until he was certain he would suffocate on the shame and regret and self-loathing.

"I fucked up," he said hoarsely. "I fucked up so bad."

For the briefest moment, the hurt that he had dealt her was visible on her face. It hit him like a kick in the stomach. She quickly shuttered it into indifferent blankness, looking away from him.

"You did what you thought you had to do."

"No, I didn't."

She looked back at him, brows drawn together.

"I thought I should have killed you—that it would've been a mercy." He was quiet for a long moment. "I couldn't do it."

"Then you're cruel *and* weak," she said flatly.

She got up and ripped the comforter off the bed, nearly dragging Max off with it, before disappearing into the bathroom. He heard the sound of towels being wedged against the gap beneath the door, then the screech of the shower curtain as she crawled into the tub for her daysleep.

Max let out a long, slow breath, astonished he could still do so after she'd plunged that jagged knife into his heart. She was right. She was absolutely right. He was a monster and a coward and he didn't know if he could ever make things right. He desperately wished he could go back in time and undo everything. Even if it meant he couldn't have Jules, couldn't be with her, if there was anything he could do to spare her the pain and suffering he'd inflicted on her, he'd do it.

But he couldn't do that. It didn't work that way. What he could do, though, was to ensure that her future would be safe and happy and peaceful. Which meant he had to have some hard conversations.

He dug his phone out of his bag. He'd shut it off after Indiana, bombarded by calls from both the Cry Lake pack and his own pack. He'd turned it on periodically over the last few days while Jules was in her daysleep to send a single text to his parents, letting them know he was safe, and then immediately shut it off again.

But everything he thought he knew had changed in the span of an hour, and the only people he could think to discuss it with were his family.

He called his mother first, knowing she'd be frantic.

"Maxim!" she sobbed his name as soon as she answered. "Where are you? What are you doing? The Cry Lake elders say—"

"Mom, wait," he said calmly. "Just listen to me, okay?"

She choked into tense, expectant silence.

"I found Jules."

"*Maxim*," she breathed, distraught. He could hear shifting background noise on his mom's end, and he knew she was rushing through the Spruce to find his dad.

"I didn't slay her. I have her with me."

"What are you doing, kochanie? This is insane!"

"Please listen. Please try to hear what I'm saying, okay?"

"I'm listening," she said quickly, obviously panicked. "Talk to me. Tell me what this is."

"Jules is a strigoi, that's true. She was turned."

His mom let out a little sob.

"But she's still herself. She's still Jules. She needs blood to survive and she sleeps during the day, but she's not a monster. She's not a killer."

"Maxim—"

"She's still Jules," he said emphatically. "She has all of her own memories—her family, the place she grew up, me..." He winced. Those memories had likely been poisoned by his idiocy. "She's still herself, mom. She gets excited about meteor showers. She found a robin's egg this morning and it made her so happy."

He wanted to tell her that he'd let Jules feed from him, that she'd had every opportunity to try to kill him, and instead, she'd done the opposite. But telling his mother about the intimacy of being fed on felt a bit like telling her about his sex life. And even if he could convey how pleasant and unthreatening it had been without embarrassing himself, he knew the mere fact that he'd willingly given his blood to a strigoi would still have the pack up in arms. They'd doubt his sanity more than they likely already were.

"Maxim..." His mother sighed. "I think you should speak to your father."

There was the brief sound of the phone being handed over.

"Max?" His dad's voice was steadier than his mom's had

been, but the worry in his tone was no less urgent. "What's going on?"

"Dad... she's still Jules. I need you to believe me."

His dad was quiet for a long moment. Finally, he said, "Son, you know they can mess with people's minds."

Max glanced at the closed bathroom door. "I don't know how to make you believe that, from the truest core of myself, I *know* that she's still Jules—that she's not a monster, and that she deserves to be loved and protected."

"Your compassion is what makes you a good guardian for the pack," his dad said carefully. "And I want to believe you. But everything we have ever known about them flies in the face of what you're telling me."

"I know," Max said heavily. "I know it does. And if anyone else was saying these things to me, I'd think they were letting grief and wishful thinking confuse them. But I'm not confused, Dad. She hasn't tried convincing me of anything. She hasn't really been talking to me, to be honest," he said, ashamed. "She wants to get away from me. And I kept letting myself believe she was just a monster acting in self-preservation. But I can't lie to myself anymore—she's not a mindless killer. She's not a parasite using Jules's body. She's just *Jules*."

"Even if she *is* Jules, what's your plan? How do you think the pack is going to react to this?"

"*Tell him to come home!*" his mother's voice whispered urgently from the background.

"I won't come home without Jules," Max said. "I can't."

A stunned silence met that. "Are you telling me you expect to bring a strigoi into pack territory?"

"No." He had very low expectations there. Maybe with time, a small handful of pack members might come around, but he doubted he'd ever get enough on his side to return to his old life. The grief of choosing between his pack and Jules hit him hard, a sharp pain in his heart, but the choice was obvious for him. Jules. Always Jules.

"What are you saying?" his dad asked.

"I don't expect the pack will accept her. But I can't leave her."

His dad let out a harsh breath. "You're leaving the pack? For a *strigoi?*"

"Not leaving. But I know that I won't be allowed to return." It was a subtle distinction, but it seemed obvious to Max. "And it's not for 'a strigoi.' It's for my mate."

"You claimed her?" His dad's shock ratcheted higher.

"*He what?*" his mother gasped in the background.

"No. Not yet. I think... I don't know if she'll ever let me. I betrayed her." He scrubbed at his face, shame and regret choking him. "I have to earn her trust back. I hope I can. Someday. But until then, I'm going to spend every waking minute making it up to her."

"What are you going to do?" his dad pressed. "Where are you going to live? How are you going to survive?"

All valid questions. The pack had structured their finances collectively—everyone who earned outside income pooled their resources for the community so that those whose labor didn't bring in wages were equally provided for. The outside world's system of individual incomes was foreign to him, but it was something he would need to figure out. He'd have to find a job and a place to live. He couldn't spend the rest of his life hopping from motel to motel, making Jules sleep in bathtubs. They needed a place that wasn't within any pack's territory, but where there also wasn't much of a strigoi presence. That excluded the remote wilderness parts of the country, but also all of the larger cities. He needed to find a city of fifty-thousand people or less to avoid strigoi, but near enough undeveloped land so that he could shift and let his wolf run.

"I'll have to figure it out, won't I?" Max answered.

"I wish you'd come home," his dad said, sorrowful but resigned.

"*Arthur!*" his mother objected. There was a scuffling sound as she apparently wrestled the phone away from his dad. "Maxim? Don't do this. Please. Please come home. Don't slay the strigoi if you don't want to, but come home to us. *Please.*" Her voice broke, and he knew she was crying.

He swallowed a wolfish whine. "Mom, I know you're scared, but I'm staying with Jules. This is the right thing to do. In time, you'll understand. I know you will."

"Maxim," she whispered brokenly. "This is madness."

"It's not, Mom. I'll call you every day. I promise. You'll see that I'm fine."

She let out a shaky, tearful breath. "I'm scared for you, kochanie. I don't want you hurt, or... or worse."

"I won't be, Mom. I know it's hard, but trust me. I'm doing the right thing."

He was eventually forced to say goodbye without having come to any kind of peace with his mother. It pained him that she was so distraught, but he knew time would prove him right.

CHAPTER 29

Jules awoke the next night with Max's scent enveloping her. It smelled more doggish than usual. When she sat up in the tub, she found a large russet wolf curled up on the bathroom floor, sound asleep. She stared at him for a while, a confusing mixture of emotions running through her. The sight of him curled up like a big old guard dog in front of her sleeping place made her chest tight and her eyes burn, but she couldn't tell if it was a good tightness and a sweet burn, or if it was just grief.

"Max," she said quietly.

He woke immediately, instantly alert, ears pricked. He looked first to the door, listening, smelling. When he detected no danger there, he swiveled back to look at Jules. His ears relaxed and his mouth opened, panting gently in a wolfish smile.

It wasn't fair for him to take this form. Nobody disliked animals. Especially not a giant, goofy wolf who looked so happy to see her. Regardless, she didn't allow herself to give into the softness. It would only hurt more later when sharp edge of his anger returned.

"What are you doing?"

He shifted, his wolven form compacting and elongating into a man—a beautiful man, naked, crouching before her with a solemn expression on his face and wary hopefulness in his eyes.

"I slept in here. Is that okay? If something happened, I wanted to be close by."

The same confusing storm of emotions continued to buffet her. "Oh."

Max tilted his head, gaze tracking intently over her. "You look good. Healthy. Did you know you don't breathe when you sleep? Or have a pulse?"

She blinked. She hadn't known that. "I... what?"

"I was worried the first day, but then you woke up that night. Then the next day you were the same—no breath, no pulse—so I just assumed that was normal."

Jules shook her head. "I don't know." She didn't know that that happened. It was terrifying. She breathed and had a pulse when she was awake. The idea that she basically *died* during her daysleep was anxiety-inducing. What if she didn't come back one of these nights? What if she just stayed dead? She'd faced death too many times in the past few months. She was tired of it. She just wanted peace. *Living* peace.

Max must've read the disquiet in her expression because he slowly, cautiously inched closer to the tub. "It's alright, Jules. You're alright. You're here now, awake and safe."

That surprised a bitter, sharp-edged laugh out of her. "Safe?"

Max's face hardened—not with anger, but with resolve.

"We didn't get a chance to talk properly before your daysleep. There wasn't enough time. But I need to say something to you, Jules."

She was still sitting in the bathtub, knees hugged to her chest, swaddled in the scratchy, dusty bed cover. She regarded him gravely, waiting, wondering what new way he'd find to rip her heart apart.

"I'm sorry," he said heavily, holding her gaze. "There are no words to express how sorry I am. Even if there were, words are easy and cheap. I can't ever make up for the suffering I put you through. But, if you'll let me, I'll prove that you can trust me. I'll protect you and care for you the way you deserve."

Jules stared at him. "Why would I do that?"

Max hesitated, jaw clenching as he considered his words. "Because you need me. I can give you blood so you don't have to hunt humans. I can protect you from other strigoi."

If she could just figure out how the hell Ragnvaldr had gotten blood bags, she wouldn't have to hunt anyone. But being protected from others like him was, unfortunately, a crucial consideration. Jules was quiet for a long time, thinking on it. Now that she had her strength back, she could probably escape Max. But then she'd be alone in a world she didn't understand anymore, at risk of running into other vampires or wolf kin who didn't have Max's personal connection to prevent them from killing her on sight.

She breathed out a heavy sigh. "Where would we go? Based on *your* reaction, I doubt your pack wants me around."

Max's gaze darkened. "No. We wouldn't be able to go to my pack. But I thought... do you remember when we talked about all the things you never got to see? Like the National Parks?"

Jules was annoyed by the hopeful flutter in her chest. Something in her expression must've given her away, because Max sat up straighter, eyes bright, coming even closer until he was leaning against the edge of the tub.

"Most of the National Parks are surrounded by wolf kin territory, but the parks themselves are neutral ground. Too many tourists and scientists and all that. Wolf kin steer clear. And strigoi—"

"Stop calling me that."

Max blinked. "That's what you are."

She could only hear his loathing in that word. "I'm a vampire." That's what she and Bee had called themselves, even before Ragnvaldr had found them.

Max nodded. "Alright." He cleared his throat. "Vampires rarely go into rural areas. But between the two of us, we could take on a single stri—vampire pretty easily. It probably wouldn't be an issue though. You almost never find them outside of cities."

She looked away from him, staring down at her knees, not speaking, just thinking. If she was being as objective and pragmatic as possible, she had to admit that Max was right. He was a safe source of blood and decent protection from becoming the prisoner of another Ragnvaldr. If she could trust him to live up to what he was promising her. Part of her wanted to, so badly. But a larger part of her, the part that had convinced her to divorce Eric and move home and stay away from men—the part that Max had already overridden once before—was terrified. And yet another part of her was still resentful and angry. She didn't want to give Max what he wanted when he had taken so much from her.

In the end, objective, pragmatic Jules won. She heaved

out a sigh. She could always change her mind, she told herself, and make a break for it later.

For now, she nodded minutely. "Alright."

Max's brows shot up. "Really?"

"Yeah. Really," she said flatly. "But this isn't forgiveness. This isn't a fresh start for us. The only thing I want from you is blood. No sex. No other touching."

"I understand," Max said solemnly. "But speaking of blood, do you need—"

"No." The thought was tempting in the way that any indulgence is tempting, but she wasn't hungry yet. She'd wait until she absolutely needed to feed. No matter what she told Max, feeding from him was its own kind of intimacy. Not quite like sex, but still primal and urgent and vulnerable. She held her breath for a moment, resisting the desire to inhale deeply and draw in his scent. There was a sense of possessiveness that came with feeding on him, not unlike love, but much more animalistic, greedy, and violent than the pure, sweet, selfless feelings she'd once had for him.

Jules didn't want any of it. That feeling was dangerous, in so many ways. But Max was right. She didn't have a choice —she needed him. He was her best shot at survival. So she'd stay with him as long as she needed to, until she figured things out, and then she'd leave when it was safe to do so. Staying with Max longterm would never be the safe option.

He considered her for a moment, his beautiful face both sorrowful and pensive. "I wish I could undo it all," he said quietly. "But I can't, so I'll do better. You'll see."

He got up and padded to the bathroom door. Jules had to consciously avert her eyes. His body wasn't hers to admire anymore. They were strangers, and they were going to stay strangers. When she heard the sound of his clothing rustling in the other room, she got out of the tub and followed him.

He turned to look at her as he finished pulling his shirt over his head. "We're a few hours' drive away from Hot Springs National Park. What do you think?"

"I've never even heard of Hot Springs National Park." She refused to be excited or grateful. It would be so easy to let go of her anger, give in to the desire for peace and affection. But if she did, she'd only be setting herself up to be blindsided again. At some point, the reality of what she was would become too much for him. Or his allegiance to his pack would force his hand. Either way, however good Max's intentions were, they couldn't be trusted. He couldn't be relied upon. It had taken her thirty years and immortal undeath to realize it, but she'd finally accepted that the cynics were right—the only person she could trust was herself.

"Well," Max said brightly, undeterred by her lack of enthusiasm, "Let's check it out. After that, we can either head south, towards Big Bend and start working our way clockwise to hit all the parks in the west. Or we could head up north to the Badlands and go counter-clockwise. What sounds better to you?"

Damn that excited flutter in her stomach. She kept her face blank. "I don't care."

"We'll figure it out later. Let's get going. We can stop on our way to Hot Springs to get you some clothes. You're probably sick of wearing mine."

"I don't have any money."

"Don't worry, I do."

Jules followed him out to the car, fighting a tangle of

emotions. She got into the passenger seat and as she pulled the seatbelt across her chest, she suddenly froze.

Max slid into the driver's seat. He glanced at her still form, then followed her gaze to the dashboard where the pretty little blue egg was sitting.

"You dropped it yesterday," he said. "I didn't want you to lose it."

Jules couldn't resist reaching for it. Despite being dropped, it was still in near-perfect condition. She turned it in her hands, examining it quietly. When she looked up, she found Max watching her intently. He immediately looked away, pretending to be engrossed in adjusting his side mirror. Jules stared back down at the egg, trying to find the will to crush it, to toss it out the window.

She couldn't. Suppressing a tiny sigh, she opened the center console and tucked the eggshell in a safe corner.

<hr>

THEY HAD TO SKIRT AROUND LITTLE ROCK ON THEIR WAY TO HOT Springs, adding a little more time to the drive.

"Little Rock is big enough to have a sizable stri—vampire," Max corrected himself quickly, "vampire presence."

"Okay." Jules wasn't eager to meet any other vampires. She was worried about Bee, but there was nothing she could do about that—she had no way of contacting Bee and she wasn't about to return to Chicago and risk being recaptured by any of Ragnvaldr's cronies. She just had to hope the girl had gotten out of Chicago and found somewhere safe to hunker down.

"There's a smaller city coming up—Pine Bluff. We'll stop there and get some clothes for you."

She was still dressed in Max's oversized t-shirt and athletic shorts with the house slippers she'd been wearing when she killed Ragnvaldr. After three days of wearing his clothes, his scent had faded from them. But in the car with him, and in small motel rooms, she was never far removed from the all-encompassing embrace of his scent. She wasn't *hungry*, exactly, but every time she inhaled deeply, her fangs throbbed and saliva pooled in her mouth.

When they finally reached Pine Bluff and found a shopping center with a cluster of clothing stores, Jules dove out of the car, gratefully hauling in lungfuls of the car exhaust and the dusty, concrete and metal-laden scent of city air. When she felt back in control, she turned to look at Max and immediately froze. He had his back turned to her as he scanned their surroundings, his attention diverted as he inhaled deeply, cataloguing scents. The urge to creep up on him, attack from behind, and sink her fangs into his neck, was so overpowering that she had to grip the car door to stay herself. Her fangs throbbed and her mouth flooded with saliva.

Max suddenly turned back to her. "Ready?"

She nodded, swallowing hard. With concerted effort at looking normal, she closed the car door and followed him into the nearest store. Under the glaring fluorescent lighting of the store, the predatory urge faded, but Jules's horror didn't. Appalled at herself, she walked mutely, rigidly beside Max.

He glanced at her. "Are you okay?" he asked under his breath.

She tried not to stiffen, not to give anything away. "I'm fine."

"You're not struggling with all these people?"

"What?" Jules looked around, suddenly aware that there were other people in the store. She'd been so hyper-focused on Max, she hadn't consciously registered their presence. She laughed, relieved that he hadn't picked up on the real reason. "No. I don't care about them."

Max's brow furrowed. "Then what is it? The lights? The openness?"

Jules shook her head.

"I can tell you're uncomfortable," Max pressed.

"I'm fine."

"Jules, you can tell me—"

"It's *you!*" she hissed angrily. "Your scent and your blood and—" She cut herself off on a frustrated snarl.

Contrary to her expectations, Max quirked a smile at her. He looked almost... smug. "Am I that good?"

"Oh, god, shut up." Embarrassed, Jules speed-walked away from him, plunging into racks of athleisure wear.

Max caught up to her, not saying anything, but radiating self-satisfied smarminess. Jules ignored him as best she could—which wasn't very well at all—and pretended to be engrossed in athletic shorts.

When she'd settled on a few pairs of shorts and a few shirts, Max gave her a skeptical look. "You're going to need more than three outfits. And you need shoes."

At Max's urging, they finally left the store with three big bags full of athletic clothes and jeans and t-shirts and a few cold-weather staples, even though she'd told him the cold didn't affect her anymore.

Back in the close quarters of the car, with Max's scent

enveloping her, the predatory urge came back over Jules. She watched him out of the corner of her eye as he put the car in gear and navigated his way back to the highway. She couldn't deny it—she wanted to attack him. But it was more than that. She wanted to stalk him, take him unawares, fight him for the upper hand, and then immobilize him as she drank from him. She wanted to see the aggression and alertness in his eyes and body die away to glazed, helpless, feeding-induced bliss. She wanted to bite him so deeply that her mark would be forever branded on him. She wanted to own him, body and soul.

But as much as she wanted that, she feared it more. Max already thought she was a monster. He'd somehow convinced himself she was a monster with a conscience. If he knew the true extent of her hunger, he wouldn't be able to convince himself of that anymore.

"Do you need to feed soon?" Max asked.

"No," Jules lied in instinctive self-preservation.

Max was quiet for a second. "Okay," he said.

Jules could almost convince herself he sounded disappointed.

They reached Hot Springs around two in the morning. The park had closed to traffic hours ago, so Max left the car in a public lot outside the park's boundaries and he and Jules walked in. They avoided the manmade structures of the bathhouse—closed to visitors anyway—and walked into the woods, following the gentle serpentine of Gulpha Creek.

At first, Jules was somewhat begrudgingly enjoying the walk. She had on a pair of comfortable sneakers and jeans and a t-shirt that actually fit her. It'd been months since she'd been out in nature. She'd spent most of the summer trapped in Ragnvaldr's house in the middle of Chicago, and since then, she'd only seen highways and motel rooms. The feel of fresh night air—a little humid, but rich with the scent of loamy earth and the clean scent of fresh creek water—was a welcome balm. She inhaled deeply, accidentally pulling in a heady sampling of Max's scent.

He was slightly ahead of her, and as she stared at his back, she was stricken by two things at once. First, that he trusted her enough to give her his back, repeatedly. And second, the sudden impulse to attack. Not to kill—just to subdue. To consume. To use.

She was exactly the monster he'd thought she was.

She pushed those thoughts away, tried to focus on the trees and the water and the soft wind and the sounds of night creatures. It wasn't really the same, but it reminded Jules of home a little bit. For a brief moment, that was a comforting thought. Then, with a sudden pang of loss, she staggered to a halt as she realized that she'd never be able to return home. She'd never again swim in the lakes or walk in the woods where she grew up. She couldn't. The Cry Lake Pack would kill her.

"Jules?" Max turned to face her. "What's wrong?"

"I can never go home," she answered, unable to keep the heartbreak out of her voice.

Max's face fell. "I'm sorry," he said. "I'm sorry so much has been taken from you."

You're the one who took it, she thought resentfully. She moved past him, trudging steadily along the creek's banks.

• • •

Max followed Jules silently through the forest, his chest aching with the need to comfort her, despite being well aware that she would not welcome his comfort.

Hot Springs National Park had been a poor choice for the start of his grand National Parks tour. Most of the park's appeal was the town and its historic bathhouse, which was all shut down after dark. There was little Jules could do except wander around the woods. He knew she liked walking in the woods, but she could do that anywhere—well, she used to be able to. Max wanted to give her things she hadn't been able to have in her human life—travel, adventure, sights she'd never seen before. He wanted to show her that her new life could be happy and fulfilling.

Instead, he'd only reminded her of everything she'd lost.

He forced himself to hang back, staying out of her way as she walked. He didn't ask what she'd found when she stopped to examine things along the creek bank. He didn't ask her where she was going. He simply followed.

In the wee hours of the morning, they stood atop Hot Springs Mountain, gazing out over the surrounding forest and hills and sprawling city streets. Jules was silent, still, as she looked out, silhouetted by the glow of distant city lights.

"The sun will rise soon," she said, her voice distant, flat.

"I've got a motel room booked. When you wake up, we can set out for somewhere else. We could go south to Big Bend. Or we could head up to South Dakota and the Badlands."

Jules wouldn't look at him. "I don't care."

CHAPTER 30

They had to cross Texas diagonally to get to Big Bend. And Texas was... a lot. There was just so much of it. So much land and so much sky for hours and hours and hours. Alaska was bigger, but Max had never driven the breadth of it.

They were in the middle of the Hill Country when Jules suddenly brightened. It was subtle—just a straightening of her spine, more intensity in the way she gazed out the side window. Max looked past her, curious as to what had caught her attention. They were on a two-lane county highway in the middle of nowhere and hadn't seen another vehicle in over an hour. All he could see beyond the road was a field. A big, broad, wide-open field that undulated over irregular hills all the way to the horizon.

"What is it?" he asked.

"Don't you see all the fireflies?" Jules must've really been engrossed if she'd answered him so readily.

"No," he admitted. "Not at this speed. I don't think my night vision's as good as yours."

"They're pretty." She was quiet for a second. "There's so many of them," she said quietly, wistfully.

Max slowed down, pulling over onto the wide gravel shoulder.

"What are you doing?" Jules asked, frowning at him.

"We're in no hurry. Let's go take a look."

He parked and killed the ignition. Jules watched skeptically as he unbuckled his seatbelt and got out of the car. He bent down to peer at her through his open door. "Come on, Jules. It's beautiful out here."

Warily, she unclipped her seatbelt and got out of the car. Max eased himself to sit on the hood, watching as she stepped cautiously off the shoulder and into the tall grasses. He didn't follow. He'd already imposed too much on her.

Jules stood amidst the open, grassy plain, taking in the dusty scent of the earth and the verdant aroma of the plants she'd trod on. In full darkness, her vision was still acute, but there was a different quality to how she saw things. Black was deeper, richer, more nuanced. It lent everything a surreal, jewel-like quality.

As she gazed at the land around her, it took her breath away. There was nothing but rolling hills in every direction, covered in swaying grasses and wildflowers, and dotted with the slow, fading pulse of thousands of fireflies. There was no moon in the sky, so instead, the infinite stars twinkled like a celestial mirror to the earthly magic of the fireflies. Jules felt like she was in a dream, or a genie's bottle, or a faerie queen's jewelry box, surrounded by lush color and fragrant scents and twinkling lights.

She drew in a sharp breath, amazed, and sank down to

sit amidst it all, tilting her head back to take in the sky, the flowers, the fireflies. The night air coasted gently over her skin, teasing the ends of her hair, bringing with it more of that dry, spicy, verdant scent. Time seemed to suspend itself, the world caught in one quiet moment of peace.

She heard footsteps behind her—Max was approaching. He sank down beside her, not speaking. They sat for a long time, quiet, peaceful. Max didn't press her for anything, didn't bother her. She hated herself for being so foolish and soft-hearted, but she couldn't deny that his presence was comforting. She was glad she wasn't alone.

After some time, she broke the peaceful spell. "The sun will rise in a couple hours."

"I know," he answered quietly. "Didn't want to rush you. We can go back to that town we passed a few miles back. I saw a sign for a motel."

Jules nodded. She took a few minutes to find the courage to say, "I... I need to feed soon."

His scent had been tormenting her in the car. And in the open air of this beautiful, quiet spot, it was less acute, but no less alluring.

Max didn't outwardly react to her words, but she could sense his sudden intensity.

"Right now?" he asked, his voice dipping into a near-growl.

"Well, no. Not in the open like this."

Max looked around. "Why not?"

"Because it's not safe," she answered, fairly certain that was obvious. Her instincts urged her to be somewhere private, sheltered, protected.

"There's nobody for miles around," he said, tracing the horizon with his gaze. "This isn't wolf territory. There are no vampires this far from any decent-sized city. We're as safe as we can be."

We. He'd said *we're* safe. Jules shouldn't have been moved by that. She was weak and silly and she was setting herself up for more pain. She shoved away the soft feelings.

"Alright then," she said roughly, moving too fast for him to react, shoving him onto his back. He stared at her with wide eyes, his heartbeat racing, the pheromonal lure of his scent growing stronger.

The aggression had come from her attempt at emotional distance mixing catastrophically with the temptation of feeding. Appalled at her lack of self-control, at her violence, she jerked back from Max, scrambling backwards.

"I'm sorry!" she gasped, struggling to her feet as Max pushed himself up to sitting. "I'm so, so sorry. I'll leave."

"Jules—"

"I'm sorry. Just let me leave and I won't ever bother you or anyone else. I just—"

"I liked it."

She froze.

"Jules," he whispered her name softly, beseechingly. "Come back."

Something wicked and dark and dangerous unfurled in her chest. "You what?" she asked hoarsely.

He smiled, the curve of his mouth shameless and tempting. Moving with the grace of a slinking panther, he crawled through the wildflowers to close the distance between them.

"I'm a wolf, Jules. When we play, we use our teeth and claws. You can't scare me with a little roughhousing."

She couldn't believe what he was saying. She blinked, frozen like an idiot while Max continued to prowl forward, slowly pushing her onto her back and bracing himself above her. Jules stared up at him, paralyzed by the ardent ferocity of her hunger. It twisted her up, hot and sweet instead of sharp and painful. How was she supposed to resist that feeling? Especially when her prey was staring at her with such heat in his eyes.

Jules reached for him, wrapping her arms around the back of his neck and rolling until he was on his back and she sat astride him.

"Oh *no*," Max drawled. "I am at the mercy of a dangerous, but incredibly beautiful apex predator. Whatever shall I do?"

"You'll lay there and take it like a good boy," Jules whispered.

Max's eyes went wide as his pulse skittered erratically. He opened his mouth to say something, but there was no way Jules was going to let him have the last word. She bent down and swiftly sank her fangs into his throat. Whatever he'd been about to say died on a wordless groan.

His blood was hot and rich on Jules's tongue, his big body pliant and warm beneath her. His hands had grasped her hips, gripping hard, urging her on while his head was thrown back, throat bared to her. Feeding from him was satisfying on so many levels—the primal gratification of survival, the predatory desire to hunt and subdue, and the terrifying emotional intimacy of Maxim Freeman and everything he entailed. He was wolf kin. Baring his throat to her, letting her bite him there... she knew what it meant. She knew, and she couldn't deal with it.

But she couldn't pretend it wasn't there. That emotional charge. That weighted history. Max's scent and taste and his very essence filled all her senses. The flow of vital energy, the reciprocal exchange of pleasure for blood, connected them on every level—physical, emotional, spiritual—and it was terrifying. Jules never wanted it to end, and yet the need to protect herself, to put distance between them, made the very act itself feel like she was throwing herself off a cliff.

When she eased her fangs from his throat, she couldn't help but linger, tongue stroking over the wounds she'd made, soothing as they healed. Max was a helpless puddle beneath her, hauling in ragged, moaning breaths that made her whole body flush with a different kind of hunger.

"Jules," he gasped. "Fuck. It's so—so—" He arched up restlessly beneath her, lifting her so that her weight was no longer borne by her knees on the ground, but instead by the tender flesh between her thighs pressed against his abdomen.

She gasped at the sudden pressure, an unmistakably sexual sound. Max growled, hands rising along her sides as he tilted his head up to capture her mouth in a fierce kiss. He had to taste his blood in her mouth, but he didn't recoil. He only growled low in his throat, his hold tightening. Jules rocked herself against him, a surprised moan torn from her as his tongue teased the points of her fangs. Even though she'd already sated herself on his blood, the temptation to bite down, to taste him again, to send him back into that drunken languor, was hard to resist.

But she had to. She couldn't quite remember why, not when Max's tongue was in her mouth and his hands were roving over her body—but she knew, in some vaguely uneasy way, that she shouldn't be doing this. That sense of disquiet managed to allay the mind-shattering lust for just enough time for Jules to remember—

She hated Max.

Didn't she?

Just now, she didn't feel anything close to hate, but—

"Jules?" Max asked, cupping her cheek.

She jerked away from him, scrambled off of him. "No. We are not doing this," she said breathlessly, backing away from him. She couldn't let herself love the man who'd ripped her heart out and stomped on it. The man who'd condemned her to misery beyond anything she'd ever known. "I told you we weren't doing this."

Max had the grace to show his shame. "I'm sorry. I wasn't thinking. I shouldn't have—"

Jules waved away his apology. In truth, she couldn't lay the blame entirely at his feet. Maybe he had initiated the kiss, but she had returned it without any reservation. There was something about the raw physicality and intimacy of feeding that made sex feel like the natural outcome.

"Let's just... not talk about it." The spot where Jules had bit him had closed over, but the skin was still shiny and pink, and the sight of her mark on his neck did weird things to her chest. She had to look away from him.

Max regarded her for a moment. Finally, he nodded. "Yeah. Okay." He got to his feet. "We should get back on the road. That motel was at least a half-hour back."

CHAPTER 31

Jules woke the next night to the familiar scent of Max in his wolf form. She instinctively reached for him, intending to cuddle, but her hand met the hard wall of the bathtub, jarring sense back into her. She sat up abruptly, hauling in a sharp breath.

An inquiring whine came from the floor and a second later, a big, shaggy brown head regarded her over the lip of the tub. It took everything Jules had to resist petting him. Every night when she awoke, it was the same struggle. It was hard to remember that the giant wolf who looked at her with such hopeful adoration was also the man who'd broken her heart and abandoned her when she'd needed him the most.

"Shoo," she said lightly, as if she weren't suffocating on messy, conflicted feelings. "I need to wash up."

With a canine grumble, Max hauled himself to his feet and padded out of the bathroom.

Jules took a quick shower. After, while she stood in front of the mirror, combing her hair, she couldn't help but be impressed with how healthy she appeared now compared to how she'd been before feeding from Max. Looking at her, nobody would ever guess that she'd technically "died."

She leaned closer to the mirror, examining the texture of her skin. She glanced up, looking herself in the eye and suddenly froze. She'd always had dark brown eyes, but there was a faint reddish tinge to them now. Almost like Ragnvaldr's eyes. Like the eyes of all his monstrous cronies.

A tap sounded at the door. She nearly jumped out of her skin, whipping around to face the sound.

"Jules? You going to be much longer? I need a shower, too."

"Just a minute," she answered weakly. Dressing quickly, she pretended to still be combing her hair as she exited the bathroom, keeping her face averted from Max.

"Thanks." He went in, his scent washing over her as he passed by, awakening that predatory urge again.

She held her breath so that she couldn't smell him, fear and anxiety twisting in her gut. How long until her eyes turned completely red and she became the monster Max knew she'd be? Should she run now, while she still had some degree of self-control? With Max occupied in the shower, she'd have decent odds of escaping him—sparing him.

But then what? Where would she go? What would she do?

She spent too long dithering. The water cut off, and a few seconds later, Max emerged from the bathroom with only a small towel wrapped around his hips. Water beaded and ran down the firm plane of his chest, dripped from his hair, slicked his big body with a lascivious sheen. Jules wanted to tackle him to the ground and bite him *everywhere*. She wanted to cover him in her marks, render him senseless and groaning.

Those were the desires of a monster. She spun away from him, afraid to let him see her eyes—both for the redness and the insatiable hunger that had to be gleaming in them.

"Jules?"

"Hm?" Despite the fact that she hadn't even opened her mouth to utter that single, wordless syllable, her voice managed to quaver.

"Sweetheart, what's wrong?"

She sensed his approach, but she kept her back turned to him. "Nothing."

"Did I do something?" There was a ghost of feeling on her back—as if he'd started to reach for her, but drew back at the last second.

"No."

"I can tell that you're upset. Please tell me what I did. I need to fix it if I can."

Jules realized that she wasn't going to be able to hide it from him forever. She might as well get it over with. Turning to face him, heart like a stone, she met his gaze.

"My eyes are turning red," she whispered.

Max was quiet for a moment, intently searching her eyes. "Isn't this normal?" he finally said, anticlimactically unconcerned.

"Normal? My eyes are brown!"

Max gave her a sympathetic look. "As a human. But str—vampires have red eyes."

"Red eyes and fangs and a merciless lust for death and violence, right?" she demanded, frightened, angry, confused, ashamed.

"I was wrong about a lot of stuff, Jules," he answered her calmly. "But it looks like red eyes are just part of the deal."

"You weren't wrong," she snapped, acting out of fear and some self-destructive impulse. "I have to fight the urge to attack you all the time. I want to jump you from behind, pin you to the ground, and drink from you until you're helpless and moaning."

Max should've been horrified, but instead, a wicked half-smile tugged at one corner of his mouth. "Yeah?"

Confused by his reaction, Jules frowned. "I want to stalk you in the dark and take you against your will! I'm exactly what you thought I was!"

"It would never be against my will."

"What?"

"When you feed on me, it's one of the best feelings I've ever experienced."

Jules stared at him.

Max's smile grew into a feral grin. "I told you wolf kin play rough. If you want a fight, I can give you a fight. But just know that even if you take me down, have your way with me, I've won. Because I got exactly what I wanted."

"*Max*," she growled, a surprising sound that came from deep in her throat.

"Fuck, I'm getting hard just thinking about it, Jules. You want to use me in other ways while you're getting the blood you need, feel free."

AN HOUR LATER, THEY WERE ON THE ROAD, AND JULES WAS STILL stuck in stupefied silence. The hungry monster inside of her had been temporarily subdued—caught in a confused muddle of arousal, shock, intrigue, and dismay. Max glanced at her periodically, not saying anything, but seemingly unalarmed by her speechlessness.

His phone suddenly lit up on the center console. He glanced at it, then let out a sigh.

"I have to take this. I forgot to call them yesterday."

Jules watched mutely as he brought the phone to his ear.

"Hey, mom."

"Maxim! You didn't call! You said you would—"

"I know, I'm sorry. There was a lot going on yesterday. We—"

"What does that mean? Are you hurt? Did the strigoi—"

Max snarled, cutting his mother off. Wide-eyed, Jules turned to look at him.

"Maxim!" his mother gasped, sounding nearly as shocked as Jules was.

"You know her name," Max said tersely.

His mother was quiet.

"We're both fine," Max said after a tense pause.

His mother was still quiet. Max didn't bother to fill the silence this time. From the corner of her eye, Jules discreetly observed the tight clench of his jaw, the hardness in his gaze as he stared at the road ahead.

"She's going to kill you," his mother whispered brokenly.

Jules's heart clenched and she had to look away, staring hard out the window as her eyes burned.

"I'm still alive," Max said gently.

"But for how long? Please, please *come home!"*

Max was quiet. Jules stared at the passing scenery—more hills, more wildflowers, more fireflies. It turned into a blur as tears welled. It was bad enough when she knew Max hated her and wanted her dead. Until now, she hadn't fully comprehended how deeply the revulsion for vampires was ingrained in wolf kin. Just months ago—a lifetime ago, to be honest—Jules had spoken to Natasha over video chat, and even across that distance, she'd felt instantly embraced by the other woman.

Now she was a soulless monster who was going to destroy Natasha's son.

"My answer to that hasn't changed," Max said tiredly.

"*Max...*"

He sighed heavily. "I don't want to fight with you, Mom. But I can't keep having this conversation. If it's easier for us both, I'll go back to texting—"

"*No! Don't stop calling!*" Natasha pleaded. "*I'm sorry, kochanie. You know I love you. You know I just want... I just want you safe and...*" Her words dissolved into a sob.

Jules couldn't fight it anymore. Her tears spilled over. She turned further away from Max, trying to wipe discreetly at them.

"I know, Mom," Max said hoarsely. "I have to let you go, okay? I'll call tomorrow."

Jules blinked hard, willing the tears away, as Max bid his sobbing mother goodbye.

"I'm sorry you had to hear that," Max said. "I'll call when you're in your daysleep from now on."

"It's fine," Jules said, proud of how normal her voice sounded.

"It's not fine." A growl rumbled in his throat. "I can smell your tears."

"Oh." Jules swiped hastily at her cheeks, no longer trying to be discreet.

His grip tightened on the steering wheel, his gaze fixed on the road. "I never want to be the reason you cry, Jules, but I can't seem to stop hurting you."

This time, truly, it wasn't him. "I cry when I see or hear other people cry. I've always been like that." Sure, her heart was aching at the fresh reminder of how reviled she was by people whose good opinion meant too much to her. But it was Natasha's grief over her losing Max that had really gotten to her.

Max reached over, his big hand closing over hers. He squeezed gently. "It'll take time, but my parents will eventually understand. I know they will. So, don't cry for them, okay? You've been through enough. You don't need to take on other people's pain on top of it."

He squeezed once more before releasing her. Jules's hand felt suddenly cold without his touch. Rubbing them together, she gave him a casual nod, pretending his words hadn't affected her deeply.

───────

They reached Big Bend shortly after midnight. The air was comfortably cool, but there was a lingering heat radiating from the dry earth that warned of hot, hot days. They drove through the desert landscape with the windows down, taking in the sights and scents of the park as they meandered along empty roads. At a fork, Max rolled to a stop and looked to Jules.

"To the river or to the mountains?" he asked. They were the first words he'd spoken in several hours, and it almost startled Jules to hear his voice again.

She looked up at the signboard at the side of the road. "The river?" she suggested.

In all her years, she'd never set foot outside of the United States. Eric had occasionally gone overseas for conferences, but even though lots of academics took their spouses on those trips, Eric had never brought Jules. If she and Max went to the Rio Grande, she could look across its banks and at least *see* another country.

Max nodded, taking the right fork. The route to the river took them along a scenic drive that wended its way through desert and mountains. It was so different from the landscape where she'd grown up. Everywhere she looked, there was something new to goggle at. Huge cactuses growing out of the ground, when she'd only ever seen them in decorative pots on people's windowsills. Flat-topped mountains whose raw cliffsides were made of infinite stripes of ruddy volcanic rock. Even the air was different—dusty and spicy compared to the green, woodsy smell of home.

"It's beautiful," Max said, echoing Jules's thoughts exactly.

"It's strange. I've seen things like this in pictures. On the internet. On TV. But now I'm... *here*. I'm in it."

Max nodded. "I've felt that way since I left home."

Her chest tightened. *Home*. The home he'd said he would never return to—for her.

"You never left Alaska before?"

"No, I did. A few times as kids we flew to Poland to visit my mom's family. But it's a small town in the middle of nowhere. It really only felt 'foreign' because everyone was speaking Polish and the weather was so warm I thought I would melt."

"Polish weather?"

Max laughed a little. "I'm from damn near the Arctic circle, Jules. Summer in Poland is a lot hotter than summer in Longtooth."

"Well, Texas is going to cook you alive, then."

He smiled. "I'll survive."

Eventually, they reached a parking lot for a trailhead that led to the river. The vegetation shifted from desert scrub to thick, colorful grasses and small, sprawling trees. Big fluttering moths and small flies danced along the tops of the grasses, while the buzz of tree frogs and cicadas and other creatures surrounded them on all sides. The hike was short and easy, and within minutes, Jules was standing on the sandy bank of the Rio Grande, staring straight across at Mexico.

"I've never been to another country," she said.

"Want to cross?"

Jules turned to look at him, skeptical. "We can't cross. I don't have a passport. I'm legally dead!"

Max shrugged. "I don't see a customs office. We could swim over, sit on the bank. Then you'll be in another country."

"We can't do that!"

"Why not?"

"Because... because, what if we get caught?"

Max looked pointedly up and down the empty river banks. They stood at an open expanse, surrounded by tall grasses and low trees, but further upriver, huge cliffs enclosed each side of the water. There were no buildings, no lights. Jules could hear the sounds of night creatures, but no humans.

"What if we drown?"

"Jules," Max said, giving her a wry look. "You know that's not going to happen."

She grimaced, conceding that one. She'd yet to try swimming in her new afterlife, but she instinctively knew she'd be even better at it than she'd been as a mortal.

"If you don't want to, we don't have to. We can just walk along the river."

Now she felt like he was very gently calling her a chicken. "No. Let's do it."

"You sure?"

"Yeah." She toed off her sneakers and socks. After a moment's hesitation, she shimmied out of her jeans and pulled off her t-shirt. She might be impervious to hypothermia, but wet clothes were still unpleasant to trudge around in.

She could feel Max's discreet ogling, like fingers trailing up and down her exposed skin, but when she turned to look at him, he was busily removing his own shirt. When they were both stripped down to their underthings, Max was the first to wade into the river.

"The surface looks calm," he said, "but the current could be deceptive. Be careful."

Wasn't he the one just telling her she wouldn't drown? She followed him nervously into the water. They waded out further and further, the sand soft beneath their feet. When they were waist-deep, Max dove forward, beginning a smooth, powerful front crawl.

Jules was a good swimmer, but she'd never cared much for the overhand strokes. They felt like way more work than her lazy sidestroke. So she did her usual thing, as inelegant as it might look, and followed Max across the wide, wide expanse of the Rio Grande. The current grew stronger in the middle, pulling them faster downstream. Jules swam against it, easily done with vampiric strength.

As they neared the opposite bank, Jules put her feet down on the sandy river bottom. She walked out cautiously, listening for the sounds of humans. There was nothing but the night.

Max stood on the bank, hand held out to her. She took it unthinkingly, and he pulled her the rest of the way onto dry land.

"There. You're officially in another country."

"Technically, I am *very unofficially* in this country."

Max shrugged. "Maybe in the ordinary world. But you're not ordinary, Jules."

"Not anymore."

"You never were."

Stupidly, her heart fluttered. Max drew closer until she felt the heat of his body against her back. She stared down at the Mexican sand beneath her feet, unable to move, unable to breathe. Max's breath ghosted against the nape of her neck, soft and hot. The monster inside her awakened with a dark, twisting, stretch. The scent of him made her mouth water. The nerve-endings in her fangs throbbed.

"Max," she said thickly. "You can't stand that close. It's been two days since I fed."

"So?"

"So, I told you that I'm... I'm not nice, sweet Jules when I'm hungry."

A growl rumbled deep in his chest. She could almost feel the vibrations of it against her back.

"And I told you that I like it. You want to overpower me, Juliana?"

She shivered. The monster rose up in her, wicked and gleeful. "Max, don't."

"You want me to run from you?"

"Max."

"You want to hunt me down?"

"*Yes,*" she sighed, trembling with the effort of resisting her monster.

He let out a soft laugh, a puff of breath against her already-sensitive skin. "Alright."

Suddenly, he gripped her shoulders and threw her to the side. She landed on her rear end with an outraged gasp.

"You asshole!"

He laughed as he sprinted away from her, plunging into the tall grasses as he headed upriver.

Jules couldn't fight it anymore. His flight triggered a predatory response that filled her with an exhilarated, instinctive need to chase. She scrambled to her feet and raced after him. In his wolf form, he might have posed a challenge to her, but in his human form, he was no match for her speed. She caught up to him in seconds, her gaze focused on his neck as she prepared to tackle him.

But Max wasn't going to be easy prey. He twisted suddenly, juking hard to the left. Jules overran his sudden turn, forcing her to spin around and double back. But by the time she did, he was diving beneath the surface of the Rio Grande. With a snarl, she raced after him, churning through the shallows before kicking off to swim.

Max surfaced on the American side of the river, shooting her a wolfish grin as he scrambled onto the bank. Despite the hunger, she couldn't help an answering smile. It might have looked a little crazed to someone else, but it made Max laugh as he turned forward, surging into the cover of a small copse of spindly trees.

Jules clawed her way onto the bank and leapt into a sprinting run. She was forced to slow down to maneuver between the narrow, twisting trunks of the trees. She got flashes of Max as he darted through them, his scent taunting her, the heavy thud of his heart calling to her. Her stomach clenched pleasantly and her fangs throbbed. Her hunger was a potent, sensuous thing—no longer painful, but thrilling. No longer terrifying, but intoxicating. She wanted Max's blood just as badly as she wanted to make him weak and needy from her bite.

The trees thinned, and Max lost the slight advantage their twisting cover had given him. He tried to race for the water again, but Jules anticipated it this time, and cut him off with a diving tackle.

Strong as she was, though, Max was stronger. She unbalanced him, but he managed to stay on his feet. With a twist and growl, he flung her off. She landed on her hands and knees less than a yard away, and surged right back for him. He was ready for her this time, wrapping his arms around her and bringing her to the ground. They rolled through the grass, struggling against each other. Max caught her wrists, preventing her from grabbing hold of him, and used his body weight to bring them to an abrupt stop.

He sat astride her, grinning recklessly, with her wrists pinned to the ground on either side of her head. His pulse ticked frantically in his throat, visible even beneath the thick dark scruff on his neck, calling to her like a beacon. Sweat streaked his skin, and she wanted to lick it off of him just as badly as she wanted to bite him.

"What now, mighty huntress?" Max taunted breathlessly.

Jules planted one heel and shoved with her hips, managing to flip Max on his back, reversing their positions. She didn't need her hands to bite him. She dipped down, intending to take his throat, but Max twisted abruptly, throwing her off of him.

He scrambled to his hands and knees, but Jules was already on his back, one arm wrapped around his chest, fingers splayed over sweaty skin and hard muscle, while her other hand fisted in his hair, pulling his head back, exposing the long line of his throat.

"Got you," she taunted with a cruel laugh.

Max tried to buck her off, but she only tightened her hold on him as she brought her mouth to his throat. She tasted the salt of his sweat, the earthiness of his skin, and then her fangs pierced his jugular and the rich, decadent taste of his blood flooded her mouth.

Beneath her, Max stiffened, then groaned. The fight went out of him in a slow, downward slide until he was sprawled on the ground, helpless and moaning as Jules fed from him. She kept hold of him, one arm wrapped around his chest, one hand in his hair, while the rest of her body relaxed against his, savoring the warmth of his broad, strong back pressed against her. The pleasure of possessing him so completely eclipsed the base pleasure of feeding, filling her with a deviant kind of arousal. She wanted to clench her thighs around him, grind her clit against the hard plane of his back. It was a separate urge from hunger, but the two were inextricably intertwined. Feeding from him nourished her, but possessing him aroused her.

When she'd satisfied her hunger, she remained draped over him, gently tracing the bite mark with her tongue, stroking his hair instead of pulling it. But as Max's dazed euphoria wore off, reality set in for Jules. She'd just shown him exactly what she was, and she'd taken such sick pleasure in it.

She slid off of him, backing away nervously.

Max pushed himself up to sit, his gaze still a little foggy as it landed on her.

"Are you okay?" Jules asked in a small, fragile voice.

He gave her a slightly loopy smile. "Better than okay, sweetheart. Are *you* okay?"

Jules's brows shot up. "*Me?*"

His gaze slowly sharpened, the last of the feeding haze lifting. "Yes, you. I know you're scared of how it feels to want... this. I can see you're freaked out."

"I'm..." She trailed off uncertainly, taking in the sight of him. His big body was still sheened with sweat and river water. Sand and bits of grass were stuck in the hair on his chest, and a bit in his beard. As far as she knew, he hadn't shaved since he'd found her in Chicago, and his beard was getting scruffy, his hair a little long. It all combined to make him look so beautifully rugged and masculine and the fact that she'd caught him, taken him for her own, spoke to too many different parts of her.

"Turn your head," Jules said faintly, unable to stop herself.

Max's brow furrowed in confusion, then sudden understanding dawned. He twisted his head, lifting his chin to bear the swiftly-healing marks she'd left on his throat. She felt his gaze burning through her while she stared at the marks, some unnameable feeling swelling inside her. It felt brutal and sweet at the same time, and she didn't know quite what it was. All she knew was she wanted to bite him again—harder, deeper. Make it so he'd never heal. So he'd bear her mark forever.

"Jules," Max said gruffly.

The sound of his voice snapped her out of whatever

animalistic trance had taken hold of her. She blinked away the daze. "Sorry."

"Don't be sorry. I loved every minute. I want to play like that every night with you."

She tilted her head. "Play?"

"You weren't actually trying to kill me?" he asked wryly.

"No, of course not!"

"Then it's play. Hunt me all night, pin me down, do whatever you want to me. I like it all."

"Whatever I want?" she teased, not certain why she did.

Max shifted his position, leaning back and letting one knee splay downward, revealing his lap—where his hard cock jutted upward, encased by the wet cotton of his briefs. "Whatever you want," he assured her.

It was too much. She tried to tell herself she didn't want anything but blood from him, but it was an absolute lie. She was a soft-hearted idiot with no sense of self-preservation.

Forcing herself to be smart, she looked away from him. "I got what I wanted."

"I can smell that sweet pussy, Jules. I know you didn't get *everything* you want."

She gasped, shocked by the crudity, but also by the sharp bolt of arousal that spiked through her. "I— You— No! We're not doing that."

Max shrugged, but the heat in his eyes could have burned her. "Well, let me take care of this before we go back for our clothes." He got up and walked back into the cold river until the water rose past his waist. He sank out of sight for a moment, then bobbed back up several yards downriver before swimming back to shore and climbing out.

"Good enough," he declared, still obviously half-hard.

It took all of Jules's self-discipline to not constantly stare at it while they walked back to where they'd left their clothes.

"We've got a few hours until sunrise," Max said as he stepped into his jeans. "Should we follow the river for a bit? Or do you want to drive through the mountains?"

"I want to drive through the mountains," Jules answered readily.

"Then to the mountains we go."

CHAPTER 32

In the days that followed, Jules knew she was slipping. She was losing hold of the determination to keep distance between them. She couldn't help it. She couldn't spend every waking minute in Max's presence and not lose some of the barriers she'd built.

After Big Bend, they had to cross a significant chunk of Texas again to get to the Guadalupe Mountains, where Jules hunted Max through narrow canyons and scrub pine forest. He put up more of a fight this time, using his strength against her, and she knew it was because it ratcheted up her own excitement—made the arousal that much sharper and sweeter when she finally subdued him.

He didn't try to kiss her, didn't offer sex, but after she slid off of him and the feeding haze lifted, he leveled her with an incinerating look that said everything his mouth hadn't. Jules squeezed her knees together and reminded herself of the pain she'd endured under Ragnvaldr, but the problem was, that horror was starting to feel like something disconnected from Max. *This* Max, with his playfulness and consideration and patience, felt like a different person from the snarling, enraged man who'd sent her away. Just like cheerful, good-mood Eric had always felt so different from criticizing, impatient, insulting Eric.

She didn't want to be the sort of woman who lived with the constant threat of punishment just for the hope of a few scraps of pleasure.

Max isn't like that, a small part of her insisted.

Then why did he send you away when you needed him most?

And for that, she had no answer.

A COUPLE NIGHTS LATER, JULES STOOD AT THE WIDE-OPEN, glittering White Sands in New Mexico, taking in the view. Beside her, Max glanced around as if checking for something.

"What's wrong?" Jules asked.

"Nothing." He peeled his shirt off, then his jeans, and shifted into his wolf form. Eyes bright, he ambled up to Jules and nudged her hip with his head, pushing her.

"What are you doing?"

He leaped back and dipped into a playful bow, tail wagging, and then jumped forward to bluff charge her. She looked at him in abject confusion as he head-butted her hip, pushing her again, and then dipping back into a play bow, an unthreatening growl rumbling in his throat.

If he were an ordinary dog, Jules would assume he wanted to play. But he was anything but ordinary, and so far, their "play" had been a bit on the rougher side.

When Jules simply stared at him, he charged her again—and this time it wasn't a bluff. He shoved his shoulder against her hip, sending her to the ground.

"*Oof.*" She landed on her ass. Max stood over her, panting happily. He skittered a few yards and glanced back at her, tail wagging, as if to say *come get me.*

He wanted to be chased? Jules had just fed from him last night, so the predatory desire wasn't really there, but a juvenile impulse was urging her to give chase anyway.

She gave into the impulse.

She was faster than Max, even in his wolfskin, but instead of tackling him like she would to feed, she jumped in front of him, cutting him off, and forcing him to leap to the side instead of crashing into her. He rolled in the sand, then scrambled to his feet, racing back towards Jules with a crazy gleam in his eyes. Did he think he was going to outrun her? Jules turned and raced away from him.

But it turned out, running up a dune of sand really slowed a vampire down. While running on four clawed feet, with a lower center of balance, made it a lot easier. Max closed the distance between them, nipping playfully at her ass.

"Hey!" She objected, spinning around.

Max darted off like a hyperactive puppy, loping merrily down the dune. He couldn't laugh in his wolf form, but everything about his body language said he was incredibly pleased with himself. Rubbing the sore spot on her ass, she sprinted awkwardly down the sandy slope.

Their game lasted for hours. By the end, Max was panting with almost worrying effort, and Jules was streaked with sweat and sand. They collected Max's clothes and got back in the car, tracking sand everywhere.

Back at the motel, after they'd both showered, there was only a little time left before sunrise would drag her into her daysleep. Jules hesitated at the foot of the bed, debating. Max had bought the big sun reflectors meant for car windshields and blackout curtains at a Wal-Mart in northwest Texas, and he'd duct-taped them over the windows at every place they'd stayed since then. She could probably safely sleep in the bed.

But there was only one bed.

Max watched her, saying nothing, but she knew he was aware of her internal debate.

Smart Jules, cautious Jules, won the debate. She pulled the comforter off the bed. The bathroom was all humid and damp after their showers, so she had to towel the tub dry before she could crawl in.

"You sure you want to sleep in the tub?" Max asked through the closed bathroom door.

"Yes."

A soft silence. Then, "Sleep well, sweetheart."

Jules's throat tightened. She didn't reply.

From White Sands, they drove on to the Petrified Forest, where Jules walked among the colorfully striated badlands with Max at her side in his wolf form. It was easier to be with him like this. There was no talking. No weighted silences. She was just an anonymous explorer, roaming the night with her wolf sidekick.

From the Petrified Forest, they made their way to Mesa Verde, where, even in his wolf form, Max made it hard to forget who he was. As Jules stood at Long House Overlook, staring in awe at the remnants of the cliffside dwellings, Max nudged gently against her hip. She looked down at him—he had something in his mouth.

It was a giant pinecone. She took it from him. It was easily the largest pinecone she'd ever seen in her life, nearly the size of a football.

Max chuffed, and then looked away, gazing at the ancient dwellings. He didn't want the pinecone back. It was... it was for her?

She should drop it. Forget about it.

But she couldn't. She wanted it.

"Thank you," she said quietly.

AFTER MESA VERDE, THEY CROSSED THE BORDER INTO UTAH. In the middle of nowhere in the Great Basin Desert, they lay side by side on the coarse ground to watch vivid purple heat lightning arc across the clouds. It took everything Jules had not to reach for Max's hand.

As they lay peacefully together, a rusty, stuttering sound reverberated in Jules's chest with each exhalation.

Max lifted his head, a surprised grin on his face. "Jules, are you *purring?*"

That's exactly what she was doing, she realized. Mortified, she said, "No!"

"Yes, you are. You're purring." He reached over and patted her head. "Good kitty."

"You're going to lose that hand," she threatened—though the threat lost some of its weight when that stupid purr wouldn't stop rattling in her chest.

THE WATERS OF LAKE POWELL WERE A WELCOME RESPITE AFTER days of desert sand. They swam in a remote part of the lake, under a sky so bright with stars, they seemed close enough to touch. The night was so quiet and undisturbed, it was easy to feel like they were the only two people in the world.

"Marco," Max said suddenly, softly.

"What?"

"No, you say 'Polo'." He paused. "*Marco.*"

"Polo?"

Max started swimming towards her. Moving as quietly as she could, she drifted away from where she'd been. Even though his eyes were closed, Max turned, precisely attuned to her direction.

She gasped in outrage. "Using your nose is cheating!"

"Says who? The International Council of Pool Party Games?"

"Yes!"

Jules started swimming in earnest, trying to shake his pursuit. It turned out vampires weren't nearly as fast in water as they were on land. Max caught up to her easily, wrapping his arm around her waist and hauling her against him.

"Got you," he said, blinking his eyes open.

Jules was caught in the heated pin of his gaze. His body was warm and strong against hers, both of them stripped down to underwear. His face was close enough to kiss and, inadvertently, her gaze dropped to his lips.

"Jules," Max said, his voice dipping into a soft growl.

It was the sound of her name that broke the spell. She

pushed against his chest and he released her. She fluttered her feet, putting yards of water between them. Her heart thundered in her ears, so loud, she was sure Max must hear it.

He held her gaze intently, saying nothing.

———

NO MATTER HOW HARD SHE TRIED TO STAY DETACHED AND objective, her masochistic heart wouldn't be told. It wouldn't listen when he let her hunt him, when he ran from her as fast as he could, fought her attack so earnestly, only to surrender to her bite so beautifully. But it was so much more than that. It was everything that made her fall in love with him in the first place, and she was terrified of the weak, needy part of her that wanted so badly to just give in.

It was the way he took care of her without being asked. It was the way he looked at her with such longing in his eyes. It was the way he'd made so much effort to show her places she'd always dreamed of seeing. It was the way long drives were made short by comfortable conversations and easy laughter, just like they used to have. It was the way she woke every night to find him sleeping as close as he could to her in his wolf form.

And every night, her heart softened a little more. But her heart wasn't in charge. Her mind was. And in her mind, she hoarded every hurt she'd accumulated, and kept her foolish, soft heart on a short leash.

So when she lay tangled with Max as he came down from the euphoria, both of them panting and sweating, she always found the strength to pull away from him without giving in to the overwhelming desire. When he stood close to her as they both took in some new and stunning sight, she resisted the impulse to take his hand, to lean against him. When she prepared for her daysleep, she ignored the urge to make space for Max to sleep beside her.

She told herself she was being strong, smart, pragmatic. But, deep down, she knew what it really was.

Fear.

THEY WERE AT A QUIET LITTLE MOTEL IN THE MIDDLE OF NOWHERE, Utah, when Jules woke to hear Max's voice.

"I wish you could meet her in person. You'd understand."

It took Jules a second to realize he was on the phone. She remained utterly still, listening.

"Won't you come home? At least for a little while?" It was his mother's voice, softly accented, cautious and faint.

"Jules is my home," Max answered simply, calmly.

Jules remained silent and still, holding her breath until Max's conversation with his mother came to a bittersweet end.

"I gotta go. Jules is going to wake up pretty soon. Love you, Mom."

"I love you, my baby. You know I do. Please—please be safe."

"I am. I really am."

When he hung up, he sat with his back against the tub, head hanging, a long sigh gusting out of him. Jules waited, holding her breath, giving him time to collect himself. When enough time had passed, she finally let herself breathe.

Max turned to face her. The stark, stressed expression fell away as his gaze met hers. He smiled so easily, it made her heart lurch.

"You're awake. Ready to go?" He held his hand out to her.

She should have done what she always did—given him a polite smile that promised nothing and got up on her own.

Instead, she took his hand and let him pull her to her feet.

CHAPTER 33

"What's the endgame with all this?" Max raised his eyebrows in question, eyes still on the road.

"You know—all the traveling. We can't do this forever. Unless you've got a trust fund, you're going to run out of gas and motel money."

"I mean... I don't know if it's technically a 'trust fund,' but I have, uh... an account."

Jules sat back. "Are you telling me you're secretly rich?"

He smiled ruefully. "No. But my cousin Jess and a few others manage the financials for the pack. Everyone's got a personal account. I don't know the ins and outs, but it's basically... I mean, as long as I don't go buy a Lamborghini or something, the balance is more or less self-sustaining."

"Are you serious? How much money do you have?"

He winced, looking mildly ashamed. "I don't actually know. Like I said, Jess handles it."

"Millions?" she prompted.

"No. Not that much. A few hundred thousand, though." He shrugged.

Jules was still flabbergasted. To just have a few hundred thousand in spending money... she could've escaped Eric a lot sooner. She could've... well, she could've done a lot of things she never got to.

But I'm doing them now.

"So, what's the plan then, Daddy Warbucks?"

Max choked on his own breath. "*Daddy?*" he asked hoarsely.

Jules couldn't help laughing. "Not like *that*, you perv. It's from *Annie*—the orphan who gets adopted by a rich guy." She paused as something occurred to her. "Wait, did you like that?"

Max looked stunned. Too late, she realized that the question implied she cared about his sexual tastes—as if sex were at all relevant for them. Which it wasn't.

Well. It wasn't supposed to be.

Cheeks hot, she quickly changed the subject before Max could say anything. "You never answered my original question—what's the plan, here? Are we just supposed to wander aimlessly forever?"

Max paused, thinking. "Well... not forever. Just until we get tired of traveling. Or we find somewhere that feels like a good stopping place. I can find a job and I probably have enough money to buy us a small house."

Us. Buy us *a house.* She let herself imagine it for a brief moment before unexpected resentment rose up and viciously crushed the fantasy. She wasn't going to build her whole future on Max. She wasn't going to build her future on *any* man. She'd figure things out, learn how to be independent, and then she'd set him free to return to his pack, where he belonged.

"Oh." But she couldn't tell him that there was no future for them. She'd told him already. She'd told him too many times and she couldn't force the words out anymore. But she also couldn't just meekly agree with him. "Well, what if *I* want to work?"

"I don't know, Jules. You're sort of... legally dead, remember? I mean, I guess if you found some kind of remote work where they never had to see your face, you could use my name. But that might call unwanted government attention if I'm filing taxes for two full-time jobs."

"Well, maybe I'll work under your name and you'll be my little house—" she almost said *husband* "—pet."

Max's mouth quirked faintly. He caught the slip but didn't call her on it. "I'll fetch the paper every morning and chase off intruders."

"Perfect." She looked away, cheeks still flushed, pretending to watch the scenery go by. In truth, she was hyper-aware of Max's gaze burning into her.

Eventually, he had to look back at the road, and Jules could breathe again. They sat in charged silence until lights appeared on the horizon—a small mountain town.

"Pull off the highway up here," Jules said, grateful for a new conversational topic. "You need to eat."

Max had been living off of an irregular combination of fast food and hunted game over the last few weeks, and while he looked perfectly healthy, Jules worried that he wasn't getting enough. He was losing a couple of pints of blood every few days, thanks to her.

He took the next exit, slowing as they rolled down the

town's main street, past brick and stucco buildings with flat roofs and steeply-angled sun shades. There were no fast food places in the tiny town, but there was a small motel with an attached restaurant that had beer signs glowing in the front window.

When they finally found a space to park in the packed lot behind the bar, Max glanced at Jules. "You sure you want to go in here? It's going to be loud and crowded."

Jules hesitated. Occasionally, the hyper-sensitivity of her enhanced senses took her by surprise, overwhelming her. Out in the wilderness, it was fine. But when they came through towns and cities, she often had to squeeze her eyes shut and plug her ears against all the stimuli.

"I'll be fine," she finally said, steeling herself. "You need to eat."

"I can always hunt."

"You need more than wild game. You ever heard of rabbit starvation?"

"We call it 'mal de caribou,' but I take your point. Just... here." He reached across her to pop open the glove compartment, taking out a container full of little foam bullets and handing it to Jules.

"What is—oh. Earplugs?"

"I bought them after that gas station in Colorado. Thought it might help."

A few days ago, before crossing into Utah, Jules had had to duck out of a gas station where Max was buying snacks because the lights were too bright and the music was too loud and the coolers were making a buzzing sound that made her want to rip her own skin off. It hadn't even occurred to her that there might be a way to accommodate the oversensitivity.

She stared down at the earplugs, overwhelmed by a wave of something both soft and crushing.

"Jules? Are you... is this okay?"

"Yeah," she said gruffly, twisting the container open to fish out a pair of earplugs. "Yeah, good thinking. Thank you."

He tapped a little overhead compartment that swung open to reveal a pair of sunglasses. He handed them to Jules. "Take these, too. In case there's flashing lights or something."

She hung the sunglasses from her shirt's collar, swallowing past the sudden tightness in her throat. "Thank you," she said again, faintly.

"Of course."

As they walked up to the door, Jules fitted the earplugs into her ears. Inside, the bar was small and dimly lit, but packed full of people. Along the back wall, there was a small stage where several middle-aged men were in the process of setting up speakers. The din of dozens of conversations came through the earplugs like a distant hum. It was surprisingly tolerable.

After weaving through the crowd, they were able to find an empty pub table in a less-crowded corner.

"You going to be able to handle all this noise?" Max asked.

Despite the earplugs, she could hear him well enough. "I think so."

"If you want to leave, just tell me. We'll go right away, okay?"

That tightness squeezed her throat again, but Jules kept cool, giving him a mild smile. "I'll be alright."

A second later a harried waitress appeared with a notepad. "Hi! What can I get for you guys?"

Jules looked around the bar as Max put in an order for the both of them. She wouldn't eat anything, but Max would easily eat both portions. The waitress left and, a moment later, Jules became conscious of Max's gaze on her.

"When you're around other people, do you ever... do you want to feed from them?"

Jules looked at him, surprised—not by the question, but by the tone of his voice and the look in his eyes. He wasn't worried about the safety of everyone around them. He was jealous.

That shouldn't have pleased her so much.

"No," she answered truthfully. "Nobody smells as good as you do."

Max only smiled at her, but she could swear she saw his wolf looking back at her, hazel eyes turned to molten gold.

The food arrived and while Max ate and Jules people-watched, the men who were setting up speakers returned to the stage with mic stands and instruments.

Max lifted his head at the sound of a few test chords, looking over his shoulder at the stage. "Live music?" There was an eagerness in his expression that Jules wouldn't have expected for some middle-aged cover band in a rinky-dink bar in the middle of nowhere.

"Looks like it," Jules said.

"We *never* get live bands in Longtooth. If you want to hear live music, you have to fly out to Anchorage. *Maybe* Fairbanks if you're lucky."

Jules looked back at the gray-haired, goatee-sporting, dad-sneakers-wearing band members with new appreciation. "Let's stay for a while."

Max swiveled back to face her, brows drawn together. "We were supposed to get to Bryce Canyon tonight."

Jules shrugged. "It'll still be there tomorrow night."

An hour later, Jules found herself being coaxed by Max to join the rest of the small crowd on the dance floor. He'd had two beers, downed in quick succession when the chicken wings turned out to be hotter than he'd expected, and while he was not terribly drunk, there was a reckless edge to his smiles.

"I'm not much of a dancer," she protested weakly.

"Nobody's going to care. Come on, just one dance. Please?"

The band's repertoire seemed to consist mostly of classic country songs, and they were in the middle of an admittedly good cover of "Help Me Make It Through The Night."

"Come on," Max said softly, eyes beseeching as he held out a hand to her.

Without thinking, Jules took it. A radiant smile lit up his face as he tugged her off of her stool. She let him lead her to the dance floor and then found herself suddenly reeled in close to him. She stumbled, her hands flying to his chest to brace herself. Smooth as butter, Max caught her left hand in his, slid his other hand to her waist, and swept her into a slow, swinging two-step. As the song slipped into the chorus, he pulled her close and deftly turned them both, his knee pressing briefly between her thighs as he did.

Jules's gaze flew to his, her eyes wide. "*Max*," she said unsteadily.

He grinned rakishly and turned her again, keeping her moving in that slow, rocking, sway, with his big warm body pressed close to hers, his hand holding hers, his guiding touch firm on her waist. By the time the song ended, Jules was breathless, even though all they'd done was sway together.

She started to pull away from him, but as the band played the opening notes for the next song, Max kept hold of her and tugged her in close again.

"One more dance."

She should have said no. She shouldn't have agreed to even one dance in the first place. But instead of doing the sensible thing, Jules found herself falling back into rhythm with him, letting herself be guided by his comforting strength as they swayed along to "Slow Hand."

Max managed to keep her on the dance floor for the next song—a faster one, in which it was all she could do to keep up with Max's lead—and the next, and the next, and the next, until they were both panting and sweaty. Max had another beer, and then they were back on the dance floor, his guiding touch growing more intimate, his knee sliding between her thighs with each step.

"Max," she tried to say his name as a warning, but it came out like a breathless plea.

He bent his head, pressing his nose to her hair and inhaling. "Hm?"

Pressed in a noisy, sweaty crowd, surrounded by music and bodies and so many scents and heartbeats, she should have been completely overwhelmed. But Max consumed the entirety of her focus. She heard only *his* heartbeat, smelled only *his* scent, was aware only of his strong hands and his dangerous smile and the heat in his eyes.

Her fingers curled into his shirt, gripping him with a shaking hand. "I need—" She couldn't bring herself to say it.

Max brought his mouth to her ear, lips brushing the edge as he asked, "What do you need?"

Hunger surged up, hot and hectic and needy. She pulled out of his arms.

"Jules, are you—"

"Come with me." She turned her back on him and walked off the dance floor, unable to suppress the sinuous stride of a hunting predator. She glanced back over her shoulder, through the wake she'd parted in the bar, to see Max staring after her, looking just as hungry as she felt. She touched her tongue to the tip of one fang, and a visible shiver ran through Max. Turning away from him, she wove through the crowd to the dark hallway that led to the bathrooms and an employees-only exterior door.

The door opened into a quiet little alley on the side of the building. Max came through the door a split second after Jules, and she reacted instantly—shoving him up against the building and pressing her whole body against his as she sank her fangs into his neck.

"Fuck!" He stiffened at first, but as the effect of her bite worked its way through his veins, he sagged against the wall. He gusted out a heavy breath. "Jules, honey," he said unsteadily, reverently.

One big hand came up to cup the back of her head, the other arm wrapped around her waist, holding her close, urging her on. His blood was rich and hot, flooding her mouth and filling her senses. His heavy breaths turned into moans, each one louder than the last, forcing Jules to cover his mouth with her hand—the music was loud inside, but somebody in the parking lot might hear him. It felt rude, but also wickedly hot, to be gripping his face with one hand, his shirt with the other, while she took what she wanted from him. And apparently Max thought so, too. She could feel his rising erection pressed against her hip and she couldn't help but grind against him a little. Behind the seal of her palm, his moans turned into thick, muffled pleas.

The heady pleasure of it all made her feel a little off-kilter, a little drunk. The loss of control startled her, and she pulled back from him with a gasp as it dawned on her—she was getting drunk from his blood. Max was still lost to the feeding high, eyes closed, face a mask of pained ecstasy. Looking at him like that made her head spin, her stomach dip.

"Max," she breathed his name, half demand, half plea.

His eyes fluttered open, vague and blissed. His pupils were blown wide, the irises just thin rings of gold. As he focused on Jules, his gaze gradually sharpened. The heat there could have incinerated her on the spot.

This time, *she* was the one who forgot. She couldn't help herself. She rose up onto her tiptoes so that she could press her lips to his. He met her with an eager growl, his firm embrace becoming crushing as he opened his mouth against hers, hot tongue tracing along the seam of her lips. The kiss was overwhelming in its intensity. Weeks of pent-up desire, frustration, and longing, poured into that kiss, stealing her breath and lighting up every one of her senses. She rocked against the hard ridge of Max's cock as she kissed him, making them both moan with agonized need.

"A room," Jules gasped against his mouth.

"Hm?" He leaned down, trailing hot kisses along her jaw as she gasped for breath.

"Need a room," she panted, pointing weakly at the *Vacancy* sign glowing above the bar.

Max dropped down to a crouch suddenly, unexpectedly.

"What—"

He slung her over his shoulder, making her gasp, then

stood up and started towards the attached motel. She thumped him on the back, giddy and breathless. In answer, his free hand landed on her ass with a hearty smack. He set her back on her feet before they went into the office where the motel's front desk was located. Getting a room was the work of a minute, and just as quickly, they were back outside, Jules slung over Max's shoulder again as he trotted towards their room.

He carried her inside, kicked the door shut, and threw her down on the bed. He stood over her breathing raggedly, but not from exertion. Jules was breathing just as hard as she met the dark intensity of his gaze. He put one knee on the bed, then the other, bracketing her legs between his own. He loomed over her, bracing his hands on either side of Jules's head, before sinking down to take her mouth in another soul-searing kiss.

Slowly, he eased his body down until she was trapped beneath the full weight of him. She spread her thighs around his hips, circled her arms around his neck, clinging to him tightly as she let the kiss burn her from the inside out.

He broke the kiss suddenly, his weight still bearing down on her, his forehead pressed to hers. "Tell me this is real, Jules. Tell me you want this."

"Yes," she panted against his mouth. "I want this. I want you. Please, Max."

He kissed her again, a fierce claiming of her mouth. His hands went to her jeans, unbuttoning them, unzipping them, pulling them down her legs along with her underwear. He slid down her body, giving her no warning before he buried his face between her thighs.

"Ah! God!" she cried out, clutching the bedding for support as he threw her legs over his shoulders. His mouth covered her pussy, tongue stroking hungrily through her folds, and his beard abraded her thighs. He went down on her the way he kissed—deep, thorough, open-mouthed kisses lavished over sensitive, slick flesh.

"Fuck, I missed this taste," he said desperately, licking straight up her center like she was a lollipop.

Her head fell back, one hand reaching to thread her fingers through his hair. He growled against her, the vibrations going straight to her clit, making her cry out again. His tongue stroked over that sensitive peak, and then his lips closed over it so he could suck in rhythmic pulses that made Jules's whole body clench and her spine arch. She came apart with a gasping cry, hips rocking against the stunning pleasure of his mouth, fingers curled tightly in his hair.

When she'd come back down from her climax, Max kissed his way up her belly, pushing her shirt higher and higher as he went. She lifted herself up and pulled her bra and shirt off over her head, baring herself completely to him. He was still fully dressed, and there was something so incredibly hot about the contrast in vulnerability. She reached for him, and he came to her, sinking down over her as he met her in another scorching kiss. She tasted herself on him, scented herself on his beard, and it made some dark and possessive part of her brain light up with greedy pleasure.

That same part of her brain made her rip his t-shirt off his body.

"*Fuck*, Jules," he gasped as her hands roved over his bare chest.

She slid her hands down his abdomen, reaching for the button on his jeans. She managed to unfasten it without ripping it clear off. The zipper she eased more carefully, breath hitching as she felt the hot weight of his erection brush against her fingers. Max groaned at the contact and his cock pulsed.

"I need to be inside you," Max said, kissing urgently along her jaw and her throat. "Let me in, sweetheart."

"Yes," Jules breathed, already arching up against him. "I need you. Please, Max."

He shoved his jeans and underwear down his legs and settled his weight between her thighs. The head of his cock brushed along the seam of her pussy, finally finding her entrance and sinking in.

"Oh god," Jules panted, clinging to him, legs wrapped around his hips. "So good—you feel *so good*."

Max moved inside her, long, deep thrusts that filled her all the way up. Her clit was still sensitive from his mouth, and now the rhythmic press of his pelvis was enough to have her spiraling towards another climax.

"Oh god, I'm coming already," she gasped, tightening her thighs around his waist. "Don't stop. Don't st—*ah!*" Her whole body tensed and trembled as her orgasm crested. Max rode her through it with the same deep strokes that got her there.

When she came back down, he was still there, steady and strong, his weight pinning her down as his hips rolled against hers, his cock filling her with perfect ease. His mouth found hers in a heated collision, lips sucking, tongues sliding. He felt so good on top of her, inside her. So right. She arched beneath him, a sated moan rising in her throat. Max's thrusts came faster, shorter. His breathing hitched, turned ragged. With a desperate groan, he shuddered, pulsing hotly inside her as he came.

Spent, he slumped to the side, half sprawled over her,

breathing gustily into the comforter. "My Jules," he murmured, pulling her against him. "I missed you. Needed you."

She lay weakly in his arms, content for now, but aware there was a reckoning coming.

CHAPTER 34

When Jules woke, she was still in Max's arms. The rightness of it, the overwhelming comfort of being held by him, warred with the panic and self-loathing.

"Are you awake?" Max asked in a sleep-husky voice.

No sense in lying. "Yeah."

"Good." He dropped a kiss on the top of her head. "I didn't want you to wake up alone, but I really want to take a shower."

"I need one too," Jules admitted.

Max nuzzled his face into the crook of her neck. "Come take one with me, then."

She shook her head, drawing away from him as she curled up into the blankets. "I'm going to be lazy for a little longer. Go ahead." She needed time to think.

Max regarded for a moment, his expression carefully neutral. "Alright," he finally said. "I'll just be a few minutes."

Jules lay on the bed, staring up at the ceiling, while she listened to Max turn the water on, then the sound of the spray hitting his body. His scent permeated the blankets, and she couldn't help pulling them to her face to breathe in.

She had to acknowledge that she'd been fooling herself. She was still completely in love with him. But she also still hated him a little bit, and she didn't know how to reconcile the two. She wasn't sure she could ever forgive him, but she also knew she couldn't hold onto this anger when she loved him. Both felt impossible. And she hated herself for it. She hated that she was so weak and so desperate for love that she was willing to overlook the way he hurt her.

She could try to convince herself that she was simply being blinded by sex and bloodlust, but it was more than that. So much more. It was the way he slept beside her during the day. The way he stood up to his family and his pack for her. The pleasure he took from her pleasure. His humility and willingness to admit wrongdoing and apologize. His dedication to making sure all her needs were met—not just blood and sex, but the comfort of her daysleep and the clothes she wore and the sights she wanted to see and the places she wanted to visit and...

It was too much. *He* was too much.

The shower was still running when Max's phone lit up on the bedside table. Stirring herself to finally sit up, she leaned over to read the screen.

Mom.

Jules stared at the phone, her heart in her throat, her pulse thundering in her ears. Just as it should have gone to voicemail, Jules found herself picking it up and answering it.

Except, she couldn't speak.

"Hello?" Natasha asked after a beat of Jules's trembling silence. "Max?"

Still, no words would come.

"Maxim," Natasha said, sounding a little more urgent. "You are worrying me. Please answer."

Jules swallowed. "Um... Max is in the shower right now," she said, her voice a faint whisper.

"Oh!" Natasha breathed in sharply. "Oh—this is... this is..."

"Jules," she provided faintly. "Juliana Wolfe."

Natasha was silent for a moment. Finally, almost apologetically, she said, "Juliana Wolfe is dead."

"Well, briefly," Jules conceded.

A small, surprised snort of laughter came from the other end of the line. A beat of silence followed, then a sigh. "I can't trust this conversation. How do I know this isn't a trick of some kind?"

"What kind of trick?" Jules asked, genuinely perplexed.

"I don't know. Tricking me into believing what Max believes, so there's one less person to suspect you?"

"Why would I do that?"

"Because..." Natasha sighed. "That's what strigoi do."

Jules cringed at the hateful word but didn't say anything about it. "Hang on," she said instead, "I'm going to send you a photo." Keeping Natasha on the line, she went into Max's photos and flicked through them until she found the one he'd taken of the two of them at Arches National Park, standing in front of Delicate Arch, with the La Sal Mountains in the background. The moon was full overhead, the red rocks bleached to midnight blues. Max was smiling happily at the camera while Jules covered a laugh with her hands—he'd caught her off-guard by telling her, "Let's see if you show up on camera."

She *did* show up. In all her silly, smitten, soft-hearted vulnerability.

There was silence on Natasha's end for a long time—so long, that Jules started to wonder if the call had dropped.

"You both look very happy," Natasha finally said, her voice tight with emotion.

"I love him," Jules admitted in a whisper, eyes burning as tears welled. "I know he misses you. He misses his pack."

"If you love him, then you want the best for him—tell him to come home."

Jules almost scoffed. "Do you think he would listen if I did?"

Natasha let out a small, rueful laugh. "He's stubborn like his father."

"He told me he was persistent like his mother."

Natasha laughed again, a warmer sound this time. "Perhaps." A beat of silence. A sigh. "I want to believe him. I want to believe you."

"Then do it," Jules said softly. "You know you can't change his mind, so why agonize over it? Why let yourself be torn up by future what-ifs when you could just be happy in the present?"

A thoughtful, "*Hm.*" And then, "Are you talking about me, or yourself, myszka?"

Jules hesitated. "I don't know."

Suddenly, the water turned off in the bathroom.

"I have to go," Jules said quickly, not sure why she felt the need to hide their conversation. "But if you call back in a few minutes, Max will take the call."

"Thank you," Natasha said quietly.

WHEN JULES GOT OUT OF THE SHOWER, MAX WAS SITTING ON THE edge of the bed with his phone in hand.

"You talked to my mom?"

She froze. "Um..."

"Did it go okay?"

He wasn't mad. Her heart returned to its normal rate and she let out a slow breath. "It went better than I would've expected," she said. "I sent her a picture of us."

"Yeah?" He smiled. "Which one?"

"In front of the arch. When you made that insensitive joke about whether I'd show up on camera."

His grin sharpened. "You thought it was funny."

She couldn't help but return his smile. He was so goddamn irresistible, in every possible way. He was funny and sweet and charming and handsome and strong and sexy and protective. Except when he hadn't been.

Slowly, her smile died.

With it, Max's died too. "Is it possible for you to ever forgive me?" he asked quietly, eyes dark with shame and regret. "I don't mean immediately. I know you'll need time. But... eventually? Some day?"

Jules sank down to sit beside him on the bed, an arm's length of open space between them. "I'm still so angry," she whispered, her voice breaking on the last word. "I understand why you thought the way you did. I get it, especially after hearing your conversations with your family. But... I never got to work through the anger, because I was too scared of you when it was at its worst. But now that I'm not scared of you anymore, it feels too late to do anything. But the anger's still there... poisoning everything."

Max listened quietly the whole time, looking haunted when she said she was scared of him, but not reacting otherwise.

"You deserve to feel angry, Jules. It's not too late to... to do whatever you have to about it. Do you want to fight me?"

"What?"

"You want to beat the shit out of me? I wish someone would. I deserve it."

That admission should have soothed her anger, but it only added to it. How did he know what she needed or what he deserved? "You don't even know the extent of what happened."

He turned to her, keeping space between them, but holding her gaze with heavy intensity. "Then tell me."

And like that, the floodgates opened. Max listened in bleak silence as Jules detailed every cruelty and torment she'd suffered under Ragnvaldr. By the time she was done, he was blanched and tense, his gaze distant.

"Fuck, Jules," he said hoarsely. "Of course you're angry. You should hate me."

"I don't hate you." She realized with some surprise that it was true. In telling her story, in seeing him face the truth of what had happened to her, it was like the poison she'd been carrying had been drawn out. She didn't want to punish Max. She just wanted him to understand. And now he finally did. She took in a breath and let it out, feeling lighter, unburdened.

But when she glanced at Max, he was the opposite. She'd had weeks—months, even—to come to terms with what had happened to her. Max was just learning so much of it now. He hadn't lived it, but she knew how seriously he took his responsibilities to those he cared about. She knew he'd be feeling it like a knife in his heart. And she was sad that he had to take that pain in order for her to heal, but she wasn't sad enough to soften the blow. Pain could be cleansing, renewing.

"Do you need to feed?" Max asked. There was a darkness in his voice that she wasn't used to. Not the usual wicked eagerness. Instead, there was something almost angry in the question. His anger didn't scare Jules—she knew it was directed at himself.

And she knew what he wanted. He wanted the cleansing purge of pain. He wanted punishment for his sins. He wanted Jules to absolve him by taking her pound of flesh.

"I just fed last night."

"You stopped early."

She had. The realization that she was getting drunk off his blood had shocked her, and then lust had distracted her.

"We can go out to the middle of nowhere," Max said, still with that simmering anger in his voice. "I'll give you a good chase."

He wanted to suffer? He wanted to be hunted and hurt and used? Jules wasn't principled enough to deny him.

"Alright. Let's go."

They set out from the motel on foot. Just a mile outside of the small town was an undeveloped state wilderness area. The land was a strange mixture of rocky cliffs, red desert sand, and scrubby, sparse forest. When they'd gotten far enough away from any roads, Max turned to her, that bleakness still in his eyes. She wanted to comfort him, to will it away—she'd gotten what she needed. She didn't want any more suffering. But Max didn't want comfort. She knew that. He wanted punishment. So she'd give him what he needed.

She bared her fangs in a cruel smile. "Better run, wolfie."

He didn't shift. Instead, he remained in his human form —his slower, weaker form—as he sprinted down into a shallow canyon where small, twisting trees grew along a mostly dry riverbed. Jules sank down to sit on the lip of the canyon, letting her legs dangle in the empty air, giving Max a good head start. He wouldn't want it to be over too quickly.

When he'd had enough time to put at least a mile between the two of them, Jules slid off the ledge, hopping nimbly down the canyon's sloping face until she stood at the riverbank. Max's footprints marked the sandy, hard-packed earth. Jules followed them at a casual stroll, letting the predatory pleasure of the hunt take over her awareness. She could follow his scent, have him in an instant, but where would the fun be in that? She'd rather make him sweat. She wanted to hear his heart pounding as he realized she was closing in on him.

But Max wasn't without his tricks. Only a quarter-mile upriver, Jules realized the bastard had laid a false trail, and she'd fallen for it like a complete rube. Suppressing an irritated growl, she backtracked, circling the path until she found another scent trail. Less cocky now, she followed it with intense focus.

She ended up following two more false trails—one that circled back on itself, and another that stopped dead in the middle of nowhere. The frustration only fueled her predatory impulses, which she suspected was exactly what Max wanted.

After the third false lead, she gave up on tracking him by scent. Closing her eyes, holding her breath, she simply listened. She heard the wind rustling the scrubby desert plants, nighttime critters skittering over the sandy soil, the buzz of insects, and the chirps of bats. She heard a thousand little heartbeats coalescing into a sound like a gentle rainstorm. And beneath it all, she heard the steady drumbeat of the one pulse she wanted most. Smiling her satisfaction, she set out again, ignoring his footsteps and his scent, following only the siren call of Max's heart.

It didn't take long to find him, still steadily moving, laying a circuitous track that would have frustrated her endlessly if she'd still been relying on her nose.

Keeping to the shadows of the trees, just out of range of wolf kin night vision, she called, tauntingly, "Hello, darling."

Max froze. His heartbeat accelerated. It called to Jules like the Pied Piper's melody. Max may have been a wolf, but Jules was the apex predator here. And just like any startled prey animal, Max did the predictable thing—he ran.

Jules laughed. Even if he shifted into his wolf form, he wouldn't be able to outrun her. In a matter of seconds, she was on him, tackling him to the hard ground. Max rolled, managing to use momentum to fling her off his back. But she landed easily on her feet, returning to him before he even found his footing.

Jules was fast, but Max was stronger. He bucked her off and managed to get to his hands and knees before Jules was on his back again. She could've easily bitten him, subdued him, but she was enjoying the game. Max was breathing hard, struggling to meet her speed with his strength. But this wasn't a match of brute strength—it was a match of agility, and Jules had the edge. So she played with him, letting him escape for a few seconds, again and again, before taking him back down each time, gradually exhausting him. Sometimes she let him get to his feet before she took him down. Sometimes she even let him run a few yards. Sometimes she stopped him with a tackle. Sometimes she simply hooked his ankle.

When he collapsed beneath her weight for the last time,

failing to rise from the ground, his heart was a thunderous beat in the quiet of the night, making her fangs ache and her stomach clench. His big body trembled beneath hers, his face pressed to the dirt, gasping for ragged, rasping breaths.

Jules was not exactly at her peak, either. Despite her advantage in speed, wrestling a full-grown wolf kin man to the ground over and over again took its toll. Sitting astride his back, she gripped his hair roughly with hands whose trembling she had to hide. She pulled his head back, baring the long line of his neck. His pulse ticked rapidly beneath his skin, a hypnotic temptation.

He groaned, defeated, as she lowered her face to his sweat-sheened skin, licking across the tic of his pulse.

"This is going to hurt," she whispered against the shell of his ear.

He groaned again, a shiver chasing over his skin.

Before her own weakness could show, Jules brought her fangs to his pulse, and bit. Max cried out, a wordless objection, or plea, or apology—she didn't know which. She pulled harder on his hair, stretching his neck for her own ease, and bit into him again, opening a new wound, giving herself more blood flow. She bit him a third time and closed her lips over the wounds, letting his hot, rich blood flood her mouth. She drank him down in lavish, careless gulps. He moaned with each one, the sound carrying down the canyon as his body remained limp and helpless beneath her.

She gorged herself on him, and when she couldn't draw anymore, she lay atop him, tracing her tongue over the mess she'd made of his neck. The wounds healed beneath her ministrations, and when no more blood was flowing, she let herself relax against him, face tucked into the crook of his neck, arms stretched along his.

They lay like that in the quiet of the night, both breathing hard, Jules's breaths underscored by the deep thrum of her purr. Something had changed between them. Something had shifted, cracked apart, and then sealed together again in the correct configuration, like a broken bone finally being properly set.

The still silence was peaceful, healing. The moon had traveled some distance across the sky when Max finally stirred beneath her, moving gently until they were both sitting up and Jules was cradled in his lap. Scooping her into his arms, he got to his feet and began walking. She didn't question him. Didn't press to escape his hold. She let him carry her for the long walk all the way back to the motel.

In the dim light of their motel room, Jules was shocked by the mass of dried blood she'd left on his skin.

"Max," she said gently, apologetically, reaching to cup his neck.

He twisted his face away from her touch. "Wash it away with me," he said, carrying her into the bathroom.

He set her down, and they stripped away their clothes in silent accord. Max started the shower, then gathered Jules against his chest and stepped into it with her. He picked up a folded washcloth and wet it in the shower spray, then gently wiped the dirt and sand and sweat from Jules's face. When he was done, he let her take the washcloth and clean the dust from his face and the blood from his neck and shoulder. Using the cheap motel soap bar, she lathered up the cloth and washed the rest of him, then patiently took her turn as Max washed the rest of her. They stood under the hot shower spray, letting it rinse away everything, leaning against each other, eyes closed.

When the bathroom had filled with steam, and their

fingers had turned to prunes, Max turned off the water and found a towel to wrap around Jules. He dried himself off roughly with another, then carried her to the bed, where he set her down as if she were made of spun sugar and spider silk. Jules opened the towel and spread her arms, beckoning him. He crawled into her embrace, meeting her mouth with his, and sank all his hot, hard weight on top of her.

They moved slowly together, the kiss deepening. When he slid inside her, it was gentle, easy, unhurried. It reminded her of the first time they'd been together—how he'd been so careful with her, so patient, so attuned. It filled her heart near to bursting. She held onto him as tightly as she could, moving her body with his, gasping his name as her orgasm pulled her under. He surrendered to his own pleasure, breath ragged, body exhausted.

The night passed in slow, lazy lovemaking, strung together by contented stretches of peaceful, dozing quiet, before they turned to each other again and again in healing need.

CHAPTER 35

Jules woke up wrapped in Max's arms. At her first breath, he lifted his head.

"Awake?" he asked.

"Yes."

He gently eased his hold on her, moving away to sit tentatively on the edge of the bed. "Are you alright?" he asked in a low voice.

She pushed up from where she was laying and moved behind him, stretching her legs on either side of his hips, wrapping her arms around his waist, and pressing her face into his back. She inhaled his scent, taking comfort in it.

"I'm more than alright. Are *you* alright?"

"I don't know how to come back from what I did to you," he said gravely.

"There's nothing to come back from. You spared me when everything you knew about vampires said you should kill me. You came back for me. I was angry," she admitted. "But I'm not anymore. When you listened to me—when you *heard* me—I forgave you."

He sighed. "That's too easy."

She tightened her hold on him. "Then let it be easy. I don't want to struggle anymore. I don't want to fight. I deserve a little peace, after all this."

Max flinched, his whole body stiffening. After a moment, her words seemed to sink in, and slowly, he eased against her.

"You do deserve peace," Max agreed, "But it doesn't seem fair that I should get any."

"It won't make anything better if you stay miserable. In fact, it'll make me unhappy, too. So really, you're just making things worse."

Max twisted to look at her over his shoulder. His gaze swept her face, thoughtful, as if searching for something. He seemed to find whatever he was looking for, the tension easing from his features.

"I'll spend the rest of my life making it up to you," he vowed.

With a pang of dismay, Jules suddenly realized that the rest of Max's life would be much shorter than hers. He was mortal, and she was... not. Briefly, it crossed her mind that the thralls seemed to be more or less immortal. But she dismissed the thought instantly. Even if she knew how to make a thrall, she would never do that to anyone, let alone Max.

"What's wrong?" Max asked, expression tensing again.

"I just..." She couldn't say it.

He turned to face her fully. "Tell me."

Her time with Max was limited. She couldn't waste another minute of it. "I still love you, Max," she said solemnly. "I never stopped loving you."

His eyes widened. That obviously hadn't been what he was bracing himself to hear. "Jules—I—what?"

She wrapped herself around him again, holding as tightly as she could. "I love you."

His arms came round her, crushing her to him so tightly she couldn't breathe. He buried his face in her hair. "God, I love you, Jules. I love you so much, I don't know what to do with myself."

"Stay with me."

"Of course. Forever, Jules. You're mine forever."

Forever's a long time, she thought sadly. But she kept her fears and her sorrows to herself, and instead focused only on the good—Max was here. Max was hers.

"Does this mean..." he paused, seeming nervous. "Does this mean—someday—you'd want to matebond?"

Another pang of sadness struck her. "I don't think you can matebond me. I heal too quickly. Your mark would never stick."

"Wolf kin heal quickly, too, but our claim marks are still permanent. And, um..." he hesitated, clearly choosing his next words carefully. "Well, wolf kin bites affect vampires in ways that ordinary injuries don't. You wouldn't—er... you wouldn't heal as quickly from my bite."

Max sounded deeply apologetic, but the news gave Jules hope. "Well, we can try."

Max nodded, deeply relieved. He cuddled against her. "When you're ready."

"I'm ready now."

Max stiffened. "*Now?*"

"Unless you don't want to?"

He clutched her tightly. "No, of course I do, I just didn't

expect you to want it so soon. Are you sure, Jules? I don't want to rush you. I don't—"

"Claim me, Max." She lifted her chin, baring her throat to him. Unexpectedly, there was something incredibly thrilling about the thought of being bitten by him. It made sense that, as a vampire, she'd enjoy doing the biting. But to be the recipient? Maybe it was just because she knew what a claiming bite meant to wolf kin, or maybe it was because she was a weird, masochistic vampire. Either way, she wanted Max's bite desperately.

Max rolled so that Jules was on her back and he was on top of her. He nuzzled her bared throat. "It'll hurt a little, I think." His lips brushed her skin as he spoke.

A low purr resonated gently in her chest. "I don't care. I want it."

Max kissed the side of her neck. "Here? Where everyone can see who you belong to?" he asked huskily.

Her insides clenched with excitement and arousal. Her purr deepened. "Yes."

He kissed her there once more, and then he bit down— hard. Jules's eyes flew open wide, her mouth open in a soundless O as the feeling of his teeth breaking her skin, sinking in deep, overwhelmed her. It was painful, yes, but more potent than that was the shocking intimacy, the vulnerability, of giving herself over to him in this way.

Threading beneath her skin, through her veins, arrowing towards her heart, was a connection deeper than anything she'd ever felt with anyone before. It coalesced in the center of her chest, warm and dense, growing more and more intense until it seemed to explode outward. Jules gasped, clinging to Max. The explosion began to slow, reaching an apex, and then gradually began to condense back inward, faster and faster, until it settled deep in her chest, entwined around her heart—Max's warmth and love and devotion, a constant presence within her.

"Oh my god," she breathed. "I didn't—this is so—*Max.*"

"I know," he murmured against her skin, tongue stroking over damage he'd left. "I'm here. I feel you, Jules."

After a long, peaceful moment of basking in their new connection, she turned to face him. "I wish I could put a claim mark on you," she said wistfully. She already knew he'd heal from it—no matter how deeply she bit him, it never remained, never left a mark.

"You bite me when you feed. It feels like I'm being claimed every time you do. I almost like that better. Other wolf kin only get to feel a claim bite once."

Jules smiled softly, comforted. Her purr resonated sweetly between them.

"You like that, kitty cat?" Max teased.

"You know I do, *puppy dog*," she replied, a little acerbically. "Kitty cat" was *not* going to become a thing. She grinned anyway, too happy to hold onto irritation for even a second.

Max chuckled. "I used to think of you as a rabbit."

"What? Why?"

"So shy. So skittish. I wanted to catch you."

"And eat me?" she asked sardonically.

Max gave her a suggestive look. "Among other things."

Surprise, surprise—after all they'd been through, Jules was still capable of blushing.

"But now I know you're a lovely, dangerous panther. I still want to catch you." He nipped at her shoulder. "But I like it when you catch me, too."

They lay tangled together, content merely to hold one

another. But the night was young, and as Max had once informed her, wolf kin have *excellent* stamina. They came together again and again, each time as intimate and heated as the last, taking the whole night to celebrate their new bond.

In the quiet, pre-dawn dark, they lay together in perfect peace.

"I love you, Max," Jules said softly.

He turned to her, tracing his finger delicately along the wound he'd left on her neck. "I love you so much, Jules."

As the light around the edges of the curtains softened, the last thing Jules was aware of was Max pulling the comforter over her, protecting her from the sun.

"I love you," he whispered, pressing a kiss to her forehead.

"Love you," she answered sluggishly as her daysleep pulled her under.

CHAPTER 36

Weeks passed in that unbelievable, contented joy. She and Max traveled the Rockies, exploring places she'd always dreamed of visiting, but never expected to be able to—Pike's Peak, the Badlands in South Dakota, Yellowstone National Park, the Grand Tetons, Flathead Lake, Glacier National Park, Granite Peak. They were in the Cascades now, sitting high above Crater Lake, watching the moonlight reflect on still water, when Max's phone lit up with a call from his mother.

"I have to tell her that we're matebonded," he said quietly.

Jules nodded. "Of course."

"If she's upset, don't take it personally. She's just—actually, maybe I should take the call later when you don't have to overhear it."

Jules shook her head. "Just answer. She'll worry otherwise."

He looked down at his phone, uncertain. Finally, he

accepted the call. "Hello?" he answered softly, trying not to disturb the peace of their surroundings.

"Hello, Maxim," his mother answered briskly. "How are you?"

"I'm good, Mom. Real good. Jules and I, ah..." he glanced at the healed claim mark on Jule's neck. "We, uh..."

"And how is Jules?" Natasha interrupted his stammering. "Never mind. Let me speak to her."

Max's brows shot up. "You want to speak to Jules?"

"Yes. Is it so shocking that I would want to speak to my son's... partner?"

"I mean... yeah."

Natasha made a scoffing noise on the other end of the line. "Let me speak to her."

Max handed over the phone, non-plussed.

"Hello?" Jules asked uncertainly. After their last conversation, she'd felt better about where she stood with Natasha, but she hadn't thought they'd reached the comfort level of casual phone conversations.

"Hello, myszka. How are you?"

"I'm... good," Jules answered with a nervous glance at Max.

He shot her a look that was just as confused as she felt.

"That's good. What have you been up to since we last talked?" Her tone was friendly, bright, with none of the grief from last time. Still, there was something studied about it— like she was forcing herself to sound carefree.

"Um, well, there's some big news that maybe Max should be the one to tell you."

"Oh?" A thread of worry had broken through the cheerful veneer. "And what's that?"

"Um..." She glanced at Max for guidance.

He shrugged, then mouthed, *Tell her.*

"Well, we're matebonded now."

Natasha drew in a sharp breath. "You're... what? How is that possible?"

"Um, well, he—" she flushed. Explaining the mechanics of a matebond felt a lot like talking about sex. And Natasha was essentially her mother-in-law. "I've got his claim mark," she said, her face on fire.

"Oh." Natasha was quiet for a moment. "I see. And... he has your mark as well?"

Oh, god, when would this conversation end? "No. I don't think I can give him one. Whenever I bite him, it just heals right away."

"It heals?" Natasha sounded surprised. "Strigoi bites don't heal quickly on wolf kin."

Max grabbed the phone for a second. "Mom, don't call her 'strigoi.' She's a vampire." He handed the phone back.

"Oh, no, you don't have to—" Jules stammered uncomfortably.

"Sorry, myszka," Natasha said, unruffled. "That's the word we've always used. I will remember not to use it." She paused. "So, you say your bites heal quickly on Max?"

"Yes," Jules answered, pretty sure she was going to die of mortification.

"Hm... that's strange. I will have to tell Margaret about it." Another thoughtful pause. Mercifully, when Natasha spoke again, it was to change the conversation. "So, what have you been up to besides joining my family?"

It was a huge overture for Natasha to frame it that way, and Jules felt it in her heart like a warm hug. "We've been traveling," she said. "I never got the chance to travel much before, so Max has been taking me to a lot of the places I always wanted to see."

"My Max is treating you well, then?"

"Of course."

"Mm. Well, where have you traveled to, then?"

Jules detailed the places they'd been, describing the beauty, and the legally dubious tactics Max had occasionally employed in order for Jules to see certain things after hours.

"And you cannot be awake in the daylight at all?" Natasha asked. "Ever?"

"I don't think so. Once the sun rises, I can't stay awake, no matter how hard I try."

"And how do you... eat? Max said you don't harm humans. Do you hunt animals, instead?"

Jules flushed again, back to mortification, but also fear. She didn't want to lie to Natasha, but she was afraid of how the truth might destroy this fledgling peace between them. "Er, actually... I survive on Max's blood." She and Max shared an uncomfortable grimace.

There was a prolonged silence. "You will have to explain that to me," Natasha finally said, her words flat and stiff.

"I don't need, like, gallons at a time," Jules said quickly. "Just a pint or so, every few days."

"A pint," Natasha repeated incredulously. "Just a pint and you're satisfied?"

"Um... yes?"

"And this is normal?"

"I don't really know. Before Max found me, my living situation wasn't exactly normal. But, I mean, it feels normal for me."

Natasha let out a slow breath. "I'm glad you're well, myszka. Can I speak to Max again?"

Jules handed the phone over.

"Hey, mom."

"Maxim," she said flatly. "Why didn't you tell me that she was taking your blood?"

Max turned bright red. "Because it's... intimate," he said, flustered and wincing.

"Oh!" A shocked breath, followed by a chuckle. "I *see*."

"Mom—" he began warningly.

"I'm sorry, kochanie, but this is important information for the pack. That a strigoi—"

"Vampire."

"—*vampire*, can feed without killing? That it isn't necessarily harmful?"

Max sighed. "Yeah. You're right. Tell the pack."

"I will. But before I do, you should tell your father. He would want to hear from you that you've claimed your mate. And that you're... *safe* with her."

Max nodded. "I'll call Dad right after this."

"Good," she said firmly. "I'm happy you're safe. I'm happy that you're happy. I hope someday we can meet your mate."

"I would like that. Jules is wonderful. You're missing out."

"I see that. But I will let you go now so you can speak to your father."

They assured each other of their love, and bid one another goodbye. Max sat for a second, arms crossed over his knees, staring out at the starry sky. His phone hung limply in his hand.

"Aren't you going to call your dad?" Jules asked.

"Yeah. Dad's harder to talk to about this. Mom wasn't raised wolf kin, so she's a little more open-minded about the whole vampire thing. Dad was raised his whole life believing that vampires are irredeemable monsters."

"Oh." Jules looked down at her hands, folded nervously in her lap.

"On top of that, my mom was attacked over the winter by a str—vampire. She would've died if Grace hadn't seen her and raised the alarm. Dad's been hyper-protective of her ever since."

"Oh." Jules clenched her hands together, knuckles turning white.

"I can call him later, when you're in your day sleep."

"No. I think I'd rather know what's being said."

Max nodded. "That's fair." He woke his phone up and pulled up his dad's number.

After a few rings, a man's deep voice answered, "Hello, son."

"Hi, Dad. How are you?"

"Worried about you."

"I wish you'd trust me. You've always trusted me before."

Arthur Freeman sighed. "I know. It's hard, Max. This is—it makes no sense. How can I trust a strigoi?"

Max didn't bother correcting his dad. Jules didn't blame him—he obviously wasn't at the point where that sort of thing would even sink in.

Even so, a faint growl rose in Max's throat. "You'll be careful how you talk about her," he said harshly. "Especially considering she's my mate now, and your bond-daughter."

Arthur said flatly, "You claimed her?"

"Yes."

"That's not possible."

"Well, there's a claim mark on her neck that says otherwise."

"*Max.*" His dad was appalled. "You matebonded with a stri—"

Max cut him off with a snarl. "*Don't* call her that."

His dad said nothing.

Max cleared his throat. "She calls herself a vampire," he went on in a more conciliatory tone. "But think about it, Dad. Wolf kin can't matebond with anything other than *people*. We can't matebond to animals, or plants, or inanimate objects. If I can matebond Jules, that means she's like us. She's sentient. She's a *person*."

His dad was quiet again. Jules was getting the sense that Arthur wasn't a real big talker.

"Dad?" Max prompted after the silence had gone on for too long.

"You make a fair point," he said heavily. "I'll have to think on it."

"Talk to mom," Max said. "She's spoken to Jules a few times, and she knows details that, when you're ready to hear them, might give you some peace of mind."

After another beat of silence, Arthur said, "I'll do that." Another silence, then, "Have you considered the ramifications of matebonding an immortal? Because wolf kin don't live forever, son, and regardless of what I think about her kind, it seems cruel to sentence somebody to an eternity without their mate."

Both Jules and Max froze. Jules could feel Max's alarm through their matebond and she wanted to comfort him, but she was stricken with her own guilt. She had already considered the consequences and decided to take them.

"I... I have to go, Dad," Max said hoarsely.

"Take care of yourself, son."

Max bid his dad a stilted goodbye, then dropped the phone. He turned to look at Jules, jaw tense, face pale.

"I'm so sorry, Jules. I didn't think of that. I didn't—"

"I thought of it," she admitted.

"What? *Why?* Why would you accept a bond when you knew—"

"Because I'd rather miss you for an eternity than never have you at all," she said simply.

He stared at her, conflicting emotions warring turbulently along the matebond. Joy and grief and pride and shame and pleasure and guilt. "*Jules,*" he said heavily. "It didn't have to be all or nothing. We could've—"

"I wanted *all*, though. I want all of you, Max. I want to be your mate. I want you here," she placed her hand over her heart, "where I can feel you always."

He shook his head, lost for words.

"I'm sorry," she said quietly.

His eyes widened. "Don't be sorry. I'm the one who—god, Jules. I get to have you my whole life, and then you're going to live forever with a severed bond? This isn't fair to you."

She shrugged. Vampires were technically immortal, in that they were exempt from aging, but they could still die by other means. She knew that firsthand. And Max had a good long life ahead of him—she'd make sure of that. Maybe, when Max's time was up, her time would be up, too. It could be arranged.

"Jules." Max edged closer to her, pulling her into his arms and pressing his lips to the top of her head. "Your expression is worrying."

"What's my expression?"

"Just calm acceptance. And the feeling in the matebond is... resigned. It's adding up to a really dark answer."

She wrapped her arms around him, holding him back. "You're young. It's not something we have to worry about for a long time."

"*Jules.*"

"*Max,*" she imitated his stern tone.

That drew a reluctant smile from him. He sighed and kissed the top of her head again. "You're right. We don't have to talk about it right now."

"We should talk about more pressing topics—like where we're going next?"

Max accepted the change of topic gracefully. "If we keep going south along the coast, we'll hit the Sequoias and the Redwoods."

Images she'd seen of the massive, ancient trees filled her mind, a soothing distraction from thoughts of mortality and death. "Alright," she said, leaning against him. "That's what we'll do."

CHAPTER 37

Over the next week, they followed the Pacific Coast Highway, with a detour to explore Yosemite, then continued south before cutting eastward towards the Grand Canyon. They'd made a massive loop of the western half of the continental U.S., and as they neared their final big destination, the conversation turned to future plans.

"East of the Mississippi is more densely populated by vampires," Max explained, "but the West has more wolf kin territory."

"I like the mountains," Jules said, looking out the window at the distant Spring Mountains. "What if we lived near one of the National Parks? You said wolf territories give the parks a wide berth. You could probably find seasonal work at one of the parks. And I could try to find remote work that I can use your name for. Like, medical transcribing, or something." They didn't need a lot of money. They had fewer needs than ordinary humans.

Max considered it. "It's not a bad idea. Which park did you like the best?"

"I won't know until we've seen the Grand Canyon." Even though the southwest was beautiful, she was fairly sure she preferred the more northern parks, like Glacier and Mount Rainier. But she wasn't going to rule anything out yet.

"We're almost there," Max said, nodding at a highway sign.

THEY REACHED THE PARK WITH LESS THAN TWO HOURS UNTIL sunrise. They already had a room reserved at one of the park's hotels, but instead of going straight there, Jules insisted on driving to one of the scenic overlooks.

"I can't wait a whole day," she said impatiently. "It's right *here*. Let's go see it."

Max glanced at the clock nervously, but conceded. "Just for a few minutes. Then we should check in to the hotel and make sure we can sun-proof the room."

"Deal."

As they pulled up on the overlook, Jules's jaw dropped. No matter how much beauty she saw, each new sight continued to awe her.

"Oh my god." Pictures couldn't do it justice. She'd seen dozens, hundreds probably, but none of them prepared her for the real thing. As soon as Max pulled into a parking spot, she was flinging herself out of the car.

"Jules!" Max raced up behind her a second later, harried and nervous. "Watch for the edge!"

"There's a rail," she said pointed out, coming to a stop in front of it.

Max drew up behind her, caging her between his arms as

he gripped the rail in front of them. "You're strong, but a fall from this height would probably be the end of you," he said quietly. "Please be careful."

She turned her head to kiss his jaw. "I will."

She felt his consternation settle along their bond. This early in the morning, they were the only ones at the over-look. Together, in peaceful quiet, they surveyed the great, unbelievable chasm in front of them. Jules had thought the Columbia River Gorge was impressively deep when they'd driven alongside it. But it had nothing on *this*. She breathed out a wondering sigh.

A moment later, they heard the sound of another vehicle pulling into the parking lot.

"The early birds are getting started," Max said, glancing at his watch. They'd noticed at every park and wilderness area, there were always a few type-A hikers out on the trails well before sunrise. They always had the most expensive gear and these sort of fixed expressions that suggested they were running a competitive race rather than actually existing in and appreciating their surroundings.

"Patagonia or Northface?" Jules asked. They'd started a game of guessing what brand the aggressive early birds' hiking packs would be.

"Marmot."

Jules pressed her lips together to hide her smile as the newcomers got nearer. They paused a few yards down the rail, two women. Surprisingly, they weren't dressed like hikers at all. One woman, tall and athletically-built, was wearing a simple yellow sundress that warmed her pale skin and complemented her chin-length coppery-red hair. She had her arms wrapped around the other woman, a shorter, curvier South Asian woman with long black hair, wearing a casual blue romper. They noticed Jules and Max noticing them, and waved. Jules waved back.

A moment later, the women came closer. "Good morning," the red-haired woman said softly.

"Morning," Jules and Max said automatically.

"Wolf kin?" the redhead asked mildly.

Max stiffened. "What?"

"It's alright—"

Max grabbed Jules, about to drag her back to the car when the shorter, dark-haired woman stepped in their way. She moved too fast for a human—too fast even for wolf kin.

"Do you need help?" she asked Jules, speaking with a soft accent.

"What? No." She gripped tightly to Max's arm, frozen with fear. "Just let us go. We'll leave. I promise."

"It's okay," the dark-haired woman assured her. "If he's not hurting you—"

"No! He's—we're mated."

"Jules, don't tell them anything," Max said desperately, his body tensed as he calculated their odds of escaping.

"A vampire and a wolf?" The redhead asked, unbothered.

Her lack of alarm gave both Jules and Max pause.

"Er... yes," Jules answered, despite Max's earlier warning.

"We are too." The tall redhead reached up to tuck her hair behind her ear, exposing a silvery claim mark high on her neck.

Max tilted his head. "You're a vampire?"

Both women laughed. "Does that make me wolf kin?" the dark-haired woman asked. She was so petite, Jules found it hard to believe. Wolf kin, both men and women, tended to be tall and rangy and muscular.

Which meant the redhead was wolf kin. But she had a

claim mark. How had her vampire mate managed to leave a permanent claim mark on her?

"I can see you have a lot of questions." The redhead let her hair fall back over her mark. "If you want, we can try to answer some of them."

"It's nearly sunrise," Max said flatly, distrustfully.

The dark-haired woman nodded. "We can meet you here again tomorrow night? Just us. Just to talk."

Jules could sense Max wanted to say no. But she wanted answers. "Alright," she said before Max could object. "Tomorrow after sunset."

"I'm Rachel, by the way," the redhead said.

"Ishani." The other woman gestured to herself.

"I'm Jules. And this is Max," she added, since she could feel from Max's prickly defiance that he wasn't going to say a word.

"A pleasure to meet you, Jules and Max. We'll see you tomorrow night?"

"Yes," Jules assured them as Max hustled her back to the car. "Tomorrow."

THE NEXT NIGHT, JULES AWOKE TO AN AGITATED MAX.

"What if it's a trap?"

"A trap for what?"

He ran a hand through his hair. "I don't know! Vampires?"

"Ishani's a vampire. And before you suggest it's a wolf kin trap, Rachel's wolf kin."

"Jules this is *strange*. Wolf kin and vampires together is not normal. *We're* not normal. And the fact that we just happened to stumble across two other people like us? And they weren't alarmed or suspicious? There's something else going on here, and I don't trust it."

"Max, they have really valuable knowledge. Rachel had a claim mark! Ishani was able to put a claim mark on her. Do you know what I would give to be able to claim you the way you've claimed me?"

Along the bond, his outrage mellowed. Gentle understanding reflected back to her. He sighed. "Fine. But if I say run, you need to sprint back to the car and drive as far and fast as you can."

And leave you? She wouldn't do that, but she didn't bother telling him so. "Alright."

He leveled a narrow gaze at her. "You agreed too easily."

"I'm an agreeable person. Now, come on, let's go."

When they reached the overlook, there were dozens of other people there—ordinary humans, who'd watched the sun set over the Grand Canyon. It seemed to put Max at ease.

"They won't try anything with this many witnesses around," he muttered as they pulled into a parking space.

Up at the rail, Rachel and Ishani were in the same place they'd been last night, looking out over the canyon. Max kept Jules clutched tightly to his side, his body placed firmly between Jules and the other two women.

"You came," Rachel said, smiling. "We were afraid you'd balk. Newcomers often do."

"Newcomers?"

Ishani and Rachel glanced at each other, sharing a confused look. "Yes. You came here looking for us, didn't you?"

Jules looked past Max's bulk, just as confused as the other women. "We have no idea who you are," she said.

"You... you just *happened* to be here?"

"We were planning on seeing the Grand Canyon, so it wasn't an accident. But we weren't looking for *you*."

"Oh." Ishani bit her lip while Rachel frowned.

"This changes things," Rachel said quietly.

"It doesn't have to," Ishani said.

"We can't break Silence if they don't already know."

"Well, how are they supposed to know if somebody doesn't eventually break Silence?"

Rachel puffed out a rueful laugh. "I swear, one of these days, I will win an argument with you."

Ishani smiled indulgently before turning her attention back to Jules and Max. Max's grip tightened almost painfully around Jules's shoulders.

"We're part of a community of both wolf kin and vampires," Ishani said, picking her words cautiously.

"Bullshit," Max said flatly.

"I know it sounds too good to be true. We thought so, too, when we first found them."

Rachel nodded. "I was in the same boat as you," she said to Max. "I wanted to run. Isha wanted to hear them out." Rachel shrugged. "She made the right choice."

"Just a whole pack of wolf kin bonded with vampires?" Max asked with heavy skepticism.

"No. At least half the wolf kin are bonded to other wolf kin or ordinary humans. And some of the vampires are bonded to ordinary humans."

"Vampires can bond to humans?" Jules asked, surprised.

Max shot her a scowl. "You're already bonded."

She poked his side. "I wasn't looking for other options. I was just curious."

"He's going to be twitchy and easily agitated until you

complete the bond," Rachel said, tapping her own claim mark.

"We don't know how," Jules admitted. "He heals too quickly."

Ishani's expression flickered briefly. "It seems there's a lot you don't know. How long have you been a vampire?"

"A few months."

"And your sire or dam?"

"She was only a vampire for a few days before she accidentally turned me."

"That's... not ideal. But not unusual, either. What about *her* dam or sire?"

Jules went rigid, and Max's hold on her gentled, became comforting rather than protective.

"He was a monster," Jules said faintly.

"I'm sorry to hear that," Ishani said gently. "It sounds like there's a lot you need to learn about our kind. Why don't we find somewhere comfortable where we can sit and talk?"

Max's suspicion had eased enough for him to agree to it. The four of them found a wooden picnic table far enough from the other visitors that they didn't need to guard their conversation.

"First things first," Ishani said briskly, her glance darting between Max and Jules. "Max is your bloodmate—or, your intended bloodmate, anyway. Right?"

"Bloodmate?"

"Your mate. The one you want to be with forever. The only one whose blood you'll ever want or need."

"That's normal?" Max asked.

"Bloodmates? Yes. As normal as matebonds are among wolf kin."

He sat back, looking stunned.

"Yes," Jules said. "Max is my bloodmate. Or, I want him to be. But every time I bite him, it heals within minutes."

"That's because you're using venom when you do."

"I'm... what?"

"You don't know about venom?" Ishani asked, not unkindly.

Jules shook her head.

"Vampires produce venom. It serves multiple purposes. The first is that it slightly intoxicates whoever you're feeding from—"

"*Ohhh*," Jules and Max said in unison, a shared realization dawning over them both.

Ishani grinned at them. "Yes, *that*. From a predatory standpoint, it subdues our prey. But from the perspective of a mutual partnership, it... well, it enhances the experience. But another crucial purpose is that it heals your prey. Again, from a survival perspective, it helps us avoid detection. But with your partner, it assures that they're not harmed. And its regenerative properties mean that your bloodmate will have the same lifespan as you do."

Max and Jules were both silent.

It couldn't be.

"Is that... that can't be true," Jules said hoarsely, feeling tears pricking the corners of her eyes.

"It is," Ishani said, smiling gently. "I met Rachel forty years ago."

"I'm seventy-five," Rachel, who looked no older than mid-thirties, said cheerfully.

"And I was born in eighteen-ninety-nine," Ishani added. "In Mumbai—though it was called Bombay then. I was turned when I was twenty-seven. My dam was like yours—" she nodded at Jules. "A young, freshly turned vampire who was starving and had no idea what she was doing."

"Oh." Jules thought of Bee, wondered where she was, and if she was alright.

"But the life span," Max said, still shocked. "How? I can't believe it. It's not possible."

"When she bites you to feed, don't you heal from the wounds even faster than you usually would?"

Max considered it for a second. "Yeah. I do."

"That's her venom. It accelerates cellular regeneration. It heals you at a faster rate than your body ages. So, as long as she feeds regularly from you, you won't age."

Max and Jules stared at her, stunned into silence again.

"There's a whole industry of vampire bio-engineering attempting to understand the process and replicate the effect in lab conditions," Ishani added.

"Vampire bio-engineers," Max repeated, sounding a little dazed by the idea.

"I know it's hard to fathom after spending your whole life thinking one way about them," Rachel told him sympathetically. "But vampire society is just as culturally complex as wolf kin society."

"That's..." Max scrubbed at his beard, agitated and appalled. "That's not good. It means wolf kin have been killing..."

"The animosity isn't one-sided," Ishani said regretfully. "Vampires generally believe wolf kin to be dumb, violent brutes—and that killing them is a necessary means of protecting vampires."

"People need to know," Max said urgently. "This needs to stop."

"It's not easy," Rachel said. "But that's one of the things

our community is trying to change. We have to protect ourselves, for obvious reasons, so we can't be as forthright and vocal as we'd like to be. But we're doing what we can with anonymous information campaigns."

While Jules agreed with them and was saddened by the needless violence, there was a more pressing concern on her mind. "So if my venom heals him, how am I supposed to leave a permanent claim mark on him?"

"When you're hungry, or close to feeding, you feel it pool in your mouth, don't you?" Ishani asked.

"I thought that was saliva," Jules admitted.

"It's a bit of both. The venom comes from reservoirs in your fangs. They feel sensitive when you want to feed."

Jules nodded, knowing exactly what she meant.

"If you draw on them, the same way you'd try to pull saliva out of your mouth and swallow it, you'll deplete them. You'll know they're empty when you can't pull any more from them."

Jules sucked against her cheeks the way she would if she wanted to swallow too much saliva. As she did, she felt a faint tension on her fangs that she might have never noticed if she hadn't been given explicit instructions. She swallowed again and again until that tension seemed to vanish. Was that it?

"You'll only have a minute or two before the reservoirs restore," Ishani continued. "So, as soon as they're empty, that's when you bite. He won't heal from it. At least, not as quickly. In fact, wolf kin are more susceptible to a dry bite than ordinary humans are. It may take him *longer* to heal than an ordinary human."

"Oh." Jules didn't like the sound of that, but the knowledge that she *could* claim him was overwhelming. She wanted to do it *immediately*, regardless of witnesses. Her gaze went to his neck, then rose to his face, only to find Max watching her just as intently, his eyes dark.

"It looks like our visit's over," Rachel said, amused.

Jules tore her gaze away from Max, an embarrassed flush creeping up her face.

"You should visit our community tomorrow," Ishani said, suppressing a smile.

Max, ever wary, said, "I don't know enough about your pack to take that risk."

"Then ask," Rachel replied. "For the safety of our people, there are some things we can't tell you. But there's a lot we can."

"Why did you expect us to know you yesterday?" Max asked.

"That's part of our effort to dismantle the wolf kin and vampire enmity," Ishani explained. "We know there are other matebonds like ours out there, trying to live in secrecy, always worried about being discovered. We have a *very* discreet network that directs those bonded pairs to meet us at the outlook if they need shelter or aid. It's not always Rachel and me waiting for them. There's a rotation. This week is our turn. We thought you had come to us on purpose."

Max seemed satisfied with that answer. "And your community? If we visit, will we be allowed to leave?"

"Of course."

"Then why all the secrecy?" Max demanded.

"For our safety," Rachel answered, almost impatiently. "You have to know that if other wolf kin found out there was a pack that included vampires, they'd attack us in order to 'save' their brethren. And if vampire communities knew their own kind were intentionally mingling with wolf kin, they'd have to act in what they considered the best interests of vampires. So we do not broadcast our existence, and we do not welcome strangers lightly. We only welcome those who can be trusted not to share our location. Can we trust you?"

"Of course," Jules said at the same time that Max said, "Yes."

Ishani and Rachel seemed to accept that.

"You can come tomorrow if you like. I can't give you our location, for safety reasons. But if you meet us here—" Ishani pulled a small card out of her pocket with an address printed on it and handed it to them "—then our sentinels will meet you and decide if you'll be welcomed."

"You'll be welcomed," Rachel put in confidently. "They don't turn people away unless they're suspicious weirdos."

"Just yesterday I would've thought our relationship was grounds enough for anyone to consider us 'suspicious weirdos'," Max said with a rueful shake of his head. He turned to look at Jules. "I think I know your answer, but what do you think we should do?"

"Let's meet them."

Max nodded. "Alright." He pocketed the card with the address. "We'll leave at sunset tomorrow."

"I'm happy to hear it," Rachel said sincerely. "See you tomorrow, then."

CHAPTER 38

Back at the hotel, as soon as their door was shut, Jules shoved Max up against it. She wrapped her arms around his neck and jumped up to straddle his hips. He caught her easily, hoisting her up and grinding her hot core against his erection.

"You're mine," she told him fiercely.

"Always," he promised.

Her eyes flashed bright with joy. "*Literally*, Max. You're mine forever."

He couldn't really believe it. Maybe it would sink in ten years from now, when he wasn't aging the way he should be. But for now, he was content to accept that Jules was his mate and that he'd have the rest of his life with her, however long that turned out to be.

"Make me yours, then," he said roughly, pulling her tighter against him.

"The bed," she gasped, her mouth meeting his in a possessive, needy kiss.

Max carried her blindly across the small, sparse hotel

room, dropping her onto the bed and coming down on top of her. Jules clung to him the whole time, kissing and stroking and nipping. Max teased the points of her fangs with his tongue, making her shiver and gasp, making her pupils grow large, like a hunting cat's. Her irises had gradually turned more red than brown over the last few weeks, and now they were deep red rings around her blown-out pupils.

They broke apart to undress each other in urgent, clumsy movements that ripped seams and sent buttons flying. Jules laughed while Max growled as he struggled with the hook on the back of her bra.

"When did they become this complicated?" he snarled.

Jules peeled the whole thing over her head and flung it away. "There is no clasp," she told him, giggling. "It's a sports bra. That was just a decorative bit you were trying to rip open."

Max growled again, tackling Jules to the bed, silencing her laughter with a punishing kiss. Soon she was writhing against him, gasping against his mouth, hands tracing urgently over his body. Her thighs fell open, allowing him to sink between them and grind his cock against the slick heat of her pussy.

"Inside me," she gasped.

He hastened to obey, fitting the head of his cock against her entrance, and then pushing in on a long, slow slide.

Jules's head lolled back, a pleasured moan torn from her throat.

When he had filled her completely, Max went still, hips pressed to hers, cock throbbing inside her. "Bite me," he insisted hoarsely. "Drink from me."

He wanted the feeling of being taken by her while he was inside her, to feel as connected to her as possible.

She lifted her head to his throat, tongue stroking over thin, tender skin. When she found the spot she wanted, she bit down, fangs sinking into him. Her venom spread through him, turning his mind off, making his body loose and languid. The pleasure of being inside Jules demanded movement, and he obeyed heedlessly, hips rolling as he thrust into her, lost between two incomparable ecstasies. Jules rolled with him, hips rocking against his as she drank from him. Her inner muscles tightened around him, clenching like a fist, and she tore her mouth from his neck with a sudden, gasping cry.

Her climax pulled him into his own, and Max stiffened as blinding pleasure overwhelmed him. He spilled in hot pulses into Jules's body, feeling as bound to her as if he already bore her claim mark.

But he wanted the mark—*needed* it. As both of them caught their breath, the dizzy pleasure fog of her venom slowly receding, Jules nuzzled against the healing bite mark on his throat.

"Are you ready?" she whispered.

He nodded, clutching her tightly to him and rolling so that he was on his back and Jules sat astride him. He lifted his chin, baring his throat for her.

Her cheeks hollowed as she sucked the venom from her fangs and swallowed it away. When she was satisfied, she brushed gentle fingers along his throat. A hot shiver ran over his entire body. She lowered herself down, bringing her lips to his neck. The tips of her fangs traced faintly over his skin, and then they were sinking in.

The pain was shocking. After weeks of experiencing the bliss of her venom, being bitten without it was starkly different. There was nothing to allay the pain except for the knowledge that this was his mate, finally claiming him—completing their matebond. He gritted his teeth, remaining still as she bit down harder, teeth sinking deeper than they usually did for feeding.

And then, suddenly, the pain vanished as glowing warmth suffused him, spidering through his veins much like her venom did. But this wasn't the feeding high. He was as clear-headed and sharply focused as he'd ever been. This was *Jules*. The purest essence of his mate, her soul bleeding into his, encircling his heart, and anchoring herself there. He'd thought the connection when he claimed her was the greatest thing he'd ever felt. But no—*this* was the truest form of joy that could possibly exist. His claim on Jules mirrored by her claim on him. A mutual bond, tying them together forever.

"Jules," he breathed her name, more reverent than a prayer.

She clung to him, tongue tracing over her claim mark.

"Don't let your venom heal it," he said hoarsely. He'd rather spend eternity with a ragged, open wound on his neck than risk losing this connection.

She laughed softly, as if reading his thoughts, and drew back, resting her head on his chest.

"You're mine," she whispered, her purr vibrating gently against his chest.

"And you're mine," he answered, kissing the top of her head.

CHAPTER 39

The address Rachel and Ishani had given them took them out to an abandoned bus depot on the edge of the Mojave Desert.

"Good place to dump two bodies," Max observed darkly.

Jules slanted an amused glance at him. Since they'd completed the matebond, he seemed much mellower. If the bond were still incomplete, she was pretty sure he would've just turned the car around.

"They're protecting their pack," she said mildly.

"And I've got to protect mine." He reached out to take her hand.

She squeezed his hand and held on. "This could be the safest choice for us. A whole community. Safety in numbers."

"I know. I know. I just... I can't let anything happen to you. Not again."

Jules squeezed his hand again. "We'll be fine," she said, more sure than she had any right to be.

As they pulled into the dusty lot in front of the depot, Rachel and Ishani stepped out of the building, followed by two men, both tall and rangy in the way that wolf kin tended to be.

Max eyed them speculatively. "Stick close to me, okay?"

She nodded.

They got out of the car and approached the waiting strangers.

"Jules! Max!" Rachel greeted them brightly, as if this were a picnic between old friends and not a huge risk for both sides.

"Hi," Jules replied with a smile, unable to resist Rachel's cheeriness.

"I see things are settled between you two," Ishani said with a mild smile, her gaze on the bandage Jules had taped over the raw, red wound she'd left on Max's neck. If he was going to heal slowly from a "dry" bite, she'd wanted to make sure he didn't end up with an infection.

"Yes," Jules said happily.

Max smiled briefly, a flash of joy shimmering through the bond.

"We're glad to see you," Ishani said.

She turned to the two men standing beside her. Both of them were dressed in dark but lightweight clothing—black, long-sleeved t-shirts and black hiking pants.

"This is Rhett." She gestured to the pale, brown-haired man whose blue eyes tracked critically over Max and Jules. "And this is James." She gestured to the other man, who had medium-brown skin and long, thin locs tied together at the base of his neck. He looked at Max and Jules with deep red irises.

"Oh!" Jules brightened. "I thought you were wolf kin."

"He's big enough," Rachel agreed.

"Yeah, but not slow enough," James said, nudging Rachel

playfully when she shot him a wounded look. "Pleasure to meet you both," he said to Max and Jules.

"Well, let's get the preliminaries out of the way," Rhett said, unsmiling. "Why are you here?"

"Er... we were invited," Jules said uncertainly.

Max found her hand again and took it in his. "I just want to keep my mate safe. And if you have a community where she'll be safest, I'll do whatever it takes to get her a place there."

Rhett held Max's gaze for a long moment, assessing. He nodded and turned his attention to James. "You have questions?"

James gave him an indulgent look. "You know they're good, man. Look at them."

Rhett sighed, looking heavenward for a moment. "You could at least do a little due diligence."

"We've got a wolf and a vampire holding hands like somebody's going to tear them apart, asking us for safe haven. What more can we do? Check their ID?"

Ishani and Rachel stood to the side, lips pursed and eyes bright. Something told Jules this was an old argument.

"Fine," Rhett said, aggravated. "Back in the vehicles." To Jules and Max he said, "Follow us. It's about a two-hour drive from here."

"If it's okay with Max and Jules," Rachel said, "We'll ride with them."

Jules looked to Max. He considered it for a second. "Sure. Hop in."

An hour later, they passed through a secured gate onto a private road. An hour after that, they were rolling down the main street of a dusty little desert town. The town itself sat in a deep bowl, surrounded on all sides by red rock cliffs. Flat-topped adobe buildings made up most of the structures, with an occasional sun-beaten, wood-sided building here and there. The whiteish adobe was bright under the nearly-full moon, though red desert dust had stained it a slightly orange color along the bottoms of the walls.

Despite the late hour—midnight—the town was fairly active, with lights on in most of the shops, and people walking and chatting on the sidewalk. After weeks of driving through sleeping little towns, it was surreal to be in one that seemed wholly awake.

"This is Rose Valley, our only town," Rachel explained. "Most of the pack live in town, but a few of us live up in the surrounding mountains. As far as the rest of the world is concerned, this is nine hundred acres of private land, owned by a real estate company, or something. I don't really know the details. Debbie and Shane and Luis all handle that stuff. All I know is, we don't show up on maps."

Max nodded as he alertly scanned their surroundings.

"You can park up here by the building with the mural," Rachel pointed. Up ahead, a large adobe building had beautiful red designs worked into the walls—stylized renderings of howling wolves and flying bats and leaping hares and scurrying gophers and fluttering moths.

"This is the Commons," Ishani explained as Max pulled into the lot beside it, following the dusty gray SUV that Rhett and James were driving. "It's our community center, our town hall, our gathering place. It also has rooms for visitors. If you want time to think on it, get to know the town, decide what you want to do, you can stay for as long as you like."

Jules and Max shared a glance.

"I think that would be... yes. We'd like to stay here for a while, maybe?"

Max nodded tightly.

"Well, we'll go inside and introduce you to some more of the pack."

They piled out of the car into the cool, dry desert air. The town was alive with the sounds of people—conversation and movement and mild traffic. Even after seeing it, it was strange to hear. Jules had become so accustomed to living in a world that slept around her, she hadn't realized how much she'd missed the presence of other people.

"Oh," she said faintly, reaching for Max. Comforting warmth reached to her along the matebond, and she leaned into him for a second.

Rachel and Ishani led them to a pair of double doors on the side of the building. They garnered a few looks from passersby on the sidewalk, but nobody approached them or interrupted their path.

"Come in," Rachel said specifically to Jules, issuing the invitation she needed to cross the threshold.

The entryway was a wide hall, with bathrooms on either side, that opened into a large open space with windows on the front and back walls. The ceiling was high, with huge wooden timbers crisscrossing to support the roof. Up high, the walls were whitewashed adobe, while a colorful tile mosaic spanned the bottom four feet, running along the entire space.

"This is the Great Room. It's where we have community gatherings—celebrations, committee meetings, elections, all of that."

Waiting in the center of the Great Room, was a small

gathering of elder wolf kin and vampires who could have been any age.

Their guides led them to the elders.

"This is Max and Jules," Rachel introduced them without any ceremony, though the waiting elders projected an air of authority. "The ones we told you about yesterday."

A wolf kin man with silver-white hair and tan skin stepped forward, holding his hand out to shake. Jules and Max accepted it in turn.

"Hello, Jules. Hello, Max," the man greeted them in a deep voice, lightly inflected with a Spanish accent. "I am Salvador. Welcome to the Cereus Pack."

One by one, the other elders introduced themselves. Another wolf kin woman named Dolores, who didn't really look old enough to be considered an "elder." A vampire woman who looked mid-forties (but was likely older) named Arlene. Two more wolf kin men, Simon and Manuel, and then two more vampires, Alecto and Augusta.

"We are the Cereus elder council," Salvador explained, completing the introductions. "Our sentinels have granted you entrance to our territory. We trust in their judgment, and we welcome you. It is our hope that you will find comfort here, and perhaps choose to join our pack. There is safety and power in numbers. And the stronger we grow, the better we can fight to change things for vampires and wolf kin across the world."

"Thank you," Jules said after a beat of silence. "We were looking for a home, and it's a relief to find a safe place."

"We'll need time," Max said, his tone guarded. "We need to think on it. Discuss it."

"Of course." Salvador nodded his understanding. "So long as you bring no harm to our people, you are welcome for as long as you wish to stay." He glanced at Ishani and Rachel. "See them settled?"

"Of course," Ishani answered.

They made their goodbyes to the elders, and then Ishani and Rachel led them across the Great Room to another set of doors near the back wall, which opened into a narrower, quieter hallway. The hallway came to a T. At the juncture, their guides stopped. Up and down the cross hall, plain wooden doors lined the walls.

"These are the rooms for visitors," Ishani said. "They're sun-proofed, of course, and they all have private bathrooms. There is a small kitchenette in each, though you can get hot meals at Rosa's place, across the street, or groceries from the community pantry."

"Don't worry about costs," Rachel added, "Our pack shares what we have with each other."

For the first time, Max's posture seemed to ease. "That's what a pack should do," he said approvingly.

Rachel led them to a door at the end of the hall. "We don't have any other visitors right now," she said as she opened the door. "So you'll have a lot of privacy."

The room was small, but cozy and tidy, with none of the homogeneity of a motel room, furnished instead with mismatched, well-worn pieces from different eras and styles.

Ishani went to the nearest window. "These shades are one hundred percent light blocking," she explained, rolling one down the metal track. The shade was solid steel. It looked like something that would be used as a security measure on ATMs and bank windows. "But as a precaution, the windows all have blackout curtains that you can draw as well."

"What do you think?" Rachel asked brightly, standing in the doorway.

Jules and Max looked at each other, brows raised.

"I think it's... good," Jules said faintly, finding it hard to believe how good it actually was. She didn't share Max's wariness, but after so much struggle, something this easy seemed... wrong.

Max pulled her into him, arm around her shoulders. "It seems almost too good," he said, echoing her thoughts.

Rachel and Ishani smiled ruefully.

"We thought the same thing when we first got here," Rachel said. "It's not perfect. We are essentially living in hiding from the rest of the world. And not everyone you meet is going to welcome you with open arms here. But, for our circumstances, it's a blessing."

Max nodded, seeming to accept that.

Ishani and Rachel helped them carry in their few possessions, which was mostly just clothing and toiletries, plus Jules's eclectic collection of "things." When they had their belongings put away in drawers and cabinets, the two women took them on a walking tour of the town. They were greeted by other pack members—wolf kin and vampires alike—hearing story after story that echoed closely to their own. A human mate who was attacked and turned, and the wolf kin mate who stayed by their side. Occasionally, there were gentler stories—cross-race friendships that weren't steeped in grief and suffering, that gradually turned into love.

They went to Rosa's, a cafeteria-style canteen run by a wolf kin woman who was mated to a vampire, who couldn't cook for her mate, so instead cooked for the nocturnal wolf kin of the pack.

"Half the pack live fairly normal daylight lives," Rachel explained. "Basically anybody who doesn't have a vampire mate. You'll still meet them, though. Our waking hours overlap in the evening, and sometimes even in the very early morning."

"How long has the pack been like this?" Max asked while they walked along a narrow, graveled road lined with snug little adobe homes. "Wolf kin and vampires living together, matebonding?"

"For about fifty years now," Rachel said.

"We got here thirty years ago, and things weren't operating quite as smoothly then as they are now."

"What happened?" Jules asked. "I mean, what made the pack start taking in vampires?"

"*This* pack has always taken in vampires," Rachel explained. "But they splintered from a different pack. One of the original—pre-vampire, that is—pack members had a skinlocked mate. Her mate was attacked and turned when they were on a weekend trip to Las Vegas. Once he awoke as a vampire, he didn't know what happened, and he tried to come home. His mate didn't have the heart to kill him, so she hid him for several weeks, maybe even months.

"There was a big blowout when it finally came to light what she was doing. It just so happened that there was a bit of an internal power struggle going on within the pack at the time. And those who resented the current leaders favored her. She was a respected member of the pack, a sentinel, and expected to join the elder's council when she was old enough. So, the people who were sick of the pack's old ways, who respected this woman, they left their pack and followed her to find new territory and they founded a new pack—a pack that accepted vampires as members."

"The Cereus Pack," Max concluded.

"Yes."

"And that woman—is she still in the pack?" Jules asked.

"Oh, yes, you met her," Ishani said. "Dolores. Everyone calls her Dolly, though."

Jules called up the memory of the middle-aged woman from the elder council. She had seemed so quiet and unassuming, but she had broken away from everything she knew to start a new life and a new system where she and her loved ones could be safe.

IN THE WEE HOURS OF THE MORNING, IN THE MINUTES LEADING UP to sunrise, Jules and Max lay together in their bed, the sun shutters drawn and the blackout curtains closed. Max's claim mark was still healing, helped along with plain old antibiotic ointment and bandaging. Jules traced over it delicately with the tip of her finger, making Max hum with pleasure, while her purr reverberated in her chest.

"I think we could be happy here," Jules said softly.

Max nodded, but there was a faint hint of grief in the matebond. Joining a new pack would mean leaving his old one—his family, his friends, everyone he'd grown up knowing and loving.

"We could just stay as guests," Jules said gently.

Max shook his head. "That wouldn't be fair to them. The right thing to do is to join the pack. I just... I need a little time to come to terms with it."

"I understand. And I'm sure they do, too. Plenty of them had to leave their original packs."

He pulled Jules closer to him, hugging her against his chest. "As long as you're with me, I can live anywhere."

She tilted her head up, meeting his lips in a soft kiss. "It'd be nice if you could be with your family. I know you miss them."

He shrugged. "No more than you miss yours."

Jules wasn't so sure about that. She loved her family, and it grieved her not to contact them, no matter how much it made sense for both her safety and theirs that she not do it. But Max's connection to his family, the supernatural bond to his pack, went beyond mere kinship. There was something almost spiritual about the connections wolf kin had to their pack, much like the matebond between lovers, and severing that connection had to feel in some ways like a loss of faith.

She kissed him again as she felt the sunrise creeping up, pulling her into her daysleep. Maybe with time, things could change. If there was one thing they had a lot of, it was time.

CHAPTER 40

"That's right, sweetheart," Max panted, pressing a kiss between Jules's shoulder blades. She was on her knees beneath him, face pressed to the bedsheets, ass up, as he sank into the soft, slick heat of her pussy.

"Oh, god, *Max*, please—yes, please—*ohhhh!*"

When she wasn't in a predatory mood, his mate was more than happy to relinquish control to him. He wound one hand into the length of her hair, twisting it around his fist as he thrust into her. She gasped and arched for him, rocking back to meet each one of his thrusts. Their coupling was fast, fierce, desperate. Not because their days were numbered, or because they feared the loss of each other. Max just had sentinel duties in twenty minutes, and Jules was expected at the community greenhouse to help with a propagation project for several endangered Mojave plants.

"Max!"

He loved when she cried his name like that. He thrust harder, forcing more cries from her, watching her fists curl into the sheets. When she came, her inner muscles squeezed his cock like a fist, tugging him into a sharp, blinding orgasm that doubled him over and robbed him of breath.

When the powerful climax released him, he slumped bonelessly to the bed. They lay sprawled together for a few minutes, savoring the closeness, catching their breath. Jules was the first to stir with a reluctant moan.

"I have to go. I promised Ella and Tom I'd help with the foxtail cactus today."

"Wait—before you go." He levered himself up from bed, going to the dresser to grab a dusty plastic bag from the top. "I found this on my watch rotation yesterday. I forgot to give it to you last night. I was a little distracted."

Jules flushed. She'd pounced on Max as soon as he'd gotten back and rendered him senseless while she fed from him. The venom high had turned into sex and then Jules had insisted on bringing Max to Rosa's for food immediately, since she'd gotten a little carried away with feeding.

"Here." Max handed her the bag.

She opened it and reached inside, pulling out a rock about the size of a russet potato, rounded on one side, flat on the other. As she turned the flat side up, she gasped. It was an intact trilobite, preserved in precise detail.

"Oh my god." She traced a fingernail lightly down the segmented body. "Max. This is— I can't—" She drew in a shaky breath, lifting her shining gaze to meet his. "After everything that's happened, I can't believe you remembered something so... so... inconsequential."

Max bent down to kiss her cheek. "It's not inconsequential if it makes you this happy."

Jules threw her arms around his neck, trying to drag him back into bed as she kissed him.

"Jules, honey, I know I told you wolf kin have amazing stamina, but I might need more than two minutes—"

She silenced him with a deep, demanding kiss. "I know. But I'm warning you now, as soon as you get back from your rotation, you better be ready."

Her feral little snarl almost had him ready right then and there. But a small pang of guilt forced him to pull out of her arms and continue getting dressed. They hadn't yet joined the pack, despite living here for months now. If he couldn't fully commit to joining, the least he could do was not shirk his duties to the community that had given them safe haven.

They were still living in a guest room at the Commons, but it was very gradually starting to feel like a home. The room smelled like them, like it was theirs, and not some random, oft-inhabited, liminal space like every dingy motel room they'd stayed in. Jules had begun accumulating interesting rocks and other desert treasures, and they lined the shelf above the bed, along with the other things she'd gathered on their travels—the eggshell that had made Max understand the truth of her, the pinecone he'd found for her in Mesa Verde, a bit of petrified wood she'd taken from the Petrified Forest.

Max had gotten the picture of them in front of Delicate Arch printed and framed, and it sat on the bedside table, a constant happy reminder. Jules had decorated the kitchenette wall with pretty little vintage floral plates that she'd gotten from a pack member who was clearing out some old things. A handmade Afghan blanket was spread across the foot of the bed, a gift from another pack member.

They were starting to make a home here, but they hadn't quite made the full leap.

With every passing week, they discussed their future—

including Max's inevitable severing from the Teekkonlit to join the Cereus Pack. But, though he knew he'd have to do it eventually, he couldn't quite bring himself to pull the trigger. Jules was patient and understanding, assuring him that there was no rush. But he wanted more than just temporary sanctuary for her. He wanted a real home and a real place in the pack. And to get those things, they'd have to actually join the pack. Until then, they'd remain guests with no real role in the community.

Max wasn't totally discontent with what they did have. They had safety. They had the comfort of others like them. While Jules admitted that she didn't love living in the desert, she'd still found purpose in working with the pack members who took care of the land. She spent hours each week assisting with anti-erosion work, and habitat protection for the Mexican Spotted Owl, and efforts to cull and eradicate invasive plants.

For his part, Max had been accepted as a sort of probationary sentinel who'd get full recognition when he finally joined the pack.

And, yet, he still couldn't quite do it.

July turned into August turned into September, and Max still hadn't managed to find the will to do it.

"It's like ripping off a bandage," Rhett—one of the sentinels who'd originally welcomed Max and Jules—told him. "It hurts like hell, but then it's over."

"I know," Max sighed. "I've just got to do it."

The problem was, even though Max knew he'd never be able to take Jules home to Longtooth, there was incremental growth with his parents that made it impossible for him to totally give up hope.

Jules and his mother chatted on the phone regularly—

more often even than Max did. And his dad had come around enough to accept that Jules wasn't going to hurt Max, even if he still wasn't convinced that vampires in general weren't dangerous monsters. But the rest of the pack?

"Does everybody else think I'm a psychopathic killer who's controlling Max's mind with my evil powers?" Jules had asked his mother on their most recent phone call.

His mom had laughed. "You make us sound like hysterical old hens. Maybe we are," she'd conceded. "Yes, most of the pack thinks that you are tricking Max and that he's in danger from you."

"Most of the pack?"

"Arthur is coming around. Margaret... well, she listens when I talk, at least."

"But everyone else—"

"Will need time," his mother had said firmly. "Just time, myszka."

Max and Jules had all the time in the world. But he still didn't think it would be enough.

So when he got a call from Margaret Huditiltik—the Teekkonlit pack's Voice, he was more than a little surprised.

And when he answered the call, surprise turned to shock.

"Maxim, it's Margaret. You need to come home and you need to bring your mate."

He was shocked that she was telling him to come home. He was infinitely more shocked that she wanted him to bring Jules.

"Margaret, what—"

"If you can get to Seattle, Caleb can pick you up there and fly you into Longtooth," she said urgently.

"*No*," Max snarled the word. "I wish I could come home, Margaret. I wish I could return to the people and the land that made me who I am. But I don't trust anybody not to hurt Jules, and I will never risk her safety."

"Maxim," Margaret said gravely, "I am speaking to you as the pack's Voice. Your mate, Juliana Wolfe, will not be harmed."

Max was shocked yet again. The pack's Voice could not lie. Which meant that not only did Margaret have no ill-intent against Jules, nobody in the pack did. "Margaret, what's going on?"

"I think we need your mate's help."

EPILOGUE

They had to fly at night, for Jules, of course. The flight from Seattle to Longtooth was nearly five hours. When they finally touched down in Alaska, it was three in the morning. Caleb had said very little to either of them. After what Caleb's mate, Grace, had gone through at the hands of a malevolent, cruel vampire, Max had been tensely prepared for a confrontation with his pack-mate and old friend. But Caleb had only given Jules a brief, wary once-over, before turning his attention to the plane.

"We're not landing in town?" Max asked as the plane dipped down to a rough, grassy runway about twenty miles north of Longtooth.

"No. The— They're holed up in the old foresters' cabin," Caleb said, sounding both wary and resigned.

Max held out a hand to Jules as they disembarked, helping her down. It was unnecessary, given her supernatural agility, but he liked to do those little things for her, and he could tell that she liked it too.

From the simple runway, it was a short hike up forested

foothills to a sprawling, ramshackle wooden cabin that had obviously seen better days. Margaret Huditiltik was waiting for them outside the cabin.

"Maxim," she greeted him. "I'm glad you're home. Your pack has missed you."

Max nodded, still not quite ready to make nice.

"Introduce me to your mate," Margaret prompted.

"Ah, right. Margaret, this is Juliana Wolfe."

"Jules," Jules added.

Margaret extended her hand. It felt like a momentous moment, and Max watched with held breath as Jules reached out to accept. The two shook and released each other without issue, and suddenly Max could breathe again.

"So," Max said, looking to the cabin. "They're all in there?"

Margaret sighed. "Fourteen of them. The fifteenth one just... vanished. We think she's still on Teekkonlit territory, but she's hard to track."

"And Connor?"

Margaret pursed her lips. "I'll let you see for yourself." She turned to the cabin door and knocked heavily. "Coming in!" she called as she swung the door open.

The inside of the cabin was dim, lit only by a handful of battery-operated lanterns. It was essentially just one room, and that one room was filled with—

Jules's eyes grew wide. Her already pale face blanched. "*Thralls*," she gasped.

Also by Heather Guerre

Tooth & Claw series:

Paranormal Shifter and Vampire Romance

Cold Hearted

Hot Blooded

—

Hellbound series:

Paranormal Incubus Romance

Demon Lover

—

Forbidden Mates series:

Sci-fi Alien Romance

Star Crossed

Moon Struck

Heart Song

About the Author

Heather Guerre writes sexy-sweet fantasy, sci-fi, and contemporary romances. A hopeless romantic and an unapologetic nerd, Heather loves everything to do with romance, aliens, shifters, cyborgs, monsters, and magic.

For more from Heather, you can subscribe to her newsletter at heatherguerre.com/newsletter. Subscribers receive alerts for new releases as well as newsletter-exclusive bonus material.

bsky.app/profile/heatherguerre.bsky.social

instagram.com/authorheatherguerre

goodreads.com/heatherguerre

bookbub.com/authors/heather-guerre

www.ingramcontent.com/pod-product-compliance
Lightning Source LLC
Chambersburg PA
CBHW011125190726

48289CB00012B/2902